# Contents

# PERFECTIBILITY
# AND RESURRECTION

CHARLES NODIER (1780-1844) was one of the pioneers of French Romantic prose; his salon at the Bibliothèque de l'Arsenal, begun in 1824 and known as *Le Cénacle*, brought together many of the key figures in the Movement and spun off other *cénacles* in which it was anchored, including Victor Hugo's. His best work consists of short stories and novellas.

BRIAN STABLEFORD (1948-2024) was a British science fiction writer, translator, and literary scholar who published over one hundred and twenty volumes of original fiction and over two hundred volumes of translations. He also wrote under the pseudonyms Brian Craig and Francis Amery. His original fiction includes the Hidden Swan series of novels, which began with *Halcyon Drift* (1972) and ended with *Swan Song* (1975), and the novels *The Werewolves of London* (1990) and *The Cassandra Complex* (2001). Among his important translations are *Monsieur de Phocas* by Jean Lorrain and *Mephistophela* by Catulle Mendès. He furthermore published numerous volumes of nonfiction, which include *The Mysteries of Modern Science* (1977) and, in four volumes, *New Atlantis: A Narrative History of Scientific Romance* (2016).

# CHARLES NODIER

# PERFECTIBILITY AND RESURRECTION

TRANSLATED AND WITH AN INTRODUCTION BY
**BRIAN STABLEFORD**

THIS IS A SNUGGLY BOOK

Translations and Introduction
Copyright © 2025 by the Estate of Brian Stableford.
All rights reserved.

ISBN: 978-1-64525-179-8

# Introduction

This collection of works by Charles Nodier (1780-1844) juxtaposes three essays with six items of fiction, all the items being concerned to some degree with what he called the *fantastique*, a genre of literature that he helped to define and in which he was greatly interested. Such a mixture is useful because it is impossible fully to appreciate his relevant works of fiction—of which the items included herein are a very limited sample—without some knowledge of the philosophical and psychological context by which they were inspired, and which their composition helped him continually to reformulate. Two of the *contes* are incomplete, but a knowledge of the nature and subject matter of the essays enables conjectures to be formed as to how the stories might have developed had they been continued, and perhaps also why they were not.

As an ensemble, therefore, the stories and essays provide a spectrum illustrating and embodying the awkward evolution of Nodier's ideas in the course of his troubled life and career, offering insight into the way that the development of his personal philosophy both assisted and impeded the exemplary contributions he made to the literature of the French Romantic Movement. For a brief but significant period in the evolution of that Movement, he provided a fulcrum of sorts for its dynamism, hosting a salon at the Bibliothèque d'Arsenal, of which he had recently been appointed as the librarian, which he called a *cénacle*, in which several of the leading figures in the movement met to exchange and discuss their ideas. Two of them—Victor Hugo and Théophile Gautier—swiftly founded *cénacles* of their own, which provided further cauldrons of argument and ambition that were important in helping to shape the work of those writers and their associates, and both became far more important as practitioners and exemplars of Romanticism, but their giant status within the history of French literature owed at least a little to the discussions they had with the cenacle and examples set by their fellow participants. Nodier's ideas and narrative strategies were among the most important initial contributions to that melting-pot of ideas.

Charles Nodier was born in Besançon in south-east France, nine years before the Revolution of 1789, by which Besançon, although a long way from Paris, was inevitably transformed. His father, Antoine-Melchior Nodier, was a leading member of the local Jacobin Club, which assisted him to obtain an appointment as the town's chief magistrate after the Revolution. Caught up in the fervor of the moment, Charles also joined the Jacobin Club, and became its precocious star, but he soon reacted against the violence of the Revolution, even more violently than his father, especially the employment of the guillotine; he developed a lifelong hatred for the fatal instrument in question, which is continually echoed in his work, and came to consider the Revolution as a great historical catastrophe, whose political reorganizations were a catalogue of disasters.

Initially educated at home by his father, and later confided to the supplementary tuition of friends of the family, one of whom was an ardent naturalist, Nodier developed a strong interest in natural history, particularly entomology, and developed a lifelong fascination with the French language and its Latin origins, before beginning more formal studies at the École Centrale of the *département* of Doubs. There, he was supposed by his father to be preparing for a career in the law, but he found it very difficult to concentrate on that supposed vocation, dabbling in literature and playing politics in a rather vague fashion, protesting against the Directoire, which had assumed control of the government in Paris in 1795. The activities of the skeptical Jacobins of the École Centrale—including the public performance of a satirical play, in which Nodier was involved—got them into trouble, compounded in Nodier's case by personal scandals to which he referred back continually in his writings, without ever specifying their exact nature, but which earned him a reputation as an incorrigible "bad lot." The first employment he obtained, as the librarian of the college, did not last long before he was sacked, and he never completed his legal qualifications.

In 1800, when the replacement of the Directoire by the Conculate appeared to offer new opportunities, Nodier left Besançon for Paris in search of employment, and although he did not find a position and was forced to return home after three months when his money ran out, he could hardly wait to resume the experiment in the autumn of 1801, hopeful that he might be able to make a living with his pen. He published his first novelette, *Les Proscrits* (tr. as "The Outlaws"), which he had written before leaving Besançon, in 1802, and followed it swiftly with another, *Le Peintre de Saltzbourg, journal des émotions d'un coeur souffrant* (1803; tr. as "The Painter of Salzburg"), similarly written under the influence of the German Romantic Movement, especially J. W. Goethe's *Die Leiden des jungen Werther* (1774; tr. as *The Sorrows of Young Werther*). Many of the vignettes collected in *Les Tristes, ou Mélanges tirés des tablettes d'un suicide* (1806; tr, as "Sorrows") must have been written at the same time, in a similar mood, but in 1803 he also published, anonymously, an item of libertine fiction, *Le Dernier chapitre de mon roman* (tr. as "The Last Chapter of my Romance"), to the authorship of which he never owned up publicly, regarding it as alien to his higher literary ambitions and excluding it from the set of his collected *Oeuvres* that he published in 1832.

All of the work from that first phase of Nodiers career is translated in the collection *Outlaws and Sorrows*,[1] which also contains another brief text published as a pamphlet in 1803, which brought the phase to an abrupt end: the satirical "ode," *La Napoléone*, satirizing and criticizing the First Consul. Although it was issued anonymously, Nodier owned up to its authorship when the publisher was arrested. He was only imprisoned briefly, several friends of his father having supplied letters pleading for his release on the grounds that he had been out of his mind when he wrote the ode—a defense that he employed himself, claiming to have been briefly unhinged by grief following the deaths of two close friends, although his friends added, helpfully, that he had also been deranged by over-indulgence in opium. He also wrote a new ode glorifying Napoléon in order to curry favor. He was released, he was but banished from Paris and placed under official police surveillance; although he continued to publish non-fiction sporadically, the fruit of his various continuing studies, he published no fiction for ten years, except for *Les Tristes*, which presumably accumulated fragments written some time before their publication.

Understandably, Nodier's early fiction does not exhibit any conspicuous sympathy for the Revolution, not merely because he was thoroughly sickened by its violence, but also because he disapproved strongly of the National Government's persecution of religion. His work is very sympathetic to the priests, monks and nuns whose functions and way of life had been temporarily abolished in France by the Revolution—an abolition carried forward by Napoleon in the course of his

---

1 The introduction to that collection and its companion volumes contain a more detailed account of Nodier's life than the one contained in synopsis here, adapted in each case to providing a context for the specific inclusions of the collection, as this one is.

conquests—and to all of the *proscrits* of what he considered to be a new tyranny even worse than that of the *ancient régime*. The heroes of his fiction are often aristocrats, or at least royalist sympathizers, and his readiness to identify with such characters seems to reflect a sense that he was an outcast of sorts himself, never afforded the social status of which he felt himself unjustly deprived.

Although Nodier's protagonists frequently rail against the "prejudice" that allowed people with *particules* in their name to look down on people who had not, even when notionally stripped of their titles, he gave the strong impression of never having forgiven the unjust Providence that had failed to equip him with aristocratic status in real life, or with some ready means of substituting for its effect. Not that he criticized Providence explicitly while displaying its relentlessly tragic effects—quite the reverse—but his perennial insistence that God must know what he was doing, and has to be trusted to settle all moral accounts in a satisfactory fashion eventually, has more than a hint of desperation about it. Although it would be an over-simplification to say that his literary work and his idiosyncratic philosophical essays are merely an expression and elaboration of that desperation, it was certainly the principal driving force of his endeavor, and, in particular, the principal source of his interest in the *fantastique*.

Stripped down to its bare essentials, Nodier's argument in favor of religion, mounted against the revolutionary agents who were actively trying to destroy it during his formative years, was that it was necessary as a means of consolation for the fact that human life is, for the vast majority of those condemned to live it, utterly miserable. The imagination functions, in his view, as a protective shield against the vicissitudes of reality, and the more oppressive reality becomes for particular individuals, the more assistance they require from the imagination, and the more assistance the individual imagination requires from manufactured imagination, whether produced by the cottage industries of folklore and superstition, the automated factories of religion or the idiosyncratic productions of art. In his view, based on what he saw happening around him as he grew to adulthood, the kind of "positive" thinking that led the Revolutionaries of France to oppose the Church, backed ideologically by the *philosophes* of the Enlightenment, was an oppression of consolation, the brutal denial of a palliative essential to psychological wellbeing.

In spite of the efforts of his many biographers, we do not know how extensive Nodier's use of opium was as a means of palliating the illnesses from which he suffered periodically throughout his life, nor whether, as one of his ardent defenders alleged in pleading for his release from prison, he also used the drug as a source of literary inspiration. It was something he did not like to talk about—not frankly, at any rate. One could argue that its effects are very evident in his fiction, but only obliquely, always deceptively, with the aid of a long series of improvised masks. He had a lot to say about the God of religion, and a lot to say about the delusions of amour and madness, but almost all of what he had to say came down, in the ultimate analysis, to lachrymose regret for the fact that civilized human life is wretched, only providing woefully inadequate answers to the hopes and ambitions of a sensitive man. Rational analysis of the problem, he thought, could not provide a solution to that existential predicament, in spite of all the significant intellectual rewards that could be obtained from the study of nature and the study of language, but imagination could at least make the quest for a solution more colorful, and lessen the pain.

*Les Tristes* includes "Une Heure, ou Le Vision" (tr. as "One o'Clock; or, The Vision"), which is generally regarded as Nodier's first venture in the genre of the *conte fantastique*, and which established a fundamental template in which mental disturbance occasioned by grief formulates a consolatory hallucination. That narrative strategy was employed to formulate further stories throughout Nodier's career, including several exemplars included in the present collection, culminating with the last *conte fantastique* he published during his lifetime, "Lydie, ou la resurrection" (1839; tr. herein as "Lydie; or, Resurrection"), which is also the most elaborate, embellishing the motif with the aid of a number of theses formulated by degrees throughout his career. The three essays translated in the present collection constitute the hard core of an extensive series of essays, in the course of which the author tried to work out what he was and ought to be doing his literary endeavors—a question that he could not separate from the question of what he could and ought to believe about the nature and future of the world, and his situation within it.

The narrative formula of "Un Heure" was not only redeployed in further endeavors by Nodier but in many other stories produced in the context of the French Romantic Movement and its descendants, especially the Decadent Movement of the *fin-de-siècle*. Those stories form a whole subgenre of "hallucinatory narratives" central to the tradition of the French *conte fantastique*, all of them employing literary ambiguity and uncertainty as a rhetorical device, far more interested in the elaborate psychological effects and functions of fantastic visions than the crude matter of their objective reality or unreality. The genre in question, and the Movement that produced it, have been subjected to a great deal of analysis and commentary over time, in which Nodier made a substantial and crucial start, in his seminal essay on *Du Fantastique en littérature* (1830; tr. herein as "The Fantastic in Literature"). That publication was swiftly followed by a succinct tripartite categorization of different types of the *fantastique*, which he employed as the introduction to an exemplary story, which he thought it necessary to distinguish from his other *contes* by allotting it a separate category, "Histoire de Hélène Gillet" (1832; tr. herein as "The Story of Hélène Gillet"). Nodier routinely combined his fiction and non-fiction in various ways, emphasizing the lack of any firm boundary between the two in his thought and in his practice.

Nodier's tripartite classification of fantastic stories was echoed, with variations, in many subsequent analyses, including Tzvetan Todorov's *Introduction à la littérature fantastique* (1970), which represents the "pure" *fantastique* in terms of a hesitation between a hallucinatory interpretation of extraordinary events and a supernatural one, which conserves its ambiguity rather than allowing it to settle conclusively in the *merveilleux* or the *étrange*. That hesitation is essential not only to many of Nodier's literary works, as a narrative device, but also to his life and his personal philosophy. While perfectly content, if the whim took him, to write stories in which the marvelous is simply taken for granted, and stories in which it is taken for granted that that the strange requires rational explanation, his most typical work is very careful not merely to maintain ambiguity but to celebrate it, regarding it as vital component of the *fantastique* and the essential mystery of existence.

Nodier's sense of the great psychological value of the fantastique was intimately associated with his conviction that he was unusual, perhaps even alone, in appreciating that value, which he never tired of preaching. He was always preoccupied—it would not be going too far to say that he was obsessed—by the notion that the *fantastique* was in decline in contemporary French society and literature, under siege from "positive" thinking and held in contempt by the majority of contemporary critics and philosophers, and his involvement with it became emblematic of his perennial self-representation as an outsider in society in general and literary society in particular: a *proscrit* metaphorically, even when his literal legal proscription was called off, ten years after its imposition. In his more optimistic moments—which seemed few and far between, but stubbornly recurrent nevertheless—he thought that the tide was turning and that the *fantastique* was beginning to make a comeback in France, shown the way by German Romanticism and, to a lesser extent, by English Romanticism, and he saw himself as one of its champions, forced by evil circumstance to be more prophet than pioneer, but doing his utmost for the cause in whatever way he could while waiting for the tide to turn.

Having led a somewhat peripatetic existence for some years during his banishment from Paris, Nodier married, and made a resolute attempt to settle down. He obtained a position as secretary to Sir Herbert Croft (1751-1825), an elderly English exile who had been involved all his life in esoteric literary projects, some of which intersected with Nodier's linguistic interests, and whose epistolary novel *Love and Madness* (1780), also found echoes in Nodier's fiction. Croft was living in Amiens with another elderly writer, Lady Mary Hamilton (1736-1821), the author of a strange feminist utopia, *Munster Village* (1778). Nodier assisted her as well as Croft, translating *Munster Village* into French and helping her to write her last novel, *Le Duc de Popoli* (1810) in French (which she could not speak). He found the demands made on him by the couple taxing, although it was probably their inability to continue paying his salary that eventually induced him to seek employment elsewhere following the birth of his daughter Marie in 1811.

The new employment he found was even more baroque than his eccentric secretarial position; his future brother-in-law, a diplomat stationed in Illyria—a region in the Balkans that had become a province of Napoléon's Empire in 1809—obtained a position for him with the region's official newspaper. The position did not last long—a matter of months—before the Empire lost its grip on the region and he had to return to

France with his wife and child, making a very difficult journey across war-torn Europe, but the experience provided him with fuel for a good deal of non-fiction and provided the backcloth to the next substantial work of fiction that he published, anonymously, *Jean Sbogar* (1818; tr. as the principal item in *Jean Sbogar and Other Stories*). In the meantime, he obtained employment in Paris in 1814 with the *Journal de l'Empire*, which was rapidly forced by Napoléon's abdication to mutate into the *Journal des Débats*, for which he worked as a reporter and political commentator until 1823.

Nodier's practical involvement with the *fantastique* took a substantial step forward in Jean Sbogar, which does not feature any explicit supernatural intrusions but builds to a remarkable phantasmagorical conclusion replete with Gothic hallucinations, attributed to madness, although hindsight, aided by the insights into the drug's psychological effects provided by Thomas De Quincey's *Confessions of an English Opium-Eater* (1821), loosely translated into French in 1824 by Alfred de Musset, a member of Nodier's cénacle, certainly allows the suspicion that they reek of opium. A further step, trivial in itself but highly significant in its consequences, was taken when Nodier was recruited by the director of the Théâtre de la Porte-Martin to assist with the rewriting of a translation of an English drama based on "The Vampyre" (1819), a novelette misattributed to Lord Byron, but actually the work of Byron's one-time private physician John Polidori. *Le Vampire*, prèmiered in 1820, was a huge success, and a key work in the development of Parisian theatrical melodrama.

1821 was a crucial year in Nodier's career and life. It was the year in which he published the first of his extensive literary exercises in the *fantastique*, the vivid hallucinatory fantasy *Smarra, ou les démons de la nuit* (tr. by Ruth Berman as "Smarra; or the Demons of the Night" in the Black Coat Press collection *Trilby; The Crumb Fairy*, 2015), which adapted the motif of the vampire—by which he had become fascinated—in a novel fashion; "Smarra" is an Eastern European equivalent of the French *cauchemar* [nightmare], which he had learned in Illyria. His melodrama *Bertram, ou Le Pirate*, based on a Byronic play written in English by Charles Mathurin, was successfully produced, cashing in on the vogue launched by *Le Vampire*. He made a journey in the summer to Scotland with two friends, including Baron Isidore Taylor (1789-1879), with whom he collaborated on several theatrical enterprises—an expedition that helped supply the backcloth to a folkloristic fantasy novella, *Trilby, ou le lutin d'Argyll* (1822; tr. in the Berman collection). That minor peak in his literary success was, however, offset by tragedy in his personal life; his wife gave birth to a son, who died before the end of 1821, an incident presumably not unconnected with the furtherance of his obsession with the *fantastique*, in reverie and fiction, as a possible source of consolation for grief.

Nodier subsequently reported that he had made a decision at that time that he would specialize in future in *contes fantastiques* and not write any other fiction. It was a resolution he certainly did not keep, if he ever really made it, but the *fantastique*, as he now conceived it, certainly played a central role in his fiction thereafter, ambiguously ever-present when not explicit, invariably reveling in its own ambiguity. He was credited by many subsequent bibliographers with having made a swift start in his contributions to supernatural fiction in an anonymous collection of anecdotal tales entitled *Infernaliana* (1822) but it seems probable that he merely helped to edit the collection for the publisher and wrote the apologetic introduction, but did not write many, if any, of the anecdotal inclusions. The collection borrows extensively from Dom Augustine Calmet's documentation of the vampire legendry of Eastern Europe, first published in 1746, and from Jacques Collin de Plancy's recent collection of diabolical anecdotes *Le*

*Diable peint par lui-même* [The Devil as Depicted by Himself] (1819), which supplemented the latter's very popular *Dictionnaire infernal* (1818; augmented in later editions; tr. as *Infernal Dictionary*).

In the early 1820s, Nodier formed a close friendship with Victor Hugo, and Hugo's disciple Émile Deschamps; together with the poets Alphonse de Lamartine and Alfred de Vigny and the critic Charles-Augustine Sainte-Beuve, they formed the core of a group of writers who held regular meetings and founded the short-lived periodical *La Muse Française*, with a declared mission to revive the spirit of French Medieval Romance in a new and revitalized form. The meetings of the group became the "cénacle" that Nodier hosted at the Bibliothèque d'Arsenal when he was appointed its librarian in January 1824. Théophile Gautier soon joined the cénacle, with his friend Gérard de Nerval, and so did Alfred de Musset, Prosper Mérimée, Jules Janin, Alexandre Dumas, Honoré de Balzac and Pierre Lacroix, who preferred to sign himself "P. L. Jacob le Bibliophile." Parallel meetings were soon being hosted by Hugo, while Gautier and other younger writers formed a splinter group they dubbed "le petit cénacle."

In 1825, Nodier and Victor Hugo were both invited to the coronation of Charles X, and the two of them subsequently traveled together to Switzerland, stopping off on the way to stay with Lamartine; the three of them agreed to collaborate on a travel book, and found a publisher, but they never completed it. The cénacle at the Arsenal continued for many years, but its location within the Movement gradually lost its centrality, and Nodier's position was marginalized by degrees. Although he published a collection of *Poésies* in 1827 he was never highly reputed as a poet, and his guests—many of whom thought themselves possessed of poetic genius, correctly in some instances—undoubtedly felt entitled to look down on mere journalists, in which category writers of prose fiction were still included. In his own estimation, however, Nodier remained the French Romantic's Movement's most important founder and its principal guide, and it was with that self-estimation that he began to publish a series of theoretical essays in 1830 outlining his notion of social and psychological functions of literature, and the crucial role within those fictions of the *fantastique*.

Practicing what he preached, however, was not so easy, in the face of the indifference or hostility of editors, critics and readers throughout the 1820s. It is probable that some of the material he published in the 1830s, when conditions eased, were written during that period, but exactly what he wrote and when is now impossible to determine. It is highly likely that his third long *conte fantastique*, "La Fée aux miettes" (tr. as "The Crumb Fairy") was written not long after "Trilby," but it did not see publication until he included it in the twelve-volume set of *Oeuvres* that he issued in 1832.

Nodier's journalistic and scholarly work generated a number of books in the 1820s, but his fiction had to contend with a marketplace subject to stern censorship, and publishers working in constant fear of prosecution for the slightest political or religious offense. Modern literary history looks back on the members of Nodier's cénacle as a spectacular constellation of stars, but at the time many of them were struggling to scrape a living, and the ensemble was faced with the constant hostility not merely of the censors but of a literary "old guard" entrenched in the Académie, who looked upon their progressive pretentions with extreme disapproval.

Nodier's own problems were probably compounded by recurrent illness, complicated by palliative self-medication. "La Fé aux miettes" is a delusional fantasy, albeit of a milder stripe than "Smarra," but the phantasmagorical element of Nodier's work reached a bizarre extreme in *Histoire du roi de Bohême et ses sept chateaux* (tr. as *The Story of the King of Bohemia and His Seven Castles*), written in 1828 and published in 1830, which seemed quite incomprehensible to many contemporary readers and critics, although modern readers can see an obvious kinship with Alfred Jarry's "pataphysical" fiction and Guillaume Apollinaire's "surreal" fiction of the *fin-de-siècle*. That was, however, a kind of *fantastique* fiction far ahead of its time, and the book marked the end of a phase in Nodier's work rather than a new beginning.

A new beginning did, however, suddenly become practicable, and Nodier seized the opportunity eagerly. The July Revolution of 1830 changed the political and economic situation of Parisian authors dramatically, almost overnight, and Romantic authors in particular; new periodicals soon began to appear in profusion, and the existing periodicals that were explicit products of the Romantic Movement became far bolder in its promotion, seized by a new spirit of liberation and opportunity. The one that rapidly became the principal organ of the Movement was the *Revue de Paris*, which became Nodier's principal market for both non-fiction and fiction after 1830. By that time, at fifty, and one of the few writers in the Movement who had lived through the Revolution, as a child and a teenager, he might have been regarded in private by many of his younger colleagues as an aging eccentric rather than a great figurehead and spokesman for *Romanticisme*, but he had not yet had his say freely on that subject, and he was determined to have it.

It was in the *Revue de Paris* that Nodier published the series of essays that developed his personal and literary philosophy fully, albeit in fragmentary fashion. *Du fantastique en littérature*, which was also published as a booklet, was one of the most important. The essay is undoubtedly a summary of ideas he had entertained for a long time, a long-pent-up polemic in favor of its subject, balanced between celebration and resentment, which develops a quasi-sociological argument to explain, albeit a trifle inconsistently, not only why the *fan-*

*tastique* seemed to have fallen into bad odor in France but why it was now undergoing a renewal—or a "palingenesis," to use a term that he appropriated from his friend Pierre-Simon Ballanche—in the specific context of the Romantic Movement. The essay was of seminal importance, not so much in persuading the readers of the *Revue de Paris* of the merits of the *fantastique* in literature—few of them would have needed such persuasion—but in providing them with a significant argument in support of its historical necessity.

"The fantastic requires," Nodier argues "a virginal imagination and beliefs that secondary literatures lack, and which are only reproduced therein following revolutions whose passage renews everything," and "when religions . . . shaken in their foundations, no longer speak to the imagination, or only bring confused notions to it, obscured . . . by an anxious skepticism, it is necessary that the faculty of producing the marvelous with which nature has endowed it is exercised in a more vulgar genre of creation, more appropriate to the needs of a materialized intelligence." He adds: "The apparition of fables recommences at the moment when the empire ends of the real or conventional verities that lend a residue of soul to the worn-out mechanism of civilization. That is what has rendered the fantastic so popular in Europe in recent years, and what has made it the only essential literature of the age of decadence or transition that we have reached."

The notion that contemporary European society was decadent and approaching a kind of inevitable terminus had first been popularized by the Baron de Montesquieu, who analyzed the decline and fall of the Roman Empire as an instance of an inevitable life-cycle that all cultures follow, but Nodier filtered it through the ideas of more recent writers, including Ballanche. The latter had put a strong emphasis on the processes of renewal and regeneration that enable cultures to carry forward a heritage of sorts from their predecessors, albeit not endlessly, as there is bound to be an eventual culmination, either in a stable state that would no longer decay—what Nodier called the hypothesis of "perfectibility," embraced by the majority of philosophers of progress—or in a radical change of state that would change the game completely.

The change of state envisaged for contemporary European society by the devout Ballanche was a version of the large-scale redemption promised by Christ but not, as yet, completed. Nodier had a notion of the eventual Resurrection markedly different from Ballanche's, and more elaborate. He was also far more interested in the consolatory role that the fantastic might play in the meantime, in both literature and life, in an era of cultural decadence. He had little faith in individual palingeneses, at least insofar as they could provide personal redemptions in the context of contemporary history, but when he considered, like Ballanche, the notion of an eventual apocalyptic transformation of the world, he did so in his own defiantly eccentric fashion, plunging into new imaginative territory.

Nodier followed the preceding citation by asserting that the contemporary re-emergence of the fantastic was "a spontaneous benefit of our organization, for if the human mind did not still take pleasure in vivid and brilliant chimeras, when it touched nakedly all the repulsive realities of the true world, this epoch of disillusionment would be prey to the most violent despair, and society would offer the frightful revelation of a unanimous need for dissolution and suicide," and he added that without the *fantastique* "I scarcely know what would remain to us today of the moral and intellectual instinct of humankind." In his opinion, however, the plight of contemporary degenrate Western civilization was so extreme that traditional orthodoxies could no longer be adequate to its palliation; innovation of some sort was necessary.

Nodier's argument was not widely taken up by other

writers of *contes fantastiques*, but it did make an impact on them, and they remembered it, especially the one who was most interested of all in their production, Théophile Gautier. The Decadent Movement of the *fin-de-siècle* rightly traced its ideological origin back to Gautier's introduction to the third edition of Charles Baudelaire's *Les Fleurs du Mal*, published in 1863, which elaborates, albeit hesitantly, the notion of a Decadent style, the description of which is applicable to his own work as well as Baudelaire's; the justification for calling it "Decadent" comes directly from Nodier. Baudelaire's fondness for the term was derived from an argument in the pages of the *Revue de Paris* between the critic Desiré Nisard and Victor Hugo as to whether the Romantic Movement in general and Hugo's work in particular were "decadent"—an accusation that Hugo construed as an insult (as it was intended to be) but Baudelaire, with assistance from Nodier's arguments, chose to reinterpret as a compliment in applying it to his own work. In all probability, Nisard would not have made the accusation had he not found encouragement in Nodier's recently-published thesis, but Baudelaire's deliberate reinterpretation merely had to look at the thesis from a different angle. Nodier's essay is, in fact, the true source of the deliberately paradoxical philosophy of literary Decadence.

Perhaps ironically, Nodier did not take as much encouragement from his own argument as Gautier and Baudelaire eventually did, let alone the wholehearted exponents of Decadent style who flourished in the *fin-de-siècle*. He did go back to writing *contes fantastiques*, and published them in some abundance in the 1830s, but they are distinctly hesitant, especially by comparison with the flamboyantly experimental *Histoire du roi de Bohême et ses sept chateaux*, seemingly haunted by the notion that they are swimming against a forceful tide of fashion in an inimical marketplace; they often fail to follow through in their intentions, sometimes breaking off and remaining unfinished—although in some instances, at least, that did not prevent Nodier from seeking to publish the teasing fragments, successfully in the case of "M. Cazotte." The present collection also includes "Zerothoctro-Schah, mystagogue de Bactriane," which languished in manuscript until Pierre-Georges Castex edited an omnibus collection of his shorter *contes* in 1961.

Nodier followed up his essay on fantastic literature with two other essays reiterating and amplifying his thesis that contemporary civilization was entering a phase of terminal decadence; he was particularly enthusiastic to argue against the hypothesis of "human perfectibility," which he considered to be an error on the part of the philosophers of progress who took their lead from the Marquis de Condorect and Jacques Turgot. Nodier was a philosopher of progress of sorts himself, and the idea of progress is central to his interpretation of the history of the earth—but his particular idea of progress argues very strongly that the human species is merely a phase in a much larger pattern, which can only be completed by the future emergence of what he calls a "comprehensive being," a new phase of life on earth destined to supersede not merely humankind but the whole of the animal realm.

He argued that case extravagantly in "La Fin prochaine du genre humain" (*Revue de Paris* 1831; tr. herein as "The Imminent End of the Human Species") and its flamboyant sequel "De la palingénésie humaine et la resurrection" (*Revue de Paris* 1832; tr. herein as "On Human Palingenesis and Resurrection"), concluding the latter essay with a remarkable exercise in speculative fiction, in which he tries to imagine what the "comprehensive being" fated to replace obsolete humankind might look like, and of what it might be capable. In between, he published a number of short stories, including "Histoire de Hélène Gillet" and "Jean-Francois-les-Bas-Bleus," which seem extremely tentative by comparison in their employment of the *fantastique*. The prefatory "advertisement" of the belatedly posthumous collection *Contes de la veillée* (1868), in which they figured as the two lead items, alleges that the latter was one of Nodier's favorite *contes*, by which he was "impassioned," and that assertion is easier to comprehend if the story is juxtaposed with "De la palingénésie humaine et la resurrection."

Nodier's use of the *fantastique* became briefly bolder after the publication of the latter essay; in particular, he set out to dramatize part of its thesis in a series of satirical futuristic fantasies begun with "Hurlubleu, grand Manifafa de Hurliubière, ou La Perfectibilité, histoire progressive" (*Revue de Paris* 1833) and "Léviathan le Long, Archikan des Patagons de l'Île savante, ou La Perfectibilité, pour faire suite à Hurlubleu, histoire progressive" (*Revue de Paris* 1833), translated herein collectively as "Perfectibility." "Zerothoctro-Schah, mystagogue de Bactriane" appears to have been intended as a continuation of the series, but breaks off just as the resurrected Zoroaster is about to explain his prospectus for the future evolution of mind, leaving that tale to be taken forward, doubtless in a different direction as well as a very different style, by Friedrich Nietzsche in *Also sprach Zarathustra* (1883-91; tr. as *Thus Spake Zarasthustra*).

The two stories constituting "Perfectibilité" must have seemed bizarre to their contemporary readers, who had few examples of futuristic fiction available for comparison,[1] and

---

1 Félix Bodin records in the prefatory material to his unfinished *Le Roman de l'avenir* (1834; tr. as *The Novel of the Future*, although *The Fiction of the Future* would be more appropriate [*mea culpa*]) that he discussed the issue at length with Nodier, evidently before the publication of "Perfectibilité," and agreed that all previous works set in the future had either been satires of "apocalypses," none actually attempting to prove an example of the fiction of the future. There is room for some contest regarding that conclusion, but what is certainly true is that the readers of the *Revue de Paris* had few works to which they might readily relate Nodier's diptych, with the notable exception of a novella by X. B. Saintine published the

even more so to anyone who read them independently as *contes*, although they are more comprehensible when they are read as addenda to the two essays. What Zoroaster would have explained to the time-slipped philosopher of progress Berniquet had the third fragment continued, we can only guess, but it would surely have been derived from the explanations offered in his essay on palingenesis and resurrection, and would presumably have expanded that thesis even more colorfully had he not felt unable to carry it through within the broader narrative framework. He did not return to it in his fiction, but he did not abandon the project entirely; although he reverted to the production of *contes fantastiques* of a much more moderate kind, often pastiches of what he called "contes de veillée"—which I have translated a "fireside tales"—he never lost sight entirely of their metaphysical backcloth. He eventually elaborated a new version of it in "Lydie," which is an appendix to his essays as well as a recapitulation of his first Wertherian *conte fantastique*, thus rounding out the present collection as neatly as it rounded out his career as a writer of fantastic fiction.

Nodier had the distinction of being elected, in 1833, to the Académie Française, a signal that the Romantic Movement had definitely "arrived" in the Literary Establishment, although Lamartine already had an armchair there, having been elected in 1829, and Victor Hugo could not long be refused one. Some of Nodier's contemporaries, however, might have regarded his election rather as a sign that Nodier was now a has-been, a member of the old guard rather than a representative of a new and dynamic literary force. Even the much younger Victor Hugo, once he was an Academician

---

previous year, also based on a theory of cultural cycles in which the march of civilization leads inexorably to a kind of degeneracy marked by fantastic extravagance, "Histoire d'une civilisation antédiluvienne" (tr. as "The Story of an Antediluvian Civilization"). Like Bodin, "Saintine" (Joseph Xavier Bonface) was a member of the cénacle.

in 1841, automatically began to seem like a member of the establishment rather than the heroic rebel against it that he had appeared to be in 1831, at the première of *Hernani*, made legendary by Théophile Gautier's famous account of turning up with a gang led by Petrus Borel, equipped with free tickets supplied by the author, spoiling for a fight against a claque rumored to have been hired by disapproving Classicists. Nodier had not been included in that escapade, apparently being considered by his friend to be too old or too sick to bear arms, a literal librarian already ripe for his election to the figurative Museum.

Although Nodier continued to publish a few *contes* in the later 1830s, much of his effort was by then directed toward the *Bulletin de Bibliophile*, founded in 1834, which fit very well with his profession as a librarian and his evolving bibliomania, but served to emphasize the fact that his interests had become increasingly antiquarian, as befitted his own antiquity. "M. Cazotte" ought perhaps to be regarded as spinoff of that interest, a bibliomaniac fantasy of sorts, which he simply did not have the energy to complete. By the time Nodier published that fragment in 1836, the Golden Age of *La Muse Française* must have seemed very far away; although a decade as remote as that seems to be a short time in retrospect, it certainly did not seem so to those living through it, and it included a Revolution that really was a Revolution for the Romantic Movement, however little consequence political historians now attribute to the accession of Louis-Philippe, by comparison with the upheavals of 1789 and 1848.

Although the other *contes* that Nodier published in the 1830s—a few of which are translated by Ruth Berman along with the classic items in *Trilby, The Crumb Fairy* (2015)— are certainly not without interest—and enough mostly-untranslated material, some of which features the *fantastique* at least marginally, remained after the Black Coat Press volume to make up two further books in parallel to this one, *The Memoirs of Maxime Odin* and *The Four Talismans and Other Stories*—the items in the present collage definitely warrant separate consideration and aggregation as an ensemble, entitled to special consideration. The juxtaposition of the fiction and non-fiction not only enables the individual pieces in the collection to be better understood, but also the works in the two parallel collections and the three volumes of earlier work. The ensemble comprising the whole of Nodier's work is far too various in its methods and themes to have a single connective thread, but the implicit argument of the present volume, and the exemplars it provides, certainly represents the heart of his enterprise, supplying the arterial blood of argument to much of the remainder, and vital oxygen to the functioning organism. Wherever it is read within the sequence—and it is arguable that reading the volumes in chronological order is not the best way to approach them—it is the one that casts the most light on the others, without which the significance of the whole picture remains ungraspable

The translations were mostly made from the copies of the *Revue de Paris* reproduced on the Bibliothèque Nationale's *gallica* website and on Google Books, with the aid of the 1961 Gallimard collection of *Contes* assembled and annotated by Pierre-Georges Castex.

# PERFECTIBILITY AND RESURRECTION

# On the Fantastic in Literature

If one seeks to know how the human imagination proceeds in the choice of its first enjoyments, one naturally arrives at believing that the first literature, esthetic by necessity rather than by choice, was confined for a long time in the naïve expression of sentiment. Later, it compared sentiments with one another, it took pleasure in developing descriptions, in grasping the characteristic aspects of things, in supplementing words with figures. Such is the object of primitive poetry.

When that genre of impression was modified and almost worn out by long habitude, thought was elevated from the known to the unknown. It fathomed the occult laws of society, it studied the secret mechanisms of universal organization; it listened, in the silence of the night, to the marvelous harmony of the spheres, and invented contemplative sciences and religions. That imposing ministry was the initiation of the poet into the great work of legislation. He found himself, by virtue of the power that he had revealed within himself, to be a magistrate and a pontiff, and instituted above all human societies a sacred sanctuary, from which he only communicated with the world by way of solemn instructions, from the depths of the burning bush at the summit of Sinai, the heights of Olympus and Parnassus, the depths of the Sibyl's lair, through the shade of the prophetic oaks of Dodona or the boscage of Egeria.

Purely human literature found itself reduced to the ordinary matters of positive life, but it had not lost the inspirational element that had divinized it in the first age. Only, as its essential creations had been made and the human race had received them in the name of verity, it went astray by design in a region no less rich in seductions, and, to put it bluntly, it invented lying.

That was a brilliant and illimitable career, in which, abandoned to all the illusions of a credulity that was docile because it was voluntary—to the ardent delusions of enthusiasm, so natural in young peoples, to the passionate hallucinations of sentiments that experience had not yet disabused, to the vague perceptions of nocturnal terrors, to fever and to dreams, to the mystic revelations of a spiritualism tender to the extent of the abnegation to which all fanaticism leads—it rapidly augmented its domain of immense and marvelous discoveries, even more striking and more greatly multiplied than those it had furnished to plastic society. Soon, all those fantasies were embodied, all those artificial bodies acquired a trenchant and special individuality, and the intermediary world was found.

Of those three successive operations—the operation of the inexplicable intelligence that had founded the mysterious world; the operation of the divinely inspired genius that had divined the spiritual world; and the operation of the imagination that had created the fantastic world—the vast empire of human thought was composed. Languages conserve faithfully the traces of that progressive generation.

The culminating point of its flight is lost in the bosom of God, which is the sublime science. We still call "superstitions," or *the science of elevated things*, those secondary conquests of the mind, on which even the knowledge of God is supported in all religions, and the name of which indicates in its elements that they are placed beyond all vulgar scope. The purely rational man is on the bottom rung. It is on the second—which is to say, the median range of the fantastic and the ideal—that it is necessary to place the poet in a good philosophical classification of the human race.

I have said that the knowledge of God was based on the fantastic or supersubstantial world, and that is one of those things that it is almost unnecessary to demonstrate. I shall only consider here the borrowings it has made from fantastic invention in all nations, and the narrow limits I have prescribed myself do not permit me to multiply examples that will, in any case, easily present themselves to all minds. Who does not recall, to begin with, the mysterious loves of the angels with the daughters of men, barely mentioned in the Scriptures; the evocation of the shade of Samuel by the pythoness of Endor; the other vision, formless and nameless, scarcely manifest as a confused vapor, the voice of which resembled a breath; the gigantic and menacing hand that write a prophecy of death on the walls of Belshazzar's palace during a feast; and above all, the incomparable epic of the Apocalypse, a grave and terrible conception, as overwhelming for the soul as its subject, the last judgment of the human races, hurled before the eyes of the young churches by a genius of prevision who seems to have anticipated the entire future, inspired by the experience of eternity.

The religious fantastic, if it is permissible to use that expression, was necessarily solemn and somber, because it had to act on positive life via serious impressions. Purely poetic fantasy dressed itself, on the contrary, with all the graces of the imagination. It only had for its object presenting in a hyperbolic light all the seductions of the positive world. The mother of spirits and enchantresses, it was able to borrow from the enchantresses the attributes of their power and the miracles of their wand. Seen through its illusory prism, the world only seemed to open up to uncover rubies with vibrant fires and sapphires purer than the azure of the sky; the sea only rolled at its shores over coral, amber and pearls; all flowers became roses in the garden of Saadi, all virgins became houris in the paradise of Mahomet. It is thus that Oriental tales were born, in the country most favored by nature, a resplendent gallery of the rarest prodigies of creation and the most delightful dreams of thought, an inexhaustible treasure of jewels and perfumes that fascinate the senses and divinize life. The man who seeks in vain for a temporary compensation for the bitter ennui of his reality has probably not yet read the *Thousand-and-One Nights*.

The capricious muse with cheerful adornment, beamed veils, magical songs and dazzling apparitions, paused in her first flight from India over nascent Greece. The first age of poetry finished with its mystical inventions. The mythological sky was populated by Orpheus, Linus and Hesiod. The *Iliad* completed that marvelous chain of the sublime world by attaching to its last link the heroes and demigods, in a history devoid of a model until then, in which Olympus communicated for the first time with the earth, by means of sentiments, passions, alliances and combats. The *Odyssey*, the second part of that great poetic duology—and I need no other proof that it was conceived by the unrivaled genius who had conceived the first—shows us humans in rapport with the imaginary world and the positive world in the adventurous and fantastic voyages of Ulysses.

There, everything reeks of the system of invention of the Orientals, everything manifests the exuberance of the creative principle that gives birth to theogonies, and which spreads the superfluity of its fecund polygeny abundantly over the vast field of poetry, similar to the skillful sculptor who relaxes by molding bizarre, naïve and characteristically grotesque forms with the residue of the clay with which he has formed a statue of Jupiter or Apollo, and who improvises, under the deformed features of Polyphemus, a classic caricature of Hercules. What prosopopeia is simultaneously as natural and as bold as the story of Scylla and Charybdis? Is it not thus that ancient navigators must have represented those two monsters of the sea, and the frightful tribute they imposed on inexperienced vessels that dared to tempt their reefs and the baying of the waves that hurled themselves, bounding, upon their rocks?

If you have not yet heard mention of the insidious melodies of the Sirens, the more seductive enchantments of a sorceress who holds you captive with floral bonds, of the metamorphosis of the reckless curious who suddenly find themselves seized, on an island unknown to travelers, by the forms and instincts of a savage beast, ask for news of them from people, or from Homer. The descent of the king of Ithaca to the Underworld recalls, in gigantic and admirably idealized proportions, the ghouls and vampires of Levantine fables, for which the savage modern critics reproach our new school, so far are the pious sectators of Homeric antiquity, to whom the guardianship of good doctrines is so risibly confided nowadays, from understanding Homer, or even remembering having read him.

The fantastic requires, in truth, a virginal imagination and beliefs that secondary literatures lack, and which are only reproduced therein following revolutions whose passage renews everything; but then, and when religions themselves, shaken in their foundations, no longer speak to the imagination, or only bring confused notions to it, obscured from day to day by an anxious skepticism, it is necessary that the faculty of producing the marvelous with which nature has endowed it is exercised in a more vulgar genre of creation, more appropriate to the needs of a materialized intelligence.

The apparition of fables recommences at the moment when the empire ends of the real or conventional verities that lend a residue of soul to the worn-out mechanism of civilization. That is what has rendered the fantastic so popular in Europe in recent years, and what has made it the only essential literature of the age of decadence or transition that we have reached. We ought even to recognize in that a spontaneous benefit of our organization, for if the human mind did not still take pleasure in vivid and brilliant chimeras, when it touched nakedly all the repulsive realities of the true world this epoch of disillusionment would be prey to the most violent despair, and society would offer the frightful revelation of a unanimous need for dissolution and suicide. It is therefore necessary not to cry out against the romantic and against the fantastic. Those pretended innovations are the inevitable expression of extreme periods of political life of nations, and without them, I scarcely know what would remain to us today of the moral and intellectual instinct of humankind.

Thus, at the fall of the first order of social things of which we have conserved the memory, that of slavery and mythology, fantastic literature surged forth like the dream of a moribund, in the midst of the ruins of paganism, in the writings of the last Classical Greeks and Latins, Lucian and Apuleius. It had been forgotten since Homer, and even Virgil, whom a tender and melancholy imagination transported easily into the regions of the ideal, had not dared to borrow from the primitive Muses the vague and terrible coloration of the Underworld of Ulysses. A short time after that, Seneca even more positive, went so far as to deposit the future of his impenetrable mystery in the chorus of the *Troades*;[1] and then, stifled by his philosophical hand, the last spark of the last torch of poetry was snuffed out.

The Muse only reawakened momentarily, eccentric, disordered and frenetic, animated by a borrowed life, toying with

---

1 In Seneca's pastiche of Greek tragedy *Troades* [The Trojan Women], the women of Troy, following the destruction of the city and the slaughter of its men, are to be shared out among their Greek conquerors. After much lamenting, the chorus of women draws some consolation from the fact that the misfortune is shared, because there is solace in companionship—but that only leads to the further complaints that the drawing of lots will separate them.

enchanted amulets, clumps of venomous herbs and the bones of the dead, to the light of the torches of the witches of Thessaly, in the *Ass* of Lucius.[1] All that remained of it thereafter, until the Renaissance of letters, is the confused murmur of a vibration that was increasingly extinguished in the void, and which awaited a new impulsion to recommence. What happened to the Greeks and Latins had to happen to us. The fantastic takes nations in their swaddling clothes, like the *roi des aulnes* so feared by children,[2] or comes to sit beside their funereal bed, like the familiar spirit of Caesar; and when its songs end, everything ends.

Our modern literature is no less submissive than Latin literature to the spirit of imitation. But the invasion of the Moors, so favorable in this respect to the moral development of the Middle Ages, had already transported to our soil the vivacious and productive genius of young poetry. Without that event, Classical literature, carefully perpetuated as far as our era by the admirable zeal of monks, would not have recovered entire and without intermediary from the bosom of barbarity, at the first appeal of a society avid for intellectual enlightenment; that is what happened later, when printing threw into circulation the harvest of the works of antiquity—which is to

---

1 The reference is to the *Metamorphoses* of Apuleius, who was sometimes called Lucius Apuleius; the proto-novel was insulted sarcastically by Saint Augustine as *asinus aureus* meaning that it was a decorative stupidity, but the judgment let to the work being frequently titled *The Golden Ass*. The confusion was encouraged by the fact that the hero is accidentally transformed into a donkey, Apuleius having borrowed his plot from an earlier Greek story often attributed—probably apocryphally—to the satirist Lucian.

2 *Le Roi des aulnes* [the King of the Alders] is the title employed by the French translation of J. W. Goethe's poem *Erlkönig* (1792), set to music by Schubert. A boy being carried on horseback by his father is convinced that he is being harassed by a supernatural entity; the father offers a series of natural explanations for all the child's supposed hallucinations, but the boy eventually dies. The poem is a classic of the ambiguous fantastic, never specifying whether the natural or supernatural account is "true."

say, a ready-made literary creation—a singular epoch in which a generation of scholars and poets suddenly reproduced the sophists of Alexandra, the grammarians of the later Roman Empire and the versifiers of the Roman decadence, like a population of Epimenides,[1] inspired by a religion, a civilization and a dead language, who only differed from themselves, in a way, by virtue of the languor of the organs of the imagination, which betrayed the inertia of a long slumber.

At their aspect, the fantastic vanished, but it illuminated Europe alone for several centuries. It was what invented or embellished the history of the equivocal ages of our young nations, populated our ruined castles with mysterious visions, evoked on the keeps the figure of protective fays, opened an impenetrable refuge in the fissures of rocks or under the crenellations of abandoned walls the formidable family of wyverns and dragons. It was what ignited on their foreheads the fires of the carbuncle when they traversed the sky as rapidly as a falling star; which led travelers astray on the banks of stagnant waters on the capricious trail of the will-othe-wisp; which consoled their rustic old age in the woodcutter's hut, in the nook of a hospitable fire, by means of the inoffensive games of sprites; which maintained with tender promises the credulous hopes of young women, and the mild leisure of the sedentary reveries of old men.

The fantastic was everywhere then, in the most severe beliefs of life as in the most gracious errors, in its solemnities as well as its fêtes. It occupied the bar, the pulpit and the theater; it sat down with Albertus Magnus in the stalls of the sanctuary with Agrippa in the philosopher's study, with Roger Bacon and Paracelsus in the chemist's laboratory, and introduced necromancy and judiciary astrology into the councils of kings. Its influence will never be forgotten in literature, where

---

1 Epimenides of Cnossos was said to have fallen asleep in a cave for fifty-seven years and to have woken up with the gift of prophecy.

it produced the naïve tales of legends, where it animated with such an imposing pomp the chronicle of tourneys, battles and crusades; where it spread with full borders in the gossip of old story-tellers and the fables of troubadours.

It is to the fantastic that we owe the romances of chivalry, an unnamed species of epic, in which all the scenes of amour and heroism of the Middle Ages are confounded with an inexpressible harmony: an amour without example, in which the modest tenderness of the beloved and the passionate enthusiasm of the lover were more greatly admired; an ideal heroism, which had everything to combat—the bravery of warriors; the wrath of paladin kings; the ambushes of treason; upheavals of nature tamed by magic; the intervention of a thousand unexpected powers modified under ever-new aspects at the whim of the inventive imagination of the romancer; all the possible accidents of fatality—and which triumphed over all of them.

There was no longer Juno, Neptune or excited Venus, as in pagan theogony, to doom a man; there was the universe entire, personified in a multitude of different individualities, struggling against a warrior covered, for all defense, by his courage, his amour and his righteousness. There was no longer the shameful and bloody quarrel of two peoples determined to destroy one another for a cause or for the reparation of abduction and adultery; there was the moral trial of the just and the unjust, struggling in the general interest of humans between Heaven and Hell, under the eyes of a Helen who was the prize and not the object thereof, and who, more fortunate than the other, could unveil herself without blushing before the two camps. There was, it must be agreed, a marvelous poetry therein, an order of interventions such that, if the ancients had had the likes of Amadis, we would probably not talk about Achilles; an imagination simultaneously grandiose and charming, that will not be renewed and will be regretted forever, like Roland's mare, which was so beautiful, so strong and so agile, which imprinted her hooves so forcefully in the sand of the lists and the field of battle, whose blanket and harness had been embroidered by the hands of princesses, and which is dead.

If I were capable of feeling a stir of hatred against Cervantes, perhaps I would reproach him for having contributed more than anyone else to the theft of those delectable fantasies of the genius of the intermediary centuries, which he broke as easily as Don Quixote broke Ginesillo's marionettes; but I am obliged to agree that the work of destruction in question, which has given us one of the finest books that the modern imagination has produced, was probably the indispensable condition of its literary destiny.

When the fables of a people have grown old, the pitiless instinct of change that resides within it will manifest itself in its day and its hour, and it will manifest to the people, by certain signs, that it is necessary to recommence social life afresh, without regard to the traditions and sympathies of the past. It then unleashes spirits of derision, impelled by an irreflective hatred, which makes baubles of everything that anterior centuries had venerated, and toys with the debris of an expiring civilization, proffering words of irony and disdain, like Hamlet, weighing the ashes of the dead and analyzing the springs of intelligence in the skull of a fool, in Yorick's grave. It is thus that Lucian was sent at the end of paganism, Cervantes after chivalry, Erasmus and Rabelais with the Reformation, and Voltaire toward the political revolutions that were about to accompany the great conflagration of Christianity. When an order of things dies, there is always some ingenious demon who watches its agony, laughing, and delivers the *coup de grace* with a fool's bauble.

The first fantastic genius of the Renaissance, by order of date, and also by order of superiority—for in the masterpieces that reveal themselves, genius is not progressive—was Dante.

He arrived of his own accord, and all alone, in the last twilight of a finished society and the first light of a commencing society, and although he had opened the quarry, he filled it entirely. It is true that he placed the theater of his terrible phantasmagoria under the protection of the beliefs of his time, but he made it his own by means of the passions, the actors and even the details of the stage, which is neither Homeric, nor Virgilian, but Dantesque. One often finds today tasteful critiques that deplore the error of that magnificent imagination and the apparent confusion of the poetic fable, in which the Virgil of the Middle Ages takes for his introducer to the Christian Inferno the Virgil of paganism. That idea is, however, the pivot of his composition, and that is what renders it sublime.

The Inferno of a particular theogony would be too narrow for such a large invention. It was necessary that Dante precipitate himself therein on the torrent of the centuries, without consideration for the circumscribed forms of a timid epic, and what he conserved of universally received ideas is, on the contrary, a very ingenious and very legitimate concession to the mythism of his epoch, the nature of which was itself one of the essential components of the Divine Comedy, but which could not form the exclusive soul of that gigantic conception. So Dante's Inferno does not resemble any of the innumerable Hells that the somber melancholy of poets has invented, and which recall more or less, collectively, the *vade in pace* of monachism and the torture chamber of the Inquisition. In its colossal architecture it contains all Hells, and it is appropriate to receive all the generations of the wicked through the eternal centuries. That atrabiliary creation ought not to be measured by the compass of the artist and the unities of the rhetor; its grandeur is in its unrestrained liberty, in the conquered right to make all the reflections of thought and all the radiance of the soul play incessantly upon the thousand-faceted mirror of the imagination.

It is necessary not to seek therein, I do not say a model, but a comparison, as in the Apocalypse of Saint John; it is even less necessary to seek fortunate imitators in the centuries that have followed it, for it is the special work of an epoch, and only the man of genius who conceived it was the expression of a century, from which his individuality cannot be separated without mutilating it. What has passed from him into modern writings, like the dream of parricide in *Les Voleurs*,[1] the despairing prosopopeia of Jean-Paul, where Jesus Christ comes to reveal eternal annihilation to the innocent souls of limbo, and the incomparable vision of the condemned man in the psychological romance of Victor Hugo,[2] is a local, partial, inextensible emanation, incommunicable today, which acts with all the power of the principle from which it emerged, but on a limited point, in a rare circumstance, and through an insensible milieu, like the fire of an eclipsed sun, which still sets fire to gunpowder through a glass lens. The world that civilization has made for us does not permit more than that.

Thus, the revered tradition of the *Divine Comedy* has not produced a remarkable work of the same genre among the people of the earth best able to appreciate it. It has remained, like an inviolable and inaccessible monument of remote times, on the extreme frontier of Italian literature, as the respect that is attached to sacred things appears to defend it forever against the impotent temerity of copyists. The new mine of invention that was to be exploited by turns in the same land by intelligence, imagination, genius and the infallible industry of imitation that attaches everywhere to the retinue of the creative muses, and which ended up in the times we call Classical by virtue of ornamenting their crowns, was common to Europe

---

1 *Les Voleurs* was the title given in French translation of Friedrich Schiller's archetypal Romantic melodrama *Die Raüber* [The Robbers] (1781; French tr. 1795].
2 Victor Hugo, *Le Dernier jour d'un condamné* (1829; tr. as *The Last Day of a Condemned Man*).

entire, but Italy alone had the privilege of stamping is discoveries with a immortal seal, because its language was ready-made. It belonged to it to enrich our chronicles and romances with the facile beauties of a free and gracious versification, and by submitting them to the harmonious meter of its octaves it also freed them from the most serious reproach of a peevish criticism, which will tolerate until further notice, by virtue of condescension for antiquity, rhythmic lies.

To make use of the familiar language of that poetry, it would be as easy to count the stars in the sky and the sands of the sea as the chivalric epics of the most ingenious of all the literary ages. The curious conserve more than a hundred anterior to Ariosto, and which Ariosto has caused to be forgotten, just as Homer caused the rhapsodies of his unknown predecessors to be forgotten. What imagination, in fact, would not pale before that prodigious imagination, which made use, playfully, of combinations full of grace, freshness and originality, of the traditions of an obscure history and the delightful reveries of a new, unjustly neglected mythology?

It was said that Hesiod was nourished with honey by the hand of the daughters of the Pindus.[1] In that case, it was the fays who nourished Ariosto with a more intoxicating ambrosia, which communicated to his divine writings the invincible seduction of their enchantments. How can magic be doubted when the poet, a magician himself, draws you at his whim into spaces less familiar to human intelligence than those into which the hippogriff strayed, when his songs resonated with a supernatural inspiration, and seemed to come from another world? Penetrated by the study of the ancients, he did not disdain to steal a few shreds from their remains, but it was never without mixing them with the air, the physiognomy of his character and the free play of his composition. He is still independent when

_______________

1 The Pindus mountain range includes Mount Parnasus, the abode of the Muses.

he obeys, still new when he imitates, and only submits himself to the invention of others in the satiety of his own inventions, the profusion of which wearies and discourages him. That is because he had stolen the jewel-case of Alcina or the secret treasures of the mines of Cathay, and the modesty of opulence instructs him to mingle vulgar riches from time to time with those that he dispenses with to much facility.

After Ariosto and his feeble copyists, the fantastic almost did not show itself again in Italian literature,[1] and nothing is more comprehensible; it is because he had exhausted it.

Who would have believed that the muse of the ideal, an elegant and sumptuous daughter of Asia, would take refuge for a long time beneath the mists of Great Britain? Perhaps frightened by the melancholy pomps of the North, the lugubrious theism of which had penetrated all the way to the throne of Odin, and the vaporous fictions of Scotland, where the bard's harp was only mingled with the clash of claymores and the roar of tempests, it soon sought repose in one of those vivid and cheerful imaginations that had enlivened with their voluptuous songs the first fêtes of her cradle. Shakespeare came along, who scarcely knew within the enclosure of his island, *orbe toto divisa*,[2] in Virgil's expression, the marvels of the physical world, but who had perceived them in some sublime vision, and who understood the prodigies of the realm of the sun as if he had strolled there in a dream on the arm of a fay; for Shakespeare and poetry are synonymous.

Spenser had only traced the path; he enlarged it, prolonged it, embellished it with new spectacles, filled it, inundated it

---

1 This judgment, seemingly reducing Torquato Tasso to the category of "feeble copyists," would have surprised many French readers, familiarized with the epic poem *Gerusalemme liberata* [Jerusalem Delivered] by virtue of its frequent use as a standard text in French schools, although it does indeed borrow extensively from *Orlando Furioso*.
2 This Latin phrase, more often rendered as *toto orbe divisa*, although Virgil actually has *toto divisos orbe*, means "separated from the continent."

with new figures, fresher, more aerial and more transparent than the fugitive apparitions of morning dreams; there he led the romantic dances of Oberon, Titania and spirits who, with a step lighter than that of Camille,[1] similarly touched the grass without curbing it; there he sowed the flowers embalmed with celestial perfumes that open to the warmth of dawn to receive the nocturnal population of spirits and close upon them until evening, like enchanted tents; the spread unknown luminaries in the atmosphere, strung celestial lyres that had never vibrated for human ears, suspended the melodious orchestra of Ariel from the stirred branches of the bush, hid the invisible nest of Puck in a rosebud, and caused a concert of magical voices to spring forth from all the pores of the earth, all the atoms of the air and all the profundities of the sky. In the innumerable colors of the palette and in the multitude of shifting sympathies that speech stirs in the depths of the soul, everything belongs to Shakespeare. When his brush has finished caressing the seductive forms of a sylph, it is to him alone that it is reserved to trace the gigantic and gross proportions of a gnome under the features of Caliban, to disguise the antique satyr under the burlesque apparel of Falstaff and to suspend the sketch of Michelangelo from the delectable tableau of Correggio. If Dante and Ariosto have not offered you all the essential conditions of the individuality of a demigod, stop at him: *incessu patuit*.[2]

What all the world knows only too well of our national literature reasons in advance to the questions I might be asked about the progress that was promised here in fantastic poetry. It is not to the academic and Classical soil of the France of Louis XIII and Richelieu that that literature, which only lives on imagination and liberty, could be successfully acclimated. The brilliant lies of genius would have been as poorly received

---

1 Possibly a reference to *Camille, ou Le Souterrrain* (1791), an *opéra comique* by Nicolas Dalayrac, with a libretto by Benoît-Joseph Marsollier.
2 The phrase is from Virgil: *Vera incessu patuit dea* [the true goddess was revealed in her stride].

there as the truth. The empire of thought belonged, via the Sorbonne and Aristotle, to the servants of a stilted muse, who trailed with the privilege of the king over the theater of the court and the salons of the Hôtel de Rambouillet,[1] the rags of travestied antiquity. Racine, inspired in his old age by the genius of the holy books, once dared, by exception, to throw into a bold story the great figure of the specter of Jezebel, and Voltaire thought he had pushed quite far the audacity of a leader of a social opposition who sought novelty in everything, when he howled a few Alexandrines through a loudspeaker via the tragic shade of Ninus.[2] We have had our chronicles and our romances of chivalry, but those respectable spokesmen of the Middle Ages spoke an obsolete language that no one was any longer capable of understanding, and the Knights of the Round Table waited a long time to obtain from the *oeil de boeuf*[3] the welcome to which they had been accustomed by Charlemagne, because an elegant introducer would have substituted a Franciscan habit for their heavy iron armor, and a red heel for their noisy spurs. The characters thus accoutered by Monsieur Tressan only resemble their heroic and naïve type as the lantern of the clown in the *Midsummer Night's Dream* resembles moonlight.[4]

---

1 The Hôtel de Rambouillet was where Catherine de Vivonne, Marquise de Rambouillet, hosted a literary salon between 1620 and 1648, which became the model for all future literary salons, dominated for some time my Mademoiselle de Scudéry, who became the most popular writer of her day with a series of episodic novels that laid the foundations for modern fiction and who inherited the salon from its original hostess. The members of the salon were parodied by Molière in *Les Précieuses ridicules* (1659), which led to its members being insultingly described as *précieuses* [precious women].

2 Voltaire's Ninus features in his tragedy *Semiramis* (1746). It is perhaps odd that Nodier gives no credit to Voltaire's prose romances as important contributions to French fantastic literature, and that he also fails to mention in this essay the fantastic fiction of Jacques Cazotte.

3 The *salon de l'oeil de boeuf* at Versailles was the antechamber to the king's bedroom.

4 After retiring from a military career, the Medievalist and Academician

It would, however, be unjust to refuse the great century the sole palm that its much-vaunted triumphs lacked, even though it rejected it outrageously; a more just future might perhaps glimpse in compensation the aborted glory of Chapelain, and slightly amortized admirations that once crowned the sonnet of Voiture, the triolet of Ranchin and the madrigal of Saint-Aulaire.[1] That production, worthy to make and epoch in the finest literary ages, that ingenuous masterpiece of the natural and the imagination, and which will doubtless survive with Molière, La Fontaine and a few fine scenes of Corneille, all the monuments of the reign of Louis XIV, the book without model that the most fortunate imitations have left forever inimitable, is Perrault's *Contes des fées*.[2]

---

Louis-Elisabeth de la Vergne, Comte de Tressan (1705-1783) wrote several neo-chivalric romances, including adaptations of *Amadis de Gaule* and *Roland furieux*.

1 The references are to the poet Jean Chapelain (1595-1674), author of a long-gestated and much-parodied epic poem, *La Pucelle* (1656), about Jeanne d'Arc; Vincent Voiture (1597-1648), an habitué of the Hôtel de Rambouillet; the obscure Jacques de Ranchin, known primarily for an oft-cited exemplary triolet dating from the 1690s; and François-Joseph de Beaupoil, Marquis de Saint-Aulaire (1643-1742), whose appointment as a long-serving member of the Académie française did little to redeem his mediocre reputation.

2 This judgment and its attempted justification illustrates a confusion that had become endemic by the early nineteenth century. The original *contes de fées* were an invention of female writers in the Parisian salons of the 1690s, imported to Versailles thanks to the enthusiasm of Louis XIV's eldest daughter, the dowager Princesse de Conti; they were "tales of fays" in a narrow sense, borrowing the imagery of French Medieval romance but deliberately placing enchantresses center stage with a calculated feminist agenda, in a fictitious world devoid of any trace of the Christian God or Church. Only four of the eight tales in the first version of Charles Perrault's *Histoires ou contes du temps passé* (1697, better known as *Contes de ma mère l'Oye* [Tales Mother Goose]) feature fays, all four derived from *contes* by female writers that he had heard read aloud in salons; the generic label, which Perrault did not employ, was only used as a title by Madame d'Aulnoy, whose works were suppressed at the time of their composition and only became well-known some twenty years later, after her death, when they became the leading items in an illicitly-printed anthology. *Le*

The composition is not exactly in conformity with Aristotle's rules, and the somewhat mannered style has not offered the compilers of our rhetorics, so far as I know, many rich examples of descriptions, amplifications, metaphors and prosopopeias; one would even have some difficulty, and I say this to the shame of our dictionaries, in finding in those ample archives of our language positive information about certain unaccustomed locutions that, at least for foreigners, still await the cares of etymology and commentators. I cannot deny that there are some in that number, like "*tirez la cordelette et la bobinette cherra*"[1] which might give grave concern to future Saumaises, but what is certain is that their innumerable readers understand them marvelously, and it is visible that the author had had the modest bonhomie not to work for posterity. What a vivid attraction, moreover, there is in the slightest details of those charming bagatelles, what truth in the characters, what ingenious and unexpected originality in the peripeties, what a frank and gripping verve in the dialogues. Thus, I have no hesitation in affirming that, so long as there remains in our hemisphere a people, a tribe, a hamlet or a

---

*Cabinet des fées*, juxtaposed with Perrault's stories. Genuine *contes de fées* were consistently refused the royal privileges required for licit publication after a handful of collections appeared in 1697, and were thus driven underground, while Perrault's stories, Christianized and adapted for reading to children, continued to be reprinted legally, thus acquiring an illusion of originality that was entirely unwarranted. In England, Madame d'Aulnoy's label was translated as "fairy tales," although her human fays are quite distinct from the supernatural fairies featured in Elizabethan poetry and *A Midsummer Night's Dream*. By the time Nodier wrote his essay, however, the term *contes de fées* had been adapted in French to apply loosely to a wide range of mock-folktales, and Nodier used it very broadly with reference to his own fantastic stories.

1 This phrase occurs in *Le Petit chaperon rouge*, known in English as "Little Red Riding-Hood," pronounced by the protagonist's grandmother and then repeated imitatively by the disguised wolf. A bobinette is a door-latch, in this case lifted by pulling a string, for the convenience of the bedridden old lady.

tent in which civilization finds a refuge against the progressive invasions of barbarity, there will be talk by the light of the solitary hearth of the adventurous odyssey of *Petit Poucet*, the conjugal vengeances of *Barbe-Bleue* and the clever maneuvers of the *Chat Botté*; and the Ulysses, the Othello and the Figaro of children will live for a long time after the others.

If there is something to put in comparison with the stainless perfection of these miniature epics, if one can oppose a few fresher idealities to the innocent charms of the Chaperon, the mischievous graces of Finette and the touching resignation of Griselidis, it is among the people themselves that it is necessary to seek those unperceived poems, the traditional delights of the firesides of villages, from which Perrault judiciously drew his stories.

I do not deny that there have been scholarly dissertations in our day on the *Contes des fées*, which have tried to find distant origins for them, and that we are led to believe on the faith of erudite men that *Peau d'âne* is a importation from Arabia, that *Riquet à la houppe* did not exercise the right of fief over his old domains without a title of investiture stamped in the name of the Orient, and that the galette and the pot of butter, in spite of their false appearance of locality, were brought to us one fine morning by some other Sindbad on the shoulders of an afrit from the land of the *Thousand-and-One Nights*. We have become so accustomed to imitation, since the establishment of the Aristotelian dynasty by which we are still governed from the height of the Institute, that it is almost received in literary dogma that nothing is invented in France, and it is probable that the Institut does not lack good reasons for engaging us to believe it. My submission to its edicts cannot go that far.

Our beneficent fays with wands of iron or hazel-wood, our rebarbative and peevish fays with carriages drawn by bats, our utterly amiable and utterly gracious princesses, our stupid and ferocious ogres, our giant-killers, the charming metamorphoses of the Blue Bird, and the miracles of the Golden Branch,[1] belong to our old Gaul like its sky, its mores and its monuments, too long misunderstood. It is to take too far the scorn of an intelligent nation that has launched itself so far forward in its own movement in all the routes of civilization to contest it the merit of invention necessary to put on stage the heroes of the *bibliothèque bleue*.[2]

If the fantastic had never existed among us, of its own inventive nature, an exception made of all ancient or exotic literature, we would not have had a society, for there has never been a society that has not had its own. The excursions of travelers have not shown them a savage family that does not relate a few strange stories, and which does not place in the clouds of its atmosphere or the smoke of its huts some mystery, surprised in the intermediary world by the intelligence of old men, the sensibility of women and the credulity of children.

The passionate Orientalists who steal the fables of our nurses in order to pay homage to the choreographers of almahs and bayaderes from beneath the peasant's thatch, or the nomadic hut of the woodcutter, or the joyful firesides of gleaners or wine-growers, are sometimes unfounded. Far from accusing Perrault of plagiarism, they ought perhaps to complain of the miserly parsimony with which those surprising chronicles of ages that never were and never will be, which are

---

1 The Blue Bird and the Golden Branch are both featured in stories by Madame Aulnoy, not Perrault; the previously-cited Finette was also employed by Madame d'Aulnoy, but was probably borrowed by her from a tale by Mademoiselle L'Héritier, which had appeared in print before Perrault's collection. Perrault—a distant relative of Mademoiselle L'Héritier—appropriated two of his key motifs from another of her tales.
2 The *bibliothèque bleue* was originated in Troyes, and consisted of cheap popular pamphlets that included almanacs and cookery books, but also recycled old literary materials, including adaptations of many verse and prose romances; it still existed in the early nineteenth century but had been superseded by sturdier and more substantial cheap books.

nevertheless so present and alive in the memory of the troubadours of our hamlets, were distributed to our ancestors. How many beautiful narrations they might have heard, imprinted, with so much vivacity, with the customs, mores and names of countries, on hearing which the most intrepid etymologist is obliged to pause at the incontestable course of inventions and things, and which he has never succeeded in attributing in his thought to another nature and another society.

Since the sentimental old woman, a dreamer and perhaps something of a sorceress, who first took it into her head to improvise these poetic fables, by the blazing glare of a bundle of dry juniper, to lull to sleep the impatience and pains of a poor sick child, they have been repeated faithfully, from generation to generation, in the long evenings of spinners, to the monotonous noise of their wheels, scarcely varied by the clink of the hooked iron that pokes the fire, and they will be repeated forever, without any new people deciding to dispute them with us; for every people has its stories, and the creative faculty of storytelling is fecund enough in every land for there to be no need to go far in search of what it possesses itself, as well as guiriots[1] and calendars. The penchant for the marvelous and the faculty of modifying it, flows from certain natural and fortuitous circumstances, and is innate in humans. It is the essential instrument of the imaginative life, and is perhaps the sole truly providential compensation for the miseries inseparable from social life.

Germany has been rich in that genre of creations, richer than any other country in the world, without excepting the fortunate Levantines, the eternal suzerains of our treasures, in the opinion of antiquaries. That is because Germany, favored by a particular system of mental organization, bears in its beliefs a fervor of imagination, a vivacity of sentiments and

---

1 "Guiriot" is a French transliteration of "griot," the label attributed in various parts of West Africa to storytellers of high status in various tribal societies.

a mysticism of doctrines in the universal penchant toward idealism that are essentially appropriate to fantastic poetry. It is also because, more independent of hidebound conventions and the formal despotism of an oligarchy of pretended scholars, it has the good fortune to deliver itself to its natural sentiments without fear that it will be checked by the imperious customs-officer of human thought which only receives ideas duly weighed and stamped by pedants. The meditative, impressionable and original individuality that characterizes its inhabitants has been manifest since time immemorial in the innumerable monuments of its fantastic library, and there, contrary to our literary habitudes, in which everything is subordinate to the aristocracy of intellect, it is popularity that consecrates success.

Germany still enjoys, in that regard, the same frankness as it did in the century of Goëtz de Berliching.[1] It is indebted in that to the multitude of local circumscriptions and particular usages that have maintained the precious ingenuity of primitive people there, which have saved it from the devouring avidity of the monstrous Medusa of centralization, whose arms, inert for any other usage but seizure, are only occupied in satisfying the insatiable hunger of the Gorgon, and which will maintain it until the end of our present civilization, whatever the theoreticians of clubs and cafés might say, in the first rank of free nations.

Since the beautiful story of Faust—admirably poeticized by Goethe, who has added nothing to the philosophical ideality of the invention, the profound allegory of the adventurer who sold his soul to the devil, which the latest rhapsody that

---

1 Götz von Berlichingen (1480-16562) was a mercenary and poet whose autobiography supplied the raw material for an eponymous play by J. W. Goethe in 1773, which made famous a phrase attributed to him and still in common in the USA, translated into American English as "he can lick my ass."

has collected it has only reduced to the dwarf form of the novel—all the way to our own day, Germany has been the favorite domain of the fantastic. It has completed the psychic history of humankind so magnificently opened in *Genesis* by the truly divine emblem of the tree of knowledge and the seductions of the serpent. Faust is the Adam of the terrestrial Paradise who has come to believe himself equal to God. The *Dream* of Jean-Paul is the solemn denouement of that sad drama, and that other apocalypse, the terrible key to the enigma of our material life.[1] Outside of those three fables, there is no absolute truth on earth.

The ever-increasing woes of the new society presage so visibly its imminent ruin that the trumpet of the angel of the last days will not announce it more distinctly to the condemned generation. At this moment, the fantastic is irrupting into all the paths that lend sensation to intelligence; and now it has entered, in spite of Aristotle, Quintillian, Boileau, La Harpe and I know not who else, into drama, elegy, the novel, painting and all the games of the mind as well as all the passions of the soul. And then there was a cry of shrill and ignorant anger against the unexpected invasion that threatens the beautiful forms of classicism; and it is not understood that there was a broader, more universal and more irreparable form, which is about to finish; that the form in question, which is that of a worn-out civilization, of which classicism is only a partial, temporary, indifferent expression, and that it is not astonishing that the puerile bond of the stupid unities of rhetoric is loosening, when the immense unity of the social world is breaking apart everywhere.

---

1 The reference is to *Blumen- Fucht- und Domerndtücke, oder Ehentand, Tod, und Hchzeit des Armenasvokalen Sibenkäs* [Flower-, Fruit- and Thorn-pieces; or, the Married Life, Death and Wedding of Siebenkas, a poor man's lawyer] (1796-97) by Jean Paul (Johann Paul Richter, 1763-1825), often abbreviated to *Siebenkäs*, a hallucinatory fantasy famous for its invention of the word *doppelganger*.

Among the men of election whom a profound instinct of genius has thrown, in recent times, to the forefront of literature, there is not one who has not sensed the muse's warning, of a society that is falling, and who has not obeyed her inspirations, like the imposing voice of a dying man whose grave is already open. The romantic school of Lewis, the romantic school of the lackists,[1] and above all, the great masters of speech, Byron, Walter Scott, Lamartine and Hugo, have precipitated themselves thereinto in search of the ideal life, as if a particular organ of divination that nature has given to the poet had enabled them to foresee that the breath of positive life was near to extinction in the decrepit organization of peoples.

I have not named Monsieur de Chateaubriand among them, who has remained, consciously and by choice, at the terminus of the old world, like the pyramid in the sands of Egypt, like the ark of the deluge on the summit of Ararat, or the pillars of Hercules on the shore of unknown seas. Walter Scott, also enchained by memories, studies and affections, has placed the bases of his renown a little further on between the two societies, but not with more solidity and power. He is a lighthouse who casts a few gleams indistinctly over the port, and some over the abyss. The abyss! Byron is lost there under full sail, and no human gaze has been able to follow him.

The German fantastic is very popular, and that is explicable, I repeat, by a long fidelity to mores and tradition, to institutions emerged from the land, often defended and saved at the price of the citizens' blood; to a system of education that is more general, more extensive and more appropriate to the needs of the times. It is explicable, above all, by a pronounced repugnance for purely material innovations, from which the intelligent and moral principle of nations has nothing to gain. The people, who have touched the fringes of all the sciences,

---

1 This term appears to have been coined by Nodier in the present essay.

who have produced almost all the essential inventions whose impulsion has completed the civilization of Europe, and who are occupied delectably in the mild possession of a liberty without ostentation, the sedentary contemplations of astronomy and the enrichment of natural nomenclatures, have the merit of conserving for a long time the innocent and sensate taste for children's stories. Thanks ought to be rendered to Musaeus, Tieck and Hoffmann, whose fortunate caprices, by turns mystical and familiar, pathetic or comical, simple to the point of triviality or exalted as far as extravagance, but filled everywhere with originality, sensibility and grace, renew for the old age of our decrepitude the fresh and brilliant illusions of our cradle. Their reading produces, on a soul fatigued by the agonized convulsions of unquiet peoples who are struggling against an inevitable crisis, the effect of a serene slumber, populated with attractive dreams that rock and relax. They are the imagination's fountain of youth.

In France, where the fantastic is so decried today by the supreme arbiters of literary taste, it has perhaps not been useless to search for its origin, to mark in passing its principal epochs and to fix to names consecrated with sufficient glory the culminating titles of its genealogy; but I have only traced the bare outlines of its history, and I will refrain from attempting its apology against the prejudiced learned minds who have abdicated the first impressions of their childhood in order to retrench themselves in an exclusive order of ideas.

The questions of the fantastic belong to the domain of fantasy themselves. God preserve me from awakening, on their subject, the miserable disputes of the scholastics of the last century and transporting a theological quarrel on to the terrain of literature, in the interest of the grace of enchantments and the free will of the intelligence. What I dare to believe is that if the liberty about which people speak to us is not, as I sometimes fear, a deception of tricksters, its two principal sanctuaries are in human religious belief and in the poetic imagination.

What other compensation can you promise to a soul profoundly sickened by the experience of life, what other avenue could be prepared henceforth in the anguish of so much disappointed hope, which revolutions bring with them, I ask you, free men who sell the cloister of the cenobite to masons and carry the pick-ax into the hermitage of the solitary, where he took refuge alongside the eagle's nest? Have you joys to render to the brothers who reject you, which can compensate them for the loss of a single consoling error, and do you believe yourselves sufficiently certain of the verities for which you make nations pay so dear to evaluate their arid bitterness at the price of the mild and inoffensive reverie of the unfortunate, who go to sleep with a happy dream?

However, everyone enjoys among you, it is necessary to say, a liberty without limits, except for conscience and genius. And you know that your triumphant march through the ideas of a vanquished generation has nevertheless enveloped the human race to such an extent that only a few men remain around you who need to occupy themselves with anything other than your theories, exercising their thought on a progression that is doubtless imaginary, but which is perhaps no more than your material progression, the prevision of which is no more grounded than that of the attempts of your social perfection under the protection of the liberties you invoke.

You forget that everyone has received, in living Europe, the education of Achilles, and that you are not the only ones to have broken the bones and veins of the lion in order to suck the marrow and drink the blood. That the positive world belongs to you irrevocably is a fact, and doubtless a benefit, but break, break that shameful chain of the intellectual world with which you are obstinate in garroting poetic thought.

A long time ago we have all had, each in our turn, our battle of Philippi, and some did not wait for it, I swear to you, in order to be convinced that truth was only a sophism and virtue only a name. Those require a region inaccessible to the tumultuous movements of the crowd in which to place their future. That region is faith for those who believe, the ideal for those who dream, and who prefer illusion to doubt for all compensation.

And then, it is necessary, after all, that the fantastic returns to us, whatever efforts are made to proscribe it What is most difficult to uproot in the people is not the fictions that conserve it but the lies that amuse it.

# The Story of Hélène Gillet

The winter will be long and sad. The aspect of nature is not joyous. That of the social world is scarcely more so. You dread the ennui of spectacles. You dread, in particular, the ennui of salons. It is a matter of making a big fire at home, very bright, lively and crackling, of lowering the lamps slightly, which have become almost unnecessary, of ordering your domestic—if, by chance, you have one—not to come in again unless you ring; and having made those dispositions, I engage you to recount stories, or even to listen to them, in the midst of your family and friends, for I do not suppose that you will be alone. If you are alone, however, recount stories to yourself. That is yet another pleasure, and well worth its price. I have tried a little of everything, and I have never really been amused by anything else.

But if you are curious with regard to fantastic stories, I warn you that the genre in question requires more common sense and art than is ordinarily imagined; and for a start, there are several genres of fantastic stories.

There is the false fantastic story. the charm of which results from the double credulity of the storyteller and the audience, like Perrault's *contes de fées*, the excessively disdained masterpiece of the century of masterpieces.

There is the vague fantastic story, which leaves the soul suspended in a pensive and melancholy doubt, lulls like a melody and cradles like a dream.

There is the true fantastic story, which is the first of all, because it shakes the heart profoundly without costing the sacrifice of reason—and I mean by the !true fantastic story," for such an alliance of words is worth the trouble of being explained, the relation of a fact held to be materially impossible which was, however accomplished, to the knowledge of everyone. It is rare, in truth; so very rare that I cannot recall any other example today than the story of Hélène Gillet.

With regard to a true story, the merit of the storyteller is doubtless very little. If his imagination is mingled with it, the embroidery risks spoiling the canvas. His principal artifice consists of hiding behind his subject. If anyone examines, he must clarify, if anyone argues, he must offer proof. Then the emotion will increase, like that of a spectator of a scene of illusions, who extends a hand mechanically to deflect a phantom, and stops, chilled by horror, at a living body that palpitates and cries out. But the story of Hélène Gillet would require on that account a volume of written development, and I have an excellent reason for not providing it, which is that it has been done, and done in a superior fashion, by one of the most learned men of the epoch in which we are living.[1] It is taken from the eleventh volume of the of *Mercure François* of Richer and Renaudot,[2] the *Life of the Abbess of Notre-Dame du Tart, Madame Courcelle de Pourlans*,[3] and the authentic manuscripts

---

1 Author's reference: "*Histoire d'Hélène Gillet, ou Relation d'un évenement extraordnaire et tragique survenuu à Dijon dans le dix-septième siècle, par un ancien avocat*, Dijon: Lagier, 1829." The collator of the book, who sent it to Nodier with other supporting documents, was the prolific bibliographer Gabriel Peignot (1767-1849), who readily gave Nodier permission to transmute it. It can now be read on Google Books.

2 The *Mercure François*, the first known French periodical, was founded in 1605 by Jean and Estienne Richer; it was taken over in 1639 by Théophraste Renaudot (1586-1653), the founder of *La Gazette*, a newspaper of sorts, which pioneered the French press.

3 Author's reference: "By Edme-Berrnard Boutrée, oratorian of Lyon, Jean Certe, 1699." The book in question is cited by Peignot but his citation is very brief and the book certainly does not contain the wealth of detail here

of the Chambre des Comptes and the Mairie of Dijon, with the consequence that there is nothing better demonstrated, nothing more exactly analyzed, nothing more complex in details, in the testimony, so picturesque and so animated, of the stenography of the Courts of Assizes. And my friend's book is a book that I recommend to you in passing.

This is quite simply what I promised you: a fireside tale,[1] one of those entertainments for the length of which you sometimes pardon me, when they interest you: a true fantastic story, arranged and recited in my own fashion, with as little latitude as the imagination can take in the disposition of an extraordinary tableau that it would not have dared to invent. Stimulate, therefore, those firebrands ready to collapse, rock the children in your arms so that they will not wake up, close the tric-trac board,[2] if you please, and put your chairs in a semicircle while I tell you what it remains for me to say before commencing.

It is necessary for me to warn you that the story of Hélène Gillet unfolds almost entirely in a theater the mere aspect of which might revolt delicate organizations, and it has been necessary for me, in order to write it, to triumph over the repugnance of my own heart. You can follow me without danger if you are hardened by the dramas or romances of our own day to impressions of a certain nature. Otherwise, go to the piano, form a separate circle or entertain gracious thoughts with the household spirit by making sparks fly in sheaves and spurts from the fire. You have been warned.

attributed to the anecdote of the supposed prophecy, which is almost all due to Nodier's embroidery.

1 The phrase that Nodier actually uses—and employs as a generic description elsewhere—is "*conte de la veillée*," which could be more literally translated as a tale told while staying awake at night [in winter]"—the occasion when domestic gatherings used to indulge in swapping stories before generous artificial lighting made it easier for people to indulge in separate activities after dark.

2 Tric-trac was a game similar to the modern backgammon.

In 1624, the castellan or royal judge of Bourg-en-Bresse, at the foot of our dear mountains of the Jura and the Bugey, was named Pierre Gillet, a noble, upright, severe man of good renown. He had a daughter by the name of Hélène, twenty-two years old, who was adored for her beauty, admired for her intelligence and graces, and respected for her piety and virtue. Hélène was scarcely seen except in church, but even the church is, for an evil mind, a place of evil thoughts. She had the misfortune to be loved by one of those violent men who sacrifice everything to their passion, even the woman who is the object of it, when they cannot hope to marry her or to please her, and I would tell you his name if history had informed me of it.

Enticed to the home of an apostate false friend for her doom, on the pretext of some act of Christian charity, she was fascinated there, like the victims of the Old Man of the Seven Mountains, by a narcotic beverage. God knows what dreams of inexplicable and unknown voluptuousness she had during that time; the unfortunate woman was never able to recall them. She was ignorant, in her innocence, of the joys that open the door of Hell.

That event only left her with a vague sadness devoid of remorse, for no thought of crime was mingled with her memories. However, the sniggering whispers of passers-by, the coarse laughter of libertines and the profoundly attentive gazes of old women, sharpened by a bitter curiosity, and above all the daily abandonment of her dearest companions gradually informed her that she had been deprived of her reputation in the eyes of the world, and that society was rejecting her. Soon, only one friend remained to her, and she hid her head in her mother's arms in order to weep, because she had nothing to confide to her.

The mystery of her misfortune had scarcely begun to reveal itself to her mind when she was gripped by the agonies of childbirth; or, rather, she fell into a long faint caused by shame, despair and dolor. That was another dream, an indefinable dream of which she conserved no more idea than of the first. Spouse and mother, nothing remained to her of that double title but the opprobrium of having borne it without the permission of religion and the law. Those two immense joys of nature, so dearly paid for by women, had only been sterile tortures for Hélène, of which nothing redeemed the horror, not even the memory of a moment of intoxication or the smile of an innocent creature awakening to life. She had scarcely known the lover, and she did not know the child at all.

In fact, as she was surprised again by the sleep of the senses that resembles death, but which is not, a young man who had been lying in wait for some time in the epoch of the clandestine childbirth, penetrated into Hélène's room at daybreak, between the exhausted mother and an old maidservant, who were asleep. He ran to the bed, for no cradle had been prepared, wrapped the new-born in the first cloth that came to hand, deposited a frantic kiss on the forehead of the sick or dead woman, and then disappeared. The investigation proved beyond doubt that it was a student from the environs of Bourg "dwelling in the lodgings of his uncle" who had served for some months as the tutor of Hélène's young brothers.[1] He was never seen again.

When Hélène woke up and learned the full extent of her misery she doubtless searched for her child, which was no longer there. She did not dare to ask for him, because it did not seem to her that she ought to have a child. All that accumulated in her mind like the caprices of a vision.

Some time afterwards, however, she reappeared in the town and in the church, accompanied by her mother, as she

1 This is a gross exaggeration; other commentators on the story agreed with the judges, suspecting strongly that Hélène Gillet was guilty of the charges laid against her and that her account of her misfortunes was an implausible invention.

had done in the past. It was only remarked that she seemed to be ill, that her bosom had sagged and that her physiognomy bore a strange expression of astonishment and terror.

The castellan of Bourg-en-Bresse had enemies, as all powerful men have, but the beautiful and gentle Hélène had no enemies. A few days were spent collecting, exchanging and propagating sinister conjectures, but soon there was no longer any mention of them. The investigations that the law had commenced, on the basis of popular rumor, were suddenly interrupted for want of evidence. Hélène felt, however, that her destiny of misfortune was incomplete, and that Providence had more rigorous proofs in reserve for her; she resigned herself to that with constancy at the feet of altars, because she was without reproach and she had faith in God.

Now, it happened that a soldier who was walking outside the town, waiting for his mistress, was struck by the actions of a crow, which was diving at the foot of a certain wall with reiterated falls, stirring and digging in the soil with its beak, scattering it underfoot and rising again toward its branch with a few shreds of bloody cloth. Then it leapt from branch to branch, its neck extended and its gaze fixed upon the place where it had descended, and fell again like a stone, to resume digging. The soldier approached, drove it away with a swipe of his saber, enlarged with its tip the hole that the crow had commenced digging, and took out of it the cadaver of a child, rolled in the remains of a chemise marked with the name of Hélène Gillet.

With that, the investigations of the Presidial were resumed, and by a sentence of 6 February 1621, Hélène Gillet was condemned, for the crime of infanticide, to have her head cut off, for poor Hélène was noble, and it was believed then that iron ennobled execution. It has become more popular since.

Hélène's advocate appealed against the judgment to the parlement of Dijon, for her family did not intervene and the old castellan even forbade expressly that there should ever be any mention of her so much did austerity of mores and justice prevail in that Roman heart over the mildest of natural inclinations. Two archers took her from Bourg-en-Bresse to the conciergerie of the Palais des États, with no other companion but one unfortunate woman who had not been able to quit her; I hardly need to say that it was her mother.

It was not that Madame Gillet counted much on the effect of her tears on the judged of La Tournelle. Too little time had passed since she had tried them in vain on the judges of the Presidial. She was counting on a judge who reforms, when it pleases him, the judgments of the earth, and in whom the unfortunate can never place their hopes in vain. But the pious woman did not believe herself worthy to communicate with God without an intermediary. She therefore came to place herself in the convent of the Bernardines of Dijon, under the protection of the prayers of the community, and particularly her noble relative, Mother Jeanne de Saint-Joseph, who had quit the name of Courcelle de Pourlans to become the abbess of the holy monastery.

The sight of those virgins prostrate on the paving stones of the choir, imploring his pity with groans and tears, in favor of a young mother whom the law had proclaimed culpable of the murder of her child, obliged to articulate in their thoughts, in order to disarm the vengeance of Heaven, the almost-blasphemous syllables designating I know not what unknown crimes, was certainly a sublime spectacle and made to attract the benedictions of the Lord, if our vain dolors ever reach as far as him. Madame Gillet was not on her knees like the others but lying face down on the ground, and she would have been thought to be dead if she had not been sobbing.

It is necessary to say, nevertheless, because one would not imagine it, that something was lacking in the solemnity of that imposing ceremony. One of the nuns had not appeared: Sister

Françoise du Saint-Esprit, who had been called Madame de Longueval in the world, and whose infirmities had prevented her from descending to the sanctuary for many years. She was then more than ninety-two years old, if hagiological biographers can be believed, who record her death in 1633, more than centenarian, in an odor of sanctity.

Sister Françoise du Saint-Esprit had fallen, in order to use vulgar terminology, into the state of grace and innocence that old age brings to those endowed with child-like ignorance. She knew no more of things related to common life than those related to the other, for she was living in advance in the eternity that she had entered many days ago, and as her language was gradually imprinted with knowledge of the future, the great minds of the time doubted her reason; but her words still passed for revelations from on high in the convent of the Bernardines.

Why should God not have accorded prevision of his mysterious designs to a few souls proven by the long exercise of virtue? Personally, at the time of writing, I would like nothing better than to believe that. Fortunately, Hélène's mother believed it. She did not quit the sanctuary except to go up to the cell where Sister Françoise was reposing on a sack of straw, her two hands devotedly crossed over a crucifix. As she thought that the sister was asleep, because she was not moving, Madame Gillet knelt down in a corner, holding her breath in order not to wake her; but she was not there for long before she heard herself called. Sister Françoise's hand was seeking her, for the aged saint could hardly see. Madame Gillet seized it, and stuck her lips to it respectfully.

"Good, good," said Madame de Longueval, with an ineffable smile, "you're the mother of that poor child for whom our sisters were praying this morning. I declare to you that she is a pure soul, chosen before the Lord, who has deigned to listen to the prayers of his servants, and that your child will not die by the executioner's hand, since Hélène is called to lead a long life with a great deal of edification."

Having said that, Sister Françoise du Saint-Esprit appeared to forget that there was someone with her, and she returned to her customary meditation.

In the meantime—it was Monday the twelfth of May, which was the last session of the Parlement—the members were occupied in the report of counselor Jacob on the appeal of the judgment of Bourg. The sentence was confirmed by all votes with an aggravating circumstance. The court ordered that the condemned be led to execution with a noose around her neck, in order to testify by that infamy to the enormity of her crime. The execution was to be immediate, and the unfortunate Hélène had only to go from the praetory to the scaffold.

The news of the outcome of the trials soon reached the convent of the Bernardines. They were seen to spread out simultaneously into the chapels, light all the candles, expose all the relics, strike the steps of all the altars with their foreheads and confound, in accordance with their age and emotions, prayers, lamentations and cries. Mother Jeanne de Saint-Joseph ran, weeping, from the nave to the choir and from the choir to the cell of Sister Françoise du Saint-Esprit, where Madame Gillet had collapsed, devoid of a voice, without a plaint and without tears, on the steps of the prie-Dieu.

"I have told you, however," repeated Sister Françoise, whose serenity was unaltered, "that the young woman will not die, and a long time after us she will be praying for us on earth, for that is the will of Our Lord." Then she returned to the contemplation of Heaven, as if it were open before her, and Mother Jeanne de Saint-Joseph searched for motives for hope.

As for Madame Gillet, her attention was no longer on that scene; she could no longer see anything, hear anything or feel anything. Suddenly, however, she started, uttering a cry of horror, for she had just been extracted from her faint by the blast of the trumpet that was summoning the soldiers to the frightful sacrifice; even the trumpet of Judgment could not have seized the soul of the wicked with a more profound anguish.

She raised herself up on her hands, lending a mute and terrible attention to the signal of the death of her beloved Hélène, and the signal was repeated, coming closer to the convent. Gradually, other sounds were mingled with it: that of the monotonous tread of horses making paving stones resound, and which covered momentarily, like the gust of a storm wind, the rumors of the multitude.

"There she is! There she is!" cried a thousand voices, which only formed a single voice, and Madame Gillet fell unconscious again, because she understood that her daughter was passing by.

"Listen, listen, my sister," said Mother Jeanne de Saint Joseph, wringing her hands in despair next to Sister Françoise du Saint-Esprit's meager bed. "Oh, my God, my sister, can't you hear it?"

"I can hear as you can," replied Sister Françoise, turning her mild infantile smile toward her. "I can hear the trumpet sounding and the horses marching with their riders; I can hear the people talking, the penitents singing. Yes," she continued, "I can hear very well. I know that that poor innocent is advancing, and that she is here now; I know that she is being taken to death; but I tell you in truth that she will not die. You can promise her mother that."

Hélène was, indeed, marching to death, assisted by two Jesuits and two Capuchins, who presented to her by turns an image of Christ, which she kissed with candor. Never had she been seen so beautiful. Her hair had not been cut, either because the executioner had not dared to raise his scissors to

it or because the ceremonial of ostentatious executions spared
that outrage to qualified patients; it was retained at the top of
her head by a knotted ribbon, but the agitation of the march
had loosened the knot and a part of it fell in thick waves over
Hélène's left shoulder, where it covered the ignominious rope
that had been passed around her neck That circumstance is
not irrelevant to the understanding of the rest of my story.

Now, if you would care to lend me momentarily the
magic wand of Hugo or Dumas, I shall transport the scene
to another place. There was in Dijon a square whose name
indicates sufficiently its tragic destination; it was called the
Morimont, or the mountain of death. In the middle rose a
scaffold, hung with a lugubrious cloth, to which one climbed
by eight wooden steps, but which was raised by a platform of
masonry formed by four stone steps. All around, to a radius of
two and a half toises, an enclosure had been traced composed
of planks and stakes, to serve as a barrier to the crowd. The
interior was occupied by the king's *procureur général*, seated on
a folding chair, escorted by his ushers of honor, by the Jesuit
and Capuchin fathers who were making the recommendation
of the soul, and by a platoon of archers. Along the fence, six
penitents were circulating in black sackcloth, open only at
the place of the eyes, with bare feet, their waists circled by a
hempen rope, with torches in their hands, who were pleading
in lamentable voices for the souls in purgatory.

Hélène mounted the scaffold alone and stopped in front of
the block, raising her heart to God. Simon Grandjean had not
yet arrived, because he was finishing his prayers at the Conciergerie, where he had taken communion that morning. Four
o'clock had, however, chimed in all the parishes, and the people
were calling for Simon Grandjean with murmurs that soon
changed into roars. Simon Grandjean was the executioner.

He finally appeared, accompanied by the excutioner-
ess—which is to say, his wife, who served as his assistant on

important occasions. He was armed with his cutlass, and his wife with a pair of scissors half a foot long, with which she had just equipped herself in order to cut the floating hair that she had seen escaping from the knot in Hélène's coiffure. That thought must have preoccupied her profoundly, for the launched herself into the enclosure brandishing her scissors and without losing sight of them; but when she arrived next to Hélène she forgot them.

A movement and a sign made by Simon Grandjean at the front of the platform informed the spectators that he was going to speak—an event entirely new in the history of judiciary executions. The noise that was rumbling in the multitude suddenly died down, like that of a tempest at the surface of a sea surprised by a calm. It is true that everything gave that scene a horrible interest, and I shall not try to heighten it by means of hyperboles borrowed from our cold language. The formidable actor that I have just caused to appear could, at that moment, demand some part of the public pity for himself. Weakened by fasting and the mortifications that he had prescribed for himself in order to render himself capable of fulfilling his terrible ministry, he could hardly stand up, and, leaning on the point of his cutlass, his distraught features announced that a frightful struggle was going on within him between duty and compassion.

"Mercy! Mercy for me!" he cried. "Benediction, my brethren! Forgive me, Messieurs of Dijon, for I have been gravely ill for three months and afflicted in my body, I have never cut off heads, and Our Lord God has refused me the strength to kill thus young woman! On my faith as a Christian, I know that I cannot kill her!"

Lightning is less prompt than the response of the audience.

"Kill! Kill!" said the people.

"Perform your office!" said the king's prosecutor. And those words signified: "Kill!" like the other.

Then Simon Grandjean raised his cutlass, approached Helene, tottering, and fell at her feet.

"Noble demoiselle," he said, holding out the hilt of the sword to her, "kill me or forgive me!"

"I forgive you and bless you," replied Hélène, and placed her head on the block

The executioner, meanwhile, excited by his wife, who was heaping him with reproaches, could not do anything but strike. The blade glittered in the air like a lightning flash, to the acclamations of the crowd. The Jesuits, the Capuchins and the penitents cried: "Jesus! Maria!"

The blade came down, but the blow slid over Hélène's hair and only penetrated the left shoulder. The patient fell over on her right side. It was thought for a moment that she was dead, but the executioner's wife knew that she was not; she tried to affirm the cutlass in her husband's trembling hands, while Hélene got up in order to bring her head back to the block, and a furious clamor was already running over the Morimont, but the bloody impatience of the people had changed its object, and was now turning to sympathy for Hélène.

The blade fell again, and the victim, attained by a wound more profound than the first, fell unconscious, as if devoid of life, on the executioner's weapon, which he had dropped.

Do not reproach me for these cruel details, sensitive souls who take such a keen interest in the unfortunates of melodrama and tragedy; I am only reporting them in order to obey the demands of my subject, not with the design of choosing them or aggravating them. This is not, unfortunately, poetry or romance; it is, alas, only history.

And you will understand that, before continuing, I need a few oratory precautions—in the interest of the reader, who must be in a hurry to escape his emotions, and to leave the stage behind the curtain from time to time, and to recall with me, while I draw breath, that the real events of which I speak are today as if they had never been. The frightful scene of the Morimont was, in fact, prolonged by so many peripeties more frightful still that I do not know whether it is more painful to be their historian than to have been their witness. All the art that I would put into reciting them, if I had the secret of a better style, would be limited to suspending the horror frequently in reticences, or veiling it under words.

I have not said, in describing the tragic enclosure of Morimont, that it enclosed another construction than that of the scaffold; it is necessary, however, that you know it. It was a kind of brick hut, where the executioner stored his irons, his ropes, his shackles, his braziers and his entire hideous apparatus of judiciary assassination. That execrable accessory of the dungeon was known as "the Chapel," as in Spain, and it was there that the condemned finished their acts of devotion when a sudden recipience decided them, when guilty, to reconcile themselves with their judge in Heaven, or, when innocent, to forgive their judges on earth.

Hélène Gillet had no need to descend to it, but Simon Grandjean hid there in order to escape the blows of the furious crowd, which was beginning to cross the barriers, crying out in a terrible voice: *Save the patient and kill the executioner!* The monks and the penitents ran after him, presenting their crucifixes to the people in order to deflect their wrath and to ward off the hail of stones that pursued them.

The corporation of masons set about demolishing the chapel, which was locked from within; the corporation of butchers organized a reserve corps behind them, entirely disposed for murder. There is no play with words here, nor combinations of style, for they are the exact terms of the legal statement drawn up four days later in the city's council chamber, which bears the signature of Alderman Bossuet, the father of the immortal Bishop of Meaux. Finally, the men of God opened up and emerged serenely, singing the prayer for the dead, as if they were marching to their own execution, and the people killed the executioner.

While that was accomplished, Hélène's scaffold presented a scene even more frightful. The executioner's wife had sought the cutlass in vain—it will be remembered that Hélène had fallen on top of it—but, at that moment, her scissors, which she had not quit, returned to her memory, and, seizing with one hand the rope that was knotted around the poor young woman's neck, with the other she struck her six times, dragging her down the eight wooden steps and the four stone steps, breaking the cadaver, already drowned in blood, with her feet, on all the steps that she struck with the head. When she reached the bottom, the butchers had concluded their initial task, and the people killed the executioner's wife.

I can finally breathe, and I think that it is high time for all of us. Fortunately, Hélene is no longer on the Morimont now, and charitable arms have carried her to a house that forms a corner of the square, the house of the good surgeon Nicolas Jacquin, whose honorable family still exercises, after two hundred years, the same profession in our two provinces of Bourgogne. None of Hélène's wounds was mortal, and none was found to be dangerous. When she recovered her senses, her first cry was that of the innocent entering Heaven, because she imagined that she had fallen into the hands of God, to whom the secret of all thoughts is known.

At the same instant, Sister Françoise du Saint-Esprit said, still smiling and lending an ear to the noise of the multitude returning to their quarters: "That's good, that's good; it's over. The people are returning home joyfully, because the young woman isn't dead."

Among so many miracles that signaled the memorable day of May twelfth, it is necessary not to forget the circumstance that caused it to concur, as I have said, with the last session of the parlement. The fortnight that the illustrious company had to rest until it could resume its work left the action of the law suspended and the functions of the executioner without a title-holder. That delay, ordinary enough between the sentence and the execution, but which the abrupt form of the judgment seemed to have abridged by design, gave Hélène's friends all the time necessary for recourse to royal mercy in favor of an unfortunate woman whose innocence had just been made manifest by prodigies; for that was then an age of candor and faith, in which one did not suppose that the natural order of human things could be overturned, against all probability, without some secret design of Providence—and I am one of those who still hold that opinion to be reasonable in the epoch of intellectual perfectionism and immense social amelioration that we have the good fortune to have reached, since philosophy has robbed Providence of its moral influence over events on earth.

The request for mercy was covered in a moment by innumerable signatures of everyone who could lend to Dijon the recommendation of an honorable rank or a high piety, but it will easily be understood that that plea for compassion, which was carried to the throne by the elite of a sensitive population, only offered a slender chance of success to hope and to pity. Louis XIII was reigning, and that young prince, who only had strength in order to be cruel, announced at twenty-four years of age the inflexible and bloody severity that was to give him the nickname of the Just by his flatterers. A deplorable justice is that of kings who only show themselves in history to serve as auxiliaries to executioners! The delay in Hélène's execution therefore went by in prayers, like an agony of a fortnight, in the chapel of the Bernardines, between the kisses of joy and the anguish of her mother's terror, who feared at the slightest noise that someone was coming to take her away in order to kill her.

Meanwhile, Sister Françoise du Saint-Esprit continued to repeat, when she remembered Hélène, whose confused story presented itself at intervals to her memory: "I promised you that that innocent will not die!"

Hélène's first words, when the cares of the surgeon brought her back to life, had expressed the same confidence in divine protection. "Something tells me in my heart," she said, "that the Lord will help me." But her soul, impoverished by so much dolor, could not always support the alternatives with an equal constancy. Sometimes, she suddenly went pale; a great tremor ran through her limbs, still poorly cured of their wounds, and she was heard to murmur, imprinting her lips on the cross of Jesus or the relics of the saints: "My God! My God! Shall I not return to the Morimont, where I suffered so much harm? Are they going to make me die? My God, have pity on me!"

At that time a dispatch was received from Paris, which was not dated but probably arrived at the predetermined time when the law was about to resume its bloody rights, for the charity of kings limps on one foot even more slowly than that of prayer. That dispatch brought one miracle more. Louis XIII had granted mercy.

The ratification of those letters of pardon "which removed from Hélène all infamy and restitute her in good renown" was pronounced by the Parlement of Dijon on the fifth of June 1625, on the plea of Maître Charles Fevret, author of the *Traité de l'Abuse,* so well known to advocates who have studied. Charles Fevret, whose greatest merit in the eyes of philologists, is having been the great-grandfather of the savant and ingenious Charles-Marie Fevret de Fontette, the editor—or rather the author—of one of the most precious monuments of our literary history, The *Bibliothèque historique* of Père Lelong.[1] Charles Fevret was reputed to be a great orator in his time and that reputation is not usurped if eloquence

---

1 Charles Fevret (1593-1661) denounced encroachments on ecclesiastical jurisdiction in the *Traité de l'Abus.* Charles-Marie de Fontette (1710-1772) supervised a new edition of the *Encyclopédic Bibliothèque de la France,* first published in 1719 by Père Lelong.

is measured by the number of harmonious phrases and the majestic pomp of speech. It is the *dictio togata* of the Senate and the Capitol of some patrician or consul, which rises above common language by means of magnificent turns and solemn words, as the magistrates of nations distinguish themselves from the vulgar by means of the ermine and the purple. One could believe that one were hearing in prose the resonance of the verses of Malherbes, and one has a presentiment of the manner of Balzac in the profusion of images and the luxury of allusions.

It is thus that he depicts poor Hélène, humbly prostrate before the parlement, and kissing the trenchant blade of the sword of justice, which cures the wounds it has inflicted, like the spear of Achilles. This is a movement that is quite beautiful:

"What a prodigy in our days that a young woman of that age, adherent to death body-to-body, struggled with such giant power in the park of its bloodiest executions, in the very field of its Morimort, and, to say everything in a few words, that, armed only with the confidence she had in God, she has overcome ignominy, fear, the executioner, the blade, the rope, the scissors, strangulation and death! After that dire trophy, what remains to her except to intone gloriously the canticle in which she will doubtless have her part henceforth: *Exaltetur Domine Deus meus, quoniam superexaltavit misericordia judicium.*[1] What can she do except hang, for an eternal memorial of her salvation, the votive tableau of her miseries in the sanctuary of this temple of justice? What design can she choose more appropriate to her condition than to raise an altar in her heart, where she will admire, for all the days of her life, the powerful hand of her liberator, the means unknown to men by which he has broken the shackles of her captivity, and the order of

---

1 This sentence, improvised by Fevret, invites the court to praise the Lord because the cup of judicial mercy has been raised.

his dispensatory providence to enable all things to be incurred for her liberation?"

I have cited that passage intentionally among many others that are no less remarkable, because it summarizes in advance all that it remains for me to say about the life of Hélène Gillet. The destiny of meditation and prayer to which her advocate seems to be summoning her here is the destiny that was made for her. There is reason to believe that she did not return to society, and perhaps only quit the convent of the Bernadines after the death of Sister Françoise du Saint-Esprit. It is known that she ended up becoming a nun in a convent in Bresse and that she had died there "with much edification," in accordance with the promises of her protective saint, not long before Père Bourrée of the Oratory published, in 1699, the *Histoire de la Mère Jeanne de Saint-Joseph, Madame Courcelle de Pourlans, abbess of Notre-Dame du Tart*. One can suppose, in accordance with the comparison of dates, that she was at least a nonagenarian.

I have omitted—or, rather, I have reserved—one extraordinary circumstance in order to close this long narration. That is that Hélène Gillets's letters of grace were granted in Louis XIII's council "in favor of the fortunate marriage of the queen of Great Britain, his very dear and beloved sister, Henriette-Marie de France," and, if I may be permitted once again to recall the expression of Charles Fevret, "while the king and his court were spending days of delight and festivity."

Those days of festivity, whose delight was so propitious to innocence, were consecrated to the marriage of Charles I, which coincided to the day with the execution of Hélène Gillet on the Morimont. Twenty-four years later, the head of Charles I fell at Whitehall under an ax more assured than that of Simon Grandjean, and the young woman of Bourge-en-Bresse had time to pray for half a century for the absolution of his soul. The designs of God are impenetrable and the human heart is blind, but there is no need to have penetrated very far into the study of past things to recognize that there is something mysterious and symbolic at the bottom of all histories.

And as the most vulgar tales require a moral, you will not forbid me, Messieurs, to attach one to this one, which is one of the most extraordinary, and yet one of the most true, that you have heard recited. It is that it is high time that the human race reproved with a unanimous voice the impious justice that has insolently usurped the work of death from the power of God, the work that God reserved for himself when he struck our race with a judgment of death that only belonged to him.

Oh, you are great makers of revolutions! You have made revolutions against all the laws! You have made them against the most intimate thoughts of the soul, against its affections, against its beliefs, against its faith! You have made them against thrones, against altars, against monuments, against stones, against the inanimate, against death, against the tomb and the dust of ancestors. You have not made a revolution against the scaffold, for no human sentiment has ever prevailed, and no human emotion has ever palpitated, in your revolutions of savages! And you talk about your enlightenment! And you do not hesitate to propose yourselves as models of a perfected civilization! Dare I ask of you where it is, your civilization? Is it, by chance, that hideous witch who is sharpening an iron triangle in order to cut off heads? Get away—you are barbarians!

As for you, my good friends, do remember now more gracious stories, the ones that lulled us gently in the basins of the Doubs in our skiffs laden with fruits, flowers and young women, while the nearby rocks sent back in long echoes the noise of bagpipes. Those stories I would take pleasure in retelling or hearing again today, for I will not hide it from you that speech was lacking my lips more than once, as the poet says, while I was recounting this one. But we are living in a time of severe thought and sad previsions, when good people might have need, like the noble populace of the Morimont, to form a coalition against the executioner; and if they had not killed the executioner—which is also a crime—I would willingly propose that a monument be erected to their courage.

It is necessary not to kill anyone. It is necessary not to kill those who kill. It is necessary not to kill the executioner. It is necessary to kill the laws of homicide.

# Jean-François-les-Bas-Bleus

In Besançon in 1793 there was an idiot, a monomaniac, a madman, whom all my compatriots who have had the good or ill fortune to live as long as I have will remember, like me. His name was Jean-François Touvet, but he was more commonly known, in the insolent and rascally language of schoolboys, as Jean-François-les-Bas-Bleus, because he never wore stockings of any other color. He was a young man of twenty-four or twenty-five, if I'm not mistaken, tall and well-built, of the noblest physiognomy that it is possible to imagine.

His thick, black unpowdered hair, brushed back from his forehead, his bushy eyebrows, wide and very mobile, his large eyes, full of a mildness and tenderness of expression, only tempered by a certain habitude of gravity, the regularity of his handsome features, the almost celestial benevolence of his smile, composed an ensemble appropriate to penetrate with affection and respect even the vulgar populace who pursue with mockery the most touching of human infirmities.

"This is Jean-François-les-Bas-Bleus," it was said, while nudging his elbow, "who belongs to an honest family of old Comtois, who has never spoken ill of anyone, and who has gone mad, it's said, by dint of being clever. It's necessary to let him pass tranquilly, in order not to make him worse."

And Jean-François-les-Bas-bleus did indeed pass by, without seeming to pay any heed to anything, for the eyes that

I do not know how to depict never stopped at the horizon, but incessantly turned toward the sky, with which the man of whom I speak—he was a visionary—appeared to maintain a hidden communication, which only made itself known by means of the perpetual movement of his lips.

The poor devil's costume was, however, of a nature to amuse passers-by, especially strangers. Jean-François was the son of a worthy tailor in the Rue d'Anvers, who had spared nothing for his education because of the great hopes he invested in him, and who flattered himself that he might make a priest, the brilliance of whose preaching might lead him one day to the episcopate. He had, in fact, been the laureate of all his classes, and the savant Abbé Barbélenet,[1] the sage Quintilian of our fathers, often enquired during his emigration as to what had become of his favorite pupil; but no one could satisfy him, because there no longer appeared to be anything of the man of genius in the state of decadence and scorn into which Jean-François-les-Bas-Bleus had fallen. The old tailor, who had many other children, had therefore necessarily held back on Jean-François' expenses, and although he always maintained him in an exact cleanliness, he was only clad in a few random garments that his profession enabled him to acquire cheaply, or hand-me-downs from his younger brothers repaired for that usage.

That kind of accoutrement, so inappropriate to his tall stature, which wedged him into a kind of sheath ever ready to burst, and allowed more than half of his forearms to escape from the narrow sleeves of his green jacket, had something sadly comical about it. His breeches, stuck to the high and carefully but pointlessly stretched, had great difficulty joining at the knees the blue stockings that gave Jean-François his

1 Abbé Barbelenet is recorded as a professor of rhetoric in Besançon in 1785 by a historical almanac published in that year. Another contemporary source, attributing the same position to him in 1789, says that he went on to be the almoner of the Lycée, and that he was renowned as an orator.

nickname. As for his tricorn hat, a ridiculous coiffure for anyone, the artisanal appearance that it gave him and the manner
in which Jean-François wore it made an absurd contrast with
his poetic and majestic head. If I lived a thousand years I
would never forget the grotesque outfit or the singular pose of
Jean-François-les-Bas-bleus' tricorn hat.

One of the most remarkable particularities of the young
man's folly is that it was only sensible in unimportant conversations in which the mind is exercised on familiar things. If
one approached him to talk about the rain, the fine weather, a
play, a newspaper, town gossip or local affairs, he listened with
attention and responded politely, but the words that flowed
from his lips rushed so tumultuously that they became confused before the end of the first sentence, in I know not what
inextricable tangle, in which he could not clarify his thought.
He continued, however, more and more unintelligibly, increasingly substituting the natural and logical phraseology of
a simple man with the babble of a child who does not know
the meaning of words, or the rambling of an old man who had
forgotten it.

Then people laughed, and Jean-François shut up, without
anger and perhaps without attention, raising his lovely dark
eyes to the heavens again, as if to search for inspiration more
worthy of him in the region where he had fixed all his ideas
and all his sentiments.

It was not the same when the conversation summarized
with precision a moral or scientific question of some interest.
Then the radiance of that intelligence, so divergent and so
scattered, of that sick intelligence, was suddenly condensed
into a beam, like the sun's rays in Archimedes' lens, and lent so
much brilliance to his discourse that it is permissible to doubt
that Jean-François could ever have been more savant, clearer
and more persuasive had he been in the full possession of his
reason. The most difficult problems in the exact sciences, of

which he had made a particular study, were only child's play for me, and the solution sprang so quickly from his mind to his mouth that one would have taken them less for the result of reflection and calculation than that of a mechanical operation subject to the impulsion of a switch or the action of a spring. It seemed to the people who listened to him then, and were able to understand him, that such an elevated faculty was not bought too dear at the price of the common advantage of enunciating vulgar ideas in vulgar language with ease; but it is the vulgar who judge, and the man in question was nothing for them but an idiot in blue stockings, incapable of sustaining a conversation with ordinary people. That was true.

As the Rue d'Anvers ended almost at the college, there was not a day when I did not pass along it four times, going back and forth, but it was only at intermediary hours on warm days of the year, illuminated by a little sunshine, that I was sure to find Jean-François there, sitting on a little stool outside his father's door, often surrounded by a circle of students amusing themselves with the extravagance of his rambling phrases. I was alerted to that scene at a distance by the bursts of laughter of his listeners, and when I arrived, with my dictionaries under my arm, I sometimes had difficulty clearing a path as far as him; but I always experienced a new pleasure, because I believed that I had surmised, child as I was, the secret of his double life, and I promised myself to confirm that idea further with each new experiment.

One somber evening at the beginning of autumn, when the weather was threatening to become stormy, the Rue d'Anvers, which is not much frequented anyway, appeared to be completely deserted, with the exception of one man. That was Jean-François, sitting still, with his eyes directed at the sky, as usual. His stool had not yet been removed. I approached him quietly in order not to distract him, and, leaning toward his ear, when it seemed that he had heard me, I said, thoughtlessly—for I ordinarily only accosted him with regard to an aorist, a logarithm, a hypotenuse or a trope, and a few other difficulties of my double estate—"Here you are, all alone!" Then I bit my lip, thinking that the stupid reflection, which would make him fall back from the empyrean to earth, would render him to his customary nonsense, which I never heard without a constriction of the heart.

"Alone!" Jean-François replied, seizing me by the arm. "Only the insensate are alone, it's only the blind who cannot see, and only the paralytic whose weak legs cannot support him firmly on the ground."

*Here we go*, I said to myself, while he continued talking in obscure phrases, which I wish I could remember, because they might have had more sense that I imagined then. *Poor Jean-François is off, but I'll soon stop him. I know the magic wand that will free him from his enchantments.*

"It's possible, in fact," I cried, "that the planets are inhabited, as Monsieur de Fontenelle thinks, and that you have secret commerce with their inhabitants, like Monsieur le Comte de Gabalis."[1] I interrupted myself with pride, after having deployed such magnificent erudition.

Jean-François smiled, looked at me with his mild gaze and said: "Do you know what a planet is?"

"I suppose it to be a world that resembles ours, more or less."

"And do you know what a world is?"

---

1 Bernard de Fontenelle's classic popularization of the Copernican account of the solar system, which concludes with a rhapsodic speculative essay about the possible habitation of other words, *Entretiens sur la pluralité des mondes*, was first published in 1686. *Le Comte de Gabalis* (1670) is an anonymous account of the conjuration of "elemental spirits" populating other worlds in the solar system. Surely intended as a satire, or at least as a hoax, it was taken seriously by many would-be occultists and its lexicon of supernatural beings was an enormous influence on scholarly fantasy and *contes fantastiques* in France and other European countries.

"A large body that accomplishes certain revolutions in space regularly."

"And have you suspected what space might be?"

"Wait, wait," I said, "it's necessary for me to recall our definitions. Space? A subtle and infinite environment in which the stars and the worlds move."

"I like that. And what are the stars and worlds relative to space?"

"Probably miserable atoms, lost like dust in the air."

"And the substance of the stars and the worlds, what do you think it is, compared with the subtle matter that fills space?"

"What do you want me to say? There's no possible expression to compare such gross bodies with such a pure element."

"Good! And you'll understand, child, that God, the creator of all things, who had doubtless given those gross worlds inhabitants, doubtless imperfect but animated nevertheless, as we two are, by the need for a better life, would not have left space uninhabited?"

"I do understand that," I replied, fervently. "And I even think that, just as we're far advanced, in subtlety of organization, of the matter to which we're bound, its inhabitants must also be far in advance of the subtle matter that envelops them. But how could I know?"

"By learning to see them," replied Jean-François, who pushed me away with his hand, with an extreme mildness.

At the same moment, his head fell back on to the back of his three-step stool. His gaze resumed its fixity and his lips their movement.

I drew away discreetly. I had only taken a few steps when I heard his father and mother behind me, pressing him to come inside, because the sky was turning bad. He submitted, as usual, to their slightest insistence, but his return to the real world was always accompanied by the overflow of inconsequential words that furnished the manual workers of the quarter with the object of their customary amusement.

I went on, wondering whether it might not be possible that Jean-François had two souls, one that belonged to the gross world in which we live, and the other that was purified in the subtle space that he believed he had penetrated by means of thought. I embarrassed myself slightly in that theory, and am embarrassed by it still.

I arrived like that in my father's house, more preoccupied, and preoccupied above all because the string of my kite had broken, and might have landed in Monsieur de Grobois' garden. My father interrogated me regarding my emotion, and I never lied to him.

"I thought," he said, "that all these reveries"—for I had recounted to him without omitting a word my conversation with Jean-François-les-Bas-bleus—"had been buried forever with the books of Swedenborg and Saint-Martin in the grave of my old friend Cazotte;[1] but it appears that this young man, who has spent a few days in Paris, has been imbued there with the same follies. At any rate, there is a certain finesse of observation in the ideas that his double language has suggested to you, and the explanation you have made of it only requires to be reduced to its veritable expression. The faculties of intelligence are not so indivisible that an infirmity of the body cannot attain them separately. Thus the alteration of intelligence that poor Jean-François manifests in the most common operations of his memory might well not extend to the properties of his memory, and that is why he responds with accuracy when he is interrogated about things that he had learned slowly and retained with difficulty, while he is irrational regarding everything that falls unexpectedly under his senses, with regard to which he has

---

1 Antoine-Melchior Nodier could, in fact, have met Jacques Cazotte, although he certainly did not know him as well as Nodier took leave to pretend in the incomplete "M. Cazotte" (tr. herein as "Monsieur Cazotte") in which there is also mention of the mystic philosopher Louis-Claude Saint-Martin.

never had any need to furnish himself in advance with an exact formula. I would be astonished if that were not observed in the majority of madmen—but I don't know whether you have understood me."

"I believe I've understood you, father, and I'll be able to recall your words in forty years."

"That's more than I want from you," he said, embracing me. "A few years from now, you'll be sufficiently prejudiced by graver studies against illusions that only obtain an empire over feeble souls or weak intelligences. Only remember, since you're sure of your memory, that there is nothing simpler than notions that are close to the truth, and nothing more specious than those that are distant from it."

*It's true*, I thought, as I went to bed early, *that the* Thousand-and-One Nights *are incomparable more likeable than the first volume of Bezout,*[1] *and who has ever been able to believe in the* Thousand-and-One Nights?

The storm was rumbling outside. It was so beautiful that I could not help opening my little casement, which overlooked the Rue Neuve, facing the gracious fountain with which my architect grandfather had ornamented the town, enriched by a bronze siren that had often, at the whim of my charmed imagination, confounded poetic sings with the murmur of its waters.[2] My eyes were obstinate in following all the lightning flashes in the clouds, which were colliding with one another in a manner to shake all the worlds. Sometimes, the fiery curtain was ripped by a thunderclap, and my sight, more rapid than the lightning, plunged into the infinite sky that opened above, which appeared to me to be purer and more tranquil than a beautiful sky in spring.

*Oh*, I said to myself then, *if, however, the vast plains of that space do have inhabitants, how agreeable it would be to repose*

---

1 The mathematician Étienne Bezout (1730-1783); the volume cited is presumably his *Théorie générale des equations algébraiques* (1779).
2 The Rue Neuve, as it was in 1793, is now called the Rue Charles-Nodier.

*there with them from all the tempests of the earth! What unalloyed peace one might savor in that limpid region that is never agitated, never deprived of sunlight, and which laughs above our hurricanes, luminous and placid, as above our miseries! No, delectable valleys of the sky, I exclaimed, weeping abundantly, God has not created you to remain deserted, and I shall travel you one day, arm in arm with my father!*

The conversation with Jean-François had left me with an impression that frightened me from time to time; nature, however, was animated in my passage, as if my sympathy for it had caused a spark of divinity to spring forth from the most impalpable beings. If I had been more scholarly, I would have understood pantheism. I invented it,

But I obeyed my father's advice; I even avoided conversation with Jean-François-les-Bas-Bleus, or only approached him while he was wandering in one of his eternal sentences, which seemed to have the objective of frightening logic and exhausting the dictionary. As for Jean-François-les-Bas-Bleus, he did not recognize me, or did not give me any evidence that he distinguished me from other schoolboys of my age, although I had been the only one to bring them back, when it suited me, to coherent conversations and sensate definitions.

Scarcely a month had passed since that encounter with the visionary, and this time I am perfectly certain of the date. It was the day of the commencement of the school year, after six weeks of the vacation that began on the first of September; consequently, it was the sixteenth of October 1793. It was about midday, and I was coming back from college more cheerfully than I had returned to it, with two of my comrades, who took the same route to return to their parents' homes, and who were following almost the same studies as me, but who had left me some way behind. They are both alive, and I could name them without fear of being disavowed if their names, which are decorated by a just renown, could be hazarded without impropriety in a story that doubtless only has the plausibility requisite of fanciful tales, and which, in the final analysis, I am not representing as anything else.

On arriving at a certain intersection, where were separated in order to take different directions, we were struck simultaneously by the contemplative attitude of Jean-François-les-Bas-Bleus, who was as motionless as a boundary marker in the exact center of the square, his arms folded, his expression sadly pensive and his eyes fixed imperturbably on a point above the western horizon. A few passers-by had gradually gathered around him, and were searching in vain for the extraordinary object that seemed to have absorbed his attention.

"What is he looking at up there?" they were asking one another. "The passage of a flock of rare birds, or the ascension of a balloon?"

"I can inform you," I responded, while I cleared a path through the crowd with my elbows. "Tell us, Jean-Francois," I continued, "what you have noticed this morning that is new in the subtle matter of space in which the words move?"

"Don't you see it, as I do?" he replied, extending his arm and describing with the tip of his finger a long arc of a circle from the horizon to the zenith. "Follow with your eyes those traces of blood, and you'll see Marie-Antoinette, Queen of France, going to Heaven."

Then the curious individuals dispersed, shrugging their shoulders, because they had concluded from his response that he was mad. I drew away too, only astonished that he had fallen so accurately on the name of the last of our queens, that positive detail entering into the category of true facts of which he had lost the cognizance.

My father invited two or three friends to dinner once a fortnight. One of the guests, who was a stranger to the town, made them wait for quite a long time.

"Excuse me," he said, as he took his seat. "The rumor has gone around, in accordance with a few private letters, that the unfortunate Marie-Antoinette was about to be sent to judgment, and I was delayed slightly waiting for the thirteenth of October mail-coach to arrive. The gazettes aren't saying anything."

"Marie-Antoinette, Queen of France," I said with assurance, "died this morning on the scaffold a few minutes before midday, as I was coming back from college."

"Oh my God!" cried my father. "Who has been able to tell you that?"

I was troubled; I blushed. I had said too much to shut up. Trembling, I replied: "It was Jean-François-les-Bas-Bleus."

I did not think it advisable to look at my father. His extreme indulgence for me did not reassure me as to the discontentment that my recklessness would inspire in him.

"Jean-François-les-Bas-Bleus?" he said, laughing. "Fortunately, we can be tranquil regarding news coming from that direction. That cruel and futile cowardice will not be committed."

"Who is this Jean-François-les-Bas-Bleus, then" asked my father's friend, "who announces events at a distance of a hundred leagues at the moment when he supposes that they are being accomplished? A somnambulist, a convulsionary, or a pupil of Mesmer or Cagliostro?"

"Something like that," my father replied, "but more worthy of interest: a visionary of good faith, an inoffensive maniac, a poor madman who is pitied, inasmuch as he merits being loved. Emerged from an honest but poor family of worthy artisans, he was its great hope and he promised a great deal. The first year of a petty magistracy that I exercised here was the last of his studies; he wearied my arm in crowning him, and the variety of his successes added to their value, for one might have thought that it cost him little to open all the doors of human intelligence. The hall nearly collapsed under the sound of applause when he finally came to receive the prize compared to which all the others were trivial, that for good conduct and the virtues of an exemplary youth.

"There was not a single father who would not have been proud to count him among his children, nor a rich man, it seemed, who would not have rejoiced in calling him his son-in-law. I won't talk about the young women, who were quite naturally occupied with his angelic beauty and fortunate age between eighteen and twenty. That was what doomed him—not that his modesty allowed him to be deceived by the seductions of a triumph, but by the just results of the impression he had made . . .

"You have heard mention of the beautiful Madame Saint-A***. She was then in the Franche-Comté, where her family has left so many memories and her sisters have settled. She was searching for a tutor for her son, who was twelve years old at the most, and the glory that had just been attached to the humble name of Jean-François determined her choice in his favor. It was, four or five years ago, the commencement of an honorable career for a young man who had profited from his studies and had not been led astray by foolish ambitions.

"Unfortunately—but from here on I am only speaking on the faith of imperfect information—the beautiful lady who had thus recompensed Jean-François' talent was also the mother of a daughter, and that daughter was charming. Jean-François could not see her without loving her; however, penetrated by the impossibility of raising himself up as far as her, he appears to have sought to distract himself from an invincible passion that was only betrayed in the first moments of his malady, by delivering himself to studies perilous to reason, in the dreams of occult sciences and the visions of an exalted spiritualism. He went completely mad, and, sent away

90

from Corbeil,[1] the abode of his protectors, with all the cares that his condition required, no glimmer has illuminated the darkness of his mind since his return to his family. You can see that there is no foundation to be placed on his reports, and that we have no reason to be alarmed . . ."

However, the following day it was learned that the queen had gone to judgment, and two days later, that she was no longer alive.

My father feared the impression that the extraordinary co-incidence of that catastrophe and that prediction might have made on me. He spared no effort to convince me that chance was fertile in such encounters, and he cited me twenty examples, which only served as arguments for ignorant credulity, the philosophy of religion also abstaining from making use of them.

I departed a few weeks later for Strasbourg, where I was to commence further studies. The epoch was unfavorable to spiritualist doctrines, and I forgot Jean-François easily in the midst of the everyday emotions that tormented society.

Circumstances had brought me back in spring. One morning—I believe that it was the third of Messidor—I went into my father's room to embrace him, as was my custom, before commencing my daily excursion in search of plants and butterflies.

"Let's not pity poor Jean-François any longer for having lost his reason," he said showing me the newspaper. "It's better for him to be mad than to learn of the tragic death of his benefactress, his pupil and the young demoiselle reputed to be the first cause of the derangement of his mind. Those innocent creatures have also fallen under the hand of the executioner."

"Can it be possible!" I exclaimed. "Alas, I haven't said anything to you about Jean-François, because I knew that you

---

1 There are several communes in France named Corbeil, but the father's suggestion that Jean-Françoiis had spent time in Paris implies that the reference is to Corbeil-Essonnes, now a suburb of the city.

feared for me the influence of certain mysterious ideas about which he talked to me, but . . . he's dead!"

"He's dead?" said my father, sharply. "Since when?"

"Since three days ago, the twenty-ninth of Prairial.[1] He had been motionless all morning in the middle of the square, in the same place where I encountered him at the moment of the queen's death. Many people were surrounding him, as usual, although he maintained the most profound silence, for his preoccupation was too great for him to be distracted by any question. Finally, at four o'clock, his attention appeared to redouble. A few minutes later he raised his arms toward the sky with a strange expression of enthusiasm or dolor, took a few steps, pronouncing the names of the people you have just mentioned, uttered a cry and fell. People pressed around him and hastened to lift him up, but it was futile. He was dead."

"The twenty-ninth of Prairial, at a few minutes past four o'clock?" said my father, consulting his newspaper. "That was indeed the hour and the day." After a moment's reflection he continued, his eyes firmly fixed on mine: "Listen, don't refuse me what I ask if you. If you ever tell this story, when you are a man, don't represent it as true, because it would expose you to ridicule."

"Are there reasons that can dispense a man from publishing aloud what he recognizes as the truth?" I said, respectfully.

"There is one that is worth as much as all of them," said my father, shaking his head. "The truth is futile."

----

1 This date (17 June 1794) became notorious; fifty-three people were guillotined in Paris on that day in the wake of alleged assassination attempts by counter-revolutionaries made against Robespierre and other leaders of the Convention, and the month that followed was the height of the Terror.

# On the Imminent End of the Human Species

There has been much talk of the amelioration of the human species and its progressive destiny, but people never talk about its end. It is an error that characterizes human vanity in a singular manner to believe the race of Adam to be immortal in the midst of everything that dies, and to imagine that the principle of destruction that undermines suns might respectfully preserve the organization of the wretched vertical quadruped to which the empire of the word presently belongs. If a philosopher or a theologian talks to you about the final catastrophe of the globe, it is the catastrophe of the last families that immediately figures in your thought: peoples struggling against the invasion of a deluge or a conflagration; wailing women carrying their newborns away in their arms; of men reproaching the world for its haste to die because they still have a few days still to live. I would like to believe that, if our planet lives the age of a planet, it will not be so tragic, at least for our noble race of anthropomorphs, the generic duration of which is far from being essentially measured by that of a mineral sphere nine thousand leagues in circumference.

Barring accidents—for planets are not exempt from them, there will be a long time when new species will amuse themselves by recomposing human skeletons from fossil debris and searching for a convenient place for them alongside that of monkeys and bats. That is the march of nature; nothing can be done about it.

I can remember little of what I knew about physical philosophy and natural history when I thought I knew everything, but it seems to me that there are principles so rational in the factual sciences that can be put to the academies, defying them to change anything therein. Those are such that you have the right to convert them into axioms and to imprint them with the same seal of infallibility as the addition of two figures accurately made. I shall report a few, to prove the point to which the proposition is naïve; I fear that it will be only too so.

First of all, the simplest organized substances are the most durable.

Secondly, the first elementary combinations that produced a being were the simplest.

Thirdly, as the permanent elaborations of the creative agent become more complex, they lose in vitality what they gain in perfection.

And that is why the oysters of Lucris, so esteemed by Apicius, will probably be even more beautiful, red and succulent when they no longer have anything to fear, centuries hence, in the race of Apicius, the most insatiable of ostreophagic animals; and why marine algae will see generations of shellfish end; and the rocks that they embrace will see generations of marine plants end; and the world will see its rocks dissolve, and the vortex its worlds, and infinity its vortices.

Everything passes from the simple to the compound, gradually being enriched by new organic acquisitions, and everything returns from the compound to the simple, returning its elements thereto.

Thus, a complete existence is an existence that is commencing to die.

The development of a complete existence has, however, unknown limits at which it suddenly recoils, like the sap of an oak or the flight of a condor; and what is true of individuals after sixty years of observation is equally true of species. At least, it is necessary to agree that the induction is universally received, for there is no other proof of death.

Otherwise, if one admitted the indefinite perfectibility of species, which is only a theory, and one did not contest the indefinite decadence of species, which is a fact, it would be the oyster that would end up eating Apicius.

There is only one means of defending the theory of human perfectibility, which requires the intervention in the denouement of the discussion of the Greeks' tragic machine, a god. Then the paradox changes its name, it becomes dogma and I can no longer involve myself with it; you know more about it than science, and I am not even a scientist.

Under the philosophical and scientific aspect of the question—and I cannot see under what other aspect anyone would dare to consider today—it is reduced almost to nothing:

Species end, so the human species will end.

They end after having accomplished the possible conditions of their development. Do conditions of possible development still remain for the human species to fulfill? If none any longer remain, what are the marks of its decadence? What age has it reached? That is what I would like to clarify in freeing myself from the technical chaos of methods into which one falls involuntarily when one has had the misfortune to read. If I take it up again sometimes it is not my fault, for I struggle against it with more horror than the pythoness against the enigmas of her demon, because the logogriphs of that time were child's play compared with what are called the verities of ours.

In accordance with what I have said (and I do not exclude here the power of a creative spirit, whatever one wants to call it, for it could not have happened otherwise), the animals, the heavens, the earth and the waters surged forth one after the other from chaos or confused matter; then the plants dressed the world; then the inhabitants of the waters, the animals of the land, and above all, humans.

That cosmogony is not difficult to find, I am told; it is in *Genesis*.

Fortunately, it is also elsewhere; it is in the discoveries of science, which have not had the good fortune that Alphonse of Portugal envied.[1] They have not succeeded in making their universe with more good sense and skill than God. I give you that system as you please, in the name of Moses and revelation, or in the name of Monsieur Cuvier and geology.

It is true that all of it is accomplished in six days in *Genesis*, which is not very philosophical, according to the calculations of the Observatoire, but who knows by what unknown star the God of Moses, whitening the firmament with his dust, deigned to measure the days of creation? Have you seen that sun of suns, that inextinguishable torch of space, of which nothing indicates the orient or the occident, of which no creature has saluted the dawn or the dusk; that luminary of eternity, the course of which embraces forever a circle that has neither center nor circumference?

At any rate, leaving aside what is only fable in the eyes of the incredulous and hypothesis in the eyes of the ignorant, there is the human species, the culminating result of a work of Providence or hazard; humankind, submissive to all the vicissitudes of time, which damages, destroys and decomposes everything, and condemned to suffer those changes with more promptitude and intensity by very reason of the complications of its organs and the power of its intelligence; humankind, almost as vital as the angels and less vivacious than reptiles, those being essential conditions of superiority.

With that species, the ascendant scale of animal organization finishes; nothing remains but the descent toward death.

---

1 Alfonso X of Castile. Léon and Galicia (1221-1284), nicknamed the Wise or the Astrologer, was a prolific writer, who achieved a lasting posthumous notoriety for a probably-apocryphal remark to the effect that, had he been present at the Creation, he could have given God some useful advice.

Only religion has the right to suppose that another destination is reserved for it; it has done so, but while recognizing what it had lost, so manifest was the progress of its inevitable degeneration, already sensible in the time of the first religious writings. Thus, in the eyes of the Christian, as in the eyes of the philosopher, the species is summoned to die, for it is not to the father of men alone that the terrible and profound revelation of God was addressed; it was not only to each of his descendants, caught in his mortal individuality; it was to the whole human species: that it must die one day, like a single man.

That phenomenon of the destruction of beings at the end of a certain period was no longer a new mystery, according to all appearances, on the last of the six days of creation. The earth must have seen the animals roaming it, and the plants decorating it, renewed several times. The dwelling of nascent humankind was the tomb of a multitude of existences that Adam could not name in the terrestrial Paradise because they had ceased to exist before he was made. Under his feet, reunited with the reproductive humus, lay the immense forests of immense rushes, and, restored in fossils to the mineral form of matter, the families of enormous saurians, which still deliver today to scientific investigation the authentic vestiges of several successive creations that have returned successively to the hearth of eternal creations.

Among the beautiful pages of the *Génie du christianisme*,[1] There are admirable ones in which Monsieur de Chateaubriand dressed with the brilliant colors of his palette that tableau of Genesian nature, already rich in the solemn magnificence of an anterior nature. If a geologist had to place himself today in the same hypothesis, he would say the same thing, with a similar talent. That is not because the poet had searched

---

1 Chateaubriand's defense of the Christian faith was written in the 1790s while he was in exile, in reaction against the attacks of the Revolutonaries.

with great care for what philosophy and truth there was in his voluntary anachronism; it is because what there is of truth and verity on earth belongs to the inspirations of the poet.

The first generations of humans, which lasted a long time and had leisure to observe, because the earth was not yet an arena—it was always a spectacle—doubtless did not recognize, beneath the annual work of reproductions, the muted and permanent work of destruction, which moderates, obliterates and transforms everything, and makes everything disappear that has had its day. They were perhaps not unaware that the birds had once crushed fruits with sharp teeth; that snakes had once traced a path through the sand with agile feet; and that in the time of their forefathers, flocks of ostriches had sometimes covered the desert with the shadow of their wings. A tradition perpetuated from age to age, which still subsists in their sacred books, maintained, in the memory of the behemoth and the leviathan, those colossi of the living world, and that of the griffin with the beak and flight of an eagle, which had four lion's feet. Even in the human race, they could already observe a menacing declivity.

There were soon no more of those millenary giants of whom there is mention in all histories, and to whose power so many almost-indestructible monuments attest. Their ascendant mission and conquest was accomplished in a short time, either because it is the essence of our species to exhaust rapidly, in futile luxury, the superabundant fire that vivifies them, or because it suited God to build under the eyes of his sole reasoning creature the scenes that might make the latter understand the secret of its organization and decadence. It is probable that there was no question then of the indefinite perfectibility of the human race. That ridicule was reserved for five-foot dwarfs accumulated in odious cloacas to suffer and die, and who expired decrepit at sixty years of age, in an atmosphere of blood and mud, over a page where they had spilled, in a few drops of ink, the last lie of their vanity.

There are no longer any sophisms in all that, for, by virtue of getting closer to matter and seeking our origin there, we have at least found the ruins of what there was before us. There is no dendrite that does not conserve the imprint of an unknown plant. You can see flowers encased in the milky crystal of agate, like the marvelous bouquet of the bride of a genius. This amber, as pure and transparent as topaz, has hardened over an insect that Dejean[1] could not name; this fragment of marble that you are touching will never enrich the metopes of our adulatory monuments; it is the tomb of an unknown batrachian, the renown of which saw daylight for the first time under a sculptor's chisel. That sand you are treading underfoot and which is scintillating with reflections of nacre is the debris of a nautilus that is no more; that lump is maintained in solid gilded disks because it is clad, like the clever courtesans who survive revolutions, with a more solid layer of metal; it is an ammonite of a lost species.

Look, then, at what will become of the human species entire: sand to roll underfoot!

To establish a fact as absolute, as important and as essential as perfectibility, the least one can do is to support it with a few facts. Here, all the inductions drawn from fact, with not a single exception, are in opposition to the principle. If humankind were tending to perfectibility by means of the condition of civilization, very advanced civilizations would be recognized by pronounced exterior signs of conformation, vigor and vitality, and it is precisely the contrary. Look at what the race of humans were of which Nestor conserves the memory, and the Latins of Turnus, the Scots of Wallace, compared with the herd of degraded animals to which the civilization has submitted! Would you go to search today for what remains that is most appropriate to retrace imperfectly the type of the adult species

_______________

1 The entomologist Auguste Dejean (1780-1845), who served as Napoléon's *aide-de-camp*, became the world's foremost collector and taxonomist of *coleoptera* (beetles).

in those great animal sheds of frail, lurid, counterfeit cadaverous humans that you call cities? It would be necessary to inform yourself in the most hidden links of the Alpine chains of the old world, and it would be necessary, above all, for you to hurry, for civilization has perhaps reached them.

One would not dare to sustain, since the fossil world has not yet proven it, that a certain number of species of the human genre have already disappeared, and yet I am convinced that it will be proven, when geology, emerging from our quarries, can carry the sound to the plateaux of Tibet or the valleys of the Caucasus. I no more doubt the existence of the ancient titanic and the ancient cyclopean species than that of the harpy so well described by the poets, with its human face, its woman's breasts, its membranous wings and its four long-fingered hands, which would have sufficed for Linnaeus to copy them to place it methodically at the head of the *vespertilions*.[1]

Without recourse to futile conjectures, which are nevertheless far less conjectural than those of perfectibility, does one not see species of the human genre that are beginning to end, which the first revolution of the globe or society that disseminates them in the deserts of the continent or the isles of the Ocean will lead, from one transformation to another, to the condition of the brute, and from the condition of the brute to death? What is curious is that in the first rank of the funeral procession of the human genre marches the most ancient and the most perfected of all the centuries, that of China.

But does one not see societies even more advanced in their decadence, in which the human type is almost effacing before our eyes, as if to leave us in no doubt of the degenerative tendency of the race? Has it not yet attained, at some point of the globe, the age of decrepitude and degradation that announces the imminent extinction of the principle of life,

---

1 In the Linnaean taxonomy, *Vespertilio* is a genus of bats.

in species as in individuals? What, then, are those scattered tribes of savages, imprinted in an order so gradual and so regular with all the symptoms of dissolution, if not the more or less recent debris of a past civilization? It would at least require an absolute lack of philosophy to see them as anything else. Everywhere where the artifices of the simplest grammar remain, the superstitions of the most vain religion, the fiction of absolute power and the taste for a barbaric luxury, there is a society that once dreamed, like ours, of a future without limits and perhaps of perfectibility, on the eve of its eternal fall. Do not the inhabitants of Easter Island, who drink sea water like the fantastic anthropophage of Victor Hugo, have monuments intermediate between the shapeless stone of Carnac and the sacrilegious ruins of Babel? That people is a ruin too, and it will disappear from the earth before the colossi of an unknown art one erected on its shores to the memory of gods or kings.

Ask travelers who have traveled the Atlantic archipelagoes what became of the colonies of primitive civilizations. They have remarked some where the populations have decreased by half between two expeditions, others in which there only remain a small number of unhealthy children crawling over the rocks like the hideous reptiles with which they dispute their nourishment.

There are some of these tombs of the human family to which the naturalist is already tempted to give another name. The unfortunate being on whose forehead God once blew his creative breath has lost the secret there of the mechanism of speech, and can only express the two or three thoughts that compose the entire repertoire of his soul by means of confused sibilations like those of the pongo.[1] He is born decrepit and only lives thirty years. A few generations more, and you will

---

1 At the time when Nodier wrote the article the term "pongo" was attributed, somewhat confusedly, to a large species of ape, based on misleading accounts of the gorilla.

find the theory of perfectibility resolved in a layer of skeletons for which no living hand could dig a grave.

What am I saying? It is to force you to search further for the exceedingly vulgar demonstration of the only verity that it is given to humans to grasp, the proof of the degeneration and death of species, and to apply it to your own. If we travel the surface of the world, and climb the summits that bristle thereon, it will tell us the same thing. Perhaps you will not cover a hundred leagues without arriving at the foot of one of those mountains which have an incontestable privilege of anteriority over all the past forms of a human society. At the summit is the dolmen, an enormous stone raised on enormous supports, without cranes, without levers and without capstans; a little lower down there is the fortress, planted like a eagle's aerie between the earth and the sky; and if you shift the rubble that served as a base for its keep, there is the iron armor that adorned the warrior on a day of battle, and which the most robust arms can no longer break without effort. On the inferior slope is the shepherd's hut, white beneath its humble roof. You can see him emerge following his flock, a dwarf for the titan of the summit, a dwarf for the armored despot of the castle, a giant for you—and next to him, his neighbor, the chamois hunter bounding from precipice to precipice, as agile and reckless as his prey.

Descend a little. That smoke is that of a city, the noise of whose inhabitants you can hear, divided between two concerns that absorb their entire lives, that of gaining gold and that of losing time. Don't stop at their effeminate forms, their sickly pallor. The multiple knell of parish church bells, which announces that one dies quickly in these pretty green-daubed houses bordered with terraces of roses. Go into the valley and pause for a while.

That monster you can see there is a man; he still has something human about him. That full and squinting eye that gazes without seeing between two swollen eyelids, bald and bloody, is a human eye; those thick lips, twisted and foaming, form a human mouth; that discordant babble, the hoarse and disordered stammers of which sometimes burst forth, is human speech. The man you see is the cretin, who only reproduces himself rarely, but whom his fellows of the valley, the city and the mountain reproduce every day.

You have only covered half a league, and you have embraced in a very circumscribed family the complete history of the human race, from its commencement to its end; those of the heights are finished and the rest will finish.

You know all that better than me; what deceives you is the prestige of the living civilization in which you have dreamed of durable elements of existence and conservation. I understand that a well-made mask can lend the physiognomy of life to a cadaver. Open the case and I will guarantee that there is nothing within but a mummy. I have seen elegant old men who go to sleep after having been measured for a ball costume and wake up in a shroud, if they wake up.

There is something artificial in old societies, as in the vegetation of old forests, which only deceives poor observers. When a society is tending to dissolution, you will see implanted upon it a multitude of interests enthusiastic to decorate its substance, like miserly lichens and parasitic mistletoe on a tree that is only alive in its bark; from a distance you have faith in that borrowed verdure, but you are no sooner at the foot of the calcined trunk than you perceive that it is dead.

That is because there is nothing in common between the apparent perfection of the social form and the vitality of the species; or rather, there is nothing more contradictory. By virtue of living, one can obtain some advantage from the experience of life; one can refine some of one's enjoyments as their number is impoverished; one can savor with a better understood economy a few residues of fleeting days; but there is no man insensate enough to imagine that that sad benefit of age can extend the limits of his natural life, through an inexhaustible succession of ever-new sensualities that were unknown to him in the prime of life.

The error of which I speak is that of a society that really has learned something in a few centuries, but which has not yet learned that it is only the expression of an individual mortality, of which the terminus is not far distant. Thus, civilization itself, at the point that it has reached, is stronger than all my arguments against the indefinite perfectibility of the species, and it is no good crying with superb disdain that I cannot see the march of that civilization; alas, I can see it marching and running just like you; the only difference between you and me is that I can see where it is going.

The Chinese social form is the only one that has been conserved without modification in historical memory, probably because there is none more perfectly matched to the needs of the civilized man; the Chinese, who do not put their destiny to the hazard of a new trial every year, and who have no idea of that better future of peoples to which we aspire with a pertinacity that no disappointment discourages, have found a means to compensate themselves for their political inertia, by using on works of creation the activity of the revolutionary principle by which all nations are tormented in their decadence, which can be regarded as a frightful symptom of their climacteric year. They avenge themselves, at the expense of the natural organization of beings, for their impotence to trouble the intelligent organization of states.

Their skill in depressing the human head is well-known, and those of breaking the delicate feet of women in fetters that change their gracious elegance into deformity, of crossing animal races by monstrous alliances, the fortunately infecund results of which appear destined to populate a fantastic menagerie. Their deplorable instinct obtains no less dire success in the alteration of plants. They succeed in imprisoning the sap of the most vivacious vegetables in abortive channels, in stifling their development, and in reducing wooden giants to the proportions of the smallest shrubs, pygmy forests in which only the insects of the earth have a right to obtain some shelter against the storm.

Well, if those trees, stupidly embellished by a barbaric caprice, were suddenly animated by the oratory loquacity and prophetic inspiration of the oaks of Dodona, what would you say on hearing them take pleasure in their shameful stature, insulting from the height of their petty pride the robust and colossal stem that had nourished their seed to thicken the wooden face, before a sacrilegious hand had seized it in order to degrade it, and to promise their offspring, future kings of mountains, powerful branches against the tempest, and per-petual shade? Be careful, Europeans of the nineteenth century; that fable is your history; there are civilized oaks.

I said just now that society had learned something, and I shall hasten to explain that overly obliging concession, in order not to give it a false latitude. In a few thousand years, society has only learned one essential idea. It does not know any moral verity that was not vulgar in the time of Job; it has only contemplated nature from a single point of view; it has not penetrated a single mystery of the soul that was secret from Homer. It is neither more philosophical than Pythagoras nor more poetic than Alcaeus. Its lawmakers have no more dethroned Solon than its physicians have Hippocrates. The arts of the ancients will forever be the object of its imitations, and of its despair.

Even the most vulgar works of strength and industry, which experience enlightened by long practice would have easily per-fected from generation to generation, have only made partial progress, and any comparison that one might try to establish between what they have lost and what they have gained would not be of a nature to flatter or pride. Look at what the affairs of perfectibility have achieved thus far, from the foundation of Babylon to the destruction of the archbishopric of Paris; it is a balance-sheet of facts and centuries that speaks louder than theories

To reduce the conquests of society to their veritable expression, let us agree that it has learned to enjoy itself. While it speaks proudly of its future destination, a secret but universal and manifest instinct has revealed to it that it no longer has one. Fixed to the present by egotism, which is the only vehicle of transitory existences, it seeks to attach itself to the future by means of vanity, which is the only indemnity of great disappointments. As for the past, it is quite natural that it repudiates it and is devoid of all sympathy for it, sensing that it will never be the past of a new society. From that phenomenon of position, which has not been able to present itself until now, two political facts result, equally new, equally characteristic and equally appropriate to our era: the notability of gold and the social ascendancy of youth. No history offers another example; there is nothing more consequent in ours. Peoples destitute of their moral goal have to take refuge entirely in the hearth of life and to honor with a species of worship the sign of temporary enjoyments that soften for a few days more the perspective of their inevitable terminus. Heirs with a life interest in a succession that will not be collected after them, they have invested civilization in unsecured funds, and without the intimate knowledge of our imminent dissolution, by which society is penetrated, what would have informed the young people of the present generation that they will not need for themselves the respect that all the centuries have given to the old?

It is no longer the gods who are going away, as in the times of Constantine and Galerius, it is humans: society, the soul of societies, has retired from them with institutions and beliefs;

the species, its rapid degradation hastened by the impure leaven of passions, vices and infirmities inseparable from an excessive civilization, only requires a few years of barbarity to make it descend below the albino. And do not ask when the barbarity will commence; a revolution, a war or an invasion will perhaps answer for me. The first tocsin to sound from one end of Europe to the other over that crowd devoid of simultaneity, devoid of affections, devoid of laws and devoid of God, can summon it to death. Let it strive to exist for a moment longer, to devour impatiently this days without a tomorrow, and dissipate its stormy death-throes in turbulent emotions. It is witnessing Belshazzar's feast without knowing it. The noise that it is making today will not trouble the silence of creation for long. The space that it has to travel in time is not infinite, like its pride, and the improvident ardor with which it is hastening toward an unknown goal is nothing but the irresistible effect of the slope that is drawing it to its doom. Nature will doubtless produce other species, but does not preserve any of them indefinitely. Eternity only belongs to nature itself.

It is a long way from these austere considerations to the pleasant and brilliant palingeneses of optimists, who dream candidly of a new Golden Age for the decrepitude of nations, and I agree that in human eyes, a sad verity will never have the attraction of a beautiful lie; so I have not conceived the vain hope of being heeded, and causing to pass into the minds of others a conviction that is, in any case, useless. In writing, I am obeying an impulse stronger than the desire to please or the pretention to instruct: the ascendancy of a profoundly disillusioned heart that savors a bitter joy in stripping away its last chimeras, like a festival costume ill-befitting the tomb, but which makes it a scruple to dispute alone the hope of naïve souls whom time has not disabused of the joy of hope. I have been mistaken so often on the faith of sentiment that I might well be mistaken again on that of reason. Speculative errors do not, at least, lead to the deadly consequences that follow practical errors, especially when they are not recommended either be the authority of a name or the influence of a talent.

As for you, my dear Ballanche,[1] who make the strings of the lyre render effortlessly the oracles of philosophy, like the legislator-poets of the nascent word, do not wake for a long time from the sublime and consoling illusion that I would like to embrace when I hear you. And who could hear you without conceiving your scorn, and without sharing it? What am I saying? Is it really yours, rather than that of Heaven, which did not place in you without design the inspired prevision of a complete civilization, with the wisdom that forms and the eloquence that persuades, but which mistook the epoch in which you ought to have been born for the instruction and happiness of the human species? Your mission called you to its cradle, and, forced to fulfill it by a necessity of which the secret escaped you of its own accord, it is not you that it is necessary to hold to account if you only arrive for its funeral procession.

Speak, however, on the edge of the abyss into which all the peoples are about to descend, speak at least to inform them of what they have lost. Perhaps the formidable judgment that weighs upon our race had need of that revelation to be entirely accomplished, and perhaps its rigor would have been lacking if the last human family had not been condemned to reopen

---

1 Pierre-Simon Ballanche (1776-1847) spent much of his life trying to embody a curious theology of progress in a hybrid work of history and prose epic entitled *Palingénésie* [Paligenesis], which he never finished, but fragments of which popularized the term in question, referring to a kind of renewal or regeneration. In 1831 he followed up a number of lyrical essays on "social palingenesis," which attributed a divine significance to the Revolution of 1789—of which he disapproved strongly but thought destined to prepare the way for a healthy regeneration of French society— with the brief fantasy *La Vision d'Hébal* (tr. as "The Vison of Hebal"), which provided a kind of synopsis of the incomplete work in the form of a prophetic vision.

momentarily the abode of delights that was closed on the first. Do not be astonished, nevertheless, if your magnificent words find among the civilized men of this century of light, so proud of its progress and its discoveries, an audience a hundred times more insensible than the marbles of Amphion, and a hundred times wilder than the tigers of Orpheus. It is a mystery easier to penetrate than the puerile enigma of that monster of Thebes, the poetic ideal of which you have created with so much power. They are going to die, and the intelligence of the soul has already quit them.

I do not dissimulate from myself, moreover, how many difficulties the opinion that I have undertaken to sustain day would present to a more skillful reasoner, in the condition of ingenuous philautia[1] and complaisant prejudice for its doctrines and its works in which present society relaxes from its material sufferings. Perfectibility is no longer a theory abandoned to discussion like other theories; it is a philosophical fact that only requires a gloss of mysticism to be converted into a dogma. One no longer demonstrates it, one professes it; and one of the purest, most elevated and most conscientious talents of our new school, lends it in the Sorbonne the triple authority of his reason, his knowledge and his good faith. A young professor seeks the truth therein, in the interests of our social amelioration, and he would doubtless find it if the truth ever rendered to the wishes of an honest heart or allowed itself to be captivated by the attraction of an elegant and noble language. Unfortunately, the sage *par excellence* recognized three thousand years ago that all our sciences are mere vanity, and if that is not all that it is permitted to us to know of the truth, it might be that there is none. What is certain is that philosophy has not torn away a single veil since, and that reflective minds who are only content with evidence, do not seem very disposed to appeal the judgment of Solomon.

---

1 I have used the direct English equivalent of Nodier's *philautie*, although it is now archaic. Derived from Greek, it means "self-love."

One proposition of Monsieur Théodore Jouffroy[1] that my hypothesis cannot admit—and I declare that I will renounce my hypothesis voluntarily as soon as the verity is found—is that Christianity will not be followed by any other religion. As I do not foresee that the truth, which is still somewhat confused, will be put incessantly at the disposal of populations, and as, on the other hand, there are, in my opinion, too many elements of life grandeur and liberty for one to be able to suppose that it remains within the range of a humankind fallen to the lowest degree of debasement and misery, I conjecture that it will be otherwise.

Religions, revealed or not, always become more or less the expression of the society that has made them successively and which modifies them incessantly. The cult of reason was the very exact expression of our extravagant and ferocious democracy; the Revolution succeeded by the crisis of the Terror is within it entirely, with the pride of sagacity, the saturnalia of dementia, prostitution and blood. The cult did not last long, the time that the paroxysm that produced it lasted. The altar and the scaffold collapsed on the same day, and will rise again together. There is a religion which will be found when needed, and which is perhaps palpitating already in some gospel of death. If, however, as I hope, there is no longer enough brutal

---

1 As a young philosophy professor Théodore Jouffroy (1796-1842) was strongly influenced by the "eclectic" philosopher Victor Cousin (1792-1857). Cousin had been a follower of Pierre-Paul Royer-Collard (1763-1845), the leader of the "Doctrinaire" politicians of the Restoration, who continued in that role after the July Revolution of 1830. Cousin was also heavily influenced by German idealism, and hence strongly linked to the Romantic Movement; he had deserted Royer-Collard's party in 1821 to move to the political left—a move that cost him his teaching post—when Jouffroy had also shifted his position in a different direction, becoming passionately interested in contemporary Scottish philosophy. In 1925 Jouffroy published an article in *Le Globe* entitled "Comment les dogmes finissent" about the death of religions, which Nodier clearly had in mind, along with other matters, while writing the present article.

energy in the passions of the epoch to arrive at that result a second time, the cold materialism, moral atheism and avaricious personality of last societies will not search very far for another faith and other symbols.

In operating upon Saint-Simonism[1] in the manner of reform—which is to say, by retrenching carefully in its pomps and its doctrines that which a poorly effaced tradition of Christian philosophy and human tenderness has left for intelligence and the heart, that religion appears to me to be marvelously appropriate to the needs of a species impatient to abolish the feeble residues of spiritualism, in order to cross the narrow gap that still separates it from brute matter and take possession of its void. *To each according to his capacity, to each capacity according to its works.* To the world that perfectibility, civilization and time have made for us, Saint-Simon is a god. It is logically impossible to deny that consequence. I believe,

---

1 Henri de Rouvroy, Comte de Saint-Simon (1760-1825) was not long dead when the present essay was written, and his political doctrine was being carried forward vigorously by his supporters. He championed the merits of the "industrious class" (all workers whose labor made a contribution to social welfare) against the "idling class" (the aristocracy), proposing a social reorganization that would effectively abolish the latter. In his later work he also proposed a reform of Christanity as a means to the amelioration of the lot of the poor. It is not obvious, however, exactly what Nodier means by "Saint-Simonism" in this partculsr context. Nowadays, the term would be synonymous with the slightly pejorative term "utopian socialism," and that is doubtless, in part, what Nodier has in mind, including the pejorative gloss, but it is as well to remember that the Comte de Saint-Simon's secretary, Auguste Comte, really did start of religion of atheistic "altruism" complete with churches and rituals, which did indeed follow the program sketched out here, although Comtean philosophy is nowadays also stained by the pejorative associations attached over time to his stern philosophical "positivism." It is also worth nothing that the aphorism that Nodier italicizes is the direct ancestor of a central tenet of Marxism, in its more pragmatic format (i.e,, "From each according to his ability, to each according to his work," as opposed to the more frequently-quoted and more Saint-Simonian "From each according to his ability, to each according his need.")

therefore, in Saint-Simon, the god of the nineteenth century, and I shall believe in him firmly, so long as another god of the same nature des not come along to simplify the social question and reduce it to its ultimate terms. It is necessary not to discourage anyone.

# On Human Palingenesis and Resurrection

I am obliged to declare in commencing that I am not occupied in this eccentric chapter, placed outside all written doctrines, with the theory of "social palingenesis."

Those two expressions are, in my opinion, mutually exclusive, since a genesis is a work of creation that supposes the action of a superior power, and society is only a work of instinct, the accomplishment of which is attributed to the limited organism of a species.

Human have made society in accordance with their power because it was their prerogative. They were not able to do better.

I respect profoundly all the theories that people have imagined for human happiness. A thought of amelioration in the lot of humankind, when it is expressed sincerely, is the highest possible manifestation of intelligence; there is nothing more worthy of veneration.

The Saint-Simonian system is composed of rational inductions that merit being discussed, and which can sustain a profound examination. I am inclined to believe that its apostles have maladroitly turned away from his entirely material and positive paths in substituting hypotheses for calculation and the authority of mystical information for factual criticism, only forgetting the essential element of mystical information—which is to say, spiritualism. I have no less esteem for Saint-Simonians of conviction because of that. Every man who is firmly convinced of what he is saying has a right to be heard, even if he is mistaken.

Monsieur Fourier's system is much more specious, for the reason that it is simpler, more naïve, more disengaged from ceremonies and mysteries, easier to subject to the proof that judges all systems in the last resort, that of experience. I know full well what will come of it, but I am not astonished that people want to know it. That research for the best possible is, in any case, one of the necessities of our nature, one of the disappointments that in inherent in the human condition, the cause of which I shall explain.[1]

The system of Ballanche is different from those. It has the advantage over them of only being expectant, which brings it out of the category of human illusions. It is an Orphean inspiration in a century in which all inspirations of that sort end up falling at the mercy of bacchantes. It is an Archimedean calculation that depends on a small movement being imposed on the world, for which the sublime artisan only has his genius for a lever, and nothing for a point of support. It is the work of a great man on whom nature has mistakenly imprinted the seal of sacerdocy over nations, when sacerdocy and nations are obsolete. And that is not without design. Worlds that are dead remain heavenly bodies for a long time. Ballanche is one of the most powerful intelligences, as well as one of the great writers, of all ages; that is all.

No, there is no specific palingenesis for the present organization of humankind. If species had that privilege, metal would have vegetated, plants would feel, animals would think,

---

1 Charles Fourier (1772-1837) was still alive when the present essay was published and some of his works had not yet been published or widely read, so Nodier's judgment is probably based entirely on *Théorie des quatre mouvements et des destinées générales* (1808), which includes his progressive theory of history and his proposal for social reorganization by the formation of phalansteries, self-sufficient communities in which all necessary social roles were filled, respected and neatly integrated.

and I would boldly conclude from that progressive improvement that we, in our turn, are on the road to comprehension. None of that has happened since the immemorial time when creation commenced, because all beings are enclosed within certain possibilities of progress.

We have touched that barrier a hundred times; a hundred times we have retreated before it, because it does not belong to us to break it. Humans embrace the earth like Antaeus, who emerged therefrom in order to wrestle more forcefully against the god that pressed him, and like him, they get up in order to die. That fate of the Titan is the invariable history of the world.

No, there is no specific palingenesis for the present organization of humankind, because humans are approaching the time when their role upon the earth will finish, like the rest of the fantastic animals of the fossil world, unless they redescend, brutal and savage to the head of inferior species, in order to give way to a new species.

When an idea is as complex as that proposition, it is necessary to unfold it with care in order to render it intelligible to the minds that care about it. The others can leave it there; they have nothing to learn from it, and that is a petty misfortune, for a decided insouciance is probably the highest point that human reason can attain, if the hypothesis I am going to develop is in error.

But before sounding the depths of a hazardous thought, it is doubtless necessary to say how one has penetrated it, and what one hopes to get out of it, in the interests of the present species.

There are two things that I do not know, and which I am somewhat anxious to know.

This is what is personal for me in these questions. I have lived obscurely, solitary, unoccupied, indifferent to the passionate movements of society, and even the curious researches of science, since the inexorable day when, casting a despairing eye over the destination of humankind, I perceived that it was imperfect or false, and that it deceived all the conjectures I had formed when I was younger on the marvelous harmony of creation.

I retired then from the milieu of those futile discussions that occupy dolorously a swarm of unfinished or spoiled beings. I abstracted myself with bitter tears for those who suffer, and tears even more bitter for those who persecute, whose intimate misfortune is incomparably greater. I closed my eyes on society, and hid from it in my neglect. I searched for distractions, however, in study. I searched for them in meditation. I even searched for them in slumber, which is the best of human states, if that is not death.

I set forth in the footsteps of Cuvier,[1] who was an intelligent idea incarnate, into the mysteries of the ancient world, and I regretted that he had not completed the cycle of inductions into which he had fortunately entered, to unveil the mysteries of the new world or the world to come, which are no less evident, for everything that is consequent in creation is essential to it. The chain of beings had broken in his hand at the intellectual link; it was only necessary to reconnect it.

I sensed then that all the consequences of the created world had been accomplished in their time, with the exception of those that will complete human existence, and I concluded therefrom that if the destiny of humankind is not finished,

---

1 Georges Cuvier (1769-1832), the great pioneer of paleontology, to which he applied comparative anatomy in order to determine the taxonomic relationship of fossil creatures to living ones. His assertion that extinct species had been wiped out by a series of catastrophes that had overtaken the world in distant past epochs was highly controversial, attacked from two sides, by Churchmen intent on defending *Genesis* and by rival biologists who preferred theories of gradual evolution to Cuvier's hypothesis of continual creations. Nodier was not the only participant in the debate who wanted to solve the dilemma by combining the two extremes of the argument.

it is because humankind is not a goal of creation, but only a temporary episode, the denouement of which is hidden in that of the universal action. I understood that the life of derision and error that we drag out on earth, which appears to be nothing but an ironic game of an evil spirit, was, on the contrary, all that it had to be in the ever living and ever progressive system of a continuing creation.

I have finally received the perception of a complete and sublime creation whose ensemble leaves nothing to desire for the anxious doubts of our belief, so easily discouraged, which would not merit being the work of God if it were not.

And I am prostrate under the weight of that conviction, because it has succeeded in clarifying for me so many certainties and comprehensive acquisitions of thought, that I could not suppose that it came from me.

From me, great God!—from a fickle, feeble, irritable, inconsiderate being who goes astray every day in the conduct of his own life, and who struggles in the human mud as in the linen of his cradle! From a debilitated and sick heart that has embraced so many affections, and which a necessary reaction on itself can only be isolated from all of nature to lose it in chimeras! From one of those old men of a ripe age whose organic prison has importuned them for a long timed, and who have worn away the springs of their courage against life by dint of exercising them!

In truth, I am neither a sectarian, nor a thaumaturge, nor a prophet. I am not a philosopher. I do not even make a scruple of being a thinker, in the broad acceptance that is given to that word, because thought is almost always badly used. The truth has not been communicated to me in the bush of Moses or Numa's wood. It has not transported me into the heavens on the chariot of Ezekiel or the arrow of Abaris.[1] It has not

---

1 The legend of Abaris the Hyperborean, a sage and prophet who was said to have traveled the world with an arrow, symbolizing Apollo, can be found in Herodotus, but the notion that he flew on the arrow, like a witch

reached me clad in the dazzling revelation that communicated it to the evangelists, nor radiant with the inspiration of poets.

I solicited it with the candor of a simple soul, and perhaps I have found it.

If it is thus, you can recognize it by a certain sign: you will understand it. Everything that is not comprehensible to an attentive mind, everything that does not reach the soul with the clarity of a memory and the vivacity of a sentiment is only a verity of dialecticism, a verity of sophistry, a scholastic and bookish verity, a verity of convention—which is to say, an aberration, or a lie.

From the moment that one has made in oneself the departure of those two verities, and I ask no more of those who deign to read me, they will know as much as I do, if I know, and more than me if I am mistaken, and they will be able to quit me or follow me.

These commencements are more intimidating than I would have wished, but we shall soon be out of them. The inconvenience to which I am subject is inevitable when one opens a path that has not been frayed, in order to reach a door that has never been opened. I shall not break it down; I have the key.

It would be futile today to repeat at length the derisions of which *Genesis* has been the object in the sad century of philosophers. Two words will suffice to reduce them to their true value—which is to say, the expression of an ignorant pedantry, a stupid presumption.

Firstly, the days of *Genesis* were not days of twenty-four hours, as a few simple-minded scholiasts have tried to prove. The quotidian distribution of our hours is an effect of our globe, which was not made when light was made, by an intelligence that did not have, like the Institut, its orient in Bercy

---

on a broomstick, is attributed to the astronomer Heraclides Ponticus, who was presumably speaking figuratively.

and its occident on Vaugirard. The days of creation were thus calculated on the progress of another sun, which is not that of humankind, and whose course no man knows.

Secondly, the astronomy, physics and history of the Bible are not dogmatic facts; they are apparent facts. Those notions have been coordinated with a sublime measure to human intelligence, and placed in consequence within range of the median faculties of humankind. They are all that they ought to be, because they were made for humans, and for primitive humans, whose nature would have been forced by a more complete information, and it is their apparent imperfection that makes their specialty. There is a catechism for the Iroquois savage; there is one for Pelisson and Turenne;[1] there would be one for Socrates if Socrates were reborn; the Bible is for everyone.

By virtue of accommodating the story of creation to humans, without respect for the evident vagueness that its divine author had left there by design, Esdras and the other chapters of scripture have denatured *Genesis*. The further one goes back to the primary texts and their first interpreters, the more one is assured that the week of creation is not full, and that it lacks one of those days whose minutes are centuries.

This is not a reckless proposition. It struck Saint Jérôme and Saint Augustine. The oldest commentators cited by Jean Mercerius[2] thought that the empty day had been filled by the creation of spirits superior to human beings, and that the day in question must have been the second, but that is contrary to the known and progressive march of creative action, which

---

1 The references are to the historian Paul Pelisson (1624-1693) and the general Henri de La Tour d'Auvergne, vicomte de Turenne (15199-1675) cited here because they were Huguenots.
2 Author's reference: "*Commentarius in Genesin*, Geneva 1589, p.15." the author of the posthumously-published text in question (in 1598, not 1589) was Jean Mercier (1510-1570), who signed himself Joannes Mercerius

always proceeds from the simplest to the most perfect, as we shall see shortly.

Other Hebrew critics rectified their mistake in a very rational manner, by transporting that lacuna to the sixth day[1] and attributing to that supplementary day, like their predecessors, the production of the comprehensive being, with the result that the species *par excellence* of creation appeared in their hypothesis immediately after humans, as in the logical order of progression. They touched the truth without being aware of it and without knowing it, since they placed in a preterite time what was only one of the infallible necessities of the accomplishment of things, or they only revealed what it was given to them to reveal; but the principle was acquired and it subsists.

The sage Ambroise Catharin, archbishop of Gonza, explains their reticence by saying that humans were neither able nor worthy to comprehend the mystery[2]—an astonishing mystery, in fact, that the universal perception of an intelligence placed between humans and God, and which practical religion informed the faithful, although the idea does not result explicitly from any passage in the sacred books, where "angel" never signifies anything but a creature *sui generis*, which God employs for his messages.

There is, therefore, a fact of intuition, which is not a fact of revelation, and which is common to all men in all centuries and all beliefs: the necessary existence of a comprehensible species.

---

1 Author's reference: "Don Calmet, *Genèse*, chapter 2. Paris 1767, vol.1 p. 651." The reference is to the first volume of Dom Augustine Calmet's seventeen-volume translation of the Bible into French (1767-1773—posthumously, as Calmet, a Bendictine monk, had died in 1757) and presumably relates to part of Calmet's commentary.

2 Author's reference: "Nondum erat capax et dignus homo as hoc mysterium capessendum. *Explanationes in primum capus Geneseos*. Rome, 1552, p.33." Ambroise Catharin was the name assumed in religion by Lancelotto Politi (1484-1553), a Dominican friar and fervent opponent of Martin Luther.

There is a fact of sacred criticism that is recognized by Christians and Jews, by scholars and saints: the material lacuna of one day in the mystic week of creation.

What I know about these facts, and what I shall make evident, is that the comprehensive species must be, and that creation must finish in its time.

What I have just written here, I address to my brethren the Christians, whom an unjust scruple might have turned away from accompanying me in the discoveries that these premises will furnish me, and which I wish to state in order to prove that the truth which remains to me to demonstrate by itself—which is to say, by naming it—is not opposed to the teachings of Scripture, of which it is rather the essential development.

Now I am quitting the theologians, I am interrogating the scholars, I am instructing myself with those who doubt, I am arguing with atheists, and when we have borrowed a few rays from the immense spectrum of light that illuminates the world today, in order to bear a reassuring torch on the unknown route in which I am engaging, we shall march without any obstacle, for what remains for me to declare does not demand anything from my audience except attention and good faith.

Geology has not deigned to write its genesis, but that causes no difficulty, because it is written in all of nature. Geology, which is an admirable science, is, in any case, an experimental science, an exact science, a science of facts. It only teaches us about the past.

Let us deploy that geological genesis, lucid, palpable and expressive, save for filling in its final pages. Here it is:

In the beginning matter was: matter expanded in aerial fluids; matter subtilized in sonorous and luminous fluids; matter dispersed in atoms and in monads; matter penetrated in all its molecules by the faculty of being and the faculty of producing; matter agitated by the desire of progression, by fecundating amour, the *alma Venus* of Lucretius—which is to say, the principle of motion and increase, which is the immortal vehicle of all existences.

And that was the first day, the first day on the clock-face of which we can neither mark the divisions nor measure the diameter.

Matter was subject to the laws of its essence. It solicited them, sometimes anticipated them, conceived antipathies, submitted to affinities, condensed into spheres, cubes, prisms and polyhedra of all forms, became worlds or became gravel, indifferently. It increased, extended, and grew, finally, by juxtaposition; there was a commencement of life, and that was the second day.

The vital impatience that animated it could not be stopped. Its pores were enlarged by an unexpected sap, by circulation, by the new phenomenon of a nourishing intussusception. It passed from its primitive mode of increase to a mode of reproduction at first spontaneous, and then regular, and then constant. Its muted and mechanical affinities gave way to almost intelligent sympathies. It vegetated. It had birth, life and death: death, a necessary condition of the state of beings that are improving, which the mineral had not known. It formed the fecund debris of its accumulated generations, accumulated by the centuries, a virginal humus in which all the plants of the earth germinated in an incredible succession of species. And that was the third day.

The vegetal only lived; it needed to feel. By virtue of aspiring to new metamorphoses, ever-agitating matter acquired organs, sensibility, the perception of external objects and locomotion. The animals existed, and the fourth day went by like the others in passionate tendencies, in trials, in progress, in developments. The improved species were social, laborious and industrious, moved as they were by an insatiable appetite that was to torment all creatures until the day of rest.

The fifth day was that of humans, or thinking beings, and that fifth day is the last of philosophical creation. One can only go beyond it by means of inductions, and all induction would be false if humans were really, as they say but dare not believe, the culminating and complete beings of a rational creation. But alas, if that were so, humans would no longer tend to change, and no species has launched forth more impatiently toward the limits of its sphere, in order to transcend them. In revolt against the poverty of their organization, against the disappointment of their hopes, against the misery of their destiny, human beings only strive to delude themselves and others regarding the faculties they lack; and the hatred of that creation, of which they cannot penetrate the secret, has rendered them cruel toward their fellows and ingrate toward its author. They are indignant at the humiliating ignorance in which nature wants to hold them, and they blaspheme in their irritated pride, because their vain sciences have not enabled them to comprehend that they too are only a transitory creation of one of the days of the world.

All the progressions that have been summoned by the creative instinct of matter have been accomplished in their day: growth, life, sentiment and thought. The unaccomplished progression that solicits human instinct is the comprehension of the truth.

The comprehensive being will arrive.

I do not want, however, to be reproached for what one of my beloved writers reproaches himself: becoming obscure in trying to be concise. Let us follow momentarily these developments of creative matter that have just attracted our gaze in their generative progress, but do not ask too much of me, for I have little time, I have little space, and I know very little.

Mineral is divided up into various species, families and genres. It is complete in its nature. The day of its creation is tending toward its decline, but it is necessary that another dawns. So the reigning being is being modified and perfected; it has acquired two senses at once in the magnet: a tactile sense that summons sympathetic bodies from a distance, and polarity, which opened to us subsequently the routes of the sea. That is not all; it rises in stems similar to trees, deploys in wires similar to branches, thins out and becomes lacy in elegant sculptures similar to leaves, becomes frayed in hair-like fibers in asbestos, blossoms in variegated corollas in cobalt. It flocculates in cottony efflorescences in magnesium; falls in brilliant seeds in a few native metals, or twists and is hollowed out like an egg around certain crystals.

And in the meantime, the arid lichen arrives, scaly, friable to the touch, metallic to the gaze, which clings to its surface, and is indecisive for a long time, for the naturalist, between an oxide and a plant.

Now the living plant is engendered in the family of cryptogams; moss bristles in clay or metal urns; ferns fold their leaflets over ochreous cylinders like pyrites, and mushrooms overshadow their pedicles, rounding out above them like the helmet of a geode.

Matter does not relent in the investigation of its organic conquests. Plant life seeks to feel, shuddering to the touch in the sensitives; it palpates, arms itself and defends itself against the dionaeae; it sees in the heliotrope, which seeks the sun, gazes at it and follows it; it chooses, it loves, it attracts in the palm tree; it has the perception of daylight, night and the slightest divisions of time in all its species.

It will succeed in becoming a sensitive being in sea silks, in xerophytes, in polyps; it is animalized and it populates. Science will be obliged to create a name for that intermediate class of natural species, and as the name that it will invent first will be picturesque and true, it will call them zoophytes: animal-plants.

And the creative principle is further extended, enriching itself with new faculties, but by degrees undetectable to vulgar attention, scarcely modifying the type of its plastic figures; thus the stellar radiation that shines in the face of the firmament was reflected in a host of crystallizations and metals; it has already passed into the corolla of the rosaceae; it multiplies in the madrepores in elegant divisions, in petallic imprints and floccular expansions. You will find it later in the vertebrate animals and in its vertebrae themselves, which have strewn the debris of the fossil world with as many astroites.

Before long the sensitive fungus develops on the sea bed, under a forest of coral, its polished dome lined with fine and fragile sheets, like its vegetal analogue in the midst of the fresh grass of the woods; the centipede goes to seize walls of damp rock with more fingers than the hart's-tongue fern and the snake coils around light stems in more knots than a liana. That dead leaf, which hazard seems to have detached from the crown of the linden tree before the harsh days of autumn, and which falls, spinning, to the ground, look, it is a butterfly; would you not think that the pretty argus that is striking the air with its wings were a flying forget-me-not? Even a bird's egg is only a seed that the sun cannot fertilize, and which cannot hatch without being brooded by a mother.

The animals, penetrated by the common impatience of everything that exists, no more have the newly acquired sensitivity of plants and vegetation than the metallic growth, crescence or cretescence, so barbarously named crudescence by our quacks. They are agitated in their turn by the need for cogitation, but, more fortunate than humans, they are provided with it by means of regular and invariable instincts in the laborious republics of beavers, bees, termites and ants. They rise all the way to near-reflective sentiments in the elephant and the horse, as far as energetic, obstinate affections capable of memory in the seals of the polar seas, to which the observer regrets not being able to accord a soul, and of which the ancients made the siren, or muse of the reefs. However, the seal does not think, and the dog, created for humans, is even more exceptional in the chain of beings. God has given it to us subsequently, in the form of compensation, to serve as a guide to the blind, as a friend to poverty, an assiduous and tender consoler of all the ills of life. If benevolence is the foremost of resurrectional aptitudes—and who can doubt it?—I am firmly convinced that dogs will resuscitate.

On the fifth day, finally, humans suddenly rise up in the midst of some astonished tribe of orangs or pongos. They are provided with one sense more, the cogitative sense, and everything that depends upon it, the tide of ideas, the confusion of speech, the diffusibility of languages, doctrines and opinions. There they are, ignorant of the past, which they cannot know, ignorant of the future, which they will never know, ever discontented with the present, regretting a better that never was or desiring a better than never will be: the most unfortunate. I admit, of creatures predestined to be, because they are the only ones who can foresee their end, and which have no organs to comprehend it; but they are only unfortunate with a relative misfortune, a reparable misfortune, which weighs upon them like a punishment to repress their insensate haste to change nature.

I shall not recount that beautiful allegorical history, so diaphanous in its emblems and so luminous in its information; ask that of Moses.

It is doubtless rather singular that I have been obliged to envelop myself in so many logical precautions and support myself with so many proofs in order to succeed slowly in the exposition of a simple idea that is written on the first page of the first volume of the first of known books, and which can in consequence be regarded as the first of human notions. The species that appears on the fifth day of creation has thought for an instrument and comprehension for a goal, but the imperfection of its organism does not permit it to reach it. It is more than three thousand years since that was said, and for more than three thousand years it has been forgotten.

Seven or eight immortal geniuses have summarized all the sciences of the species with an overwhelming superiority: Pythagoras, Plato, Aristotle, Descartes, Charles Bonnet,[1] Cuvier and I do not know who else, the first with beautiful poetic lies, the last with material facts. What have they learned about humankind, except what Adam learned at the foot of the tree: that he had devoured the fruit of science pointlessly, and that he had to die?

The system of Pythagorean transmigrations was a comprehensive hallucination, but I am not surprised that it became the belief of a party of nations. Pythagoras would have been much closer to accessible truth if he had extended his theory to all material creation instead of restricting it to the final creature. There is no final creature so long as creation has not finished, and that is so naïve to say, that it is hardly worth the trouble of stating it.

Now, creation has certainly not finished as long as the creature retains a determined appetency for improvement and can conceive a better state, for which it lacks the comprehensible organs.

I ask humans now whether they believe themselves to be the end of creation?

---

1 Charles Bonnet (1720-1793) was a Genevan botanist and philosopher who helped to popularize the idea of a hierarchical scale of natural beings—sometimes known in English as "The Great Chain of Beings," which Nodier has just set out in a more poetic manner—and who went on in *Palingénésie phlosophique* (1769-70; partially translated in 1787 as *Philosophical and Critical Ideas Concerning Christianity*) to argue the survival of all creatures and their perfection of their faculties in a future state—a precursor of and alternative to the Chevalier de Lamarck's theory of evolution, which Nodier clearly preferred, and tried to extrapolate in the present essay.

It is necessary for me to stop for a moment to give free rein to an objection that will doubtless be addressed to me if I have been followed thus far—for I supposed in the beginning that I was dealing with a patient and resolute audience.

"What you have just said to us," someone might reply to me, "we knew, or very nearly, and you have only reestablished a species of order in a few ideas that we had conceived before you, but it is on those ideas themselves that our philosophical faith in perfectibility rests. Humans ought to become more and more comprehensive in their own species. We are already very comprehensive ourselves, for we no longer believe in anything, and that proves that we know a great deal.

"Has not civilization made enough progress to promise us more? See what a touching forbearance it has brought to mores, what clarities it has caused to spring forth in education, what a rapid and irresistible movement it has imparted to all intelligences! Justice is no longer mistaken; medicine has become, as no one is unaware, a veritable exact science; merit alone leads to honors and virtue alone to power; the harmony that regulates fraternal societies, thanks to the unlimited liberty of the press,[1]

---

1 Author's note: "I mean by the press here what it can become in a false interpretation of social necessities, what I tried to characterize a few days ago by an expression extracted from the most bitter dolor: *the fury of the press*. It is true that one can say, without being held to account, *the fury of religion* in speaking of fanaticism, *the fury of amour* in speaking of jealousy, and even *the fury of liberty* in speaking of the Terror, but the free press is not so accommodating. It has conceived such broad views of liberty that it does not accord to anyone the liberty of complaining about its license and its frenzies. One newspaper said on that occasion: 'Monsieur Nodier calls the press a fury. We wonder what we should call Monsieur Nodier, who is born of the press and nourished by it?' I am not sure what I ought to be called, if I am not called by name, but I suppose that one cannot call me a fury. My life is orderly. As for being nourished by the press, I honor it for that, as a poor and worthy worker honors an instrument that has brought him profit and consideration, and of which he has never made use in a

mutual information by the Jacotot method,[1] would be the envy of More's Utopia and the idea republic of the wisest of Socrates' pupils. Politics is still a little embarrassed in its march, but Père Enfantin[2] has cleared the fog from religions forcefully. It will be something else when we have found women liberated and organized the phalanstery. Finally, we no longer burn books, and if we submerge them from time to time, it is in truth because we have no more need of them. Oh, it is a very visible and very satisfying thing, the perfectibility of humankind. We will grant you with pleasure, Monsieur, that the comprehensive being must surge forth one day from creation, but the comprehensive being will be human."

Ironic or sincere, the picture that has just been traced is, in fact, the expression of a social statistic, but, taking that antagonism in its most favorable acception, it cannot change the logic of my proposition, which I ought to present now in a more exclusive form.

1. It is as impossible to be devoid of comprehensive organs and to succeed in comprehension as it is for someone born blind to appropriate the sensation of light and colors.

2. Humans are devoid of organs appropriate to be comprehensive.

It remains for me to prove that.

---

harmful manner. It is not the fury of the press but the muse of the press that has nourished me."

1 The "Jacotot method" of "intellectual emancipation," popularized by Joseph Jacotot (1770-1840), was briefly fashionable after the 1789 Revolution, especially in Belgium, where Jacotot thought it politic to go into exile after the Restoration.

2 The leading Saint-Simonian Barthélemy Prosper Enfantin (1796-1864) became an ardent preacher of that philosophy after the July Revolution of 1830 and soon became convinced that he had a divine mission, causing some scandal when be became the leader of a cult based in the heart of Paris preaching and attempting—very awkwardly—to practice "free love."

I believe that it is Voltaire who says somewhere, with the assurance of a philosopher and the levity of a man of the world, that the impossibility of acquiring a sense is demonstrated by the impossibility of even determining the object and the perception. Thus he refrained from acquainting us with those with which he endowed his fantastic voyager, Micromegas and the man from Sirius, so liberally. That is truly too much modesty or reoccupation. It is sufficient to think of them to offer him a dozen or more, without going to search further than the simple organization of a few poor animals that have been, in that regard as in many others, more favored than us. The sense of the annual return of bad seasons that alerts swallows so infallibly; that of the daily ascension of the sun that wakes the cock on his perch every morning; that of orientation that directs the dove with so much surety to the nest of her chicks; that of peril, which makes a blind fowl cry out in the midst of its offspring on the arrival or a hawk; that of distances, which permits the idle quail to measure its flight across the sea to an invisible point of repose; that which informs the dog and the stork of salutary herbs and remedies; that which directs and moderates the precipitate flight of the bat in the anfractuosities of tenebrous caverns; and that is only to mention a few.

If humans had received at birth some organic disposition to the comprehension of the truth, they would have tried it first on their most immediate contingencies, or, by virtue of being pressed from all directions, would have become accustomed to knowing and judging them. The most immediate contingencies of thinking beings are three in number: creation, space and time.

Creation: human beings live in it, by it, and with it; the most incontestable of their notions is that they are because it is.

Space they sense everywhere, in the steps they sketch while hanging on to the apron strings, in the running of a horse, in the flight of an eagle, in the eternal march of comets, in the immeasurable gaze with which they penetrate infinity.

Time they are subject to every day, in every hour, in every minute; they are subject to it in all their actions, in all their thoughts. There is no inspiration of the lungs, no movement of the pulse, no alternation of the systole and the diastole of the heart that does not remind them of time.

Now assemble, I do not say all men—that would be futile—but a few men that I shall name; assemble Orpheus, Epicurus, Democritus, Aristotle, Hippocrates, Archimedes, Marcus Aurelius, Cicero, Montaigne, Bacon, Locke, Leibnitz, Bonnet, Kant, Cuvier—and you too, my dear Ballanche! That would compose, I think, a rather fine intellectual society. Give them for a reporter the good Prince della Mirandola, who has engaged to sustain against all comers a thesis *de omni re scibili*,[1] and ask those people, who can scarcely be suspected, whether they know what time is, what space is, what creation is—the three immediate affairs of humankind—and whether they comprehend organically how those facts, identical to their own existence, can be or not be, can have a commencement and an end or no more end than beginning.

They will respond to you that they do not know, and that no man can know.

And it is you who expect something more!

Everything that it is permitted for a man to know, when he has studied fruitfully the secrets of his organization, is that he is infinitely imperfectible, because he lacks the essential means of perfectibility.

But the brute would have known that, if it had been able to comprehend that it was not thinking, the plant if it had

---

1 The phrase, meaning "concerning everything knowable," was used as the title of a treatise by Giovanni Pico della Mirandola. An unknown wit added *et quibusdam* ("and other things") in citing it, occasioning the oft-quoted sarcasm that the author, supposedly the last of the Renaisssance Men, was said to know everything there is to know, and a few other things besides.

been able to comprehend that it was neither impressionable nor locomotive, the metal if it had been able to comprehend that it was not alive.

Humans would know it if they were not thinking beings—which is to say, if they did not have the misfortune of abandoning their reason to extravagant chimeras.

Humans are not comprehensive beings.

Creation is not finished.

I shall return momentarily to my Christians, whose scruples I might have alarmed desperately—which happened without design, since I am convinced that their religion is the most veritable of the beliefs of thinking humans. Now, I believe that I am capable of proving to them with another authority than I employed at first, in proceeding to the gradual exposition of my principles, that my opinion is the only one that can elucidate completely the mystery of divine revelation, in what remains impenetrable. This digression will be brief.

If anyone asks me why it is that the comprehensive being is not announced in the books of Moses, which contain the full revelation of the burning bush and all that of Mount Sinai, I will ask in my turn why it is that the resurrection of humankind is not expressed either, even implicitly, and by what chance the contrary is put in question in Ecclesiastes, neither more nor less boldly than in tragic Seneca; and why the notion of the immortality of the soul, which is the most important of moral notions, after that of God, has only been an effective moral notion since Jesus Christ, instead of being a revealed notion.

There is only one solution to that difficulty, which is that holy scripture is the contract of alliance of thinking beings who recognize one another with the name of human; that it only contains the truth that is given immediately to their nature, and that the thinking being is not immediately summoned to the resurrectional state, as the comprehensive being will be. Resurrection is for the thinking being only an instinctive idea and a sentiment of anticipation. It is for the comprehensive being alone that it will be a comprehensible idea. One can draw from that an induction that will have the precision and clarity of an aphorism.

What we call mystery for the thinking being will be perception for the comprehensive being.

Add to that that the Church has recognized the necessity of an intermediate state between human life and the resurrection in two of its extra-biblical dogmas, particular judgment and purgatory, as it has recognized the existence of the comprehensive being in the extra-biblical dogma of the angel: respectable facts of belief that are not revealed, the nature and circumstances of which—the form, the time and the places—have never been converted into articles of belief.

Now, the intermediate state between the thinking being and the resurrectional state is the comprehensive state, which is in its own nature, as the Church has thought, a state of purification and judgment.

If one looks back on the ideas I have just developed, they will be found equally consequent in the system of divine creation and that of spontaneous creation, because spontaneous creation could only have been accomplished by a fortuitous succession of incredible events, in which hazard will always have made up for the absence of an intelligent direction; and the phenomenon of that perpetual throw of the dice, to make use of the witty comparison of Abbé Galiani,[1] would be in-

---

1 Ferdinando Galiani (1728-1787) is remembered primarily as a pioneer

comparably more unintelligible to thought than the existence of a creator God. The logical hazard, the hazard invariable in its combinations, and invariable in its products, is a phantom unworthy of a fairy tale.

I have been a doubter, and even incredulous, because I could not see anything in human life but unjustly unequal divisions while it lasts and a frightful void at its end. I refused, in my blind heart, to know and admit God, because his supreme wisdom had measured an incomplete revelation to our incomplete organs.

The chain of beings was interrupted, as I have said, at the link from which the uncertain destiny of human beings was suspended; and, to take the masses as I see them, stirring even in the entrails of antiquity the deplorable history of centuries and nations, I found my species well deserving of annihilation.

Since the great circle of creation has been accomplished in my eyes, since I have traveled it in its admirable regularity, from the moment it proceeds from God by matter endowed with the creative principle to the moment when it ends in God by means of the comprehensive sense, which is the very breath of God, returned to its origin, I have taken my errors in pity. Here, nothing is lacking the eternal harmony of created things, and everything that is bad in temporary things concurs with the absolute good of the accomplishment of universal facts. The faculty of belief has passed, more intense and more powerful, from the mineral into the plant, life from the plant into the animal, and sensibility from the animal into humans. Thought reaches in its turn, from humans to the comprehensive being, with the three intelligent senses of memory, imagination and judgment. Thus, humans are traversing the state of comprehension in order to arrive at the state of resurrection, in which they will always be.

---

of the science of Economics, although he was also a humorist who belied the later reputation of that discipline as "the dismal science" and aided in him being much admired by Voltaire.

Oh, if it were not thus, and the perfection of humans finished with humans, what human would dare to pretend to resuscitation?

It is thus for the irrevocable reason that it is impossible for it to be otherwise.

And if I could transport the whole human race with me on wings, stronger and more assured that of my speech, to the contemplation of the marvelous sphere that has become sensible to me, there is no soul, no matter how rebellious it might be to conviction, that would not share mine!

God is, it would say; God always will be; and humankind, purified by the state of comprehension, will always be near to God when humans have been subjected to the last of their proofs.

The rest is no more than one of those objects of vain and impotent curiosity over which the insatiable avidity of our minds will be exercised for a long time yet.

What will be the comprehensive being of the sixth day of creation, and what will become of human beings?

I do not know more for certain about these questions than those who have never foreseen the comprehensive being, but I will make you party to my conjectures.

The comprehensive beings will probably resemble humans, as humans resemble animals, although not too closely, but with a development of organs of which we cannot imagine the extent and the range. They will have all the senses that we have observed in the surplus of created beings, and a multitude of others that escape us and are reserved for them. The generative matrix only needs a few modifications to submit them to nature, so few that there is only a slight effort to make in order to imagine them: that it has the generosity to maintain, as

135

is encountered in a few exceptional individuals, the opening
of the *trou de Botal*,[1] thus maintaining after birth, the mode
of circulation established in intra-uterine life (which would
cost very little, since it is only an act of conservation); that it
reduces the usage of the respiratory apparatus to a facultative
function, as it has done in amphibians and fish, so that my
new creature can conquer the depths of the sea.

Do not be embarrassed by their almost useless lungs, which
will no longer be anything but an organ of voluntary employment; on the contrary, enlarge the space that they occupy in a
vast and solid torso, which already seems destined by its conformation to contain them, like the carcass of an airship; give
them the amplitude of an aerostat, calculated on the small
weight that it displaces in order to rise in the atmosphere, and
enveloped, instead of its heavy parenchyma, by a docile elastic
membrane. The beings that you have just invented so easily
with me will be able to traverse the air in any direction that
it pleases them to travel,[2] not in the manner of Icarus, whose
the bird-like adaptation is inappropriate to all the possibilities of our physical configuration, nor with the four wings
of Mercury, whose poetic iconography is better matched to
the equilibrium and the mechanism of our strength, but by
creating a void at will in their large pneumatic viscera and by
striking the earth with the feet, as the instinct of their progressive organism teaches humans to do in dreams.

---

1 The *trou de Botal* was the original name given to the *foramen ovale*, a
small hole between the atria of the fetal heart, which usually closes after
birth, assisting the fetus to circulate oxygenated blood obtained from the
placenta without the intervention of lungs. Nodier's suggestion that the
comprehensive being will retain the fissure in question does not explain
how oxygenated blood will be supplied in the absence of a supportive
placenta.
2 The issue of the possible dirigibility of aerostats was a niggling topic of
debate in the 1830s, but the idea that they might be directed by skipping
in this manner does not seem to have been suggested, perhaps because its
inconveniences and impracticalities were too obvious.

In the laboratory of creation, all of that requires no more than a moment, and one might ask with surprise why it has not happened already, if one did not know that it has not happened because the time has not yet come.

The elliptical expression of an idea that would probably have required a long volume of clarifications to be fully extended scarcely permits me to deliver myself today to my invincible appetite for episodes. I shall therefore not pause for long over an incidental question of scant importance, which I shall nevertheless take the liberty of submitting to the Académie des Sciences some day if I become famous enough, rich enough or a sufficiently great seigneur to raise my voice that far:

"Why do humans, who never dream of cleaving through the air with wings, like all the flying creatures by which they are surrounded, dream so frequently of rising up with an elastic power, in the manner of aerostats, and why did they have that dream for a long time before the invention of aerostats—since the dream is mentioned in all ancient oneirocritiques—if that prevision is not a symptom of their organic progress?"

The being that has reached the comprehensive state, therefore, leaves a vast career open to our conjectures, and, although it might seem bizarre to say so here, I only tolerate a conjecture insofar as it summarizes inevitably a long series of facts that can only end thus. The auxiliary conjectures that circumstantiate them are only good to amuse the imagination, and I do not represent them as anything else.

The comprehensive beings will doubtless be born beautiful, because it is for them that the catechistic instructions of the Roman Church have foreseen a *glorious body*. Matter ought to be subtilized to the point of becoming more impalpable than air and light in the resurrectional state. Suppose now—and what prevents us parading in advance the torch of poetic thought over the denouement of the greatest of poets,

over the last day of creation?—that the comprehensive beings
are born adult, that they live without aging, and that death
for them will only be a certain passage to immortal rejuvena-
tion. Suppose that they only renew themselves within their
species by means of the pure effusions of amour that are the
sensuality of the soul, and with which our vulgar life presents
a divine appearance, too quickly obscured by the poverty of
our sensualities of flesh and blood. Suppose that the beings
produce the blossoming of two memories in harmony, two
sighs that understand one another, two kisses that fecundate
one another, two souls that mingle; that they blossom as pure
as the thought that has conceived them, clad in all the features
of a physiognomy present in the memory, all the qualities that
have been cherished in what is loved the most—the friend
that one has lost too soon or the child for whom one has
shed so many tears! That is not only possible but probable, for
everything that it is possible to imagine of good is probable
in the progressive march of a creation of love that is being
accomplished.

That state, however—of which I am not prejudging anything except in order to conform to the imaginative fantasy
of minds that accompany me in a path closed to all human
prescience—will be no more exempt than all the other states
of organized matter from confusion and pain; and perhaps we
know already that there are terrible revolutions to undergo,
by way of one of the great mystical histories, the revelation of
which is not written among any people, in any sacred book, but
the conviction of which has existed since time immemorial in
all traditions: the history of the revolt of the angels. It is probably superfluous to repeat here that its preterition is only an
oratory device that is found in all prophecies of a lyrical genre.
It is undoubted therein that the comprehensive beings will be
divided into two different families for two different destinies,
and I say that on the faith of a notion of little value, since it is

my own, because I am convinced that everything that has been a general matter of credibility will become a real fact.

The rest of the game of creation concluded in its works is easier to follow until the day it has to die. The minerals will continue to render their elements to the primal matter, the vegetables their terrestrial humus to mineral matter, animals and humans their mineral and vegetal debris to the two preexistent natures. Only the sense of thought will have nothing to render, because it does not proceed from anything; it will pass entirely into the comprehensive being.

What subsists today will conclude its existence by virtue of a long series of gradual degradations. The ants will hollow out for a long time yet their covered paths with profound detours; the bees will construct their hexagonal cells, the swallows their conical nests, the caterpillars their woven sheaths, the ant-lions their traps and the beavers their dams.

Humans, taking a step back from living civilization, will perhaps continue to found, in a few savage islands, experimental republics and progressive societies, with the aristocracy of money, the protectorate of women, atheism and the guillotine. A few will gradually detach themselves from that degenerate, decrepit and dying species, like Bougainville's Tahitian or the worthy Iroquois chief that you have seen dancing at the court if you have gone there. They will arrive charged with their books, for they will still print. Some among them will be distinguished by a powerful aptitude for comprehension, I know not what Galileo, Montesquieu or Rousseau of ages to come—if they produce any—whose confused babble will excite among scholars a few humorous polemics or some affectionate interest.

That is the entire future of humankind in the human state, and it is the only idea that can console a man, when he knows that the interval that separates the thinking being from the comprehensive being is almost nothing—only death.

Although the comprehensive state is, for us, only a theme borrowed from the vague world of hypotheses, it is quite different for the resurrectional state, from which we are separated by another infinity, and which comprehensive beings will not know distinctly themselves. So see what the theologians and poets have made of it! It would be enough to inspire an appetite for annihilation in the most expansive soul that had ever invented a pleasant future of solitude and repose—for annihilation, which is not without charm for a fatigued life, only appears horrible by virtue of its opposition to resurrection, and what do we know of resurrection?

To a person penetrated by a faint perception of the mysteries of the resurrectional state, however, annihilation ought to be an object of fear and despair. Annihilation is the Hell of the wicked.

Resurrection is, like *Genesis*, a familiar object of mockery for the incredulous. I can conceive that when I succeed in shrinking myself to the narrow proportions of the Pandemonium in which they have imprisoned their souls. The resurrection that humans can promise themselves has, in fact, something paltry and ridiculous about it, because humans are not comprehensive, and because comprehensive beings, who will have a far more developed sentiment, will nevertheless only be able to form an imperfect idea of the resurrectional state, devoid of grandeur. Such as I have glimpsed it, however, through the two veils that separate me from it, its aspect, obscured as it is by impenetrable darkness, fills my heart with hopes so sublime that I am obliged to have recourse to the notion of an intelligence entirely foreign to my wretched nature, which dazzles and overwhelms me.

Resurrection! My God! The sentiment of being prolonged forever with security in an ecstasy of joy!

The invariability of a young and happy thought in a happy universe, both of which do not grow old, and an eternal love that dissolves in an eternal love!

The conception of space, duration, creation and the creator . . . that is very little! Their possession, their assimilation, their power is a purified soul, which is identified with everything that it has understood, and which enjoys everything that it senses!

The suppression of distances, of time, of individualities! The present that is always, the infinity that one touches every-where the affections to all life elapsed, which is resuscitated, amassed, which presses and palpitates in a single emotion, ever new and always the same, because eternity no longer marches!

All that it is possible to accumulate of pure and ineffable delights in all the senses of all known beings, and also in more senses than there are atoms in all the suns!

To respire in all the points of the immensity that everyone will occupy, the souls of parents, of friends, of children, of na-ture, of God, in whom everything ends in order to find itself again! To live all that endlessly, with a rapture so complete that it would extinguish with a breath the sentiment and existence in the organization of an angel!

That . . . !

Do not be frightened by the poverties of your future. I am only human; I know nothing; I understand nothing; I imagine with crippled and vulgar senses.

That . . . is not resurrection!

✳

I was far advanced in the composition of this little essay when it occurred to me that there were few idlers or thinkers in France sufficiently devoted to meditation to read it all the way to the end, and that, of the handful of readers on whom that hope is founded, there will certainly not be any who consent to occupy themselves with it in a serious manner for a day. I was about, therefore, as the poets say, to make a homage of it to Vulcan, the god to whom I have most often paid similar tributes—it would be different if I were a sage—when, at the moment of accomplishing that intellectual infanticide, oppressed by an invincible slumber, which always pursues me when I reread my work, with my head in my hands—in the attitude that you have now, that of a man who is bored—I was suddenly transported by the caprice of dreams into a German tavern, in Vienna, Gottingen or Heidelberg, next to three young students who were conversing about the future destiny of humankind, while gravely smoking their cigars around three empty beer tankards, and I thought I heard my name.

*For them*, I said to myself, *the thought that I am abandoning might not be useless! Three seeds of my ephemeral grain have fallen on a fertile terrain, and might perhaps germinate in the end, above the frivolous and deceptive ideas of humankind.*

And I finished this work in the peace of my conscience, because I had undertaken it with conviction, and I had drawn inexhaustible consolations from it during one of the bitterest days of my life.

As for you, amiable and tender, but unconscious and light souls, who are fire for lies and ice for the truth, do not castigate my flight into the psychological world into which I have just dragged you. Even the exaltation of an intimate belief and a doctrine identified with my thought is incapable of separating me from you. If you like my fiction better than my philosophy, I am entirely ready to recount to you tomorrow one of the tales that I tell . . . so poorly!

# Perfectibility

## Part One

### *Hurlubleu, Grand Manifafa of Hurlubière*

"To the Devil with you all!" cried the Manifafa.

"Does that include the Chief Jester of your Holy College of Buffoons?" asked Berniquet.

"No," Hurlubleu said. "I'm talking to that rabble of kings and emperors who murder me every evening with their salaaming and who insist on caressing the soles of my slippers with vile kisses. I like you, Berniquet; I like you, Chief Jester of the Holy College of Buffoons, because you have no common sense and you don't lack wit, without which everything is humdrum. I must have a high opinion of your worth, to have conferred upon you one of the most eminent dignities of my empire, for I remember that you fell into my house like a bomb."

"Absolutely," replied Berniquet. "I arrived in a cannonball at the foot of Your incomparable Majesty's glorious divan—and the vehicle is still there, encrusted, so to speak, in the marble on which he deigns to set his sublime feet when he is tired of lying down all day."

"That's not the half of it, Berniquet! Your arrival—which was unexpected, and even a trifle brutal—passed for miraculous, because it delivered the land from a frightful schism that had already cost the lives of a hundred million of my subjects, the reason for which I no longer recall. Charge my calumet so that I can refresh my thoughts."

"Eternal and immutable Manifafa," Berniquet continued, while stuffing his master's pipe with all the customary ceremony associated with that noble office, "the buffoons affiliated to the cult of the Divine Bat, from which your imperial dynasty is descended, and which has the infallible pleasure of covering the sun with its wings every night to procure Your Most Perfect and Most Adored Highness a cool darkness favorable to his sleep, were divided into two stubbornly-opposed parties, commanded by two pitiless jesters, with regard to the question of whether the Sacred Bat had hatched out of a white egg, as Bourbouraki proposed, or a red egg, as Barbaroko maintained—Bourbouraki and Barbaroko being, of course, the two greatest philosophers that had ever illuminated the world and other dependencies of the Empire of Hurlubière with the light of science."

"Why remind me?" replied the Manifafa, sighing from the depths of his soul. "It wasn't my fault that I couldn't reconcile Bourbouraki and Barbaroko, or all those damned jesters. I myself, practically on my own initiative, proposed a compromise to the council of my chibicous[1] by which it could have been amicably agreed that the egg of the Divine Bat was white outside and red inside, or vice versa—I couldn't give a hair of my moustache, myself—but the red buffoons and the white buffoons would never accept it, so obstinate and reckless were they in their resolve, with the result that that bitch of a question would still be hanging in suspense if you hadn't descended abruptly from the clouds to settle it."

"I replied ingeniously to Your Serene Highness that the two jesters were lying about it, and proved by demonstrative

_______________

1 Nodier appears to have invented this word, having run out of readily-available synonyms for "clown".

logic that the Celestial Tetrapod could not have emerged from a white egg, just as it could not have emerged from a red egg, since it was by nature viviparous, mammalian and anthropomorphic, neither more so nor less so than a buffoon; upon which Your Serene Highness hastened in his sovereign bounty to have the heads of the two jesters and all the chibicous cut off, to the great contentment of his people, who were impassioned with joy throughout the world."

"That memorable event was inscribed in letters of gold in the annals of my reign, with the decree by which I named you Chief Jester. I remembered right away, you see—but where the devil did you get that *viviparous, mammalian and anthropomorphic* nonsense from?"

"I knew it by abstraction, in my capacity as a qualified doctor of all infused doctrines and encyclical propagator of the perfect monopoly in *omni re scibili*—but that story is too long for it to be permissible for me to take up the precious leisure time of the great, the very great, the infinitely great Manifafa."

"Tell me your story, Berniquet. If it's long and boring, so much the better. I only like stories that put me to sleep—but spare me at least half of your formulas of obsequiousness and respect; the fact that I am superior to you, poor dust beneath my feet, is too obvious to both of us for me to forget it. For fear of losing the habit, just call me Divine Manifafa from time to time. That's much better, Berniquet—it's short, it's true, it's clear; and when I'm smoking, with my legs comfortably extended on my divan, I don't pay much attention to etiquette. Speak, Berniquet! Speak, jester!"

"Your Majesty will be aware," Berniquet continued, profoundly moved—as he should have been—by this gesture of benevolent familiarity, "that, ten thousand years ago, I lived in a sort of village, which was dirty, smelly, badly-built and disgraceful in every respect, erected on a part of the site that has since been occupied by the stables of your noble eunuchs, which was known as 'Paris' in the patois of that barbaric era. It did not hesitate to pass itself off as the queen of cities, even though it is scarcely mentioned in the ancient chronicles of the Empire of Hurlubière, whose incomparable capital of Hurlu shines today like a resplendent diamond in the world's crown."

"I've heard talk of your shanty-town," Manifafa put in, excitedly. "Stop there a moment, though. What's this ten thousand years you're talking about, with that clownish face that declares that you're forty-five at most? If you know the secret of prolonging for more than ten centuries the existence that the most vigorous of my immortal ancestors accomplished in less than a hundred meager years, I'll open my treasure and my harem to you on the spot, and I'll have you set by my sacred side, buffoon as you are, on the throne of Manifafas. Tell me this instant, jester, if you know a means of living forever! I order you, on pain of death!"

"No more than you, Divine Manifafa! We all die in our turn, ever since our miserable universe began rolling in its narrow orbit, and I have some reason to think that it will be thus until a new order emerges. I really am forty-five years old, neither more nor less, as Your Highness has granted me with his special grace. And if he takes the trouble to subtract the months of nursing, the age of cutting teeth, whooping cough and apron-strings, time at college and the Sorbonne, the enormous portion of illnesses and sleep, the days of military service, the visits made and received, indigestions, missed meetings, lectures, concerts, literary conversations and the public meetings of eighteen academies, he will easily comprehend, in his wisdom, that there remains to me a definitive quotient of one miserable year of life, just like everyone else. On my honor as Great Jester of Buffoons, I wish that lightning would strike me down, if I claim to have existed for one hour more. As for the ten thousand supplementary years that were mentioned just now, I leapt over them in the course of my biography. They lasted no longer, so far as I was concerned, than the time required for the heart to pass from systole to diastole, or for a woman to change her mind."

"That's nice," said the Manifafa. "The length of your story is beginning to bore me very nicely, although I'm well accustomed to reading all the nonsense in Hurlubière to put myself to sleep. Go on then, jester!"

In response to the Manifafa's imperious and decisive gesture, the jester squatted on his heels and continued in these terms:

"In Paris, about the year of grace 1933—which, I have the honor of relating to you, wasn't yesterday—there was a universal propaganda of perfectibility to which I was party, by virtue of my polymathic, polytechnic and polyglot erudition, and which received licensed ambassadors on a daily basis from every rhumb of the horizon. The merchandise was somewhat mixed, according to taste, but all savants, in order that no one will understand them, have to be professional imps to some extent. On one foggy winter evening, however, before sharing out the takings, they agreed that it would be rather difficult to create a perfect society if a preliminary means could not be discovered to procure a perfect man, or to produce one, the aggregate always being, according to the apt expression of peripatetics—God bless them—the complex expression of the aggregated elements, as the Divine Manifafa understands a thousand times better than his humble slave, assuming that he is not yet asleep."

"May the Holy Bat shade me with his tenebrous wings in perpetuity," cried Hurlubleu, "if I understood a single treacherous word of it! But take it upon yourself to spare me the peripatetics' aggregate and get on with it!"

"It was thus resolved that they would devote themselves incessantly to the search for the perfect man—which is to say that as soon as they found out where he might be, and having established that he was, they would make him the foundation of the universal propaganda and the regeneration of civilization."

"You were too modest," the Manifafa put in, "for your propaganda and your civilization had no lack of them—foundations, that is. You came out with that witticism willingly, although it wasn't in very good taste. But what were you expecting of the perfect man, since you had already reached the supreme end-point of science, which consists of no longer understanding anything?"

"Organic perfection!" Berniquet replied, humbly. "The complement of those innumerable faculties which God has distributed between his creatures so prodigally, but which he has restricted in our species with a malicious parsimony to the exercise of five obtuse and miserable senses, combining them, more maliciously still, with intellectual sensibility, which we only use to manufacture stupidities."

"We also use it," the Manifafa said, "to say them and print them, damn it. These considerations must, indeed, have furnished the propaganda with ample food for thought."

"Softly, softly, milord! Propaganda never thinks that which it has thought before. There was a little Chinese peasant there that you could have passed through the eye of a needle, but who knew that it was as long as it was broad, and who swore to us that the perfect man had been manufactured by Zeretochthro-Schah[1] nearly four thousand years previously,

---

1 This name (with a slight variation in its spelling, the explanation for which is not obvious) is revealed in the appended fragment to be the "real" name and title of Zoroaster, although the readers of the *Revue de Paris* could not have been expected to know that when this passage first appeared there. The inconsistencies of continuity between Berniquet's story as related there and the end of the present couplet suggest strongly that the fragment must have been written first, and then abandoned in order to be substituted by a much longer story, commenced in the two chapters making up the present story.

but no one had any idea of what had become of Zeretochthro-Schah or his automaton."

"I can't give you any news of that. Who ever heard mention of an animal of that name?"

"Zeretochthro-Schah, Divine Manifafa, was, as they say, *si res parvas licet componere magnis,*[1] a sort of incongruous cross between a manifafa and a buffoon, who lived in the time of Gustaps[2] and came from Media to indoctrinate Bactria. In addition to the Zend-Avestra and a few other books, it is generally believed that he left behind a formula well-accommodated to the most vulgar intelligence for the confection of the great work of perfectibility, which is the perfect man; but, as his luggage was being transported, it was unfortunately flooded by a bottle of ink, and has never been seen since. No other means of obtaining cognizance of it, therefore, remained to the universal propaganda but to consult tradition, making a journey to the relevant places at the State's expense. According to every indication, we would have obtained good results from that great enterprise if another manifest obstacle had not cropped up at the time—which was that Bactria was swallowed up by an earthquake between two of our meetings, taking Zeretochthro-Schah, his traditions and his formulae with it."

"Goodbye perfect man and perfectibility. I imagine that the nose of universal propaganda was put out of joint."

"I have already had the honor of telling Your Divine Highness that the impeccable propaganda never went back on its

---

1 "If, in this instance, it is permissible to compare small things with large ones."

2 The family of Gustap, allegedly contemporary with Zoroaster, is cited in *Exposition du système théologque des Perses* (1774) by Abraham-Hyacinthe Anquetil-Duperron (1731-1805), who published a three-volume version of the Zena Avestra, which he attributed to Zoroaster; the reliability of his research was challenged at the time and soon fell out of fashion with orthodox scholars, but enjoyed a renaissance of fashionability during the French Occult Revival.

decisions. A dozen of us set forth, firmly resolved to search for the Bactrian all the way to the center of the earth, into which frightful confusion, according to every indication, he must have descended by virtue of the law of gravity."

"You're putting me on the track, wise jester. Did the reputation get there by artesian well?"

"Your ever-august Majesty's immense penetration is as sudden as genius, but we were not so ingeniously advised. It seemed appropriate to complete an exploration of the entire surface of the globe before visiting its entrails."

"Marvelous! I can see you now in a speedy conveyance, like the scientists of the common people. Propaganda on the high road!"

"There was no means, sire. One could no longer travel without mortal peril, since the invention of railways."

"I had forgotten that. Continue then—for I've been making mental efforts for a whole quarter of an hour, which are waking me up."

"We embarked on the steamboat *Progress*—a fine vessel, I assure you—with three funnels and a powerful engine, which sailed so boldly, triple port, that my friend Jal[1] would not have had time to count the knots on the log line. We traveled nearly eighteen hundred leagues, at the stoker's estimate, until we were reduced, for want of combustibles, to throwing our furniture, our tools, our petty possessions, and even our hydrographic charts, our scientific textbooks and our patents, into the boilers."

"You would have been wise to begin with those, jester," said the Manifafa.

"At first, that made a bright and brilliant fire, which filled our hearts with joy, all the more so because the guardian of the valves already thought he could see land through his achromatic telescope. The fanatic would have done better to

---

1 Augustin Jal (1795-1873) published a glossary of nautical terms.

150

attend to his valves however; the three steam-engines, which I had the advantage of mentioning before, profited from the occasion by exploding all at once, with such perfect harmony that one would have thought that they had given one another a password."

"The explosion of a steamboat—the capricious and jerky speed of which has discomfited me many times—necessitates the observation, Berniquet," said the Manifafa, "that this mode of navigation is a furious demonstration of its inventor's intelligence, and has a great deal of pleasure in it."

"When one has come back, milord. We were thrown so rapidly to an enormous height that I had not time to measure it with exactitude, because there is an essential lack of objects of comparison at sea. We soon perceived, however, in accomplishing our parabolic trajectory, in the manner of projectiles, that we had had the good fortune to be steered close to shore—without which death would have been inevitable. Undoubtedly, no country so delightful had ever presented itself to the gaze of an astonished traveler. Calypso's isle, of which you have perhaps heard mention, was only a miserable sandbank by comparison, unworthy of the imagination of poets.

"As we drew closer, we were able to see developing before our eyes—and that figurative expression is quite exact in this instance, for we were falling head-first—all the marvels of an Elysian vegetation, crowned with flowers and fruits. There were none but orange-trees with golden apples, banana-trees with floating clusters, and vines with purple grapes, which linked their opulent arms with the branches of mulberry-bushes and elms; there were none but cherry-trees weighed down by the weight of a multitude of rubies, their flexible boughs swaying gently in the breeze; there were none but laurels with berries black as jet, or acacias with perfumed sprays, which mingled their intoxicating odors with those of violets, carnations, heliotropes and tuberoses, the fresh verdure of whose meadows was punctuated everywhere by streams of crystal and silver, like threads of elegant embroidery. Roses being relatively rare in the region, however, we did not notice any at first glance."

"I'm only astonished that you were able to notice so many things," the Manifafa commented, "but I presume that you decided to make landfall after having tacked for as long as you say—let's leave it at that."

"By hurtling from branch to branch, in the manner of Christophe Morin when he took the magpie from the nest,[1] Divine Manifafa. Our first concern was to count ourselves. Of the eight hundred individuals who had composed the crew only six of us remained, but thanks to the special effect of the providential wisdom that watches over the progress of humanity, all six of us were delegates of the élite of the universal propaganda."

"I have often heard it said, my friend, that people of that sort always land on their feet. But do me the honor of informing me whether the providential wisdom you mention had conserved the little Chinaman for you?"

"The little Chinaman had done his bit, Sublime Highness; by virtue of his natural extreme slenderness, one may presume with considerable assurance that he had returned, in impalpable atoms, to the perpetual fire of creation."

"So much the better!" cried the Manifafa. "He was the one who got you involved, in this interminable story, with the pursuit of Zeretochthro-Schah, and I do not feel capable of forgiving him that in this lifetime."

---

1 Christophe Morin is the eponymous protagonist of a vaudeville by "les auteurs de *M. de Bièvre*" [Emmanuel Dupaty, who had signed the earlier vaudeville " Citoyens C et C"] first performed at the Théâtre des Troubadours in year VIII (i.e. 1797) and printed in 1801, which formed the basis for a similarly-titled opera in 1800, although Nodier is more likely to have been familiar with another eponymous spinoff by Gabriel-Marie Legouvé—who is recruited as a character in "Monsieur Cazotte"—which was also published in 1801.

"We were a little bruised; that's the least one can expect when one falls from on high without preparation, but that only increased our pleasure in the midst of the happy people who were dancing in the shade. We hastened to join in their innocent games, as naively as if we had been simple shepherds, and our cheerfulness increased considerably, as you can believe, when we learned that this pastoral festival was being held to celebrate the departure of a freight-balloon for a very distant region, to which it would take us in a little while."

"Did you know, savants as you were—and you being a particularly savant jester—where this balloon would take you?"

"What does it matter where a balloon might take one when one does not know where one is going? That is the road taken by savants, empires and the world."

"Take ship for the skies, Berniquet! Go, my son, my jester, wherever the demon drives you! But an aerostat that one cannot steer is no more than a child's toy, only good for amusing kings, old women and academies."

"A mere bagatelle! The subtle perspicacity of your mind is still transporting you, increasingly extraordinary Manifafa, in advance of the discoveries of ancient civilization, as if you had divined them! The direction of balloons had become the simplest of all problems to solve, since steam-engines had been applied to navigation; the resistance of air-currents is less difficult to vanquish than that of the waters. We therefore climbed resolutely into the steam-balloon *Well-Insured*, which was an imposing vessel, perfectly equipped and armed for that great expedition because of the large number of aerial corsairs that had been ravaging the regions we were going to visit for some years, thus causing an immense prejudice against atmospheric travel, in spite of all the precautions of customs officers and the police. We were furnished with twenty-four good Siamese cannons, fifty-two feet long, and a hundred and eighty-two pounds of cannonballs, which could hit their targets at a range of seven leagues, and we had no less than six thousand fighting men, organized into troops armed with every possible weapon, save for cavalry and sappers, not counting the chiurm[1] and the boarding parties, who were stationed at the grappling-irons—with the result that we took to the air, without anxiety and without difficulty, followed by the acclamations of the multitude."

"I recommend, jester, that you keep an eye on the valves! But how did you and your fellow savants pay for your passage? Were the propagandists of perfectibility stationed at the grappling-irons or beside the chiurm?"

"Eh?" Berniquet replied. "Set aside that needless concern, Divine Manifafa! In all the terrestrial, maritime and celestial conflagrations that you can possibly imagine, the first thing the savants of my time made sure of was to carry their purses with them everywhere, and the perfect consideration they enjoyed in that distant era procured them much credit everywhere that the name of man was known. Their diplomacy was worth bars of gold."

"Might I permit myself to observe, Berniquet, that that is not the case today?"

"I agree, milord. Whatever the circumstances, we were able to go nearly four thousand leagues[2] without knowing exactly where we were, because Your Majesty is not unaware that the compass has drifted a few degrees since then, and at that height it can move randomly, turning entire circles at times, with no other motor than its own capricious oscillation, the attractive

---

1 The English word chiurm is as esoteric as Nodier's direct French equivalent, *chiourme*, but there is no ready alternative; it refers to a means of calibrating the rhythm of a crew of galley slaves—traditionally, a man beating a big drum.

2 A metric league is four kilometers; the earth's circumference is approximately forty thousand kilometers. Given that the steamboat had already carried the travelers eighteen hundred leagues, therefore, a balloon journey in a similar direction would have taken the travelers more than half way around the world, probably ending up somewhere in the Pacific.

action of the pole being considerably altered in those elevated regions."

"That was a good opportunity to graduate the scale of the blueness of the sky, which gave so much trouble to Monsieur de Saussure!"[1]

"The sky was as black as ink. However, we consoled ourselves in our isolation by giving names to the occasional clouds. It was a very ingenious pleasure, a human joy, gone with the wind like those of earth. Besides, we would have run the risk of a serious accident if we had not escaped, by means of a skilful maneuver, the eruption of an accursed volcano, which almost put the *Well-Insured* up the spout."

"I can't let that pass," Hurlubleu interrupted, "and God knows that you've made me swallow a lot over the last hour. Never, and I mean never, has a volcanic eruption climbed so high!"

"It often happens, superhuman Manifafa, that the eruptions of aerial volcanoes descend much lower, at least when the ambient rotation of the atmosphere does not transform them into pretty little pocket satellites, as I have often seen in my travels. The explosion that threatened us at such close range could have been the one that destroyed Paris. It was, to tell you the truth, that of one of those wretched provincial planets that the earth carries away, like a scatterbrain, in its stupid revolutions, like one of those baskets of plums that children whirl around in a sling without letting a single one fall, and which, being composed of inflammable elements tormented by an igneous principle, end up brutally dissolving into a rain of aeroliths when poor passers-by least expect it. Considering its apparent diameter, we judged that it was scarcely any larger than a third-class prefecture, which the least of your civil servants would not have wanted."

---

1 Horace de Saussure (1749-1799) was a physicist and geologist who invented or improved numerous measuring devices, and was one of the first people to reach the summit of Mont Blanc.

"He would have been quite right!" replied the Manifafa. "A prefecture composed of inflammable elements tormented by an igneous principle would be no favor. The description that you have given me of these aeroliths appears, moreover, to be very instructive and very amusing, and I excuse you, because of that, for having taken this route to the center of the earth, even though, looking at the thing rationally, it was not the shortest."

"That was not the only inconvenience of our journey. We had just dropped the pneumatic sounding-line into a rather beautiful depth of atmosphere—from which it brought back, entirely to our satisfaction, a mixture of oxygen and nitrogen, formed according to the proportions that the chemists consider most suitable for everything that breathes—when we were distressed to perceive that the hull was leaking air in two places."

"And there's another, damn it, Berniquet! I've heard mention of water leaking, but I never heard of leaking air."

"There's nothing easier to understand. It means that gas was escaping in abundance through fissures in the capsule, for want of repair. As Your Majesty can imagine, we lost no time sending out caulkers, but Castor and Pollux, the protectors of mariners, permitted one lad of tender age and little experience to bring the flaming tar so close to the breach that the hydrogen suddenly caught fire, decorating the balloon superbly with a marvelous girdle, which radiated a dazzling spray, and must have given it the appearance to those below—for the sun had been hidden for a long time throughout that hemisphere—of a shining meteor. On my jester's honor, I might live through my ten thousand years, so quickly passed, and ten thousand more, but time could not efface from my memory the sentiments of admiration with which I was filled by that sight of that fiery globe . . ."

"Which burned on an equal footing with planets," Hurlubleu interrupted. "I willingly put myself in your shoes at the present moment—but not otherwise, parenthetically. Admiration presumably did not absorb you, though, to the extent that you did not pay attention to anything else?"

"We made haste to disencumber the vessel of its useless cargo, for it had no excess ballast in reserve: the steam engine first, then the Siamese cannon! Their like had never been seen for the excellence of the work and the richness of the carving. After that, a whole encyclopedia, in order of topic. I did not regret them much. After that, the entire record of laws, decrees and ordinances, with all the speeches from the two chambers. That was a terrible loss! After that, someone had the impertinence to say that it would have been better to commence with the scholars. I took the plunge along with the others, but I was so fortunately favored by my particular weight—heaven be eternally praised!—that in the course of my perpendicular flight I overtook one of those aerial barges, which was foundering. As it was made in the form of a seahorse, according to the fashion of the period, current since the famous cetacean of Monsieur Lennox,[1] I bestrode it as gently as could be in such circumstances, in such a manner that I found myself firmly saddled, with my right hand in the mane, maintaining a good seat, planted like a Saint George."[2]

"And then Berniquet, you dug your spurs in, as your position demanded, and I see you with pleasure on the road to the land of Zeretochthro-Schah, if the aggregate weight is reciprocally multiplied by the square of the velocity."

"I came down, as chance would have it, in a large rut set in the exact middle of the highway, where I was only embedded

---

1 This enigmatic reference might refer to a dimly-remembered passage in Walter Scott's *The Pirate* (1822), in which the crew of a ship named the *Lennox* encounter a stranded wale.

2 The term "un Saint-Georges" is used in French to refer to a particular position in sexual intercourse, in which the penetratee sits astride the lap of the penetrator; the phrase is probably intended to imply that Berniquet's sitting position was not quite as comfortable as he suggests.

up to the neck, because I had soon recovered my courage as I recognized, from the nature of the soil and the geological configuration of the locality, that my lucky star had set me on my feet in one of the most civilized countries on Earth."

"Setting on the feet is a hyperbatic manner of speaking, to which I will gladly subscribe if it pleases you, but I warn you that I shall have more difficulty in agreeing to the indefinite perfection of a country in which there are such large and profound ruts is the exact middle of the highway."[1]

"Oh, that was because the philosophers of that country, Divine Manifafa, had something much better to do than fill in ruts."

"What were they doing, then?"

"Cookery," Berinquet replied.

"Well," replied the Manifafa, "I can't blame them—but begin at the beginning, jester, for we just left you, to my great regret, in a situation that was scarcely convenient for exploring the terrain."

"It was, however, favorable to meditation—and, as for the terrain, I knew it thoroughly, independently of my personal experience, by virtue of what I had read in cosmographies and traveler's tales, which never lie. The isle of the Patagons,[2] so

---

1 Hyperbation is a rhetorical term referring to a deliberate inversion of meaning. The French term that I have translated here with excessive literality is *prendre pied*, to which Hurlubleu is presumably objecting because Berniquet has ended up neck-deep in the mire. The other key phrase in this passage is *juste milieu* [exact middle], which had a very specific reference in the context of French politics before and after the July Revolution of 1830, when it was proposed—and, to some extent, implemented—as a means of arbitration to balance the opposed demands of the Royalist right and Republican left, involving the calculation and subsequent steering of an exactly-balanced middle course between the two. This extends a sketchy series of analogies in which the progressive savants' steamboat journey and trip in the dirigible airship, both ending in disasters, represent the Revolutionary and Imperial phases in recent French history.

2 The reference is not to the geographical Patagonia but to a legendary island inhabited by giants. An alternative image of it is set in an archipelago

158

far as I had been able to judge by sight while plunging into that mid-Atlantic empire, forms a circle about eleven hundred and thirty leagues in diameter, which gives a circumference of three thousand five hundred and fifty leagues—or should, if Adrien Métius of Alkmaar is no fool.[1] It is the fact that it has never produced any living thing that renders it particularly appropriate to civilization."

"Which remains to be explained," cried Hurlubleu, shaking his head defiantly. "An island that produces no living things, but where there are philosophers! It's true that they crop up everywhere—according to you, though, their cuisine must be rather meager."

"The most perfect that could ever be savored at a royal table. It would only be necessary to *presuppose*, if "presuppose" were admitted to the Hurlubièrean language—which depends on the Academy—that the island of the Patagons is the center of an archipelago entirely populated by philosophers, who are methodically arranged in their islets, according to the encyclopedic system of Bacon, with such technical precision that the languages of Earth merely require labels to figure in the topography of perfectibility the *universal compendium* of human knowledge.[2] This species being very populous, because

that includes the abode of a more advanced human race, in the second part of Nicolas Restif de la Bretonne's *La Découverte australe par un homme-volant* (1781; tr. as *The Discovery of the Austral Continent by a Flying Man*), a graphic fantasy based on the ideas of the pioneering French evolutionist Benoît de Maillet (1656-1738), but the coincidence might be no more than that.

1 Adrien Métius (1571-1635) was the Dutch mathematician credited with the discovery (or rediscovery) of the constant *pi*, which expresses the relationship between the circumference of a circle and its diameter.

2 This passage links Nodier's imaginary island with Francis Bacon's *New Atlantis*, as described in the first utopia (written c1609; published posthumously in 1627) to argue flamboyantly that technological progress was the key to a better life. Bacon never finished it, any more than he finished the great encyclopedia of human knowledge that he intended to produce.

it is extremely idle, it decided one day to take advantage of the proximity of the metropolitan island, where I was presently in the situation of which you are aware, and where I beg you to permit me to remain for a little while longer . . ."

"As long as you care to, jester," said the Manifafa. "Take your time."

"It decided, as I said, to send a creative colony there, and that only required laboratories, since it knew how to produce by chemical combination all that Creation produces. It was by this means that the philosophical consistory of the Isle of the Patagons devoted itself to culinary manufacture, to satisfy the communal necessities of healthy individuals who took plea-sure in eating two meals a day, when they were able to afford them—I'm not taking about poor authors, those innocent proletarians of speech, disgraced tributaries of the press, hon-est people who scrape a living when they live at all, and who have lost their pensions through the malice or ineptitude of a chibicou; they are hardly to be seen there. But suppose, for example, that Your Highness had a sudden desire tomorrow to dine on an excellent *tête de veau en tortue*,[1] as could happen to anyone; you send your menu to the mammalogical sec-tion, which makes a calf and puts the head aside for you. The section's Architriclin—that's a highly-placed official—imme-diately sends your menu to his colleague in the ornithological section, who makes you a cock, and dispatches the comb and the kidneys to the first laboratory; the same with the crus-taceological section, which concocts superior crayfish. After

---

1 *Tête de veau en tortue* is an elaborate recipe found in the pretentious gastronomic guides popular in Nodier's day. Its basic constituents are a calf's head and rice, but it also requires numerous truffles and quenelles (meatballs), twenty prepared cockscombs and a crayfish. There is a certain irony in the fact that the Patagonian food scientists produce the cockscombs, crayfish and raw material for the quenelles artificially, while apparently taking the truffles (by far the most expensive ingredient) for granted.

that, everything proceeds as normal, and it is served hot. It's a delicious meal."

"Who are you talking to?" said the Manifafa. "All that appears perfectly in order to me, and I would take great pleasure in interrogating you on a few details, if I weren't too scrupulous to retain you in that rut any longer than is appropriate to a man of your age and quality."

"I was there for a hundred hours and I don't know how many minutes, Divine Manifafa."

"Then we have time—so amuse yourself by answering me; it will give you a rest. How is it that these philosophers, who were making so many things, had not succeeded in making the man for whom you were searching with such rare intrepidity?"

"Eh! Be assured, Lord, that they were making such men very well. A man is no more difficult to fabricate than a wild rabbit when one knows his composition. The anthropological section had no other occupation from dawn to dusk, in contrast to backward and mechanized countries where people voluntarily occupy themselves with it, in a more specialized fashion, from dusk to dawn—and it must be admitted that it has not spared its efforts, since it has made the Patagons, in the least of which there is material for the dozen drum-majors of the dozen legions of your capital, including those of the suburbs. But beyond the five natural senses, it had found itself considerably embarrassed, the ideological section never having been able to furnish the intellectual sense in good condition. The intellectual sense! Divine Manifafa, you would have reduced the ideological section to rubble, because you would not have been able to obtain enough of it therefrom to make a vaudeville—and when that is distributed in equal parts between fifty million giants, it's almost as if they had none of it at all. That's why the unhappy race of Patagons is so stupid that the nations of the world have since adopted into their speech the proverbial usage *as stupid as a Patagon*."

"Heaven help us—and the Holy Bat too!" said the Manifafa. "With what did these poor people make kings?"

"That's a great pity," Berniquet replied humbly lowering his eyes. "They made them with Patagons."

"That proves, jester, that there was no great profit in this method, since the philosophers did not preserve it for themselves."

"One is careful with kings and peoples, sire, when one calculates their living expenses! The philosophers, who had continued to reproduce in the vulgar manner, because it is slightly more amusing, remained very small—which forbade them the chance of acquiring positions of public authority in the country of the Patagons, where all such positions are determined by height, including the crown. When the king dies, the population is passed beneath a hectometer, and his successor is selected by the ruler."

"With the result that the reigning sovereign," the Manifafa put in, "has a perfect right to judge himself *the Great* and receive that title from his court without anyone having grounds for criticism—which seems quite agreeable to me. But what happened, Berniquet, if some petty Patagon peasant took it into his head to grow immeasurably all of a sudden, surpassing his legitimate prince by a cubit or two, while the latter was peacefully enthroned on the word of the ruler, geometry and the philosophers?"

"He would be recognized as the heir presumptive, lord, and proclaimed Caesar, until another came along to contest his rank. I've heard it said that this had spared them many revolutions and civil wars, and they were no worse-governed for it."

"I can easily believe that, jester. It's the most reasonable electoral system that anyone has ever invented, to my knowledge, and I'll try it out on my chibicous before long. Whatever happens, I'll be almost certain not to lose by the change.

If your report is accurate, though, there are still two things that bother me. My first concern, Berniquet, is to know what becomes of Patagon women in a country where the anthropological section takes the trouble to make the children?"

"Oh, the women are very busy, sire; they discuss, they manage, they administer, they judge, they govern, they formulate plans of campaign, statistics, laws, constitutions—and, from time to time in their spare moments, write little eclectic pamphlets: treatises on ontology, epic poems in thirty-six songs. They do a great deal of harm! But what is Your Highness's second concern, Divine Manifafa?"

"My second concern, Berniquet, is to know what you did to extricate yourself from that diabolical rut?"

"I did not spend all my time reflecting on the notions recalled confusedly from my reading. I made every effort to shout at the top of my voice, and with all the force of my lungs, that I was the sole survivor of a dozen members of the universal propaganda, who had come to pay homage to the civilization of the Isle of the Patagons. I added, with a compassion easier to imagine than to express, that I would probably be the last propagandist who tried to land in that philosophical rut, especially by the route by which I had come—unless, that is, one of my comrades had succeeded in remaining in the air longer than me, and I saw no possibility of that."

"My Grand Orator could not have put it better, dear Berniquet, even though that is his profession, for which I pay him a fat salary, and he has raised his voice several times in opposition—but to whom did you address this eloquent and naïve discourse?"

"To a handful of wretched children, twenty-five or thirty feet tall at the most, who were playing follow-my-leader and other similarly puerile games on the roadside."

"On the side of the rut, you mean. And what happened after that, jester?"

"Alas, milord, you know what happened: a legion of philosophers in fancy coats and silk stockings, with gloved hands and umbrellas under their arms,[1] came to sit down around me on folding chairs to arrange the means of getting me out of it. On the first day they were not excessively embarrassed. The judged almost unanimously that I appeared to have fallen into the rut accidentally. On the second day, they decided that it would be best to extract me by means of some machine. On the third day, they contrived a marvel . . ."

"They finally got you out!"

"No, Divine Manifafa. They appointed a commission composed of scientists highly-skilled in mechanics. I thought I was lost, that time. Holding out my shaking hands, which I had succeeded in detaching from the rut, at the level of my head—where they had made themselves very useful by chasing away the flies—I renewed my futile supplications with a great abundance of tears. The philosophers were already some distance away. What saved me was that among the numerous brats that I had the honor of mentioning a little while ago, there were two who had made a monstrous seesaw out of the mainmast of a three-decker sailing-vessel and were indulging themselves wholeheartedly in that ridiculous exercise—which is, as I had made sure to tell them, unworthy of occupying human thought.

"One of these little brutes, whom I had observed paying a stupid but nevertheless rather crafty attention to the philosophers' discussion, brought his mast closer when they had disappeared, and, having carefully established the equilibrium of the large moving part on its fulcrum, set about turning the extremity towards the place where my convulsive hands were still agitating vainly. I took hold of it mechanically, but

---

1 Louis-Philippe, who acceded to the French throne after the July Revolution, was routinely caricatured by reference to his habit of carrying an umbrella with him when he went out.

firmly, to avoid a collision between my head and the gigantic joist that would probably not have been to my advantage. At the same instant, the miserable Patagon ruffian jumped up to a considerable height to reach the other end, and pulled it towards him with all his weight, with the result that I sprang forth from the rut like a dart; by letting myself slide along the beam, of which I had not let go, I landed quite comfortably on solid ground of rocks and pebbles that would not have given way beneath an army of Patagons.

"The fortunate meeting with that instinctive expedient caused me to reflect bitterly upon the misery of those unfortunate Patagons, who were reduced by the deprivation of the intellectual sense to be stupidly confined to the exercise of their animal faculties, without any hope of becoming savants, and whom civilization—ordered and gentle, to be sure, but set up like an instrument—turned perpetually like cogwheels. That is harmful."

"I recognize your good heart there," said the Manifafa, "but that's the fault of the ideological section, which is not in the land of the Patagons for nothing, and who, if I understand you correctly, diminished the intelligent and perfectible minds of these islanders. Since their civilization is ordered and gentle, however, Berniquet, and they do not lack instinctive expedients for getting themselves—and others—out of difficulties, what more, and what better could they desire?"

"Better, I don't know; but more, progress—or, to explain myself with all the precision and eloquence required in these elevated matters, I wanted them to be making progress. Good God, what good is a nation that isn't making progress? The essential destiny of man is not to furnish with simplicity his brief career in the midst of his family, faithfully fulfilling his duties to God, the state and humankind, as those miserable driveling moralists preached in ignorant antiquity. The essential destiny of man is to make progress; and, whether he likes it or not, he *will* make progress, mark my words, or he'll explain why he isn't . . .

"These Patagon children were, however, naturally benevolent. The poor little fellows hastened to plunge me into a pool of pure water, at a rather bitter temperature, which washed away the mud of the rut and restored a little suppleness and elasticity to my painful limbs. They dried me off afterwards, in the rays of an ardent and reparative sun, while fanning my forehead with a few balsamic leaves with which they had equipped themselves for that purpose; and, without further delay, they delicately peeled the remaining detritus of their breakfast, in order to prepare me a good meal—which proved very copious, for one could easily live on a Patagon's crumbs. I had scarcely expressed my gratitude, by means of gestures of which they took little or no notice, when they returned to their seesaw, after having pointed me in the direction of the city of philosophers, where I expected to find someone with whom to talk.

"As I was on the point of arrival, I saw a vast procession emerging from the walls with great ceremony, which headed towards me. I immediately recognized the objective of that scientific excursion equipped for travel. There were planks, poles, ladders, ropes, pulleys, rails, levers, weights, counter-weights, wheels, capstans, tackle-blocks, cranes, dredgers, clamps, measuring implements, pick-axes, hooks, jacks and all the movable equipment of the Conservatory of Arts and Crafts, with the exception of a seesaw. I was very flattered by the foresight of these great men, and tried to make my sentiments manifest to them in some twenty languages—of which they appeared to have no knowledge. For my part, I understood nothing at all of theirs, which made me think with admiration that they might well have invented the universal language, or at least discovered the primitive one.

"That little difficulty, which naturally injected a certain obscurity into our conversation, prevented me from making them understand clearly how I had succeeded in getting out of the tight spot in which they had found me, but they seemed so enthusiastic to honor that difficult operation, in which I saw no great inconvenience, that I gladly abandoned the attempt to compose an autoptic description for them. I consented, therefore, to the frenetic acclamations of a great crowd of Patagons, who had lined all the streets along their route—to which welcome they deigned to respond with proudly modest benevolence, smiling graciously to the left and the right, to the extent that I came very close myself to believing in the efficacy of the help that they had been taking me. In any case, I was too well-accustomed, and had been for a long time, to the traditions and customs of academies, not to do likewise.

"I was conducted in this fashion—triumphantly, so to speak—to the palace of the Supreme Consistory, where I was deposited, like an object of curiosity put on display, on the Architrichlin's green baize: a solemnity much more flattering for its object than for one who is always sure of the approbation of a Patagon audience—for these people are essentially admiring, by virtue of their great innocence."

"The innocence of the Patagons is all very well, but I'm not without anxiety regarding the anthropological section. They must have wanted to have you stuffed."

"There was no question of that for the moment, Divine Manifafa! The Great Architrichlin made a speech tailored to the Patagon audience, whose galleries were overflowing, which did not at first enlighten me as to the difficulties of that philosophical language. I had a great deal of difficulty distinguishing between the apheresis, the dieresis and the synthesis, getting past the apocope and the syncope, struggling with the contraction, making sense of the syllables and the euphony, invoking the conciliatory paragogy in which to take refuge from the tenebrous anagogy, and I could not, no matter how hard I tried, catch up with my radicals. Wise and savant Edwards,[1] if only you had been there!

"Eventually, the frequent repetition of a locution in which I had captured in passing the mystical metathesis suddenly revealed to me that this beautiful and erudite idiom was quite simply the native patois of Villeneuve-le-Guyard, where I was born, but elegantly inverted in the order of the disposition of the letters, in the manner of a boustrophedon,[2] to which I had had the good fortune to have initiated myself in my early youth, by reading signs backwards—which meant that, within a moment, I had as much mastery as the most experienced linguist of all the delicacies of the hieratic language in use in the isle of the Patagons. I therefore began speaking after the Architrichin, with an easy confidence that astonished everyone—and the due reserve that modesty imposes upon historians who are speaking about themselves cannot make me keep my mouth shut regarding the prodigious effect of my speech, since the results of that inaugural session still made themselves felt after ten thousand years of my short life.

"The thunderous applause that followed my harangue disconcerted me to such a degree that I remained as if enraptured between the four candles on the demonstration table—to the extent that that an idiotic savant, who was fulfilling the functions of a majordomo, was dispatched to the chemistry section to fetch a soothing spirituous beverage, of which they make use themselves on similar occasions instead of sugared water, to calm the senses of an orator during the heat of enthusiasm and the hullabaloo of applause.

---

1 Possibly the American theologian Jonathan Edwards (1703-1758), who commented in learned fashion on the rhetorical style of religious revivalism.

2 A boustrophedon is a document in which alternate lines are written in opposite directions, those reading from right to left being constructed in mirror-writing, but Nodier appears to be using the term here simply to refer to inverted speech.

"I only took a drop of it, but I had scarcely finished downing the potion when, instead of impressing on my physiognomy the tonic and hilarifying influence of a salutary liquor, I was seized by a frightful spasmodic yawning, which immediately caused all the spectators to judge—as was only too true—that I had just fallen victim to a philosopher's mistake. It is necessary to tell you, moreover, that philosophers' mistakes are even more dangerous than an apothecary's mistake. The Architrichlin made haste to check the suspect phial, and he had no need to go any further than the label to say, expansively: 'A fatal and irreparable mistake has been made. It isn't the water of health and rejoicing that has just been administered to our beloved colleague—it's the water of eternal sleep!'

"'Eternal sleep!' I cried—to the extent that one can cry out when one is yawning, while the hiatus assiduously punctuates one's every word! 'Eternal sleep, accursed Arichtrichlin! May the lightning strike you down, along with the entire Isle of the Patagons!'

"'Eternal isn't strictly accurate,' the Architrichlin put in, benignly. 'The dose wasn't strong enough for that. You haven't had enough for more than ten thousand years, according to the prescription, which is calculated to perfection, and you'll obtain a great advantage from this slight interruption to your academic work, since you've dedicated your life to the search for the perfect man. Who knows? Perhaps you'll find him when you wake up.'

"Meanwhile, I yawned with all my strength. 'A slight interruption!' I replied, in the most violent fit of temper that can grip a man who is falling asleep. 'Ten thousand years, a slight interruption! You don't imagine, then, pitiless Architrichlin, that I have business to take care of at home! My civil list pension is in jeopardy, for want of a certificate of life, and I was in a position to formulate a nice establishment with a rich and pretty young woman who will probably not wait for me!'

"'I dare not make you any promises with regard to her,' the Architrichlin replied. 'If she were here, and if she agreed to it, I could offer to put her to sleep with you; it wouldn't cost me anything more—but that's the only condition in which young women can await a future that has ten thousand years to sleep. It's a petty inconvenience anyway. Good-looking as you are, you'll easily find other mistresses, and ten thousand years pass so quickly when one's asleep!'"

"They aren't squeamish," said the Manifafa.

"And having said that, the gentleman bore me away, without my being able to put up much resistance, in view of the soporific state into which their infernal specific had put me. By one corridor after another, I arrived, still yawning, in the Hall of the Oneirobes.[1] They are local sect of sages who spend almost all their lives asleep.

"I perceived in the blink of an eye, beneath glass bell-jars numbered in indelible ink, a number of worthy individuals who had spontaneously embraced that vocation of centuries-long sleep, whether out of disgust for the world in which they lived, or by virtue of a quite natural impatience to see another. It was, I swear to you, a perfectly select society. There were some there who were stirring already, so near were they to resuscitation. As I no longer had any need but sleep . . ."

"Me neither," said the Manifafa.

"As I was half asleep . . ." Berinquet continued.

"Me too," said the Manifafa.

"I wished them much pleasure, internally," the jester went on. "I went unceremoniously into my bell jar—which covered a bed that was very comfortable, at least for a man who is asleep—and I went to sleep in a flash."

"Good night, Berniquet," said the Manifafa, letting his pipe fall. "Sleep well and don't have bad dreams."

---

1 I have transcribed this improvised term directly; oneiro- is a Greek preface signifying "dream".

"The first thing I did, when I woke up, was to look at my watch; it had stopped. When I was woken up . . ."

"What? Damn it!" the Manifafa put in, arranging himself on his divan. "When you woke up, I was probably asleep! At least, if the Devil doesn't take a hand, I can surely sleep for an hour or two during the ten thousand years that I've had the pleasure of granting you between the beginning and end of your long story. Not that I didn't take a certain pleasure in it, Berniquet—I was particularly amused by the naval combat between the seahorses and the genteel saraband of the four little blue guenons. It's really very amusing."

Berniquet, who had an extremely penetrating mind—as was noticeable at various points in his narration—saw clearly that the Manifafa had not been listening thus far without taking the time to have an occasional nap. "It is necessary that kings be very stupid," he murmured, in a very low voice, "else they are very ill-intentioned. Here's one with whom I've been discussing the most transcendent and abstruse questions of morality, philosophy and politics for an hour, and who takes advantage of such precious moments to dream about seahorses and sarabands of little monkeys!"

"What are you muttering between your teeth, Berniquet?" cried the Manifafa. "You look as if you're making faces at me!"

"I thought, Divine Hurlubleu, that my expedition was worth the trouble of being recounted to its conclusion—and I intend, moreover, to make it an element of a trilogy whose title will be of some consequence to my editor. That's what will make it a success."

"How scrupulous can the soul of a jester be, Berniquet? The people for whom you write are so well-accustomed to three-letter monograms that you'll risk nothing, on my word as a Manifafa, by throwing them a four-part trilogy. They'll see many others! For God's sake though, Berniquet, go to sleep and let me sleep!"

"A trilogy in four parts for a time that goes quickly! Why not?" said Berniquet, in an aside. While he reflected, biting his fists, on this new mode of composition, the sublime sovereign of Hurlubière had already snored three times. He was asleep.

The jester lay down at full length beneath his master's feet, to meditate more at his ease on the dignity of the species and its progressive improvement. He went to sleep.

I, who am transcribing this with difficulty from Berniquet's manuscripts, as three o'clock in the morning chimes on one clock after another, by the dying light of an oil-lamp whose price my grocer is clawing back with dishonest lawsuits, feel the quill slipping from my fingers. I'm going to sleep too.

What about you, Madame?


**Part Two**


*Leviathan the Long,*
*Archikan of the Patagons of the Savant Isle*


At six forty-five in the morning, Hurlubleu sneezed three times in succession. It was the signal in response to which his attentive eunuchs were accustomed to bring him his chocolate.

Berniquet, who was lying on his back, as is usual when one is asleep—at least when one is not lying on one's right side, or even the left—perceived that the Manifafa was no longer deigning to sleep, so he turned over on to his belly. That done, he sprang abruptly into a sitting position and resumed speaking thus: "When I woke up, Divine Manifafa—and I admit that I had a bit of a headache . . ."

"Is that you, jester? Ten thousand years have gone by since you were last seen! Finish, then, if you must. Tell me the rest of your adventures in detail; perhaps they'll send me back to sleep."

"At first, I was as red-faced as a bell-founder to find myself alone under my bell-jar. All the other Oneirobes had departed without the accompaniment of drums and trumpets—which was a matter of indifference to me because, sleeping as I was sleeping, I wouldn't have been able to hear them. It occurred to me that I might have been forgotten during my siesta, and I hurled myself so impatiently against the walls of my transparent prison that we both rolled along the floor. It was as well for me that it was made of a malleable, elastic and unbreakable glass invented by the Patagons, since I did myself no more harm than a man who falls out of bed wearing an excellent padded dressing-gown.

"The savant on duty came running in response to the noise, followed by his assistants, and—after having observed from my notes that I had conscientiously completed my ten thousand years, with a small surplus—he obligingly provided me with a passport to go wherever I wished. He didn't even demand the requisite declaration of witnesses to my identity, which I would have had difficulty procuring. In exchange, to keep his accounts in order, I gave him a proper receipt for my person, establishing that he had delivered me to myself duly and integrally, *in ossibus et cute*,[1] at the expiry of an interval fixed in advance at ten thousand years, healthy, safe and well-conserved—which is to say, without any apparent breakage, damage or wastage—and in working order, thanks to the expertise of the authorized conveyors, all to the general satisfaction and my own. Then I got ready to leave.

"'Wait a minute, my good man,' he said, grabbing me by the sleeve. 'You European doctors must know almost every-thing, or not far short of it.'

"'I know more than everything,' I told him, 'since I'm a delegate of the intellectual propaganda of perfectibility.'

---

1 "Skin and bones."

"'That's good,' he continued. 'We won't ask you for that much—just whether you know medicine. It's not a matter of drinking the sea.'

"'As much as is necessary,' I replied, 'to cure completely a man who is not sufficiently churlish to insist on dying. I swear to you that the physicians of my time knew no more than that.'

"'Then you're my man. Can you imagine that Leviathan the Long, who is a very imposing prince—he's more than forty cubits tall—has promised *in petto* to have us all quartered before sunset if we haven't brought him a physician capable of curing him? Of what, I can't tell you: of some trifle, the tedium of some ostentatious speech, the resentment of some ill-received ordinance, a malady of the court—but we take such things very much to heart, for kings are capable of anything.'"

"Take care, Berniquet. There were no physicians in that Academy of philosophers! What the Devil were they playing at that day?"

"Perhaps they were distributing Saint Michael ribbons, Divine Manifafa. I have had the honor of informing you, if I am not mistaken, that the Isle of the Patagons was extremely civilized."

"That's true, damn it, but I don't think so any longer. Unfortunate Leviathan the Long: a king of forty cubits, and not a single petty physician comes to soothe the anguish of his death, to administer the last rites!"

"I had no sooner examined the colossal Archikan of the Patagons than it appeared to me, pending a better opinion, that he had suffered a cut on the index-finger of his right hand."

"Don't deceive yourself, Berniquet—a cut on the index-finger of the right hand causes a sharp pain that would damn a buffoon. I was often subject to them in my childhood; that's what prevented me from learning to write."

"The diagnosis being sufficiently confirmed, in my opinion, by a strict autopsy . . ."

"Curses!" cried Hurlubleu. "Did you really have the ferocious courage to eviscerate this Leviathan for the sake of a cut?"

"Oh, no milord, I'm only taking about the kind of clinical autopsy carried out on living invalids, whose investigations stop at the epidermis, while awaiting something better. I hastened, therefore, to order eighty thousand hungry leeches from the helminthological section, and applied them to my patient."

"To your patient—I like that. He was neither more nor less than the Archikan of the Patagons—but I'll wager that you'd forgotten one thing."

"I say nothing to the contrary. One often forgets something in practical medicine. But what, Divine Manifafa?"

"A mere bagatelle—to give notice to the hereditary prince to hold himself in readiness for his enthronement. Two thousand leeches a cubit! My God, what a bleeding! I shall be quite astonished, jester, if the Archikan of the Patagons lasted much longer."

"Bah! An Archikan is as strong as a buffalo. I assure you that his cut felt better after six months. He wasn't able to move a hand or a foot."

"There's an invalid who must have owed you a great deal, Berniquet. I like to think that he died cured."

"You have arrived, Divine Hurlubleu, at the most extraordinary part of my story. My invalid did not die at all. After a further eighteen months of convalescence, and as many tons of analeptics, the least of which exceeded in capacity the giant cask of Heidelberg, I had the satisfaction of rendering him hale and hearty, save for a sort of hemiplegia, which badly inhibited the movements of half his body, and a rather disagreeable species of claudication, which completely prevented him from walking."[1]

"Which is to say that you had extracted him from the predicament in good order to the tune of seventy-five per cent. Poor Archikan!"

"The most honest man in the world. He sent for me in order to give me his thanks in person."

"Had he lost his mind, then, this Archikan of the Patagons?"

"Impossible, milord. No Archikan of the Patagons has ever lost his mind, or anything resembling it. 'European doctor,' he said to me, 'it's a pleasure to see you with the one eye of which we can still make use. With the intention in mind of awarding you a recompense proportional to your services, and having taken advice, we have resolved in our wisdom, and for your own good, to put you discreetly back to sleep. What do you think, amiable and savant foreigner?'

"At these formidable words, I shivered from top to toe, and my hair stood on end in terror."

"I imagine, Berniquet," observed the Manifafa, "that you prostrated yourself before him and embraced his knees."

"I would have liked to, but there was no way to do it. I simply embraced his ankles. 'Bright light of the world,' I cried, 'my emotion tells you how sensible I am of the gratitude that it pleases you to heap upon the least of your slaves, but that would not be in accord with the duties of my mission, which have been languishing far too long, and injurious to the propagation of a multitude of discoveries that ought to be turned to the glory and the profit of the human race. It is indispensable that I wake up from time to time to correct my proofs.'

"'That is a laudable and worthy occupation, to which I have an infinite inclination myself,' replied Leviathan the

---

1 An analeptic is a tonic; a hemiplegia is a partial paralysis (nowadays attributed to a haemorrhage in one hemisphere of the brain); a claudication is a limp.

Long, 'but what can I do for you, then, and by what benefits can I display my gratitude and your merits. Speak! Would you like to be Quasikan?'

"'The title of that office is beautiful,' I replied, 'but I do not know what it entails.'

"'It is almost self-explanatory,' he continued. 'The Quasikan is the second person in my empire, and in that capacity he has the right to adore me perpetually, to amuse me when I am bored, and to do everything I wish.'

"'I understand perfectly, light of the world—in return for which he is lodged, fed and clothed . . .'

"'Shaved, sheared and buried—with all the benefits of life, of course—and enjoying in addition the disposition of all my treasures.'

"I bit my tongue just in time. 'What astonishes me,' I said, cleverly, 'is that such a beautiful situation is vacant.'

"'By accident,' he said, shrugging a shoulder—I would have challenged him to budge the other. 'Can you imagine that that there have been fourteen on the trot that I have had impaled, in vain, to correct their distractions? Not one of them was able to remember that my left slipper must be presented to me in the right hand, and my right slipper in the left hand. It's the most express condition of the ceremony, and it is recorded as such in the fundamental laws of the Savant Isle. I too am rather distracted, and I admit that the fundamental law scares me.'

"'Mighty sun of the Patagons,' I murmured, in a tremulous voice, 'the sublime rank of Quasikan is far above my unworthiness. You would reward my feeble offices too nobly by sending me home as soon as possible, by the shortest route, provided that it is not in a boat with a triple compressor, nor a balloon armed for war, because I hold those two vehicles in execration, for reasons that are particularly personal.'

"'What!' retorted the Archikan. 'I gladly give you permission to return there on foot, if you know the secret. It's a means that my islanders have very rarely used, so far as I know, for transporting themselves to the continents. Since you are proposing to return whence you came, though, do me the favor of letting me know where that is. You will find that I have an astounding erudition in that regard. After hunting and heraldry, the subject in which we Patagon kings are especially well-informed is geography, because it opens the minds of young people wonderfully, and stimulates the appetites of sovereigns for conquest. It is no less necessary for government, at least as we govern.'

"'My intention,' I replied, 'is to go to that capital of science, that metropolis of art, that headquarters of civilization, that inexhaustible arsenal of perfectibility, Paris. It's near Villeneuve-la-Guyard, only half a day away by diligence.'

"'To Paris!' he cried, with a deafening laugh. 'It's ten thousand years and more since Paris was destroyed by a rain of aeroliths.'

"'I always suspected as much,' I riposted, striking my forehead with my hand. 'I was there.'

"'That astonishes me greatly, doctor. If you had been in Paris on that day, you would not have been sleeping for ten thousand years on the Isle of the Patagons.'

"'What! Sire, I was not in Paris; I was in the rain of aeroliths, which I did not deem it appropriate to follow as far as the ground.'

"'That was wise on your part, for at the contingent point, I would not have given straw for the difference. You should know, then, that the place where Paris was is occupied today by the superb city of Hurlu, which was founded by Hurluberlu, and which has the inestimable good fortune of now living under the most gracious, the wittiest and the most illustrious of all his descendants, the magnanimous Hurlubleu, grand

Manifafa of Hurlubière. You can verify that immediately in the *Royal Almanack.*'"

"Stop there, Berniquet," the Manifafa interrupted. "Is it really true that Leviathan made that speech?"

"May I never go back to the land of the Patagons," replied Berniquet, "if I have altered a single word of it."

"I have difficulty understanding, then, why you give so little credit to the mind of the Archikan, for those phrases seem to me to be exceptionally well-turned."

"Everything is relative, divine Manifafa; a fool may utter such phrases as would do honor to a man of genius, and the expression of so natural and so facile a sentiment is only feeble and vulgar in proportion to an eloquence and style of forty cubits."

"That's fair, jester; I'm not unduly flattered to be placed at that height in the estimation of that great personable. Continue."

"Leviathan continued speaking: 'I cannot see the slightest inconvenience,' he said, 'in sending you back to Hurlu, but I'm afraid that you'll find it a long journey if you obstinately refuse to use speedy means. It's a terrible problem to untangle.'

"'It seems to me,' I replied, 'that on a globe whose circumference is calculated at nine thousand leagues, it requires scarcely three thousand leagues by the axis and four thousand five hundred leagues by the semicircle to reach the antipodes. Now, we both understand by antipodes the two opposite points of the sphere through which the greatest possible perpendicular could be passed.'

"'I could not prove the contrary in a quarter of an hour,' the Archikan replied, 'but I have a suspicion that you are mistaken regarding the actual dimensions of the Earth—and that would be an entirely understandable illusion after ten thousand years of sleep. Observe first, savant, that you are not taking account of the gradual increase of the geological and mineral world by juxtaposition. A tree elevates a bird's nest imperceptibly while it sleeps momentarily, with its head hidden beneath its wing, but you're supposing, doctor, that you have spent ten thousand years under your bell-jar without changing your relative position in space!'

"'No, truly,' I replied to the Archikan. 'There must be something in it, or I don't understand anything.'

"'Reflect a little further,' Leviathan the Long went on. 'You have seen satellites dissolve and rain aeroliths upon the Earth. You have seen them bury cities and cover vast regions without anything of indestructible matter being destroyed but a transient form. What do you say about the geoliths that volcanoes vomit forth as they deepen their craters, a common phenomenon that will perhaps be repeated until the empty globe is reduced to an immense shell, which must necessarily gain in surface what it loses in solidity?'

"I thought privately that this accident would be very favorable to the exhumation of Zeretocthro-Shah and his man, and that it would be rather prudent to postpone to that epoch the definitive advent of perfectibility.

"'What do you say about all the organic creatures, living and sensitive, which accumulate in humus, which stand out from cliffs, which lie in ossuaries? About mountains that collapse, and which, in flattening out their abnormal unevenness, increasingly raise up the soil that serves as their base. What do you say?'"

"What do you say, Berniquet?" cried the Manifafa. "I don't understand the Patagon any better than the propagandist, or the propagandist than the Patagon, but it seems to me that there can't be much in it. When you put your story into print, don't make this huge Leviathan so stupid; he talks at least as well as the books of buffoons."

"Instinctively, milord; there is nothing as crushing as the simple reasoning of an ignoramus, but Your Majesty probably no longer remembers that these poor people have no intellectual sense?"

"I remember quite clearly, jester, that the ideological section appeared not to have found it—but if it ever does find it, against all expectations, and you still have credit in those lands, I suggest that you ask them to keep it to themselves. That can't do the ideological section any harm, and I think it would be as well for them if our Patagons did without it."

"'Finally,' said the Archikan, still talking, 'you are not taking into account certain fortuitous aggregations like the one that resulted from the fall of the moon while you were sleeping so soundly. There's a protuberance that extends your diameter a little!'

"'What!' I riposted immediately. 'The moon, gone astray by virtue of one of those perturbations to which it was so liable, has become united with its metropolis? That meeting must, indeed, have produced a rather remarkable bulge on the sphere.'

"'Don't speak any longer of a sphere, my dear doctor; the world that your century labeled thus now resembles one of those spinning-tops with irregular and unequal rhombs, which children cause to leap about on rope—or, if you prefer, it is exactly the same shape as one of those pumpkins from which pilgrims fashion gourds. The most unfortunate thing about that collision was that it struck in a horrible fashion that beautiful kingdom of diamonds in which the Regent would only have passed for a miserable paring, because they had succeeded in fabricating the richest of nature's works in enormous dimensions. We have carefully retained the recipe for them, but we have searched in vain ever since for the proportions and the procedure.'

"'That's what we lack too,' I told Leviathan the Long, 'but I ought to add that we don't have the recipe.'

"'It comes down,' he said, 'to two rather common principles: charcoal dust passed through a sieve, which can be extracted from bladder-nut trees, and a vegetable element called *fagotine*, which the botanical physiology section has discovered in bundles of firewood.'"

At this point the impatient Manifafa once again abruptly broke into the jester's interesting narrative. "I'd like to know, Berniquet, why the botanical physiology section got mixed up in it. Diamonds are losing all their value."

"Right, milord! The street urchins no longer want them for playing marbles—but bundles of firewood are priceless."

"I can't see, then," he continued, joining his hands together piteously, "what advantage one can derive, in terms of political economy, by debasing a stupid jewel whose rarity alone made all utility unnecessary, and making it impossible for good folk to acquire the joyful firewood that adds charm to winter evenings?"

"It's necessary to make a distinction, Divine Manifafa; I didn't say that it was advantageous, merely that it was progress."

"My word, you're right, Berniquet. That distinction had escaped me. Resume your story immediately, jester, for I'm finding it very instructive."

"The Archikan continued the discourse from the point at which we left him in this manner: 'You see, doctor,' he said, 'that, the world has grown unexpectedly in your absence. It will be difficult to reach the fine city of Hurlu, by the most direct route, in less than ten years, to which you must add ten years more that you will inevitably spend at custom-barriers, hospitals and police stations, and another ten years spent in waiting for passports and visas. Factor in fatigue, accidents and, most of all, the infirmities that increase every day at your age, and you'll be doing well if you only have to give yourself another thirty years. With the virile maturity that you display, strong resolution, an intrepidity proof against anything, good feet, a good eye and a little luck, you might well make your entrance into the splendid capital of Hurlubière in sixty years or thereabouts, save for submitting to preliminary inspection of the gendarmerie, the *sergents de ville* and the officials at the toll-booth.'

"'You don't say,' I replied to Leviathan the Long, in a humorous tone. 'That will make at least a century since my emergence from the baptismal font.'

"'You'll be all the more respectable. On the other hand, if you decided to take the indirect route—which is infinitely more comfortable—we would be able to offer you, in truth, suspension bridges ending in eight hundred planets.'

"'Great God—eight hundred planets! And planets with suspension-bridges! All those ruined entrepreneurs!'

"'That's where you're mistaken. All the men who grow bored on one planet spend their poor lives going in search of another. It's a perpetual shuttle; but that mode of traveling presents quite a few inconveniences, according to the celestial mechanics section. The first, savant friend, is spending your valuable spare time in journeys that are instructive but fruitless, for two or three hundred thousand solar cycles—I'm giving you approximate figures, because I don't remember them.'

"'Oh, milord,' I cried, lamentably, 'I gladly give you dispensation for the approximate figures and the other inconveniences. After a figure and an inconvenience like that, I'm quite certain of never seeing Hurlu again.'

"'You'll be there in ten minutes, if that's agreeable to you,' the Archikan replied, laughing.

"'Two or three thousand solar cycles, and the space that their revolutions embrace, in ten minutes! I must be dreaming.'

"'That wouldn't make things worse,' he went on. 'All the time one isn't dreaming is time lost.'

"'I can't deny,' I ruminated, understandably, 'that fulminating gold promised to make a very pretty projective in my youth, but these thousands of solar cycles reduced to minutes must surpass the range of the propaganda."

"'Gold! Truly a beautiful poverty. Get it into your head that we have discovered ten metals superior to gold on one planet alone, and ten thousand projectives for fulminating gold. The common people don't make matches from it.'

"'That's strange!' I replied. 'Gold was quite valuable in my time, if one can judge by hearsay.'

"'With rhinoceros-loads, hippopotamus-loads and camel-loads, dear doctor—so many years have you slept—with mammoth-loads, you would not be rich enough to buy a handful of rice, barley or sesame.'"

"Oh, how I would like," said the Manifafa, "to see that double-dyed fool Croesus resuscitated in the midst of his treasures in the Isle of the Patagons, to laugh at his idiocy! That bewilderment would do great honor to the gaiety of Providence."

"'Come on,' Leviathan continued, in an imperious voice, 'decorate this famous doctor with a ceremonial gown that will not be useless to him in the cold regions through which he will pass, and send a forced projection to Hurlu, even if it bursts the mortars. You'll answer to me with your head!' As I was carried away, he added: 'By the way, European philosopher, don't forget to present assurances of my esteem and fraternal amity to your master.'"

"I kiss his hands," said the Manifafa, "and I approve of the way he treated you, because it was quite gallant. There you are in a carriage, then."

"It was a comfortable chair, elegant, light and well suspended, but devoid of wheels or shafts—those vulgar means of vehiculation being quite useless to it. It was simply fixed in front of a horizontal metal bar—have the generosity to imagine it, for I did not have time on the way to make a drawing—the extremities of which ended in two large-caliber cannonballs at the orifices of two artillery pieces, which were placed at exactly equal distances, similar to my tilbury, with the result that I was enclosed in a sort of iron horse."

"That's rather ingenious," Hurlubleu interrupted. "I'm waiting for you at the projective."

"Behind me the openings of the two cannons were furnished with two convergent conductors, which inevitable slanted towards a common summit, geometry not having changed between here and that disposition. I was not made to wait. Scarcely was I arranged on my cushions to sleep when a lanky postillion arrived . . ."

"Match alight!"

"No, Divine Manifafa, Leyden jar in hand. The electric spark was preferable because of its synchronicity. He presented the switch to the conductors' point of contact, and I departed with a rapidity that is difficult to imagine, especially if one has only ever come from Villeneuve-la-Guyard by way of a mail-coach."

"Did the mortars explode?"

"I have never been able to find out, milord. Sound travels at little more than two hundred fathoms a minute; I would have been hard pressed to catch it."

"This means of travel, Berniquet, must be rather inconvenient for people who are short of breath."

"Not as much as you might think, Divine Highness, because the rarefaction of the air, which is incalculable at those heights, makes more than adequate compensation, and because the rapidity of the flight almost makes up for the lack of atmospheric density. The greatest danger that a traveler might run is that of encountering a body more solid than the medium he is penetrating."

"An aerolith, for example, worthy jester—that would be a dire occurrence."

"Very dire, Divine Manifafa. I almost cracked my skull on a thin grey mist of flax which was no larger than a fist, and which arrived, bobbing around insouciantly, exactly in the middle of my two cannonballs. God, what a crash!"

"You blew it away."

"I couldn't—but it was obliging enough to take its right of way, like a taxi-cab."

"What I find most irritating about this method, jester, is the monotony of the eye-blink, for nothing can be as disagreeably uniform as a route where little grey mists of flax count as events, when one is accustomed to observing as one travels, ending up reading the signs."

"The monotony! Don't believe it, milord. I took an inexpressible pleasure in contemplating the eight hundred planet-to-planet suspension-bridges that were hurtling from horizon to horizon in marvelous arcs, all charged with trophies, obelisks and statues in rather good taste, and exactly the right proportions, at least by comparison with those on the Pont de la Concorde. I can't describe it."

"No one else would be able to describe it any better than you, Berniquet. You're talking about an admirable view."

"I was enjoying it with all my heart when the shaft of my cannonballs, probably overheated by friction, and heat-sensitive by nature, suddenly dilated with a screech—and broke into two exactly equal parts, because of the homogeneity of the material and the perfect equipollence of the two projective impulses."

"By virtue of the homogeneity and the equipollence," said the Manifafa, yawning and climbing his jaw, "it could not have happened otherwise. You're now well on track to describe the world upside-down again, for I can't believe that you're the kind of man to give up the habit of falling head-first, as the variety of your tale would require."

"I beg Your Majesty to recall," Berniquet riposted, "that I fell feet first into the rut."

"My word, that's true, jester," Hurlubleu replied, "and I've sometimes regretted it slightly, for if you had struck the bedrock with your head, I fancy that the story of your travels would already be over and done with."

"It's only a matter of patience, Divine Manifafa, and we're nearing the end, if you wouldn't prefer that I start again. As I was leaning on the bar at the instant when it shattered, which is an entirely natural posture when one goes out to see the world, I had the good fortune to retain the side I was holding and to follow my flying cannonball, while Leviathan's royal chair went to the Devil. Your Sublime Highness already knows the rest. I passed over the high wall of the palace and the tenfold circle of your guards, in which I made a nasty hole, as far as the small apartments, where I was carried quite naturally to your sacred knees—which seemed to cause you some slight surprise, in view of the rarity of the event."

The Manifafa was snoring like an organ. Berniquet concluded, logically, that he had gone to sleep.

It is at this point that the jester's adventures appear to come to a stop, but it was not the end of his troubles. This great man remained human, by virtue of a few weaknessness of organization for which no one had found the remedy in his time. Several times, while he was telling his tale, he had noticed a certain trembling of the silk screens whose light hangings closed the communicating door between the harem and the bedroom, and he had rightly attributed this to a moving body more intelligent than the external air, for it surely must have heard him talking. Astonished by the unaccustomed absence of their royal spouse, and perhaps also curious to make a more leisurely examination of the unknown philosopher who had passed so suddenly through their midst in the wake of the shafted cannonball, without having time to let them see him, the Manifafa's wives had slipped furtively, one by one, to all the exits—and Berinquet even thought he had caught two or three glimpses of the crafty brown face of an odalisque, so barely mature that it impressed a singular preoccupation on his mind. That was the fortunate male's favorite sultana.

The hands of the clock had not marked out an entire quarter-hour when the Manifafa awoke with a start from some preposterous dream or other. One might perhaps have guessed that he did not find the jester nearby; on the other hand, he had scarcely passed the nearest screen when he found him extremely close to the favorite sultana, where the savant chief buffoon, surprised by a gentle and deceptive drowsiness, had yielded to the charms of a sleep similar to that of innocence.

The unfortunate Berniquet reopened his eyes to the gleam of the yataghan.

"Do you recognize the master of your body and your soul, detestable hypocrite?" cried Hurlubleu.

"Mercy, have mercy on the body of your humble and devoted jester!" sobbed Berniquet, in a stifled voice. As for his soul, the philosopher had arranged that it would require no more preparation than the fleshy, sweet and edible tap-root of *Brassica napus*, which is the third variety of the Linnaean *Asperifolia*.[1]

"This is a fine way for a spineless wretch to carry on, on the pretext of being a savant," the Manifafa said. Sheathing his blade again, he continued: "That's all right. Never let it be said that I deprived perfectibility of such a great hope merely to satisfy the vengeance of my mad jealousy. I can exploit you in a fashion more advantageous to my glory. I would gladly send you on a shafted cannonball, on my behalf, to visit that honest Leviathan who said so many nice things about me, if I had the means—but you will give me great pleasure by returning, as soon as possible, to the quest for Zeretochthro-Schah by

---

1 *Brassica napus* is rape, which does not have an edible root, although its seeds are a rich source of oil; the use of botanical analogies in the euphemistic representation of human genitalia and sexual activity was, however, commonplace in the 18th century—a circumstance not unconnected to Linnaeus' decision to classify plants according to their sexual organs—so Nodier's reference to rape's "tap-root" is presumably not intended literally. *Asperifolia* means "plants with rough leaves"—another reference that is presumably metaphorical.

way of the bottomless well that has been newly opened up in the middle of Hurlu's main square. I often thought about it during your story, and I am happy and proud to be able to offer you, within my own State, a favorable means of accomplishing your great destiny. Make an amicable will, therefore, in which you will take care to give me all that you possess, as our mutual friendship requires, and make ready, seductive jester, to depart for Bactria this evening. I am curious to know whether you will come back as easily from the nucleus of the Earth as from the most eccentric points of its rotation."

Berniquet, who was discreet, respectful and courteous, had not uttered a single word in reply to this paternal allocution. He was interred that evening.

The jester of the buffoons was as fundamentally wise as one can be when one is a philosopher, and as good-natured as one can be when one is a philanthropist. Although he was quite obstinate in his systematic whims, his adventurous voyages and his negative longevity had disillusioned him somewhat with regard to indefinite improvement, and it was noticeable that he had often spoken of it lately with a muffled laugh. It is probable that he did not arrive at the great *vade in pace* of Hurlu's main square without inwardly desiring that he had never got involved with propaganda, Zeretochthro-Shah, Hurlubleu and the favorite sultana, but he put on a brave face—and the sensitive populace, who sometimes take account of powerful people who have come to harm when none has been done to them, accompanied him with the most energetic evidence of sympathy and regret of which common people are capable in cases of noble distress; they said nothing at all.

The ceremony was pompous and magnificent. All the Hurlubierians were there—ten million individuals, not counting the women and little children. The jester, with a lantern attached to his doublet, a basket of provisions in his hand and a voluminous album under his arm—for his notes and drawings—took his place in the miner's basket with all the dignity of an ambassador thoroughly convinced of the importance of his mission.

"Irreparable man," said the chibicou who was accompanying him at the moment of his leave-taking, "if our prayers for your return go unanswered for a long time, as seems only too likely, what information will you deign to leave us, in your infinite prudence, as to what we ought to think of the utility of science and the goal of wisdom?"

"I should like to communicate to you all that I have learned in more than ten thousand years of existence," replied the Curtius of Perfectibility,[1] "saving the rectification of my judgment by new discoveries. Science consists of forgetting what one thinks one knows, and wisdom is not worrying about it."

On that sentence, in which all human philosophy is summarized—and which is sufficient for me to conclude, insouciantly, my laborious pilgrimage through this vale of tears, the inexplicable Jehosaphat[2] of the living—the activation of the cables sent Berniquet speeding into the bowels of the Earth.

A week later, the watch-officer's rope brought back a nice packet of geological rarities, the most curious of which was a fossil cockchafer which had eight legs and an inverted prothorax. The former jester informed his colleagues, by means of a missive attached to this subterranean gift, that the shaft widened out into an immense cone as it approached its utmost depths, which considerably increased the difficulties of a return journey, at least by means of ordinary ambulation,

---

1 Curtius was a legendary hero of ancient Rome; when an earthquake opened a deep fissure in the Forum he declared that the strength of Rome was embodied in the arms and courage of its citizens, and leapt into the gulf on horseback. The fissure then closed up again, as if to signify the Earth's agreement.

2 The Valley of Jehosaphat extends between Jerusalem and the Mount of Olives. In apocalyptic mythology it is where the dead will assemble for the Final Judgment.

but that he was happy to write them a polite note informing them of his determination to proceed to the central point of his excursion.

After that, all the cables were withdrawn, and the philosophical shaft was covered over by an enormous monolith in the form of a millstone, in the style of those fabricated at Ferté-sous-Jouarre, between Meaux and Château-Thierry. A regiment of Patagons could not have lifted it.

I regret now not having the pen of Tacitus—or a better one if you can imagine that—to describe the terrible events that followed Berniquet's departure. His partisans, who naturally saw his unexpected and sudden message as a sort of covert exile, gradually roused the cruel civil emotions that subsequently gave way to the bloody war of the buffoons: THE WAR OF THE BUFFOONS, which, you will remember as vividly as I do, furnished history with such beautiful pages, and over which the tragic muse has shed so many tears!

The advantage lay at first with the august dynasty of Hurluberlu, but it soon turned in a calamitous fashion; that was the effect of a particularity too memorable for me to pass over it here in silence, although the solemn dotard Attus Navius has not said a word about it in his chronicles. It appears that, as the etymology—which is the true luminary of facts—suggests,[1] official congratulations in the court of Hurlubière really did consist of tickling carried to the extreme of reducing the conqueror to helpless spasms; it is generally believed that the magnanimous Hurlubleu quit this life during one of these glorious epilepsies. It must at least be admitted that critics will be hard pressed to prove the contrary, and I am all the more enthusiastic to accept this lesson because it furnishes me

---

1 The etymology of the terms Hurlubleu and Hurlubière relate them to the verb *hurler*, to howl. The former suggests a condition akin to that expressed by the English phrase "howl [with laughter] until [one is] blue in the face". Bière has two meanings, equivalent to the English "beer" and "bier", the latter presumably being the intended one.

with a precious example of a king who dies laughing—which
has probably never happened before, and will certainly never
happen again, the way that monarchies are going.

Hurlubleu having died childless, the kingdom's Great
Charter necessarily rendered power to the buffoons, who
would have been quite content without it, in accordance with
their immemorial habit—for one never saw anything emerge
from any of that deplorable empire's revolutions but buffoons:
buffoons against buffoons; buffoons on top of buffoons; a
whole host of buffoons. The people had plumped for white
buffoons, red buffoons, buffoons of every color, buffoons with
long robes and buffoons with short robes, buffoons in buskins
and buffoons in boots, buffoons in togas and buffoons in armor, buffoons with pens and buffoons with swords, buffoons
by birth, buffoons by chance, buffoons with money, buffoons
with doctrines, buffoons of industry—but they were always
buffoons. The wretched Hurlubierians, having something of
the buffoon innate within them, always opted for buffoons
and perennially devolved into buffoons. In the final analysis,
who would vote for buffoons if he were not a buffoon?

The sovereign buffoons, as is reasonable, erected a pedestal
on the stone that closed the shaft into which Berniquet had
descended: an unequal dodecahedron depicting the dozen
continents of the known world. If ever a thirteenth were discovered, I sincerely declare that I don't know where one could
put it, but Heaven preserve me from such a great problem!

Berniquet had left a popular legacy equivalent to the
almost three hundred sesterces that Caesar had left to each
Roman citizen—which amounted, according to Monsieur
Letronne,[1] to 59 francs 61 centimes. That's what I call a good
prince! The poor jester, however, had not a single brass *uncia
sextula* to dispose—and that, more than anything else in his

---

1 Jean-Antoine Letronne (1787-1848), a contemporary polymath
particularly distinguished in the fields of geography and archaeology.

life, inspired the profoundest pity in his biographers. On the largest face of the base, therefore, in a lapidary style not seen again in the Academy of Inscriptions, the last lines of his will were inscribed:

MAY GOD DEIGN TO GIVE
TO ALL MY GOOD FRIENDS,
ALL THE PATIENCE REQUIRED
TO TOLERATE LIFE WITH LOVE
AND BENEVOLENCE,
TO RENDER IT SWEET AND USEFUL,
AND THE GAIETY REQUIRED TO LAUGH AT IT.

A statue of the jester erected on the monument was inaugurated the following day, and, as the sculpture of that improved era was naïve and bourgeois, the skillful artist represented him in a nightcap and slippers, breaking wind.

It is a beautiful piece.

# Zerothoctro-Schah,
# Proto-Mystagogue of Bactriana

### *Hypostasis*

My God, My God, what an instructive and amusing thing life is, when one has returned to it.

I had only been dead for ten thousand and a few hundred years when, one fine day after All Saints' Day—good day, good work!—the cockcrow reached me about which I have had the honor of telling you.

Although I had taken the time to sleep off our hostess's Jurançon, I was, I swear, a trifle dazed, like a man who has lost in the custom of society the habit of the open air. I had walked and walked for I don't know how long over mountains, valleys, avenues, terraces, parvises, courtyards, vestibules and steps, when I suddenly stopped before an immense portal of the Heteroclitic Order, above which as written, in phosphorescent letters:

NON PLUS ULTRA
HERE ONE LEARNS THE PURE TRUTH
THE TRASCENDENT SCIENCES
AND THE ART OF SLEEPING STANDING UP,
IN ALL LANGUAGES
*N.B. You are requested to leave dogs outside.*

After assuring myself that I had not understood exceptionally, I spotted a man of colossal stature who appeared
to be there in order to guard the door. He opened it to me
with great marks of courtesy, taking off in order to do me
that honor a sesquipedal turban with which he was gallantly
coiffed, and which had the form of a gigantic candle-snuffer.
I searched with my hand for my night-cap, with the intention of returning politeness for politeness, as well brought-up
people do, and I brought out a candle-snuffer that was no less
remarkable than his in its grenadier dimensions.

The worthy man testified his fervent sympathy again in the
fashion of the time and place, by grasping his nose between
the thumb and forefinger of his left hand, and I beg you to
believe that you have never seen such a nose. I riposted with
urbanity by seeking the tip of my own, but it was so long that
I had all the difficulty in the world reaching it.

After those paltry courtesies, to which people probably
attach too much importance in good company, we went into
a very obscure room, which closed behind us, the unique ban-
quette of which we shared. One could not see there even by
sticking one's finger in one's eye, and my nose would, in any
case, have inconvenienced me greatly had I yielded to that
ridiculous whim. By a singular good fortune, it did not occur
to me.


*Proscenium*


We immediately fell into conversation in the ordinary manner; in our attitude, which must have been a trifle mannered,
our respective noses did not permit us to speak other than in
profile.

"Will you forgive me, Monsieur," said the possessor of
one of the largest noses on earth—it was me who had the

other—"for sitting down casually beside you, by virtue of the inferences, attributions and privileges that my responsibility gives me over all resurrected individuals?"

"Not only do I not form any opposition to that," I replied, "but I have an infinite obligation to you for being so kind as to reassure me by your amicable presence in the temple of light. It is as dark there as in an oven. Your expressions, which are singularly well-chosen, prove to me, moreover, that I could not find myself in better society."

"Where will you be, then," he replied, doubtless with a smile, "when you hear, Messieurs? They are the ones who have at their disposal the fine flower of pathos, who enjoy agreeably syllepsis, hypallage and hypotyposis, and who filter speech, so to speak, through a valve. But I am not yet informed of the epoch and the circumstances of your death."

"It was the sixth of October 1834, from an inflammation of the gut, to serve you, if I can; or, in order to inform you more specifically, an enteritic phlegmasis, which signifies exactly the same thing. The physcians of my era were so decried in vulgar language that they only spoke in Greek."

"That was progress," said the man with the long nose, "and civilization profited from it. Your physicians, who spoke in order not to be understood, and who did not always understand themselves in speaking, had taken a great initiative over their century, and it is because you have not been able to cast your thought like them, if you think at all, through baroque synonyms and impenetrable jargon, that your career has been very limited, my poor comrade, and your life quite absurd. People did not know then the road to Corinth, where one arrives immediately now, with a double logogriph that is often not a word. It's a fine industry! In any case, it's necessary to resolve oneself. Here we are today, foot to foot, condemned to suffer the chastisement of our mores in the limbo of the paradise of the adroit, in the eternal spectacle of the unexpected marvels of perfectibility. Such is, in order that you should know it, the literal text of your judgment."

"Horrible, horrible!" I cried. "For I'm beginning to understand, given what you have taken the trouble to tell me, that the frightful torture to which the imperfectible resurrectees of whom we have the misfortune of being part, consists of hearing speeches and discourses eternally. Oh, the atrabiliary imagination of old Dante had forgotten that genre of torture in the Penal Code of the damned! It had not been foreseen either in the menaces of God, the fulminations of the Church, or the Ambrosian amenities of Antonio Rusca, which reek so strongly of burning, or the beautiful topography of Purgatory of Barthelemi Valverde, who speaks of that realm as if he had recently returned from it. It would be a bloody treason, a bird-call Hell."[1]

"Alas, Monsieur, scholars are capable of anything. But of what do you have to complain for a short obligatory session after so many centuries of repose for I do not believe that I have had the honor of receiving you before? Messieurs have moments of indulgence on jubilee days like this one, and if you conduct yourself well, they might well permit you to die again at your ease after the closure of the testimony, in order have a little leisure time before the next convocation. You have probably come to expiate some philosophical drollery, a doubt about the social morality of mutual information, a ludicrous objection to the orthography of Monsieur Voltaire of the Académie Française, improved by Monsieur Marle of

---

1 Antonio Rusca, a professor at the Ambrosian College of Milan, published a treatise *De Inferno, et status daemonum ante mundi exitium* [On Hell and the condition of the Demons before the End of the Worls] in the early seventeenth century. A sixteenth-century Spanish theologian named "Barthelemi Valverde" is credited in various French reference books as the author of *Le Feu du Purgatoire defendu par les passages des Pères Grecs & Latins & Orthodoxes*, but the Bibliothèque Nationale does not possess such a book.

the grammatical society,[1] or a disrespectful reticence in the analysis of the Jacotot method.[2] Perhaps you have spoken recklessly about magnetism, phrenology, eclecticism, leeches, or making bread with wood shavings; youth is presumptuous. It isn't good, but all bad cases are deniable and all ignorance merits mercy. Come on, have a little courage!"

"You're furiously inured, neighbor," I replied, abruptly, "if you suppose that one has the misfortune of resuscitating after centuries of centuries primarily in order to hear what one knows. Damn, damn! You must have some enormous sin on your conscience that forces you to accept your fate with so much resignation."

"As you say, Monsieur; I was the porter of the tower of Babel on the day of the confusion of tongues, and I gave myself a broad license to laugh wholeheartedly in the face of Messieurs when they could no longer understand one another, I was very poorly inspired in that, I can tell you frankly, because they finally succeeded."

"Succeeded? In what, porter, if you please? In building the tower of Babel, perhaps?"

I believe that you know. You've arrived on the six hundred and sixty-sixth floor above the entresol, which is the meeting-place of the members of the six hundred and sixty-sixth section . . ."

"Oh my God! Enough floors and sections! I know what you mean and I shall remember your figure exactly by the mnemonic method. It's the number of the beast, where there

---

1 Charles-Louis Marle (1799-1860) campaigned for a simplified phonetic orthography in the 1820s but with little success; among those who mocked his efforts was Alexandre Dumas, who recalled meeting him in his memoirs.

2 Joseph Jacotot's "panecastic" method of "intellectual emancipation," previously mentioned in passing in the essay on palingenesis and resurrection, was based on the notion that "everything is in everything" and that a single paragraph could thus become the starting-point for mastering an entire language and literature.

is a *lapsus calami*[1] in the autograph manuscript of the Apocalypse. In sum you were the porter of that, and you're the porter of this?

"Alas, yes, Monsieur."

"The punishment is well worth the crime, unfortunate that you are! What astonished me is that, in arriving at perfectibility, they have not learned benevolence, and they are still treating us as enemies, since we are, according to you, condemned to listen to them."

"Monsieur," replied the porter, "I'll tell you . . . it's because complete perfectibility has not exactly been found. We have Babel and tongues, just as when I was there; the maximum of perfectibility we shall only obtain today or tomorrow."

"People said that in my day, and I waited for it patiently enough, until the inflammation of the gut."

"Until the enteritic phlegmasia . . ."

"If you wish; I waited, my dear friend, and I always allowed myself to be told that perfectibility was for tomorrow, which left me with a profound suspicion in its regard."

"You probably won't have it any longer this evening, for I can tell you the program. In a little while the congress is to hear the important report of the savant Doctor Berniquet, who was mandated more than five hundred years ago to search for the perfect human, whom the philosophers had been announcing to us for such a long time, and no one doubts that he will bring him back in his collection, at least stuffed. It's probably that your palingenetic return to earth has been calculated in view of that great event, the knowledge of which will sicken you with eternal remorse."

"In truth, you're mistaken in supposing that I take tenacity to that point in my opinions. Four thousand years of sleep devoid of agitations and dreams, the probability—not to say

---

1 A slip of the pen. The number of the beast given in the current version of *Revelations* is said to be a mistranslation, the oldest known manuscripts giving the number as 616.

the certainty—that I would find in the auditorium of your sages neither the journalists nor the creditors who once made rude war upon me, and finally, the benefit of the sweet repose of the nerves, humors and passions that death has procured me, have disarmed me of all my bellicose vanity. I shall see the perfect human with a great deal of satisfaction and it will be a veritable pleasure for me to present my compliments to him."

"That desire will not take long to be fulfilled," the porter replied. "The sacred veil is tearing. Prepare your eyes for the flare of fires that will dazzle you. Light has arrived."

While he was speaking thus, Argand lamps lit up, and the curtain was raised.


### *Oramie*[1]


It was dazzling. I pulled my candle-snuffer down over my eyebrows to sheet my eyes from an excessively vivid sensation, turning them to the right and the left with the propitious shadow of the derisory nose with which I was furnished, in order to habituate them gradually to that profusion of light. The universal congress was composed of no less than forty thousand men, a thousand abreast, I was told, and forty deep—a number already symbolic,[2] which was for me a singular revelation of perfectibility. Each of those messieurs was coiffed with a magnificent cylindrical lantern illuminated by gas, and his breast was resplendent with a sun ablaze with the same light, with the consequence that through the narrow intervals between their armchairs and in the amphitheatrical disposition of their ranks, nothing could be seen but fire.

---

1 This subtitle is enigmatic, but it would be absurd to evaluate it a compound of *or* and *amie*, and the greater temptation, given the content of the chapter, is to liken it to the Latin *oremus*, meaning a call to prayer.
2 Because the Académie has forty members.

The throne on which the president was elevated in the middle of his four acolytes offered an even more remarkable spectacle. The tiara with which the pontiff of civilization was crowned rose in three pyramidal stages interrupted by multitudinous triangles, which rotated around one another with a movement appropriate to their construction, activating numerous variously colored fires before the audience like a mirror of skylarks, while the transparency that formed the back of the stage rotated about a perpetual axis, in the manner of those fires so stupidly named pyric, of which you have had the representation chez Séraphin.[1] I do not know how I succeeded in familiarizng myself with those marvels.

Suddenly, the president rose from his seat with a miraculous solemnity and took from his igneous ephos three philosophical muscades,[2] which he placed in the superior cavity of three golden goblets placed in front of him.

"Behold," he said, "one muscade, two muscades, three muscades. Under the first goblet, there is nothing. Under the second goblet, there is nothing. Under the third goblet, there is nothing." And he made the demonstration.

"Everyone knows," he continued, "that the first goblet is the emblem of the age of apprehension, the second goblet the emblem of the age of comprehension, and the third goblet the emblem of the age of perfection, which we are about to attain so happily. The three muscades are going to pass into it. One, two, three . . . behold the muscades!"

---

1 In Nodier's day the tautologous phrase *feu pyrique* [pyric fire] would have been familiar as the name attributed to a kind of magic lantern show popular in the Revolutionary era, also known as *feu Séraphin* after one of the Parisian impresarios who made use of it; Séraphin had his own theater near the Palais-Royal; he died in 1798, but his theater survived for some time thereafter, and Nodier might well have visited it.

2 The literal meaning of *muscade* is "nutmeg," but the name was applied colloquially to the small ball used in a familiar trick in which it is placed under one of three inverted cups and then seems to shift from one to another, or to disappear completely, with the aid of sleight-of-hand.

"Now, the muscades will disappear. Begone, muscades!"

And I received one of them on the only part of my face that was able to protrude outside the box of the resurrectees.

"The muscades are no longer there," he added (I knew that, of course, very well). "What do you want in their place?"

"Supreme Father," said one of the forty thousand, "I would like to see in the place of the first the symbol of the age of apprehension."

The Supreme Father turned over the first goblet and showed us a pretty wolf seven years old, whose teeth were being sawed by a rabbit with a goose-quill, by the light of an owl's eyes.

"Supreme Father," said another, "I would like to see in the place of the second the symbol of the age of comprehension."

The Supreme Father turned over the second goblet, and we saw an ugly ape with a bare backside, which had been drawing water from a well with a bottomless bucket since the age of Pythagoras, without being able to preserve a single drop.

"Supreme Father," said yet another, "I would like to see in the place of the third everything that exists of the present symbol of perfection, since we do not yet have the joy of enjoying it completely."

The Supreme Father turned over the third goblet and uncovered a little man hideous in his ugliness and stunted by old age, sitting with his knees crossed in the fashion of tailors, who appeared to be amusing himself bursting balloons in order to hear them pop.

"Victory! Victory!" cried the entire assembly. "It's our worthy colleague Berniquet, the great seeker of perfection, the man of eternal knowledge, the xenomaniac of intellectual lands, the man who is bringing us science and truth from afar!"

"Solely to accomplish the noble mission with which you had charged me, Messieurs, I did not hesitate to throw myself into the new crypt that opened to my gaze; I launched myself into it with a single bound, but the bottom of the circular well was formed by a tilting trap-door,[1] which swung abruptly on its axis and closed again over my head, while I descended into a bottomless gulf with the customary precipitation of gravitating bodies. That accident inspired to begin with, I cannot dissimulate, a few serious reflections, all the more so because I had not covered five hundred leagues in that manner without perceiving that I was heading directly for the center of our globe, which I had always been very curious to explore, but which I despaired of reaching undamaged.

"Philosophy sustained me not in the air but in my soul; the love of the sciences came to console me, affirm me, cheer me up and change my abject terrors into mild meditations. I gradually accustomed myself to contemplating assiduously the different tellurian strata whose distinct divisions were designed to my gaze, but of which, to my great regret, the rapidity of my passage did not permit me to bring back any specimens. I counted thus by means of broad zones the ages of the globe and the evolution of nature—a sublime and enchanting spectacle for a philosopher who had facile respiration, but I had unfortunately contacted asthma while climbing Mount Chimborazo.

"Finally, after fourteen and a half hours, watch in hand, I arrived at the mid-point of our terraqueous things, with a grievous anguish that it is difficult to enable you to imagine, Messieurs, upon a further four or five thousand leagues of

---

1 The phrase *trappe en chapechute* [tilting trapdoor] has a double meaning in French, because the term *chapechute* was used metaphorically to refer to a stroke of luck occasioned by someone else's negligence.

atmosphere weighs, although it is only a bagatelle relative to space; and I won't mention the volcanic heat, in relation to which the igneous philosophers have not exaggerated. I cannot tell you the exact degree because of the abruptness of that investigation and the poor state of my Fahrenheit thermometer.

"My feet had touched the ground, not without a slight sprain. I pulled myself together and got my breath back, of which I had great need. My candle was still burning within its glazed capsule, thanks to the rarefied atmosphere. I illuminated the enclosure that I had reached in all directions. It was a cavern, and I had few reasons for doubting it. The center of that universal milieu was occupied by a cippus,[1] which bore a sconce that did not bear anything, at least apparently. By dint of stirring the ashes of an old wick, over which thirty or forty centuries had passed, I succeeded, however, in extracting a tiny human figure, so pale, so worn out, so wrinkled, so paltry and so stunted that my first thought was to put him in the margin.[2]

A little squeal informed me that a breath of life still remained in the embryo; I seized him, warmed him up with my breath, rubbed him with a drop of eau-de-vie found in my traveling gourd and replanted him in the middle of his sconce, lighter than I had expected. As he stood there with his hand on his hip, with all the dignity that his two-and-a-half inch stature could contrive, I was no longer thinking of going back up where I had come from in order to find my colleagues and my carriage. That appeared difficult.

"Stop, Berniquet," the dwarf said to me, "and don't leave here without rendering to me all the life for which I've been waiting for centuries without number."

---

1 A low pillar employed in ancient Greece and Rome as a landmark or tombstone.

2 The text has "*mettre dans les machettes*" [literally, put in handcuffs] but the narrative voice must be employing the phrase metaphorically, as a writer would, to indicate the insertion of a marginal note.

I prostrated myself with admiration on seeing that he could talk. You would have done the same, Messieurs. It is so rare that an articulate idea, enunciated in such good terms, comes from a candlestick, especially when the candle is dead.

"Stop!" he continued, in a persuasive voice. "And if you find a little stone jar somewhere, in which I once enclosed the elixir of long life, give me, I beg you, an abundant foot-bath all the way to the rim of my candlestick; but take care, on your head, not to let a drop pass the edge, for we'd both be drowned in the river of science from which we could no longer draw, and which would engulf your academy along with the rest of the human race."

I had the jar in my hand, but I mistrusted my trembling hand, and, a spy-glass wedged in the orbit of the eye, I let the sacred liquid fall drop by drop, following its progress by the light of my candle, freed from its prison.

Suddenly the floating fire of the candle was lowered, as if by magic, and its pink and blue tongue came to lick the unknown liquid, which suddenly caught fire and rolled in burning waves, like a good punch-bowl of Jamaica rum. Imagine with what terror I sought then, in the midst of that conflagration, recreative to the gaze but frightening for the sentiment, the solemn figurine that I had just removed from so many centuries of death in order to roast alive on a sconce

"Organized atom, thinking and speaking," I cried, "archeological monad, living microcosm that, even stuffed, would have done honor to the finest museum on earth, sublime and rare creature that the sages of my country would have been so proud and so happy to possess in a bottle, by what fatality is it necessary that I have reduced you to ashes before having dissected you?"

"You're mistaken, Berniquet," replied the little phantom; "I'm alive, and I'm thriving like a charm. The deluge of fire with which you inundated me is my atmosphere and my element. Its warmth reinvigorates me and I feel radiant with all my old philosophical splendor. I owe my palingenesis to you and I will give you an account, if I can, of the eventual progress of the world to come."

He was, in fact, standing there, full of assurance, and his naturally imposing physiognomy stood out marvelously under the ash and the smoke. His hooded cape of bright colors, which was rounded out like a mushroom balanced on its peduncle, gave him the appearance of a badly-trimmed wick. Beneath it, his eyes were sparkling like the cotton of a damp candle, or like two little craters that had just opened up in the face of a miniature volcano.

"May I know," I said to him, "to whom I have the honor of speaking?"

"That's the least that I owe you for the services you've rendered me," he replied. "I am Zoroaster."

# Monsieur Cazotte[1]

On the third day the man cried: "Woe to Jerusalem!
Woe is me!" And a stone launched by the ballista
of the besiegers killed him on the wall.
*The prophecy of Cazotte.*

### *Advertisement*

It is not a question here of the famous prophecy of Cazotte
reported some time after the ninth of Thermidor by Laharpe.[2]

---

1 Author's note: "This fragment is taken from a novel that I began to
write in the manner of Cazotte, which Monsieur Renduel, to whom I
had promised it, had promised to publish. Obscure works, but more
appropriate to my age and my studies, forced me to abandon it. Nothing
else of it will ever appear."

2 Jean-François de La Harpe, or Laharpe (1739-1803) wrote a brief
account—found among his papers and first published in 1806, before
being separately reprinted as a booklet in 1817—of a dinner imagined
to have taken place in 1788, the guests at which include the philosopher
of progress the Marquis de Condorcet, the writer Nicolas Chamfort,
the physician Félix Vicq-d'Azur, the magistrate Aimar-Charles-Marie de
Nicolaï, the astronomer and mathematician Jean-Sylvain Bailly, the poet
Jean-Antoine Roucher and the salon-hostess the Duchesse de Gramont,
during which Cazotte prophesies what would become of them all, and of
the king. La Harpe was only making the point that the people involved
could have had no inkling, on the eve of the Revolution, of what was to
happen, but numerous readers did not appreciate the rhetorical device
and misinterpreted the *jeu d'esprit*, on which he was no longer alive to
comment, as reportage.

That is a matter settled and very nearly judged, which I could neither recommence without lacking the decency of modesty nor extend in development without lacking that of good taste. I think, like everyone, that the scene in question is in large part invention, and I am convinced that Laharpe himself never conceived the hope of giving it the authority of a veritable fact. However, it would not have succeeded so easily if it had not exaggerated, beyond all plausibility, the inspired old man's power of prevision, in characterizing the events predicted by positive circumstances, which the vague intuitions of the second life cannot grasp, if they grasp anything. Laharpe, a man of intelligence and talent, was entirely inept in relation to imagination, and it is not astonishing that he employed maladroitly an instrument to which he was not accustomed. One goes far when one does not know where one is going, and cannot see the goal that one passes. To provide illusion to others, it is necessary to be capable of providing illusion to oneself, and that is a privilege that is only given to fanaticism and genius, to madmen and poets.

With the artistry that combination demanded nothing would have been easier, I repeat, than to make the generation that had seen Cazotte accept his marvelous predictions, for that worthy man was always on the tripod, and most of the things that he announced were realized in their time in the most natural manner. There is no effort to make in order to comprehend that result, extraordinary as it might seem at first. The faculty of foreseeing the future, in a certain order of events, is quite independent, in fact, of revelations, visions and magic. It belongs to anyone who is endowed with a profound sensibility, an accurate judgment and a long aptitude of observation.

The reason for that phenomenon leaps to the eyes; it is that the future is a past that is recommencing. Everyone is able to predict the day and the spring, because everyone has seen spring succeeding winter and day succeeding night. It is the same with all consequences that have similar antecedents. Future history is no less lucid to the eyes of the philosopher, save for a few names and dates, than the most averred ancient history. Nostradamus, poor fellow, who had nothing but a very superficial and very confused almanac science, something got things right; with the science of affairs and the knowledge of men, he would rarely have been mistaken. That, as everyone knows, is what Cazotte did not lack, and it was not difficult to foresee, in his time, that a revolution of the nature of ours would pass through all the phases appropriate to revolutions.

Revolutions are not aborted, they only die of old age. There is no one in the world who has not had occasion to learn that, from experience or history, with the exception of the people who start revolutions and who strive foolishly afterwards to contain them within certain limits. What a pity!

The particularity, much more extraordinary, that is the basis of this little romance, is not, as one might believe, a simple play of the imagination.[1] I remember very distinctly having heard the principal fact recounted by Cazotte when I was at the age of childhood that is already that of keen perceptions and imperturbable memories, and I even think that it is the part of the story in which there is question of the strange longevity of Marie Delorme, designated in the *Fragment* under the name of Madame Lebrun, that prompted Monsieur Delaborde, who was very intimately linked with Cazotte, to write the singular *Lettre de Marion de Lorme aux auteurs du Journal de Paris*, which was reprinted subsequently in his *Recueil de pièces interesssante sur le procès de Chalais*, London 1781: a curiously piquant letter that caused a great sensation then, although its frivolous and bantering tone was inappropriate

---

1 This is not true. Nodier and his father were not in Paris at the time when the story is set and Nodier never met Jacques Cazotte. As the previous quasi-autobiographical fantasy, "Jean-François-les-Bas-Bleus" relates, Nodier was in Besançon in 1792.

to such an important question of biography, but the character of which suited the productions of the time.[1]

The air of skepticism and irony that the author had given it did not prevent professional scholars from occupying themselves with it with interest, and my friend Monsieur Beuchot[2] did not disdain to take account of that singular hypothesis in the *Biographie universelle*, half-protecting the adventurous temerity of the anecdote with a few reticences proving that he was not entirely convinced. I have taken my research further and with more confidence, because I am relying on the oral tradition of a witness worthy of faith, and I believe sincerely

---

1 Marion Delorme (1613-1650?), whose name is not linked with that if Madame Lebrun in the fragmentary *conte*, although it evidently would have been had the story continued, was a courtesan whose name was linked, at least by rumor, with several of the famous men and courtiers of the era. Her salon allegedly became a meeting-place for conspirators during the turbulent rebellion of the Fronde—which led to speculation that her death was faked in order to avoid arrest, and thus the flourishing in the nineteenth century of retrospective conspiracy theories. She became a figure of particular interest in the Romantic Movement; she played a leading role in Alfred de Vigny's novel *Cinq-Mars* (1826), whose eponymous hero was the most prominent of her lovers, and then moved to center stage in Victor Hugo's play *Marion de Lorme* (written 1828; first performed 1831), which was banned during the reign of Charles X but premiered after the July Revolution at the Théâtre de la Porte Saint-Martin, where Nodier must have seen it. The play was subsequently adapted into two operas. The fictitious work by the composer Jean-Benjamin de Laborde (1734-1794)—who was guillotined, like Cazotte—was first published in 1780; the 1781 collection allegedly published in London (false indications of places of publication were commonplace, as a measure protecting Parisian printers from prosecution) was actually titled *Pièces du procès de Henri de Tallerand, comte de Chalais, décapité in 1626.*

2 Aimian-Jean-Quintin Beuchot (born 1777). His article in the *Biographie universelle* reproduces the rumor that Marion Delorme had fled France in 1850 but had returned later to marry twice, latterly to an attorney named Lebrun, eventually dying in 1741, when a Madame Lebrun whose maiden name was given as Anne-Oudette Grappin was buried, supposedly at the age of 134 years, but Beuchot expresses conscientious skepticism as to whether the woman in question could have been Marion Delorme.

in what I am saying, which is a great rarity in fantastic stories, and not common in the others.

The identity of Anne-Oudette Grappin, the widow Lebrun, and Marion Delorme was evidently manifest for me at the first glance that I cast over the marriage certificate of her mother, whose name was Marie Delorme, as can be verified in a region where the names Delorme and Grappin were still common twenty years ago. As for Marion's natal village, my good brother in study and heart, Monsieur Weiss,[1] who has stitched a small number of notes to this biographical page, would not be embarrassed to recognize it, if the learned librarian of Besançon had had to hand, like me, the mortuary extract of the widow Lebrun, where he would have read Baverans instead of Balheram. I have no need to explain that the small mistake of the author of the Letter is easily explicable by the outdated orthography of the registrar, who expressed the consonant $v$ by a vowel $u$, in accordance with an old habit that grammarians have long since reformed in typography but which was abusively perpetuated almost to the present day in handwriting. As for the final $s$ that follows an $n$, everyone knows that it is easily confused in cursive letters, even under the most correct pen, with the third branch of an $m$. It is sufficient for me to understand it to visualize that word in the rapid and lazy scrawl of a sacristy scribe.

After that tedious excursion on to diplomatic terrain (I beg the pardon of the messieurs of the École des chartes) I shall return to my fantasies, which the majority of readers will doubtless dispense me willingly of clarifying and justifying by the scrupulous verification of a mortuary extract. "What does it matter," they might say, "whether your story reposes on a true or false fact, if it is able to interest or please?" It is a matter of taste. I am less insouciant or more delicate in the choice

---

1 Pierre-Charles Weiss (1779-1866), another leading contributor to the *Biographie universelle.*

of the pleasures of my imagination, and I confess that I have never been able to savor them more than when a little verity seasons them. The attraction of an anecdote so piquant and so little known is—along with the need to request from my aged memory a puerile, not to say ridiculous, but tender and vehement impression of my early years, which I shall explain in due course—the most forceful reason that has determined me to write the last of my romances. This is nothing else. More fortunate than La Fontaine, I can at least promise myself that this work is the last trouble that amour will cause me.[1]

Perhaps there is an opportunity here to consecrate to the venerable Cazotte a notice more developed than that of Monsieur Bergasse,[2] which would suit my material all the better in the present circumstance because I have sometimes been obligingly reproached for circumscribing my little compositions within excessively narrow limits, but what could I say about Cazotte that is new to a generation that has followed him so closely? What reader is not amused by his suave and cheerful stories? What sensible soul has not been moved by the idea of his noble misfortunes? It would be necessary, in any case, to borrow facts that are already familiar from works that are in everyone's hands, and I prefer to clothe my works a little tightly than to stuff them at the expense of others. And then, that fine story would certainly harm the one I am writing; I would not be forgiven—and that would be just—for only having found in a life so pure and so glorious the subject of a fairy tale of sorts.

I shall limit myself on that chapter to consigning to my preface a notion that occurred to me today, which biographers

---

1 Nodier, ever an unreliable prophet, did not keep this "promise" to himself. Nor was this the last time that he announced in a story that it would be "the last" of his romances; "Les Quatre talismans" (1838) concludes with a similar allegation, but he published two more thereafter, including "Lydie."

2 Nicolas Bergasse (1750-1832) wrote the article on Cazotte in the *Biographie universelle.*

have neglected inappropriately. The memory of the heroic Elisabeth Cazotte is inseparably linked with that of her father, but it is not known generally enough that the illustrious old man had a daughter worthy of him, whom the Restoration has omitted to summon to the honors of the peerage.[1] One of the grandsons of Jacques Cazotte, of whom the École Polytechnique has retained a dazzling memory, died a few years ago in the prime of age and life, as he was about to marry a young woman he loved, for Heaven does not exhaust its proofs on a single head in a family chosen for them. If a government more liberal than the pretended representative governments that have already emerged from the chaos of our revolutions decides one day to transport to immortal names to which posterity has contracted an irredeemable debt the smallest of political honors of which intrigue and money are now in sole possession, I will congratulate myself for having reminded it that the name of Cazotte has an heir.


# I
## *The Author's Story*

Do you not hear a voice, my friends, which rises and resounds in the posterity of next week, a voice that cries "Deliver us from the fantastic, Lord, for the fantastic is tedious"? For myself, I have found it for a long time as insipid as trivial truths that are no longer worth the trouble of being repeated; and I have traveled so far, with your fashionable storytellers, on the back of winged serpents, dragons and griffins that I would have no shame in relaxing momentarily on Sancho's warhorse, if some fortunate hazard enabled me to encounter it. It would be a poor means of being welcome among you, today, when a

---

1 Jacques Cazotte's daughter Elisabeth (1775-1800?) allegedly defended her father from the mob and then accompanied him to prison, but not to the guillotine; she married in 1800 and died in childbirth not long after.

storyteller is not willingly admitted to your firesides if he does not come down the chimney or arrive through the window; and as your capricious, fickle and sometimes incongruous taste is nothing less than the supreme arbiter of whomever is reduced to writing by his unlucky star and yours, it is necessary for me to bestride once again, whether I like it or not, one of the monsters of your hippodrome.

However, as my instinct brings me back, in spite of my métier, to the natural and the true. I dare not promise you to lose sight entirely of the limits of the promised land to which I am belated in returning. I would even be very embarrassed to say positively whether the tale I have to tell you has more of the lie that amuses you than the reality that charms me, which tells you that in listening to me until the end, if you are obliging enough to listen to me until the end, we will each sleep afterwards on our own side, if you are not asleep already. Here goes, then.

It is as well to begin with to remind you that in 1792, I was rolling gaily, as Montaigne says, through the fine days of my tenth year. I passed then for a sufficiently exemplary and studious little boy, but whose progress only responded imperfectly to the advantages of an organization from which another might have been able to extract a better dividend. That was because I had an extreme aptitude for appropriating sentiments, but a pronounced incapacity for appropriating ideas. I took in delight all the marvelous reveries with which the imagination of children is cradled, in antipathy all the positive studies with which the primary education of men is nourished; and a I have not changed since, I have become in growing old, a species of man without ceasing in consequence to be a species of child.

In the multiple scenes that have succeeded one another before me, I have only ever seized a certain ideal aspect of things, the more or less colored surface that is, to tell the truth, only the vestment of facts, and which reason often counts for nothing when it is a matter of appreciating them. While my contemporaries were laboriously amassing solid materials with which to construct history, I was building houses of cards and making up tales that I communicated willingly to others, because after the pleasure of hearing tales, there is no pleasure sweeter than recounting them. If, from time to time, I formed a slightly firmer opinion about events or people, it still retained in some way the fantastic life that I composed for myself, and which was itself only a tale, a little long, sometimes surly, sometimes cheerful, sometimes singular and bizarre. As I knew the denouement in advance, I struggled with a glad heart through the episodes of the route, occasionally hanging on to the slightest caprices and the vainest fantasies, and gathering as best I could all the individuals and scenes that were presented to my view, in the frame of my magic lantern.

That mental disposition had not isolated my young imagination so completely from the true world that I did not experience a few vivid sympathies, but you will easily understand that those predilections of instinct were attached, with a very particular complaisance, to objects familiar to my taste and my reading. Thus, nothing that enters into the monotonous combination of the events or ordinary life had the privilege of interesting me. I did not believe that a man had lived essentially if he had not sought or been subjected in a long career to other vicissitudes of fortune than those brought by the scantly varied chances of our common destination. In order to move me forcefully it required hazardous or adventurous glories; the more unfamiliar their point of departure was, and the more reckless and unexpected the ascendancy was that they had acquired over the world, the more they drew me irresistibly in their wake. I only knew the passions of their movements and results, but it was in that vehement play of exalted sentiments that I made all the realities of an enviable existence consist.

The sight of women only caused me to experience, as yet, an extremely vague emotion, which was not without some sweetness, but if a romantic event relieved the vulgar foundation of their history; if their name was mingled with touching adventures or great catastrophes; if hazard had imprinted on their life the seal of a tragic fatality, that indecisive emotion went as far as frenzy.

Forgive me these long preliminaries. They are not unnecessary to the intelligence of the rest of my story, and it requires nothing less for you to understand how it happened that at the age of ten my soul was preoccupied by a sentiment more exclusive, more passionate and more fanatical than amour, and that there was then a woman—or to put it better, a simulacrum, a phantom, a dream—who was the sole charm of my solitary walks, the illusion of my slumber and the eternal fodder of my futile regrets and my extravagant hopes. That unique lady of my thoughts—I scarcely dare, even today, finish a confidence that is escaping me entirely for the first time—was Marion Delorme.

In the epoch of which I speak, my parents suddenly decided to take me to Paris in order to receive there the sole complement possible of an education so fortunately commenced. That change of situation displeased me greatly from one point of view, because it threatened me with a more coherent system of study, and above all a more demanding surveillance, than the one to which I was accustomed. On the other hand, it brought me closer to the places where Marion Delorme had lived, and the Place Royale compensated me in prospect for all the rigors of the college.

It was in that disposition that I descended with my family at the old furnished house that accommodated then our compatriot, Monsieur Dauty, in the Rue de la Verrerie, and the corner of the Rue Barre-du-Bec, above the ground floor, where a café of rather fine appearance can now be seen, but which was then occupied by a silversmith named Monsieur Brisbart. I dare not assure you, nevertheless, that it was the same house, for the Rue Barre-du-Bec seems to me to have been considerably widened.

Independently of the principal motive for that voyage, my father promised himself the pleasure of seeing again in Paris a few friends who were the more or less celebrated, and who have become more so. Delisle de Sales, whose metaphysical romance entitled *Le Philosophie de la Nature* still conserved some vogue, had been his colleague in the order of the Oratory.[1] Legouvé[2] remembered having received from him the first elements of rhetoric and the first principles of versification. Relations formed in society, and maintained by a common taste for literature, had held him in long correspondence with Collin d'Harleville[3] and Marsollier des Vivetières,[4] who has since become the fecund providence of the Opéra-Comique.

A much narrower affection linked him to the honest Jacques Cazotte, his elder by twenty years, whose acquaintance he had made in Lyon in the home of a young officer named Saint-Martin,[5] a thaumaturge passionate about a new

---

1 Jean-Baptiste Isoard, who renamed himself Jean-Baptiste Delisle de Sales (1741-1816) was imprisoned, fined and exiled for suggesting in the monumental *De la philosophie de la Nature* (1770) that humans had evolved from orangutans. Voltaire helped raise the money to pay his fine. Thinking himself safer after the Revolution he published his utopian novel *Éponine, ou de la République* (1793), but offended the Convention and was imprisoned again, and was fortunate to be released.

2 The dramatist and Academician Gabriel-Marie Legouvé (1764-1812). His tragedy *La Mort d'Henri IV* (1806) might have been recruited to supply incidental details of the part of the present story that was planned but remained unwritten.

3 The dramatist Jean-François Collin d'Harleville (1755-1806), similarly one of the original recruits to the Institut.

4 The prolific dramatist Benoît-Joseph Marsollier (1750-1817), who preferred to style himself Marsollier de Vivetières.

5 Louis-Claude Saint-Martin (1743-1803), who signed himself "*le philosophe inconnu*" became a follower of Martinez de Pasqually, the mystic founder of the quasi-Masonic cult of Martinism, but eventually broke

philosophy, which was not very commendable for the coherence of its ideas and the clarity of its formulae, but at least had the advantage over the sad philosophy of the last century of speaking about the imagination and the soul.

My father, who was born with a certain penchant for the marvelous, had not, however, conserved a long fidelity to the theories of the Martinists. He had paused for a number of years at less seductive but much more positive theories without ceasing to love Cazotte and his reveries, on which he never contradicted him. The good Cazotte, who regarded that slightly tongue-in-cheek tolerance as a formal adhesion, congratulated himself more every day on the repentance of his strayed follower. And his visits were multiplied by reason of the opinion he formed of his progress, for no man was ever animated by a greater fervor of proselytism.

His arrival was always welcomed with the most lively satisfaction by our ordinary society, which was composed of the persons already named, a few amiable and intelligent women of my mother's acquaintance or whom hazard had brought to our house, but there was certainly no habitué of our evenings who was more agreeable to me. That is because of an extreme benevolence, which was painted in his handsome and pleasant physiognomy, and a tender mildness, which his blue eyes, even more animated, expressed in the most seductive manner. To the natural ascendancy that his age gave him, Monsieur Cazotte joined the precious talent of recounting better than any other man in the world stories that were simultaneously strange and naïve, which held the most common reality in the exactitude of circumstances, and the enchantment of the marvelous. He had received from nature a particular gift for seeing things in their fantastic aspect, and you already know

away to develop his own philosophy, heavily influenced by the German mystic Jakob Böhme. In addition to this philosophical works he wrote a bizarre novel, *Le Crocodile, ou la Guerre du birn et du mal* (1798; tr. as *The Crocodile*), which Nodier might have read.

that I was organized in a manner to enjoy that kind of illusion with delight.

Thus, when grave footfalls were heard, at equal intervals, on the flagstones of the little vestibule that served us as an antechamber; when the door opened with a methodical slowness and allowed the perception of the lantern carried by an old domestic less lame than the master, whom Monsieur Cazotte gaily called his page; and when Monsieur Cazotte appeared himself, with his triangular hat, his long frock-coat of green Camelot bordered with a little braid, his square-tipped shoes closed a long way forward over the foot by a strong silver clasp, and his long cane with a golden pommel, I never failed to run to him with testimonies of a hectic joy, which was further augmented by his caresses.

On the day that I have to tell you about, Monsieur Cazotte arrived later than usual, at the moment when the conversation was beginning to engage with a serious question. Delisle de Sales was then occupied with a great history of the human race, which was presumably part of the immense collection of his almost-forgotten works, and he was developing his theory with the pompous abundance and profusion of images and illusions that characterized his manner. When he had almost finished, my father said:

"In truth, although I have often reproached you for putting poetry everywhere, I must admit that I do not see you without pleasure attempting to renew the forms of the historic style. It seems to me that people are almost always scornful of the manner of presenting past facts that renders the life and interest of the moment at which they were accomplished. I'm not talking about old Plutarch and our Philippe de Commines,[1] who appears to us to be scarcely less old than Plutarch. Those people knew how to take possession of an action, set the scene

_______________

1 Philippe de Commines (1447-1511), a chronicler of his times much admired by Charles-Augustine Sainte-Beuve, the pillar of Victor Hugo's cénacle.

for it and summon me to the rank of spectators in the midst if the actors, to witness their debates at close range and enable me to participate more intimately in the passions that moved them. That is living history. In all those who are called historians, above all in France, I only see cold compilers of cold documents, clerks, feudists and gazetteers on the one hand and bulbous rhetors on the other, declaimers inflated by words and wind who paraphrase the legal documents of the former with oratory pathos.

"At fifty-four years of age I've seen history, and if events continue as they are today I shall be able to flatter myself before long with having seen more of it than is ordinarily made in three or four centuries. The history at which I was present has already been written in part, and I'm very surprised, when I try to read it, to find it so commonplace, so insipid, so denuded of soul and movement, compared with my sensations. I dare to affirm, with regard to the epoch that our memory can embrace, that one can learn a hundred times more in the conversation of an old man of good faith, prided that he is endowed with a little sensibility and some judgment, than in all the rhapsodies of our historiographers. It's me who gave Monsieur de Voltaire the anecdote of the Chevalier d'Assass, killed at Clostercamp on the night of the fifteenth and sixteenth of August 1760. I had it from a man named Charpin, my wig-maker, who had served in the Auvergne regiment, and who recounted it better than Monsieur de Voltaire himself."

Delisle de Sales did not reply. The name of the wig-maker Charpin had sounded badly in his ear, and he shook his head, as if to testify that the authority in question figured poorly in a period of four sections terminated by a majestic spondee.

"I share your opinion," said Monsieur Cazotte, who had not yet spoken, "even though your ordinary circumspection has frightened a proposition at the moment when it might have presented to you with the appearance of a paradox, and you restricted to contemporary history what it was necessary to say boldly of all histories, since the commencement of the world until today. Humans having always been the same, or very nearly, sagely setting aside a few modifications of time and place, it is no more difficult to represent, from an animated and dramatic viewpoint, the battle of Cannes or that of Pharsalia, than that skirmish at Clostercamp in which your wig-maker figured so fortunately for the memory of his captain. Moses, whom you have not cited among historians imprinted with an extraordinary merit of local verity, because his name is in bad odor today in philosophical discussions, owed that incontestable advantage to the oral tradition of the patriarchs, and your friend Pascal, the eagle of the Oratory, as of Port-Royal, made that remark very well.

"I suggest, in fact, that the old man of whom you were speaking just now, and whom you suppose to be provided with good judgment and a certain warmth of soul, if he has lived in his youth with old men favored with the same qualities, possesses on his own account more singular and true notions than one would find in the majority of books, and he would need no more than ten similar intermediaries to go back to the first positive days of our monarchy, only admitting the benefit of a longevity not common, but of which the centuries offer examples. The desire takes me to furnish you immediately with a proof of what I am saying, but it will be necessary for that to know first what day we have reached in the month of May."

"That's not difficult," replied my father, taking out his watch, which registered the days. Today is the fourteenth."

"The fourteenth!" said Monsieur Cazotte. "It is now a hundred and eighty-two years, neither more nor less, since good King Henri was deposited, a few hours after his death on the little stairway in the Louvre that I showed you the other day. What would you say if I were to tell you, with as much clarity as an eye-witness could, details of the murder of Henri IV that have never been written down, but regarding which it is impossible for me to raise the slightest doubt?"

At those words, our little circle tightened around Monsieur Cazotte, and we awaited his story in a profound silence.

"It is true," he said, "that these particularities are only an unknown episode of an anecdote even less known, but I have not forgotten," he continued, smiling, "that I owe you this week a story for which Charles has gained me more free play than usual, and I am at an age when one cannot dread dying insolvent. I shall therefore tell it to you, if your time is not otherwise employed, and I shall try to make it short."

Monsieur Cazotte's proposition was welcomed, as you might think, with a lively urgency. Legouvé, above all, put more expansion into his insistence than was familiar to him then, and was not promised by the slightly Jansenist stiffness that he obtained from God or his father.

"Unknown deals if the death of Henri IV," he exclaimed. "I shall take great pleasure in learning them, for that subject interests me, and I have always thought about making a tragedy of it."

"A tragedy?" replied Monsieur Cazotte. "One is no longer dreaming, then, about the amours of Astrée on the banks of the Lignon! Alas, it is the tendency of a society that is aging. After the romances of innocence, the tragedies of history! Let us talk about tragedies then," he continued, shaking Legouvé's hand. "You'll see many others!"

And he commenced.

## II
### *Monsieur Cazotte's Story*

I had reached the age of twenty without leaving Dijon, where I was born. In 1740 my family sent me to Paris, where it counted for me on the protection of a few great lords of our duchy of Bourgogne who had come to "deprovincialize" at court. I was welcomed with the elegant politeness that good people adopt for the sake of kindness and affection, and then I was left there. It was necessary to renounce a few pretentions that had never had much empire over my mind, and I resolved myself to it without effort, because the society that I had scarcely entered was beginning to weary me.

Although young and passably dissipated on occasion, deep down I loved solitude, recollection, vague and dreamy meditations, and all of that is incompatible with the movement of affairs and pleasures into which I threw myself at first. I resolved to isolate myself immediately from almost everything, even including the most common forms of exterior life. Here I am, then, in a long habit carefully buttoned to the chin, in a round flat hat with a broad brim, wearing raw leather gaiters with straps closed by steel buckles. If you combine with that unpowdered hair, cut rather short over the forehead and falling a few inches over my collar and shoulders, you will form an exact idea of Jacque Cazotte, or a hibernating student.

I had not contracted any intimate relationship in high society. That is not where one goes in search of friends. People of that status have too much to do to take the time to love. Even the persons who had seen me most frequently would not have recognized me, in any case, and I congratulated myself for that, for I had no wish to see them again. I was fortunate, and I knew that I was fortunate—an inappreciable and rare advantage without which all happiness is only a chimera.

223

I took pleasure then so delectably in the sweet liberty that I had made for myself, and I put to such good profit the hours of the day, that they always appeared to me to be too short, and I would have complained about the sleep that came to trouble me in the enjoyment of my illusions if the dreams that it brought me had not rendered them to me frequently.

I dreaded seeing people at the expense of the inexpressible voluptuousness I experienced in savoring my thoughts; the shadows never had enough thickness for my taste, the most profound retreats were never obscure enough to protect me from their encounter, to hide me in the palace of my Ginnistan,[1] far away, very far, from their passage, with my sylphs and my fays. That is because the slightest distraction dissipated my enchantments, as the song of an excessively matinal bird disperses, at sunrise, the gracious spirits who play around the pillow; as an atom gone astray in the air, where it is floating imperceptibly, breaks and dissolves by touching it, like a soap bubble more limpid than diamond and more radiant than a rainbow. It was because creation belonged to me: another creation, truly, than the one you know, far more varied in its productions and much richer in marvels.

I have heard in my life a multitude of gripping tales and touching adventures, but never anything as penetrating, as vivid and as intimate as the tales I made up for pleasure, and in which I was always, as is reasonable, the principal character. At the moment when you would have believed me to be fatigued by dragging the weight of a monotonous idleness, I was wearing away my imagination and my heart, subjecting them to passions without object, surmounting obstacles without reality, struggling against perils that were not menacing me; I animated everything, I populated everything, I made every-

---

1 Ginnistan is featured in the allegorical mock-romance *Klingsohrs Märchen* [Klingoshr's Tale] in *Heinrich von Ofderdingen* (1800) by Novalis (Friedrch von Hardenberg).

thing of nothing. There is no state that brings our essence closer to that of divinity.

That lasted for a few months, but I was too avid for emotions, too damaged by sympathies and affections, to be self-sufficient for much longer. That sad genre of sagacity has never tempted me. I only wanted to imprison my inconsiderate expansion in a small sphere, to attach to myself somewhere the gentle bonds of interior life and domestic amity; to possess, to savor my days without squandering them at random, as one does in Paris.

Fortunately, I suddenly remembered that my father had given me a letter for a certain Monsieur Labrousse, whose honest and peaceful household could pass for a phenomenon since it merited being cited even in the province. Monsieur Labrousse was a former wholesale druggist who had made a considerable fortune dealing in mechandise from India. Satisfied with his lot, he had retired from commerce while still in his prime, and he lived as the principal tenant on the first floor of the large and superb house whose façade separates the Rue du Figuier from the Rue des Nonandières. I introduced myself into his home, not without a certain shame, for it was a century since I had arrived, but I had made the decision to admit it candidly and to swallow the just reproaches with resignation.

I was received as if I had disembarked the day before, and the welcome I was given inspired regrets that were doubtless depicted with the eloquence and frankness of sentiment; I had not been there two minutes without experiencing them.

Monsieur Labrousse was a good man of an extreme simplicity; there was nothing in his attitude or his manners that indicated the delicacy of tact, the finesse of calculation and the watchful and meticulous prudence that ought, in my opinion, to characterize a consummate merchant who had become rich, and I concluded immediately that probity can lead to fortune, like the other thing, when it chances to be combined with excellent judgment. I have never known a man who had more of it, and who exercised it on fewer objects. When a question escaped at a tangent from the circle of his habitual and necessary ideas, he was not one of those imperturbable minds who grab it by the mane like a restive horse and do not let go until they have subdued and tamed it. You would not have determined him to follow it, for anything in the world; it suddenly remained as foreign to him as if the conversation had continued in Chinese; but if you reentered, fortuitously or by condescension, into a subject that his position and his affairs had rendered it useful or agreeable to him to study, you were sure of obtaining from him the most luminous, and sometimes the subtlest, solutions for all the difficulties that it could present. He left nothing to desire then in solid instruction, sage indications, precision and common sense. The most intrepid sophist, or the most peevish disputant, would not have found an objection to his judgments.

I will not spare you a portrait. That is my manner of procedure, and I am too old to adopt another. Madame Labrousse was a stout woman, rounded physically and morally, whose immutable serenity was a pleasure to see. One sensed, in looking at her, that she had been happy all her life, and one understood that marvelously; her physiognomy announced, not gaiety exactly, but contentment, the serious gaiety of the soul that is infinitely rarer, and which proves something more than a good situation of fortune and a good disposition of mind—which is to say, a good organization, good health and above all, a good conscience.

Those excellent people, about whom you will forgive me for speaking at such length although they have nothing to do with my story, but whom I love to recall, had three amiable daughters, of that utterly simple and facile amiability that owes nothing at all to education and obtains its source in an essentially benevolent nature. The eldest, who was about thirty years old was called Madame Lambert. She was a widow, and that severe state reflected in her character something grave and serene, which suited her position within the family, where she exercised a full authority by the concession of her parents. She was the true mistress of the house, for Monsieur and Madame Labrousse only figured there in reality as two aged children insouciant by virtue of confidence and taste, who were concluding their lives surrounded by the cares and caresses of the other three.

The third of the daughters was named Claire; she was reaching her seventeenth year, but the ordinary turn of her ideas and her conversation would not have given her more than twelve. Her beauty, which was quite remarkable, resulted above all from the pure and velvety freshness which is to the face what their flowery powder is to fruits and innocence is to the soul; and her mind, which appeared quite lively, owed its greatest charm to a dazed naivety that revealed continually the charming ignorance and curiosity of a child; her purity was so perfect that the most commonplace conversation about the most vulgar things of life was full of objects of astonishment for her. She had the age of modesty, but she had not yet had the savant revelation of it so precocious in women. Hers was an involuntary, irreflective organ like that of the sensitive plant, which recoils timidly at the slightest contact, although it has no reason to fear being injured.

I have not told you anything about the second of the demoiselles Labrousse, who was three years older than the latter, but Heaven is my witness that I have not forgotten her. Angélique—that was her name—did not resemble, by her features, anyone in the family; she did not resemble any other woman, and women that have resembled her are very rare on earth. She had all the generosity of her parents, however, not more sincere and more affectionate, but more expressive and more ardent. Her mind was distinguished by an exquisite finesse of perceptions, her heart by an inexhaustible tenderness of sentiments. She spoke very little, but her gaze, more animated and more eloquent than speech, sympathized like a particular language of the soul with all touching or elevated ideas. That communication of thought, which results from a mute but impotent emotion, and is manifest by I know not what mysterious effusion, was her language. She seemed to be spreading it so naturally around her that it was necessary to be unworthy of understanding her to dare to interrogate her.

Religious imaginations meditative in their faith converse thus with superior intelligences, and it is thus that they understand the sublime voices that vibrate uselessly for coarse or vulgar organs. The ancients, who attached a familiar divinity to every hearth, would have recognized one in Angélique, and you should not suppose me sufficiently maladroit to imagine that the name came to me for the occasion of a tale. That is because it is not a tale that I am telling you; it is because Angélique truly recalled the angel sent from Heaven to watch tenderly over everyone, and there was nothing in her appearance that did not confirm that suggestion: her slender and flexible figure; her noble and gracious features; her grave and soft smile; or her suave accent, as flattering as distant music heard by night.

I would not be astonished, in truth, if that memory still lent some poetry to my expressions, for everything became poetry in Angélique's atmosphere, and I cannot recall my disturbances and my delights of those times without rediscovering a little almost-extinct fire of my youth and my enthusiasm. However, the impression that was engendered most ordinarily by the sight of her and her conversation, and which has made me forget momentarily the modest and unadorned style of a fireside tale, was not joy. On the contrary, she left in the mind a long and vague sadness that one experienced without explaining it. I can scarcely tell you today what it was: an obstinate but confused notion of uncertainty and of the fugitive rapidity of happiness, an obscure but profound doubt, like a presentiment, the indefinable bitterness that corrupts an anxious felicity.

Above all, when she was animated by a sudden inspiration, when a penetrating emotion made her breast palpitate, when her forehead, dazzlingly white, and her pale cheeks were colored like a transparent cloud behind which the sun has passed, when her words trembled and died incomplete on her lips with a faint sound, with the dying murmur of a harp that has finished resonating under the fingers, one felt the cruel anxiety of a traveler gone astray who sees the distant light toward which he was heading disappear. One trembled—dare I say it?—that Angelique might be extinguished. There was so little in her that belonged to our common nature that one might have thought that she was only associated with it by an effort of complaisance and tenderness, while reserving the right to go away at any moment.

If you have slept the slumber in which suspended thought is not yet asleep; if your dubious dream has been flattered then by a cheerful illusion that you would have been glad to prolong, and which you have striven hopelessly to retain the deception ready to vanish; if, in that state, you have prescribed immobility to your limbs and silence to your breath, for fear of waking yourself up and seeing vanish with the enchanting dream that lulls you in fleeing an error a thousand times preferable to all the realities of life, then you are not very far away from comprehending Angélique.

I loved her as it was permissible to love her, like the illusion that escapes the soul, like the dream that one tries in vain to fix. God knows that I never cradled a deceptive hope in her regard, that I never promised myself that I would be able to call her my wife. Her parents decided otherwise. They were much richer than me, but they bore me an esteem and an attachment that redeemed all differences of fortune between us. My frequent visits to the house had gradually rendered me necessary there, and I was no longer designated as anything but "friend Jacques." The sweetness of that new family intimacy had even succeeded in distracting me completely from the passionate appetite that had drawn my childhood toward voyages and adventures.

You can imagine that there was no need to fathom with any great precaution my sentiments for Angélique. I had no reason to dissimulate them from her parents, and I revealed them to them continually by the impulses of a naïve admiration. Why would I have made a mystery of them? It was not a passion, it was a species of worship; but the natural common sense and the cold and serene reason of Monsieur and Madame Labrousse could never arrive at grasping that delicate nuance, perhaps almost imperceptible to more exercised minds, and which sometimes escaped me. They only attributed my timidity to the just reservations imposed upon me by the mediocrity of my patrimony and the poor success of my pretentions with regard to the protectors that I had been promised. They therefore took it upon themselves to make advances with a candor and a generosity whose examples are becoming increasingly rare every day, since the house of the civilized man has replaced the tent of the patriarch.

It seemed to me that I was going mad. My surprise, my intoxication, the disorder that the mere appearance of such an unexpected good fortune cast into my ideas, could only be manifest in tears. Their tears mingled with mine. They were so happy at my joy!

Finally, the moment arrived when that communication, changed into serious formality, had to take place before Angélique herself. I trembled. My heart was hammering precipitately in my breast, as if it were attempting to enlarge or break it; I would have liked not to be there; I would have liked a visit or an unforeseen event to postpone the conference to another occasion; I dared not turn my eyes toward Angélique because I knew that one of her glances would inform me of my fate; but I decided to do it.

She was paler than usual. She seemed to have been plunged in a profound meditation since her family's intentions had been explained to her.

Suddenly, she passed her fingers over her forehead. "Don't talk to me about that," she said, in an assured voice. Then she leaned toward me, and, seizing my hand, which was trembling in hers, she said: "I love Jacques, and if I know what love is, I love him as much as one can love. I would never have made another choice . . . if I had a choice to make. But I shall not marry him. Alas, I shall not marry him!"

I remained silent. I experienced neither confusion, nor despair, nor astonishment. On the contrary, I felt liberated from an importunate anxiety. That state is as difficult, perhaps impossible, to describe as it is to write. Angélique's response was extraordinary, and yet—I don't know why—I had divined it.

"What are you saying?" cried Monsieur Labrousse. "You love him but you won't marry him! What does this strange caprice signify?"

"A caprice?" Angélique replied, with a somber and reflective air. "A caprice, indeed! You can't think anything else. I love him and I won't marry him. My heart is free—or rather, it's his—but I refuse him, I must refuse him, my hand! Oh, that is, I agree, an incomprehensible mystery . . . an illusion or—who knows?—a folly. What if I'm mistaken about the motive, the impulse, that makes me act? What if it were still possible . . . !

"Listen, listen," she continued, excitedly. "No, no, I shan't decide anything! I'm not sure of what I'm saying. I too have need of happiness, hope, a future! I too would like to live! We'll talk about this another day, if we're all still here . . . we'll talk about it three months after the death of Madame Lebrun."

"Three months after the death of Madame Lebrun!" Monsieur Lebrun interrupted, with an abrupt and impatient vivacity that was not natural to his character. "Three months after the death of Madame Lebrun! I'd like to know what Madame Lebrun can have to do with the establishment of my daughters? I have no other interest in whether Madame Lebrun lives or dies than what is suggested to me by Christian charity. Are you being extravagant my child? Who can tell when Madame Lebrun will die? Who can tell if she will die?"

Angélique smiled.

I had heard vague mention of Madame Lebrun, two or three times at the most. She was an extremely old woman who lived on the second floor of the house, in whose home Madame Labrousse and her daughters spent at least one evening per week. Angélique often went there alone, and I remembered having seen her come down with an emotion that her expressive features could not disguise; but that observation had not left any trace in my mind at the time; it suddenly came back to me.

When I perceived that there was no longer anyone there but Monsieur Labrousse, who was squeezing my hand tenderly to substitute by means of that mark of interest for an impossible explanation, I said, sadly: "Who is this Madame Lebrun, then, whose name awakens me from all my dreams? It seems to me, as you've just remarked, that she can have little influence over your affairs, and that you hardly know her?"

"Madame Lebrun?" he replied immediately, probably glad to seize a subject of conversation that would spare him the explosion of my dolor. "Madame Lebrun? In truth, I'd be very embarrassed to say. It's more than thirty-four years—it was in 1706—that I saw her for the first time at the burial of the famous Mademoiselle de Lenclos,[1] and what I can affirm is that she appeared as old then as she does today.

"She had returned from distant voyages, in which she had not been enriched, and it was said that she had arrived one day too late to be able to have a place in the deceased lady's testament, to whose succession it was generally believed that she would have had valid rights, as a relative and as a friend; but I have never attempted to clarify that. Nor do I know what her name was, or rather what name she claimed, for her anterior life is covered by some mystery, the penetration of which she appears very determined not to allow. She married in those days, doubtless for form's sake, with the sole intention of giving herself a status, some unknown Franc-comtois named Monsieur Lebrun, who mingled in affairs and seemed to have succeeded in reestablishing his own. It is not astonishing that at her age, she had found small parts of heritages to collect here and there. So many generations have passed from life to death while she has been on earth!

"Since then I had completely lost sight of her, until one of these recent years, when she came to rent lodgings in this house. Her husband had died long before, and I don't think she knows anyone now except my family, who take pleasure in her conversation, because she is really very curious and very varied, that old woman, who was born with intelligence and who has received an education, having seen a great deal and retained a great deal. What is most certain is that she's a worthy creature, pious charitable, benevolent toward everyone,

1 Anne "Ninon" de Lenclos (1620-1705) acquired a reputation as a courtesan, like Marion Delorme, with whom she was acquainted, but was far more than that, being a writer of considerable merit and an influential salon-hostess. Voltaire's father was her notary and she left money in her will to the young François-Marie Arouet, as he was then, so that he could buy books. The Comte de Saint-Simon insisted that she never had more than one lover at a time, and that she abandoned that lifestyle entirely long before she died.

who pays her rent very exactly, and to whom I would have no reproach to make if I did not imagine that she has troubled, to our misfortune, the head of my poor Angélique with a few reveries to which persons of her age are subject. That, in truth, my dear Jacques, is everything that I know about the history of Madame Lebrun, considered in its natural aspect."

That reticence excited my curiosity keenly.

"In its natural aspect?" I said. "What other is there, if you please?"

"I don't know whether I dare talk to you about it," replied Monsieur Labrousse, looking at me anxiously. "It might diminish greatly the esteem in which you have been kind enough to hold my judgment, if you were able to think that I attach to those follies more importance than you do; but I'll give them to you for what they are worth

"Popular rumor, always borne to think that old age combines with its experienced knowledge of the past some more-or-less clear prescience of the future, has chosen the life of Madame Lebrun for the text of the most bizarre romances. She is, in that sense, a kind of female Wandering Jew who is at rest, and I cannot guarantee that the adventures that are attributed to her have not already been printed in Troyes. Although she is commonly called 'the ivory fay' because of the remarkable appearance that age has given her, and of which it is only possible to form an accurate idea by seeing her, some designate her by the name of the Princess of Egypt, others hold her to be a dethroned queen of China or Japan.

"As she talks quite familiarly of lords and princes of times past, I have known people quite convinced that she had once reigned in France, and some will sustain firmly that she is none other than the unfortunate Mary Stuart, for whom one of her women once rendered her head to the executioner at Fotheringay. All of them agree in conferring on her the gift of divination; that is the least of it; and although she is assuredly not rich, an opinion founded on the expert elegance of her costume, the appearance of a few jewels escaped by chance from her reverses of fortune, and the liberality of her alms—which are, in truth, her principal expenditure, lend her with as much foundation the secret of the philosopher's stone.

"It even seems that she takes pleasure in maintaining these ridiculous suppositions by strange singularities of language, manners and conduct. I'll only cite you one, because we're not far from the moment that is in question here. You've just learned from my mouth that she only has habitual frequentation with us, and yet, at the return of every year, she absents herself regularly for a month, without anyone knowing what becomes of her then. On the first of January, after having been very exact in giving presents to her young friends of a few curious antiquities that she has brought back from foreign lands, she departs, on the stroke of ten o'clock in the evening, accompanied by a very serious chambermaid almost as antiquated as her mistress, from whom no one has ever extracted a word, and who seems to be charged with a large basket appropriate to contain provisions. That departure lasts until the first of February, when she returns at the same hour, healthier, neater and brisker than when she departed.

"The domestics and porters—who are, as you know, an indiscreet species loquacious by nature—have tried several times to find out what she does, in spite of my express prohibitions, but they know no more than we do. They have never found her again after turning the corner of the street, and you can imagine their conjectures well enough."

I did not believe that I had heard anything more extraordinary in my entire life; and the more I reflected on it, the more I sensed a new order of ideas developing, in a way, to the eyes of my intelligence.

"What astonishes me the most," Monsieur Labrousse continued, understanding my silence, "is that the high rationality of my Angélique has been able to be taken in by these illusions, to the point of according them an importance that they do not merit."

"Oh, my friend," I exclaimed, "don't accuse Angélique of error in order to justify our ignorance and our credulity. Who can be sure that the obstacle by which she is frightened is nothing but a reverie? In prolonging the life of his creature on earth, might God have not accorded her, to compensate her for the progressive dissolution of her material being, some prescient anticipation of the future of the soul? Might he not have opened to her in advance the treasures of the unlimited science of good and evil that belongs to him in Heaven, the emanations of which he reserves for the purest? Is it impossible that a deadly fatality, which is perhaps attached to me, might have been partly revealed to a mind almost entirely freed from the vulgar bonds of matter, and that the mysterious soul of Angélique has read more distinctly than me, in the immutable decrees of destiny, a presentment that, vague as it is in my thought, often fills me with terror? Has not Madame Lebrun heard my name pronounced sometimes since I have come close to you, and might it not have resonated in her ear like the rumor of a tragic event? Alas, I have often imagined myself that the divine will reserves a bloody catastrophe for me!"

"Are you mad?" Monsieur Labrousse interrupted, looking at me fixedly. "Has a hitch, to which I hope we shall easily be able to put an end, shaken your judgment. Reassure yourself Jacques. Have courage!"

What I had just said belonged, in fact, to the ungraspable series of sentiments that feed imaginative minds, and to which his own had never paid any heed. Mine was abandoning itself to it entirely for the first time; I felt that the words had escaped me, like the impulse of an interior and spontaneous will, which did not have its source in my ordinary faculties, and which bore to my soul the idea of an intimate but profoundly unknown voice. I wondered in my turn whether my reason had not gone astray.

After a few days my imagination calmed down and my preoccupations dissipated. Angélique did not cease to treat me with tenderness in the presence of her family, and I did not see her otherwise. I thought that I found, more than once, in her speech and in her eyes, the expression of a pure amour; I became almost happy again.

However, the astonishing restriction that she had opposed to her family's wishes, and the information, even more surprising, that I had received from Monsieur Labrousse, made me desire keenly to see Madame Lebrun. That favor, rather difficult to obtain, was solicited by Angélique, to whom Madame Lebrun could not refuse anything, and the day of my visit with Madame Labrousse and her daughters was fixed for the thirty-first of December—which, you will remember, was the eve of the aged neighbor's periodic migration, always followed by a month of absence. As for Monsieur Labrousse, who had rather promptly lost sight of the motives for my impatience and my curiosity, he remained by the fireside in order to play his usual game of tric-trac with the curé of Saint-Paul.

It was eight o'clock in the evening when Madame Lebrun's door opened and I don't know why my heart was beating strangely as I passed over the threshold, as if it were closing on my last hopes as it swung on its hinges, because the perhaps-exalted but conscientious and reflective spiritualism with which I honor myself of having made a continual profession, since it has been given to me to meditate on nature and human destiny, put me far above the superstitious beliefs of the vulgar, who only know what they know poorly, because they know very little. I shivered, however, when I was named.

Madame Lebrun's apartment had nothing, however, that recalled the imposing apparatus of the abode of the sibyls; I judged it to be even simpler than I had expected. There was nothing but old woodwork, clad with the modest decoration of olden days, and furniture that was neat but long out of fashion, among the items of which, scarcely distinguishable by virtue of a richer and more antique physiognomy, were a prie-dieu singularly ornamented by a few sculptures like those Cursinet[1] had made a hundred years before and, next to it, a species of pedestal that bore a beautiful and grandiose casket wrought by Boule père,[2] the employment of which I did not seek to divine. You will not doubt that my gaze was suddenly turned to Madame Lebrun, whom Angélique strove to retain seated, in order to spare her futile and tedious demonstrations of politeness. I precipitated myself toward her in my turn, and succeeded, with some difficulty, in preventing her from quitting her place. I found, on getting up again from that attitude of insistence, the two black and profound eyes of Madame Lebrun fixed on me like iron anchors.

"O my God, my God!" she cried, falling back in her chair and covering her forehead with her hands. "Is it possible that your justice will tolerate that crime once again? Always, always, O my God!"

Then she let her arms fall back on the sides of her armchair as if they were encrusted there, her body fixed and motionless, and her face pensive. Her attention seemed to be so distracted from us that I dared to look at her more carefully, because her eyelids were lowered.

Her attire, of a very ancient taste and an elegant simplicity, only announced the negligence of a woman of high society who liked to maintain her adornment; but I was struck, like the people, by the prestige that had caused her to be nicknamed 'the ivory fay.' She had the same polish as ivory, with the pale blond reflection that time gives it. The blood and

---

1 The interior decorator Cursinet seems to be known entirely by virtue of praise heaped on him by the art historian André Felibien in the early years of the eighteenth century.
2 Presumably the cabinet-maker André-Charles Boulle (1642-1732).

the life had entirely disappeared under the smooth, taut skin, in which only a few inflexible wrinkles were hollowed out here and there, as the implement of a sculptor might have excavated them, and in which were hidden, according to all appearance, the history and dolors of a century.

It would have been difficult to decide, at her aspect, whether the ivory fay had been perfectly beautiful, but I did not doubt for a moment that she had been charming, and my mind, fertile in palingeneses, rejuvenated her thus and was representing her smiling in the midst of all her young woman's graces, when one of her hands suddenly rose up, as if moved by a spring, and slid into my hair in order to bring me closer to her, as if she had suddenly rediscovered me on emerging from a dream.

"Always? Always?" Madame Lebrun repeated. "And it has been said for such a long time that Armand-Jean Duplessis no longer reigns![1] There is, however, no mistaking it," she murmured, in a voice that was becoming increasingly faint, in such a manner as only to be heard by me, and the final articulations of which expired in my ear. "To this one the destiny of the other! Another head for Mataboeuf!"

The impression that those singular words made on me was so vague and so fugitive that I did not take the trouble to search them for a meaning, I was doubtless less astonished because I had entered Madame Lebrun's abode entirely prepared for something extraordinary, and, content to see that

1 Cardinal Armand-Jean du Plessis, Duke de Richelieu (1585-1642) was Louis XIII's chief minister and the reputed power behind his throne. He was also reputed to have had an executioner nicknamed Mataboeuf [Oxslayer]. Richelieu was a counsellor of Henri IV's second wife, Marie de' Medici, who was crowned the day before his assassination in 1610 by François Ravaillac and became regent thereafter, although the two eventually came into conflict. The writers of the Romantic Movement, particularly Alexandre Dumas, made Richelieu a great villain and Henri IV a great hero, but it required a bold conspiracy theorist to suggest that Richelieu had anything to do with Henri's murder.

her emotion had not lasted any longer than mine, I went to retake my seat.

"Mataboeuf!" she repeated, placing her ivory forehead in her ivory hands. "Where have I got that name? What has rendered me those memories? How have they reawakened so powerfully after a century has passed? By what fatality am I condemned to see again what I have seen, as if I were seeing it again?"

Her ideas appeared to be crowding in her mind and running to her lips; and everyone was listening, especially Angélique and me. Mystery has so much power over young soul that a Christian and poetic imagination has nourished with marvels!"

Madame Lebrun continued to reflect, and one of her fingers elevated toward the sky announced that she was about to speak.

"The story that she told us, I will recount to you another time," said Monsieur Cazotte, rising to his feet, "for it seems to me that ten o'clock has chimed, and under the reign of liberty it is more prudent than ever to return home early. And then, my Elisabeth is a daughter to become easily anxious about her aged father. It is said in the *Imitation of Christ* that worry corrodes those who love."

The old page, having been alerted, had risen heavily from his bench. My father showed Monsieur Cazotte out, and I leapt up in order to hang from his hand.

When he had gone, Legouvé made two tours of the room, murmuring in a rather sullen tone: "There is, however, in all that nonsense, the appearance of a dramatic motif."

"I have seen therein," said Marsollier, caressing his ruff, "the intention of two interior scenes well enough indicated, but which would have needed arrangement and style."

*For myself,* I thought silently, *I shall make good use of it one day, and I shall not lose a single one of the details that have struck me, for I shall write it down this very evening.*

"And what if you never hear the rest?" my father said to me, who had divined my design, on seeing me put my hand on his writing desk and his paper.

"Then," I said to him, "my pasticcio will be no more or less finished than the *Quatre Facardins.*"[1]

Four months later, the good Cazotte took his head to the scaffold of the Terror, still young then. Scarcely emerged from the cradle, it devoured old men.

---

1 *Les Quatre Facardins* (1749) by Comte Antoine Hamilton, a humorous Oriental fantasy left unfinished at his death, was belatedy provided by endings by two other writers, including the English Gothic novelist Matthew Gregory Lewis. The longest of the several romances that Nodier published after "Monsieur Cazotte," the pastiche Oriental fantasy "Les Quatre Talismans," might well have been written with Hamilton's model in mind, although it is moralistic in inclination rather than farcical.

# Lydie, or Resurrection

Chamfort wrote somewhere: "At twenty-five, it is necessary that the heart is broken, or made of bronze."

At twenty-five, my heart was broken.

From disgust for the positive life, I had arrived at being horrified by it. All my ideas and all my hopes were attached to the future life, which will be nothing, the materialists say, or which at least remains for us, such as we are, an incomprehensible mystery. All of its darkness was illuminated to my eyes. I penetrated into it as into reality. I sensed, and understood profoundly that God, who could not, in accordance with the immutable rules to which he had submitted his creation, destroy the smallest atom of matter, had not reserved in his omnipotence the power to annihilate the celestial fire of intelligence and amour, which is the most perfect of his works; I therefore believed strongly in the necessity of eternal compensations, apart from the revelation that promises them to us, for I was born in a century of little faith; and that conviction sustained me against all dolors.

Once I had reached that point of philosophy or that degree of illusion, the wounds on my heart gradually scarred over, but I extended all the efforts of my prudence to spare it new ones, by isolating myself as much as I could from my companions in misery. There is nothing that leads more easily to egotism than the lassitude of an embittered sensibility; I had been broken so often in my dearest affections that I made wisdom consist of no longer loving anything, for fear of losing what I loved yet again, and it seemed to me that one could live thus, as if loving and living were not the same thing.

My fortune still permitted me voyages, the mobile and rapid manner of existence that is only composed of fugitive sensations, which bears us through all the attachments of the earth without leaving us time to contract any anywhere. *Life itself is a voyage*, I said to myself, *and it is only in default of varying it by means of everyday transitions that one can be caught by a bond so difficult to dissolve. What regret could trouble the last moment of an insouciant pilgrim who has changed his family and his fatherland ever day, who has not left anyone the memory of his features and his name, who only owes tears to the memories of his childhood and who will not cost the witnesses of his death any tears? To die thus is to pass from one inn to another; it is, at the most, to be out of one's element, and I shall be well accustomed to that.*

What I ought to have said to myself is that to die thus is to die without having lived; that we are on earth in order for us to love, to serve one another reciprocally, to aid one another to bear the burdens of life; that resurrection would be futile to whomever had not accomplished that duty; and that the man who has not loved will scarcely be resuscitated, if it is permissible to express it thus, for we are only summoned to enjoy the benefit of resurrection by benevolence and by virtue. Those new ideas germinated in my heart on the occasion of an event that I shall recount to you.

Perhaps consequent with my theory, I had no titular domestic. One sometimes loves a domestic and might be loved; I changed them as I changed my domicile, or to put it better, my station, and my stations were brief. If I lost by that arrangement the advantages of an assiduous, regular and perhaps affectionate service, I gained more intelligent guides, familiar with the countries through which I was traveling, more learned in the particularities that animated the aspect of places; I traveled better and more fruitfully.

The one that I took on in Geneva to accompany me in the region of Vaud, and who was to quit me in Maetigny, his ordinary residence, was known as Little Lugon, because of the extreme exiguity of his stature, although robust and shapely, which nature had opposed, in one of those games that amuse her, like a capricious miniature to the gigantic proportions of the Alpine world. Little Lugon, in addition, combined all the qualities that make Alpine guides a species apart, a particular type. He was a living history, a biography, a Helvetian statistic, and I agree that it would not have been necessary ask any more of him; he was even better than that, for Little Lugon was fortunately neither savant nor skeptical. All the pleasure of his conversation consisted of a naïve good faith, which did not have in view either the hope of teaching or the retention of informing. He knew the names of things and the dates of events, but his modest intelligence had never striven to go back to the causes of any effects or to anticipate the effects of any causes; he said what he knew and believed what he said; that is the way I like erudition to be.

When an unexpected question surprised him in the middle of his narrations and transported him from the realities of positive life into the conjectural world of the imagination and metaphysics, he usually got out of the embarrassment by means of the exclamation that the benefit of a favored organization has informed the people of the Orient, but which fortunately belongs in all lands to the language of sensate men: "God is great!" said Lugon, and I challenge all the philosophers of earth to find a more reasonable solution to most of the difficulties that the sciences present. I do not doubt that the *Encyclopédie* will be recommenced one day under that inspiration, and there will then be means to make a good book of it—which is to say, something other than it is today—but Lugon had no thought of recommencing the *Encyclopédie*; he had never heard mention of it.

We departed from Vevey in the afternoon of a beautiful spring day, to go and visit, for want of the boscage of Clarens,[1] which did not exist and about which I scarcely cared, the Château de Chillon, about which I did not care at all.[2] Travelers imagine, wrongly, that it is good to see what other travelers have come to see before them, and that is almost always what does not merit being seen.

We were walking side by side under the shade of the road, without hastening the pace of our horses, when Lugon broke the silence in order to speak aloud of his own accord:

"That's George's house," he said, "but Lydie is no longer there. The poor creature has taken advantage of the good weather to make up a bouquet of wild flowers for George, in the wretched corner of land that she calls her garden."

We were, in fact, passing at that moment a pretty white house, closed by a green door and shutters, the entire aspect of which gave rise to an agreeable idea of calm, ease and cleanliness.

"George's house?" I said, immediately. "And who is George?"

"Oh, George," replied Little Lugon, "is Lydie's husband."

"Very good, but may I not know who Lydie is?"

"Lydie, Monsieur," replied Lugon, coldly, either because he paid no heed to the monotony of the vicious circle or because he wanted to excite my curiosity, "is George's wife."

---

1 Clarens and its boscage are celebrated in the classic love story usually known as *La Nouvelle Héloïse* (1761) by Jean-Jacques Rousseau.

2 The former prison of the Château de Chillon became a popular tourist destination—almost an object of pilgrimage—for the writers of the Romantic Movement, including Lord Byron, Victor Hugo, Alexandre Dumas and Gustave Flaubert. Nodier's claim that he did not care about it at all is a slightly perverse but typical distancing move.

"Good!" I cried, constraining my impatience, "But may I not know, once and for all, who Lydie and George are, and in what regard they have the good fortune of interesing you?"

"Lydie and George," he said, drawing his mount closer to mine and placing his hand familiarly on my saddle-bow, "that's a story."

"Tell me the story, for I have nothing better to do than hear it recounted."

We made out horses match strides. Little Lugon collected himself momentarily; he passed his fingers slowly over his forehead, as if to reestablish the order of his memories, then raised his head again with assurance, and commenced thus:

"So, George and Lydie were husband and wife, as you know, and a better matched couple in every respect was never seen, for there was no one better looking than George, except perhaps Lydie, and no one better than Lydie, except perhaps George. It was supposed that they weren't well-furnished with money when they arrived in the region four or five years ago, because they went to lodge with Mère Zurich, who then occupied a poor cottage on the hill, above those vines; and I could still show it to you if the little orchard that borders it hadn't grown so bushy now; but there would be no point, since she has given it to one of her neighbors who was poorer than her. She's a very worthy woman!

"A few days later, George came down to the shore and put himself at the service of the boatmen and the fishermen. As he was vigorous, adroit, sober, cordial and good looking, he soon had more to do on his own than all the oarsmen on the lake, but he didn't abuse his advantages, and it was known thereafter that if one of his companions had a bad day, George never failed to give him a share of his benefits, so that everyone liked him because of his generosity. What is rarer, the more he increased his petty fortune, the less jealousy he caused. It's perhaps the only time that has happened.

"You'll understand that he soon had his own boats and nets, and it was at that time, in order to put himself more easily in reach of the lake, that he bought the pretty little house that I showed you just now. It's true that it wasn't dear then, and that it's by dint of hard work and economies that he embellished it year after year. What determined him above all to quit his wretched redoubt was the death of a child he lost up there; his wife could no longer live in a place that reminded her continually of her grief, but they brought Mère Zurich with them. She had cared for the child, Mère Zurich, she had loved him; Lydie often looked at her, weeping, and they wept together. As for Lydie, she was scarcely seen except on Sunday, when she went to hear mass at the Catholic chapel, or on feast days, when she crossed the lake to go and make her devotions at Saint-Gengoux. That, Monsieur, is who George and Lydie are."

"Thank you, Lugon," I said, making a movement to urge my horse to a trot. "The benediction of God couldn't descend on a more honest house. But that isn't a story,"

"God is great," said Lugon. "It's not the whole story."

I tightened the bridle and I waited.

"As George wasn't from the region," Lugon continued, "people wondered about the place where he might have come from, and they told one another what they learned from strangers; for Monsieur isn't unaware that there's no country in the world that more travelers pass through than the canton of Vaud.

"George was born of an honest but very rich family in a seaport in France; I don't remember whether it was Strasbourg or Perpignan,[1] but I'm sure that it must be in the direction of England. His father was an owner of merchant ships, an associate in his enterprise with Lydie's father, with whom he had agreed a long time ago that they would marry the two

---

1 Lugon's geography is clearly unreliable.

children when they came of age. The poor children loved one another tenderly, and their fortunes were so perfectly equal that there was not a word to be said against the suitability. But man proposes and God disposes. A tempest, a bankruptcy and a pirate took everything.

"The two friends died of chagrin within a few days of one another, and the lovers remained so sad, so poor and so abandoned that there was no longer any question of their betrothal. George, who had been brought up for a useless métier, like that of député, author or advocate, felt that he had soul and courage. He went to work on the port, and earned his living bravely by carrying burdens, like a simple man of the people, because he was strong, as I've already told you, and because he wasn't proud. His former study companions were disdainful of him, but he didn't care about them.

"One day, he was occupied in unloading a vessel, and when he asked where he ought to take the bales he was given his father's old address. It was the only one of the ship-owner's buildings that had escaped the accident in which all the others had perished. 'That's all right,' said George. 'My father had the confidence of a lot of businessmen whose fortunes were shaken by his misfortune, and this compensates them.' So he paid his father's debts honorably, only keeping for himself the little that it pleased the creditors to leave him, after which he returned to work as before. His conduct was remarked, although it was natural, because men gladly esteem honesty even when they don't practice it.

"It's necessary to tell you, Monsieur, that George had an uncle of a great age, who wasn't married and who was very opulent, for he had taken part in the commercial affairs of George's father while they were sure, and had got out in time when they became dubious. George's uncle summoned him, and the people who reported these details to us claimed that he spoke to him like this:

"'I've heard good things on your account, Monsieur. Although your mother, who was my sister, never engaged her wealth in her husband's enterprises, because I was able to dissuade her from doing so, and you had much more to demand than hazard has rendered you, you've had the pride to pay all the creditors, as if it were your responsibility, to satisfy I know not what stupid duty of exactitude and probity for which no one held you to account. It isn't with similar politenesses that one makes a good business, but that fault only concerns you and I wouldn't care about it if I hadn't heard that you were obliged to live on the work of your hands to remedy your insensate prodigalties. You haven't even perceived that your poverty might do me harm, in a town were I'm reputed inappropriately to be rich. Do you know, Monsieur, that no other man of the blood from which you emerge has ever taken it into his head to work for the public, and that the tools of an artisan or the hooks of a porter are an eternal shame to your family?'

"'Alas, Monsieur,' said George, 'it didn't seem to me that my conduct could have such consequences. I regarded labor as the sole honest resource of those who have nothing, and you'll permit me to follow that opinion in the practical employment of my life, nothing proving to me thus far that it isn't worthy of a brave man and a Christian. I can understand more easily, however, that my unmerited indigence humiliates the pride of an honorable family, and I'll spare it without regret the shame it has received, by transporting the exercise of my obscure industry far from here. I've been thinking about it for a long time, and if I haven't executed that project sooner, it's because I needed time to amass a few economies that were very slow to accumulate in the métier that I've embraced. From now on, since you wish it, you can be assured that I'll no longer afflict you with the sight of me and the spectacle of my poverty. I'm ready to leave,'

"'Very good,' said the old man frowning. 'One could decide you to leave the city, then, by furnishing you with a few expenses for the journey? It'll be very little, I warn you, Money is so rare!'

"'No, no, Monsieur,' cried George with an indignation that he hastened to contain. 'I can quit the city, and I shall; the savings I proposed to make, I've made. One spends very little when one isn't rich enough to give. I don't want any money. Since I've been working, I've never had any need of it.'

"At those words, the old millionaire's forehead cleared slightly. 'Listen,' he said to George, in a milder tone, 'you're my nephew, the blood of my blood, the son of my dear sister . . . yes, dear, I can say that! We were very fond of one another in our childhood. One has a tender heart when one is young. It's experience that teaches us the reality of things and raises our minds to the knowledge of positive verities; but in the end, I'm your uncle, your good uncle, and I'd like nothing better than to do you good if I could. It's true that I pass for rich, but that's because no one knows my business, and anyway, taxes take it all.

"'What would you say, however, if I wanted to ensure your happiness—which is to say, your fortune? It's not that I'm thinking of letting go of my petty properties—God preserve me!—prudence forbids it, and because of the vicissitudes of time, which runs away, sage people keep what they have; but you're my only natural heir, and without reducing myself to indigence I can guarantee you an honorable part of my succession if you marry to my liking; for I'm your good uncle, my poor George, and I only have your future wellbeing in view. It's necessary to resolve oneself to some sacrifice for one's relatives. The wife that I destine for you is the widow of one of your father's creditors, a woman of order and intelligence, who has placed all the money that you have rendered to her at twelve per cent interest in superb securities that are worth triple and probably won't be withdrawn because she didn't lend them long term. You'll therefore be rich after my death and you can sustain our family's name worthily by living economically—but I'll explain that later. Go, then, to prepare everything to put yourself in a state to receive my benefits and we'll dine tomorrow with your future . . . in her home.'

"'Thank you, my dear uncle,' said George, 'for the projects you have formed to render me happy, and I beg you to believe in the gratitude that your bounty inspires in me; but it's impossible for me to collect the fruit of them. You're not unaware that before my father's death I was ready to marry Lydie, the daughter of his friend, and the misfortune that has struck us both at the same time has only rendered that engagement more inviolable. Two sacred wishes accorded in uniting us, and poverty has not separated us.'

"'You're going to marry Lydie, a daughter of nothing who has nothing!' cried the furious uncle.

'I have just informed you of it,' replied George. And he retired respectfully, for the old man's anger was manifest all the more in imprecations, and George feared being accursed.

"A week later, they did, in fact, marry, and they departed immediately, George having promised to quit the city in order not to make the honest people who bore his name blush at his debasement.

"George's uncle, whose age wasn't extremely advanced, but whom the love of gold had corroded with avarice and care, died a few weeks later, and as he was a philanthropist—a new métier that brings in a great deal—he left all his fortune to mutual education, which is the most beautiful invention of which mention has ever been made; it's a manner of knowing everything without learning, and studying without masters.[1]

_______________

1 Nodier's antipathy to the "Jacotot method" of "educational emancipation," often mentioned sarcastically in his narratives, might stem from the fact that he was subjected to it for some while as a child, but that is conjecture.

God is great! As for poor George, he prayed for his uncle as if he had inherited, but wasn't unduly afflicted by his abandonment and he worked courageously until death."

"George is dead, then?" I interrupted, squeezing Lugon's arm sharply.

"I thought I'd already told you that," he continued. "It was the sixth of October last autumn. It will be exactly eight months at Corpus Christi. George was coming back cheerfully in his boat, after having finished his day, when his eyes were suddenly struck by the sight of a cloud of fire and smoke that the wind was pushing over the lake. He immediately thought of a terrible accident and rowed hard in order to reach that little cape on the strand, which is now called Lydie's Garden.

"A fire was, in fact, devouring the house that occupied the other side of the road, the ruins of which I'll show you in a little while. He scarcely took the time to moor his boat, seized a ladder that a few old men were dragging along painfully—for the workers hadn't yet returned—and applied it under a window from which he could hear screams coming.

"An instant later he had launched himself into the flames and he reappeared with an unconscious woman, whom I received in my arms, for I'd arrived at almost the same moment, and I tried to follow him. 'She's saved! She's saved!' cried the people. But the poor creature, who had recovered consciousness in the open air, started uttering frightful moans and calling for her children.

"I had got as close to the window as I could, but I was trying in vain to hang on to something, because it was all burning, when I felt George pass me another burden, and then a third; they were the children, whom I had the great pleasure of hearing cry out, and who were passed from hand to hand to their mother; but the unfortunate woman was still lamenting, and I could no longer understand her plaints, the flames roaring in my ears like a tempest. 'The cradle! The cradle!' repeated a few voices that drew nearer and nearer to me, because they had established a chain from the edge of the lake to the ladder I'd climbed. 'The cradle! The cradle!' I shouted in my turn, in a voice almost stifled by the smoke that was suffocating me.

George went in again, and I thought for sure that he wouldn't come back. At that moment the fire had reached the uprights of the ladder and the upper rung, in such a manner that they all gave way at once, without excepting the one on which I was standing. The crowd that was pressing behind me retained me on the next rung, and the ladder leaned by its own weight against the burning wall, which was already ripped by fissures deep enough for me to be able to retain myself, but the distance that separated me from the window had increased by six feet. George measured it with a glance, swiftly took off his boatman's belt and passed it in the blink of an eye around the poor innocent that he'd taken from the cradle. 'To you, Lugon,' he shouted, 'and be careful. The child's alive! He's saved too!'

"The child was alive, in fact, he was saved, but George was lost; he was dead. Scarcely had the poor little creature emerged from my arms than the roof collapsed on the ceiling, the ceiling collapsed on George, and everything was engulfed in a horrible furnace, from which George's remains haven't been recovered. They must have been consumed entirely, or the angels carried them to Heaven. God is great!"

"Good!" I said to Lugon, linking my hand tenderly with his. "Good, my noble friend . . . but afterwards?"

"Afterwards?" said Lugon. "Oh, the children are doing marvelously, and you'd already have seen them if they weren't playing in the willow grove."

"But Lydie, you aren't telling me anything about her? Is Lydie dead too?"

"To speak to you sincerely, Monsieur, there are people who think that it would be better if she were dead. She went mad a few days later, of a strange madness. Doesn't she imagine that she's half resuscitated, and that she spends every night with George, in I don't know what corner of Heaven? Nothing can get that idea out of her mind . . ."

As he was saying that, Lugon suddenly stopped. "Look, Monsieur," he added, drawing closer to the hedge that protected the right side of the road. "There's Lydie's Garden, and that young woman walking there, with her eyes inclined toward the ground, looking for flowers, is Lydie, poor George's wife!"

He turned his horse abruptly thereafter, passed the back of his hand over his eyes, and seemed disposed to resume the agreed route.

I had dismounted.

"Wait for me here, my good friend," I said to him. "Let your horses rest in the shade of that linden tree. It's necessary that I see Lydie and speak to her."

"Don't do that Monsieur," said Lugon, trying to retain me by the arm. "The physician says that madness is sometimes contagious, and Lydie's is of that species. It must be true, since Mère Zurich believes firmly in everything that Lydie tells her."

"Can a man as sane as you," I replied, laughing, "abandon himself to such chimeras? Physicians exercise an empire over our credulity by distinguishing themselves abundantly with extraordinary propositions and false discoveries. Be tranquil on my account; I'm perfectly shielded from contagion by the ideas of a madwoman, and if that unfortunate has no consolation to received from me, at least I have nothing to fear from her."

At the same time, I reached the other side of the hedge, while Lugon, somewhat reassured, moved into the shade, whistling.

Lydie had not paid any heed to me. Her basket was full, and she had sat down in order to arrange her bouquets.

I arrived on the edge of the lake, collecting a few small flowers from the shore in order to attract Lydie's attention. "Don't be afflicted," I said, presenting them to her, "if I permit myself to glean in your harvest. Although these flowers are fresher and prettier than those I've seen in my travels, my intention is not to take them with me, and I've only assembled them in order to add them to your bouquet."

"Ah!" she said, looking at me with a smile and depositing them one by one the basket where she had amassed the others. "It's for George. He has some that are far more beautiful, and which have perfumes of which no flowers on earth can give an idea, but he likes to see again the flowers that grow on the edge of the lake, which we once picked together."

"He won't be long in coming back?" I said, sitting down a few paces away.

"Not here," she said. "He no longer comes here. He can't come here, since he's dead. Didn't you know that he's dead?"

My heart was constricted. "Pardon me, poor Lydie," I replied, "I thought you were waiting for him."

"Oh no," she cried, "it's him who is waiting for me; but I'll go soon, in a little while, when the sun has set. Oh, if one could sleep forever!"

"Your sleep is sweet, Lydie, since you desire the hour that returns it. In the meantime, at least, you're not suffering?"

"Suffering!" she said, drawing closer to me. "Who is suffering? I never suffer, never; during the day I hope and I wait. I sometimes find the days long, but I abridge them with prayer, collecting flowers for George, thinking about him, forming projects for our long happiness, which nothing will be able to trouble when we're united entirely."

"And at night, Lydie, the night that you prefer to the day?"

"Oh, at night, we're together. Haven't I told you that? It seems to me, in fact, that I haven't seen you for a long time, but I'll tell you all about it, if you want."

"The story would interest me greatly, if it wouldn't fatigue you, but . . ."

She took my hand in one of hers and passed the other over her forehead, as if to search there for a memory. Then she remained silent momentarily, while her ideas succeeded one another and were connected; at the same time, her physiognomy took on a more animated expression and her eyes lit up with a supernatural inspiration.

"You doubtless haven't forgotten the day of the fire," she said. "No one has forgotten it. It was frightful, wasn't it? The fire died down, however; the children were saved; their mother was happy. Everyone was reunited; there was only George who didn't come back. I don't know whether someone told me the reason or whether I divined it. George was dead, and at that time I regarded death as a serious thing, like an eternal separation. I thought that between George and me it was finished for eternity, and I regretted that my grief couldn't annihilate me right away.

"It seemed to me that I hadn't loved him enough, since I'd survived him; but I reassured myself by thinking that despair was perhaps a malady similar to others; that it required periods and crises, like fever, that it didn't kill like a dagger. It would be too gentle, I thought, to die of a first attack, to die almost without suffering, when George had suffered so much; but I hoped, however, at the convulsions of my heart, ready to break, that I wouldn't suffer for long. I lived like that for I don't know how long, without moving, without speaking, without eating, without sleeping, but agitated in my mind by singular illusions.

"The preoccupation of the fire pursued me. From time to time I felt its ardent vapor flowing around me like a torrent; it stifled my respiration, it burned my hair and my eyelids, and when I tried to fix my desiccated eyes around me, I saw the flames that were reaching all the exits, which were elongating, folding back, rounding out, withdrawing in order to come back, like tongues of fire licking a pyre before consuming it, and I said to myself: *That's good, I'm dying with George. Why did they want to make me believe that he had died without me?*

"Sometimes, I heard loud voices shouting next to my ear: 'Courage, courage, he's saved! See how the beams have crossed over miraculously over his head and have preserved him, like a vault!'

"'He's saved!' repeated the little girls from neighboring villages who were coming back from grape-picking, and they jumped about.

"For myself, I tried to extract an inarticulate cry from the depths of my breast, to ask who had saved him. 'It's me, it's me,' George repeated, 'Can't you hear me?'

"I could hear him very well, and I couldn't be happy enough, for his breath had brushed my cheek; but at the moment when I thought I could grasp him, I perceived that my hand had fallen into the hand of a pale, sad man who was looking at me with dry and severe eyes. 'Perhaps she won't die,' he said, 'but her reason is alienated; she's mad.'"

At that point, Lydie stopped momentarily in order to collect herself again, and then she repeated her phrase at the word where she had left it, apparently drawn by an unexpected order of ideas, but without losing the link. "Mad?" she said. "What is it, then, to be mad? Madness is the state of a mind that abandons itself without consequence and without rules to all the chimeras by which it is struck . . . a truly happy state, the happiest of all, after death, and the only one that it is permitted to the wretched to envy, since it's a crime to want to die. I wasn't mad, me! I didn't forget anything! I didn't imagine anything that wasn't true! I knew that George was dead, I knew that I was alone, I knew that he wouldn't come back. I would have liked to be mad, but I couldn't. I had more reason than I needed to comprehend my misfortune, and I understood it too well to distract myself from it.

"I said to myself: 'That horrible squeezing of the heart that I'm experiencing, it's necessary that it lasts until it breaks my heart. That anguish in which I'm dying, it's necessary that I submit to it, as long as I haven't finished dying. But dying is so easy,' I added then—forgive my despair, as God has pardoned me. 'That young woman that George pulled out of the lake not long ago, and they had so much trouble returning to life, she was no longer living, she was no longer feeling, she had no more love, no more regrets. No more pain! Another minute and she would have been at rest, poor creature, for all eternity. The repose that she found so quickly, what prevents me from obtaining and savoring like her? There's a lake so close to here, and the waters are so deep!'

"You can imagine, my friend, that that resolution had come to me because I wasn't thinking about God. Alas, I was only thinking about George! And yet, it calmed me down. I was tranquil, with the hope of soon being tranquil. I opened my eyes to see whether it was dark, for my plan could only be carried out in obscurity. The sun hadn't set entirely, but facing me, its last reflections were already dying away in the mountains. I listened, and I heard the horns of the herdsmen calling the animals back to the sheds. The twilight mosquitoes were finishing buzzing in the windows. My turtle-dove was hiding its head under its wing. I said: 'Soon,' and I felt almost well."

At that point in her story, Lydie interrupted herself again for a moment; she sighed softly, like a traveler drawing breath after a difficult journey, who is measuring with security, on a gentle slope, the rest of his way. Eventually, she continued.

"It was more than a hundred hours," she said, "that I hadn't slept, and whatever effort I made to remain attentive at the arrival of the darkness, from which I expected my deliverance, I couldn't help my eyelids closing. All the objects disappeared together, all my ideas vanished in I don't know what confused sentiment of existence, which hardly differs from death because it's calm and almost as insensible. Only there was still a vague noise around me, melodious and soft, like that of a little evening breeze expiring in the reeds, or that of the last wave that touches the shore.

"The night whose commencement I had just been awaiting with so much impatience appeared to be whitening already with the light of morning—or, rather, a light that wasn't that of day, and wasn't that of fire, gradually penetrated the transparent obscurity. As it increased gradually, I fixed an instinctive attention on the phenomenon, completely disengaged from all the preoccupations of my mind.

"I no longer had any memories, nor sentiments, and no more soul. I only had eyes. The light was still becoming brighter, and yet it inundated my eyelids without fatiguing them. I wondered vaguely how mortal organs could support being dazzled by it. Suddenly, as if my senses had woken up one after another, I thought I heard a rustle of wings that were agitating in that marvelous atmosphere, and it seemed that the noise was proceeding from a point more luminous than the rest, which was precipitated toward me from the full height of the sky, growing, developing in its fall, acquiring form and color as it approached. They were wings, in fact, wings with golden feathers, the vibration of which was more charming to the ear that all the harmonies of earth, and the angel or the god that they were about to render to my amour, you'll understand very well, was George. But in the ecstasy into which so much happiness had plunged me, I was no more capable of divining than of seeing.

"Already, his wings were rounding out above me, his arms were enveloping me in a gentle embrace. His lips were wandering from my mouth to my forehead and my eyes, the curls of his hair were floating alongside mine. 'Come with me,' he said. 'Confide yourself without dread to your brother and your beloved friend. This earth is no longer our earth; this abode is no longer our abode.'

"And we rose up at the same moment with a rapidity so marvelous that the limit of the nocturnal darkness had already been passed while I was still wondering where we were going. It was as if we were plunging into an ocean without a bed and without a shore, into the eternal ether, which never has night, and which all the stars in space illuminate with their light. Our world, which I sought with my gaze without regretting it, was no longer anything but a pale planet that scarcely whitened the black veils of the firmament with a patch ready to disappear. The sun didn't take long to be extinguished in its turn, while a new sun came to appear at the horizon, which seemed to precipitate toward us, incessantly augmenting in grandeur and brightness, and then disappeared into the depths of that infinity, where so many suns are hidden.

"A moment later, so much had our flight hastened, doubtless, as we approached our goal, those innumerable stars were passing before my eyes with lightning promptitude, like the fiery stars that one sees crossing the sky during the calm nights of a beautiful autumn. My astonished senses were insufficient to the spectacle of those turbulences, which fled from my route, and the marvelous harmony of which I sometimes thought I could seize in passing.

"Soon the movement of George's wings slowed down; they were deployed in their full extent, similar to the wings of a soaring eagle, but almost motionless in appearance, striking the air gently with their extremities at equal intervals. The last sun that had illuminated me was no longer running after the others like a meteor about to vanish; it remained fixed in the sky, but larger, more radiant, and yet milder than ours, for I could easily support its splendor and my gaze affirmed, drawing a new force therefrom. An instant later, fresh breezes, the caressant breaths of an unknown atmosphere commenced to play in my hair; I thought I heard a distant noise, in which the most gracious of earthly sounds were mingled: the murmur of branches quivering in the wind, the chirping of recently-hatched birds leaning over the edge of the nest, about to attempt flight; the eternal sigh of the lake, feebly agitated, whose little waves are coming to die among the reeds.

"The horizon, limitless a little while ago, was approaching and gradually closing. The mountains, whose summits had appeared to me at first to be similar to floating islands that bathed in an immense sea, grew alongside me under their robes of shade, verdure and flowers, for they had nothing of the austerity of our icy and granitic Alps. An instant more, and the crowns of gigantic trees lowered their flexible fronds around us, then raised them flexibly to crown us with an awning dappled with bouquets and fruits, in which colors shone, and they exhaled perfumes of which our mortal organs cannot dream.

"George finally deposited me on a bed of embalmed grass, furled his wings and let himself fall beside me, like a golden butterfly settling. Then he passed his arm under my head, imprinted a kiss on my forehead and, his attentive eyes on mine, he gazed at me, smiling while he waited for me to speak.

"'Oh, how happy I am,' I said to him, 'since I'm here with you. But won't you tell me where we are?'

"'In the world of the resuscitated,' George replied, 'in the place where fortunate souls come to take other forms and undergo further proofs, longer but less rigorous than the first, in order to render us worthy of one day appearing before God.'

"'What!' I cried. 'Is this not yet the Lord's celestial garden, which was promised to us by the faith of our fathers, and in which the unalterable happiness of the just commences, never to finish?'

At those words, George adopted a graver attitude, a more serious expression of physiognomy, like a man who has solemn things to reveal, and I felt his gaze filling me with a tender respect, for, through the sweet complaisance of amour, the majesty of a superior nature could be seen shining there.

"'Do you think,' he replied, 'that there has ever existed, among the creatures most favored by the graces of the Omnipotent, a soul chaste enough and pure enough to present itself with security before its master, at the moment when it abandons our life of opprobrium and sin. Your heart is too well inspired to have conceived that presumptuous hope. You have too often experienced yourself, in your naïve and modest conscience, that, on the contrary, the sentiment of our unworthiness is augmented with every step that it is permitted to us to take on the road to perfection, and you're not unaware that that idea is an assiduous subject of alarm for those who love God, since it frightens the uncertainty of salvation to the extent of the agony of the saints. The pride of philosophers and scholars has recoiled before that abyss; they have not dared to seek in their theories the means of filling it in. They would rather leave a limitless void in creation than admit unknown intermediaries between its author and humans, and that is why they have invented the most impossible of hypotheses, eternal death and oblivion.

"'Nothing dies, dear Lydie, and nothing can die; but everything changes form and is always being modified, until the spirit returns to spirit and matter to matter. The world to which I have brought you, although incomparably better than ours, is only one of the rungs of the immense ladder that incessantly brings us nearer to the eternal abode, the possession of which has been promised to us by the divine words of Christ. Here must be accomplished, for the chosen souls who have practiced his precept of love, the thousand year reign, the mystery of which occupied the theologians of earth for such a long time—in vain, because the explanation of it was hidden in the mysteries of death. That explanation, I know that you will not ask of me, because you have faith in my words and I could not give it to you, because the organs that could transmit it to your intelligence do not belong to the living.'

"'Great God!' I said, fearfully, 'am I not dead and resuscitated? Will it be necessary to quit you again?'

"'Calm yourself, my beloved,' George replied, smiling. 'We shall never be separated for as long henceforth as we were on earth, and that separation will not have the ennuis and uncertainties of the other. Every morning, then, after the kiss of adieu, I went to deliver my boat to the doubts of the mist and the squalls of the lake, to the hazards of a navigation that was not without perils. Now, it is you who are traveling, and I am sure of your return. It's me whom you'll allow to wait for you, and you're sure of finding me again. If we were happy, when we had a few years to live thus, how can we not be now, when the bounty of God measures us so many centuries? And that's not all, if you remember. Such a sad sentiment was mingled with our joy! It only required an accident to trouble it; it only required death to destroy it. We did not know what death is, but we know today that the only wealth that it could take from us then, it alone can give to us.'

"'It's for that reason, then,' I cried, pressing him to my heart, 'that I hoped for it with such a keen impatience! Oh, if you had not come so soon, it was me who would have arrived; more sudden than me, because your soul is worth more than mine, you have only anticipated my resolution.'

"'Stop!' George interrupted, looking at me with a tender gaze. 'If you had accomplished that fatal resolution, it would have been forever. The centuries, in their eternal succession, might never have reunited us. The soul enlightened by the clarity of faith, which despairs of God in order to embrace annihilation, becomes unworthy of all the graces of the creator, and if annihilation is possible, it's for the suicide that it is made. The suicide has broken the ban and violated the law of misery and resignation imposed upon him; he will doubtless vegetate, solitary and sad, in the obscure limbo of an unknown world until the day when the expiations of his repentance have satisfied divine justice.

"'Fortunately for us, the criminal project that you embraced was only an illusion of delirium. By means of a marvelous sense that is given to us, and which associates us with all the impressions of the cherished beings that we have left on earth. I was following with terror the chain of your thoughts when a sudden revelation told me that you were saved, because intelligence had been withdrawn from you. You were rendered to me, even in time, for such is the privilege of pure souls that God has reserved, and whose reason has suddenly been troubled by dolor. Your days seem to belong to dreams that had led you astray; your sleep elevates you to the possession of the truth, which escapes the impotent efforts of sages. The memories that you will; transport to the earth, when the moment of awakening extracts you from my arms, will make you an object of derision or pity for humans, but you alone will know the future destiny of humanity, which living men will never know Your body is enchained, I do not know for how long, by the vulgar bonds of life, but your soul is summoned in advance to savor immortality. Support with resignation, then, the ennuis of that momentary prison, the door of which will open every evening to the immense space of eternal liberty.'

"'I have understood everything,' I replied, 'and my soul, humiliated before the grandeur of God, submits with gratitude to all his will; but since it is permitted for me to see you in the moments of apparent death or anticipated reparation that God has give us for the relief of our dolors, shall I not also see my daughter, my sweet and pretty little girl? She cannot inhabit any other world than the one we are in, for what can the resurrection of mothers serve if they do not rediscover their children? The innocent heart of that poor angel was not yet open to sin, and God could not have refused the most lovable of his creatures a happiness to which even virtue has less right than innocence . . . but why are you not replying to me, and why has a tear come to moisten your eyes, at the very moment when you are trying to console me with a smile? Has God wanted to keep my little girl for himself?'

"'All beings are his,' he cried, 'and he possesses them everywhere. But God is incapable of deceiving the tenderness that he has deposited in your heart himself. Only, wiser than you are in the impatience of your love, he delays the resurrection of children until the moment when they can awaken, as if after a pleasant slumber, suspended from the bosom that has nourished them. Our little daughter is not returned to you yet, because you are not yet resuscitated, but on the day when you are reborn in my arms, however many years remain to you—for old age is only for that new life the brief twilight of a beautiful day that ends in endless daylight—at that moment of glory and happiness that can no longer escape our hope, you will see the cherished child blossom in the first of our embraces, and share her innocent caresses with us as if she had never quit us.

"'Between now and then she will continue to sleep peacefully in her little shroud, as in the sheets of her cradle, unless God sometimes admits those ingenuous souls to celestial visions of which even the resuscitated do not have the secret. Patience is one of the greatest efforts of our nature, so long as it is only supported by resignation; but it becomes easy when it is supported by faith. The day when your daughter will wake up is so close to us in the succession of days that you would be reluctant to awaken her yourself and extract her from her dreams if she were asleep on your knees. And what does it matter how long she sleeps, since she will not grow old? Seek to triumph, my Lydie, over these vain anxieties of the living, which I cannot dissipate entirely, because only death can give you the intelligent and pure senses that you lack in order to understand me. Content yourself with enjoying the aspect of the benefits that God lavishes upon us, and the certain hope of those he has promised us. Think that the hours are going by, and that we have as many hours to be separate as hours to be together. Don't go away today without having visited your domains and your gardens.'

"While speaking thus, George lifted me gently from the green carpet on which we were sitting, and drew me from one surprise to another through the delightful boscage, the marvels of which were renewed at every step, for they have the strangeness and sublimity that creation delivers to all the luxury of its divine fantasies, not being restricted anywhere to the uniform reproduction of species. Every tree, every stem, every blade of grass has its deportment, its figure and its nuance there; every flower is distinguished from all the others by its color and its perfume, but that does not exclude the privilege with which a sensitive soul can endow a beloved flower, for the slightest care suffices to perpetuate it by cultivation. I loved the columbines there, the forget-me-nots, violets and roses, so much that one might have thought that everything that has inspired a sentiment or brought a consolation to the human heart has become capable of resuscitating with it.

"The fecund and varied magnificence that God manifests here in his works of predilection, bursts forth there in the most obscure and most neglected works, if it is permitted to think and say that he has neglected anything. The grain of sand that rolls under the foot would put the rubies and sapphires of royal crowns to shame. The dust that floats in atoms in a ray of sunlight has all the splendor of diamond sparks. The streams flow over nacreous sand more brilliant, more transparent and richer in reflections than opal, and there is not one of their little waves that does not cradle all the colors of light at its surface, like a prism or a rainbow. But what can those vain comparisons tell you, my friend? What are rubies and sapphires? What are opal and diamond? What is the rainbow itself in the inexhaustible treasure of the Lord's creations?

"Bewildered by astonishment and admiration, I would not have been able to turn my eyes away from the miracles that struck my eyes in all directions, if the impressions I experienced had not all been united in George himself, who appeared to me to be the king of those celestial solitudes, and in whom I remarked, strangely, a solemn character of beauty that had almost escaped me on earth. 'O my beloved,' I cried, shedding tears of happiness, 'it is not you who would deceive your Lydie! You have measured my ecstasy with regard to the mortal organs with which I am still clad, and to protect me against the emotions that might dissolve the bond before time. No, this is not a world of transition between time and eternity, the temporary abode of a creature that must finish being once before living forever. This is the place where the Lord lavishes his eternal recompenses upon the just in eternal joys. That sun a thousand times more radiant than ours, but which strikes my eyes without wounding them, this splendid and calm nature, the repose of which no storm ever seems to have troubled, those birds ornamented with brilliant plumage that has never been seen even in dreams, which brush my hair in their flight and delight my ears with songs intelligible to thought, more harmonious than music and more expressive than speech: all of this creation, which lives, feels and loves, every movement of which, every emanation of all the voices confounded in an adorable concert, is the highest and most perfect of God's creations. You have wings yourself, George! And your wings are the attribute of the angels that surround the throne of the sovereign master of all things. What, then, is the paradise of the elect, if the world we are in is not that paradise?'

"'I understand your error,' George replied, 'and I would understand it more if death had already endowed you with the organs that you lack in order to perceive, in this tempo-rary world, a thousand sensations that escape you, and which surpass in sweetness those that you are experiencing now. You could form a feeble idea of it by seeking to take account of the emotions that matter would have experienced, if it enjoyed intelligence and thought, at each of the transformations that bring it closer to perfection. Imagine, it you can transport your mind into that impossible hypothesis, the plenitude of joy that would have filled that inert matter when it acquired the faculty of growth into the metals; of the metals when they obtained, in plants, the faculty of living and perpetuating themselves forever; the plants when they passed from the sedentary state to the state of movement in the organization of animals, and when they exchanged their captive and solitary vegetation for instincts and sentiments; and the animals, when the most privileged of all received from the divine breath an inspiration and a soul!

"'To each stage of that progress, the conquest of a creation seems to be attached, but the sensuality with which sensible matter would have been inundated every time, if it had been able to take account of its metamorphoses, has nothing comparable to that which penetrates the human heart at the moment when it takes possession of a new life, which prepares it for the assured possession of eternity. That is what you will know one day, when you have received from death the privilege of knowing; and you will forgive me then for not having satisfied more clearly your doubts and your questions, because you will understand that I was obliged to make use, in order to explain myself, of a language appropriate to the imperfection of your debilitated and incomplete senses. The knowledge of the mysteries of another life only belongs to another life, which it is permissible for me to allow you to anticipate, but which only God can give to you.

"'As for these wings, which you have noticed,' he continued, lowering his eyes toward the ground with a grave modesty, 'I must admit that they are not common to all the resuscitated, as you might have believed. God, who has established necessary differences between all his creatures, the apparent inequality of which will only be effaced on the supreme day of his justice, has maintained some hierarchy even in the intermediate world to which he summon his first elect. As all titles are not equal there, he wanted the virtues that are dearest to him to be distinguished by exterior figures and sensible advantages appropriate to inspire respect and submission. That striking manifestation of his favor is, among us, the pledge of an immutable order and the secret of a politics the principle of which nothing can alter; but no one dares to be proud of it, because the motive of the will of God is impenetrable. What it is possible to conjecture is that God has recognized by that extraordinary distinction the devotion of humans who have given their lives for the salvation of their fellows, and who have thus placed the accomplishment of the most sacred duty of humankind before the interest of their own conservation. There would doubtless be little merit in submitting to such a natural instinct without reflecting on its consequences and its dangers, but perhaps there is some pride in obeying it on the occasions that awaken it, which develop it and make it cry out in the depths of our soul like a voice of Providence, and my death would have been more worthy of envy than pity, if I had only had one life to immolate in quitting you. But you were alive, Lydie; it was not you that I was going to save, it was you that I was going to lose—and have no doubt.' George added, bearing my hand to his heart and his lips, 'that God has not recompensed my action so much as my sacrifice!'

"'That is good,' I told him, 'for my ideas are becoming clearer with every word that you pronounce. Let me tell you the rest. So, my George, you are fortunate among the fortunate, because you are good among the good, and the privilege you share with a few has nothing humiliating for the greater number, because it is the nature of beautiful souls to recognize the ascendancy of superior souls, and because God has, in any case, imprinted in your peers the manifest seal of his predilection. You are fortunate in the glorious life that divine bounty made for you in regard to my father and yours, who loved us so tenderly, and into whose arms you cannot take me as long as the bonds of life, which still enchain me to the earth, are not broken. If something is lacking in the pure felicity that you enjoy, it is your poor Lydie and your little Marceline, for whom you are nevertheless waiting with security, as in the return from a short journey that offers no perils; and although my proof will appear to me to be longer, I too am happy, for I can no longer doubt that it will end.

"'Oh, do not let the sentiment of our future happiness be obscured in your soul by the slightest anxiety, for your Lydie is savoring it with you, and the difficult days that I have still to pass in the world where you are no longer, at least lightened by a firm hope, will make you proud of my calmness and my courage. There is no one unfortunate but the wicked, who must regret in eternal suffering having counted in vain on annihilation; and I cannot hide from you that that sentiment mingles some sadness for me with the ineffable joys of resurrection. The creator had made them our brethren, and has prescribed to us to feel sorry for them and to love them, although we were hated and persecuted by them. Will those unfortunates not find grace before the pity of the Almighty? Will Hell never render them?'

"'I expected that question,' George replied, with a new smile, 'for all the secrets of your heart are known to me; but you will know one day what it is impossible for me to resolve for you, because it has only removed the first of all the veils that separate us from God; it must be thus in order for our souls not to sink in astonishment and respect in the contemplation of his mysteries. What I can tell you, and what the sages inform us in our new life, is that perhaps no one is absolutely wicked, and, in consequence, there is perhaps no punishment without remission. Other clarities will doubtless radiate a new daylight in the rebel intelligences. Other, more rigorous worlds will submit the insensate and the perverse to longer and more difficult proofs, but they will also have their merits and their crowns. Only obstinacy in the hatred of God and his works will reject the supreme judgment at the solemn moment, but for that it is necessary that the divine breath that animates the creature is absolutely annihilated therein, and that nothing human remains. There are still falls to be dreaded in this world of election to which I have transported you, for this is not the eternal life, and the good are exposed like the evil to the affliction of the passions; but those falls are very rare. There are still reparations to hope for in the world of exile where the condemned are groaning, and as the cruel hope of annihilation no longer reassures them, those rehabilitations are numerous. Nothing is finished before the sovereign bounty, because there is nothing that is complete and universal. I have spoken to you about our theories and not our mysteries. Among the resuscitated as among the living, wisdom consists of humility.'

"'May the will of the Lord be done in all things,' I said then, 'but finish reassuring my weakness in regard to one doubt to which your discourse has sometimes given birth in my mind. The revelation is true; it is not permissible to doubt it, and the language of Holy Writ is the divine expression of verities in which we ought to believe. Why are those verities enveloped by impenetrable darkness? Why has that revelation, emanated from God, who knows everything and can say everything, remained imperfect? In rendering sensible to all the future destinies that become so evident to the eyes of the dead, from which the scales have fallen, the tender mercy of the Lord would have abridged our proofs; for, since the first pilgrimage that we accomplish on earth, all souls would be launched toward him with a common accord. Why has he left us plunged in ignorance and doubt, so closely akin to despair, even when he announced himself through his prophets and gave us his son? Ought the science of faith to attempt to rise above the teachings of faith?'

"'Never,' cried George, 'for faith is not a science; faith is a virtue, the merit of which consists in its abandon and its simplicity. Those who believe because they know do not believe sufficiently, and do not believe well. Conviction is the effect of examination, and examination is a mental operation that marks ingratitude and suspicion. In order to penetrate the abyss of the will of God, humans lack organs that God has not deigned to give them. What would you say to someone born blind who offers a judgment on colors, or a deaf-mute who analyzes the effects of music? Is it necessary to remind you that these mysteries have been unveiled to Christians in the first page of the scriptures? Whoever has succeeded in discerning good and evil has already lost his innocence, for the property of innocence is not to know evil.

"'All the beings that the Lord has produced are equally dear to him, but he wanted to enclose them within just limits which they could not cross without dooming themselves. It is no more permitted to a human to conceive the mysteries of creation than it is to a plant voluntarily to change its soil and its horizon or to an animal to reflect on its existence and communicate its thought. The first inhabitants of the earth were reserved to the purest wellbeing that their species could enjoy, when a spirit of pride and dementia opened the false path of knowledge to them; they acquired the faculty of knowing, and with it the doubts consequent upon it and all the misfortunes that accompany it, from the uncertainty in which the soul went astray at the thought of the annihilation that kills it.

"'That is the result of an impatience that is proper to all created beings and bears them incessantly toward the degree of perfection that they ought eventually to attain, a natural and irresistible instinct that a stone obeys in growing and aspiring to live, a plant in living and aspiring to feel, an animal in feeling and aspiring to think, and humans in thinking and aspiring to understand; but humans had received intelligence, they knew the range of their organization, foresaw with assurance the promised ends and were not content within the limits that were imposed upon them by the divine will. They tried to become equal to God, and God punished them in their vanity by abandoning to them the fruit of the science that only taught them death.

"'That, dear Lydie, is the history of humankind. The woe would be too great if God had not left for compensation the faith that has confidence in his promises, the hope that waits and the charity that loves, three virtues that the wisdom of saints call theological, in the language of the Greeks, because they contain within them all the science of God. Believe, hope, love: that is the veritable law of Christians, and when they fulfill those conditions in their first life of proofs, they render themselves worthy of the other. If you ask me now why the revelation, which is the very expression of eternal verity, has not clarified this darkness, it will be easy for me to satisfy you.

"'Revelation has not been given either to beings of a nature superior to humans, or to humans obstinate in the sin of science, who persist in seeking the reason for things in spite of the express prohibition of God, and who thus renew within them the original sin of their race. It has been given to the simple in mind and heart, who believe because they feel and not because they know. Life would be an easy proof if the testimony of our senses demonstrated to us that life is only a proof, and that the future will compensate us sufficiently for the present, if the present were not closed; but revelation has reached us in human form, and was only able to be communicated to humans within the conditions of their nature. The truth that it gives us is the general truth that our organs can grasp and our faculties can embrace, but it is sufficient thus to the needs of our nature and the legitimate hopes of which it is the source.

"'The verity of scholars, on the contrary, is a bottomless abyss, the formidable echoes of which repeat endlessly the Lord's prophetic threat: you are dust and you will return to dust. The sin of the terrestrial paradise, Lydie, is science, the deplorable daughter of curiosity. Believe then, without effort what God and his Church have taught you, even when that information appears to you to be imperfect, for you know that the entire species to which you belong is imperfect, and cannot receive others so long as it is not enlightened by death. Death is enlightenment.

"'Listen carefully once again, sweet friend, in order that my words are not traced in sand, but imprinted forcefully in your heart. To know is perhaps to deceive oneself; to believe in the wisdom of wellbeing; to hope is the remedy and the consolation of all woes; to love is the whole of virtue. I do not know whether the sovereign judge will take much account one day of the knowledge for which you have been momentarily ambitious, but I can assure you that the most precious treasures of his grace belong to candor, to pity and to charity.'

"I leaned over George's bosom, spreading a few tears of joy there, and our walk continued in silence, for I was no longer curious. I enjoyed purer delights than those that had filled the hearts of the first living beings in the terrestrial paradise, and I did not want to renew the sin of Eve, in the paradise of the dead. I knew, in any case, that the doubts that still tormented me were the effect of my ignorance and my imperfection, and that they could only afflict my friend by bringing him back for too long from the serene sentiment of his condition to the tender pity that mine inspired in him. And then, everything continued to distract me, by virtue of sensations that humans are not even capable of naming, because there is nothing that resembles them in our ordinary sensations.

"My eyes, inundated by flattering light that astonished them without dazzling them; my ears, watered by a river of harmony that never ran dry; all my senses, overwhelmed by a wellbeing for which they were not formed, commenced to become drowsy in a delectable languor of which none of our terrestrial sensualities can give an idea, if one cannot imagine the inexpressible ecstasy of a soul that has just been ravished in God. I sensed my limbs weakening, but George's arm sustained me.

"'The moment has come,' he said. 'You are falling asleep in the life of the resuscitated in order to return to the life of the dying, and in order to drag yourself painfully during a few hours that will scarcely separate us, for my thought will not cease to follow you and watch over you. Remember to believe, to hope and to live, and do not fear suffering, for the sufferings of life are temporary, while the joys of resurrection are eternal.'

"At the same instant," Lydie continued, "I did indeed wake up on the bed of dolor where I had suffered such mortal anguish the day before, and I felt my hand pressed again in the hand of the physician, who was interrogating the movement of my blood.

"'Where is he?' I cried. 'What has become of those bright birds with golden plumage, which saluted us with their concerts. What has become of the flowers that inclined their odorous corollas toward us in order to embalm us with their perfumes? Has the Lord extinguished his sun?'

"But I remembered George's words immediately, for they had scarcely ceased to resound in my ear and to vibrate in my soul; I understood with resignation that my captivity was not finished, and I smiled.

'That's good,' remarked the doctor, in a tone of satisfied pride. 'What I foresaw has happened. The young woman is in dementia; there isn't a moment to lose to transport her to the hospital of the alienated in Lausanne, where I can observe at closer range the development and crises of her malady.'

"'To do what?' said Mère Zurich, a good old woman of the neighborhood who had assisted me in the preceding days and has not quit me since. 'To do what, if you please?'

"'To cure her,' replied the physician, taking a pinch of snuff from his golden snuff-box.

"'Alas,' replied Mère Zurich, sighing, 'God forbid that she is cured, since she is happy thus, and her forehead has resumed the angelic serenity that rendered her so beautiful in the time of her happiness. Could you resuscitate George and bring him here when she is cured? If your knowledge doesn't go that far, let's leave Lydie as she is. The poor child will be everyone's daughter, and I can guarantee that we won't abandon her!'

"While speaking thus she wrapped her arms around me as if to retain me, and I responded to her tenderness with tears of gratitude, for I would have found much to lament in quitting George's house and the people who had loved him. The physician was very afflicted, according to all appearance, at losing a subject of study who was beginning to do him honor, and I haven't seen him since. My story finished there, and now I hope and I wait."

For a long time, Lydie did not say anything more, although I was still listening to her. As for Lydie, she had returned to her flowers, without paying any heed to me, and I think she had forgotten me completely when I placed myself in her path again.

"One more word, Lydie, a word and nothing more," I exclaimed, seizing her hand with a respectful tenderness. "Since the solemn night when George transported you into the paradise of the resuscitated, has the same dream happened to you again, even once?"

"The same dream?" she said, with an anxious expression. "Do you call that a dream, as all the others do? Oh, don't be alarmed; I don't hold it against you. The living can only judge in accordance with their senses, and their senses are veiled by thick darkness. Since the night when the paradise of the resuscitated was opened to me, I spend all the hours of my sleep there, and I have penetrated mysteries even sweeter that those I have recounted to you. If it were not thus, do you think I would still be alive?"

A woman I had not perceived until then, who had arrived during the last moments of our conversation, came then to place herself in front of Lydie, who took hold of her arm. I recognized Mère Zurich, and, in fact, the sun, ready to set, had already marked the hour for quitting the esplanade some time ago.

*Poor innocent,* I said to myself, following Lydie with my eyes through the bends in the path and seeing her disappear for the last time behind a clump of verdure that was not to return her to me. *Poor Lydie!* I repeated, after a moment's reflection. *Or rather, fortunate woman, privileged among all women! You will go to sleep from the sad realities of the world, and dream, on the bosom of your friend, of the felicity that is promised to you! Sleep for a long time, Lydie, and may Heaven hasten for you the fortunate day when you will not wake up again! Thanks be rendered to you, however, for the sweet and precious consolations that I have obtained from your conversation. Where there was for me an enigma to which I could not obtain the key without research and sacrifice, you have shown me that the solution of the imposing mystery only belongs to those who are able to love and suffer. The fear of suffering caused me to fear amour, and I did not know that in removing myself from the rigorous proofs of the heart by virtue of a pusillanimous mistrust of my strength, I was adulterating in myself the most vivacious principle of my immortality, the only one that ought to acquire us a right to an eternal recompense and enable us to participate in eternal joys! Your words have reignited the torch of active charity that I tried to stifle in my bosom. I shall return among humans to aid them in their difficulties, and at least to weep with them when it is not permitted to me to aid them. I shall resume my part of the calamities that are attached to our temporary existence, I shall accumulate on my resigned head everything that it is possible for me to spare others, and if I experience some regret it is because that duty, blindly disdained for such a long time by a false philosophy, is too facile for souls of conviction that want to render themselves worthy of their destiny. There is, in fact no real misfortune for amour when it is supported by hope and faith, and if that prescience of the infallible truth were given to everyone, as to Lydie and me, my God, who would dare to say that our terrestrial paradise was closed?*

"God is great," said Lugon, for I had proffered the last words aloud while walking toward the lace where he was waiting for me, one hand passed through the bridle of my horse. "Monsieur has no doubt noticed," he added, while I threw myself into the saddle, "that it is too late this evening to go see the Château de Chillon?"

"Eh! What does the Château de Chillon matter to me, my friend, and all the residues of the Middle Ages, and all the memories of poetry, and even the marvels of nature that I was going to admire in the Alps? My friends are saddened by my absence, my mother is old and infirm, I have left a domestic ill, the poorest of our neighbors has lost his cow, the money that I dissipate in solitary distractions is lacking twenty houses in the village, and tomorrow I shall resume the road to the Jura."

That response, which only presented itself to Lugon's mind as a bizarre string of phrases devoid of order, doubtless inspired in him some anxiety as to the state of my reason, for he only replied to me with a shake of the head accompanied by a sigh. The poor fellow had not forgotten that Lydie's madness was reputed to be contagious.

"God is great," he murmured in a low voice, urging his mule forward in his turn; and we reached Vevey at a gallop.

Since then I have remained faithful to all my resolutions. I have accepted, with submission and gratitude, the part that the Lord had made for me in the dolors and tribulations of humankind; I have never complained that the cup was too full, although it has often overflowed, but I ought to repeat again that there has been little merit in my courage, for courage costs nothing to faith. There is no man who has not drawn as much as me from the same convictions, and who does not forbid himself carefully to submit his instinctive belief to the miserable quibbles of philosophical examination once he has understood that all our virtues consist of loving and that all our wellbeing consists of believing.

Those words of George's bring me back to a story of which I have promised the end. In the course of the spring that followed my encounter with Lydie, a worry of which I was not the master pressed me to see her again and inform myself of her fate. The science of the physicians frightened me, when I thought that they might have cured her, that she might have returned to the frightful sentiment of her misfortune, and was no longer dreaming. My own constancy, still unsteady, needed to be reassured by her strength against the mockeries of fine minds and the superb disdain of sages. In order to put an end to those uncertainties, I returned to Vevey, but I did not stop there. I passed before George's house, which was closed, as it had been the first time, and I thought that Lydie must be at the esplanade, for the hour was not yet advanced and the day was warm and pure. When I arrived there, I encountered a rider who was leading another horse. As I knew the man and was known to him we both dismounted at the same time. It was Little Lugon.

"Where are you going, Monsieur, without a guide and without a domestic?" said Lugon, responding cordially to my handshake.

"To Lydie's Garden," I replied. "Did you notice whether she was there?"

"She's there, Monsieur," Lugon replied, in a grave and concentrated tone, lowering his gaze toward the ground. "Madame Lydie is in her garden, and will not emerge again until the angel's trumpet summons her to the last judgment. She's dead."

"Dead!" I cried.

And the human heart is an abyss of contradictions. I do not know what imported into me then the regret of her loss or the joy of her deliverance.

"She died," Lugon continued, "scarcely a month after the day when Monsieur conversed with her for such a long time. She was in her garden, as she called that corner of the strand, surrounded by flowers that she had picked, and with which the poor woman had the custom of composing George's bouquet, Mère Zurich had come to look for her twice, and twice she had gone away because she thought that Lydie was asleep. The third time, as the night was already somber and everyone was returning from work, she decided to wake her, but she could not do it, because Lydie was dead. Then Mère Zurich uttered a scream that summoned all the passers-by. 'Look, look!' said Mère Zurich. 'She's dead, and I thought she was asleep!'

"What is strange, Monsieur, is that when they came to take away the body, around which Mère Zurich had wrapped her arms without saying another word, they perceived that Mère Zurich was dead too. Two graves were dug for then, which you can see, because they were Catholic and they couldn't have a part in the prayers of Huguenots."

"Are you Catholic, Lugon?" I said, involuntarily, for my thought was distracted by other ideas.

"Certainly, Monsieur," replied Lugon, coldly, "since I'm Valaisian."

"And what do they think in this region about two deaths, so sudden, that nothing had presaged?"

"The doctor wasn't astonished by them. He said that the young one had died of a cerebral congestion—I think that's it—and the old one of apoplexy. Oh, he's a very knowledgeable man."

At that point Lugon looked at me fixedly with a mixture of astonishment and sadness, for he had not forgotten his old prejudices entirely, and had just recalled them to memory.

"The old one," he said, "had had her time, but Lydie, so young and so beautiful . . ."

"Don't weep for her, my friend. Lydie is free now from all her dolors. Lydie possesses forever, without trouble and without awakening, the felicity of which she could only dream."

Lugon looked at me again.

"God is great," he said.

A PARTIAL LIST OF SNUGGLY BOOKS

**ETHEL ARCHER** *The Hieroglyph*
**ETHEL ARCHER** *Phantasy and Other Poems*
**ETHEL ARCHER** *The Whirlpool*
**G. ALBERT AURIER** *Elsewhere and Other Stories*
**CHARLES BARBARA** *My Lunatic Asylum*
**NATALIE CLIFFORD BARNEY** *The One Who Is Legion*
**S. HENRY BERTHOUD** *Misanthropic Tales*
**LÉON BLOY** *The Tarantulas' Parlor and Other Unkind Tales*
**ÉLÉMIR BOURGES** *The Twilight of the Gods*
**CYRIEL BUYSSE** *The Aunts*
**JAMES CHAMPAGNE** *Harlem Smoke*
**FÉLICIEN CHAMPSAUR** *The Latin Orgy*
**BRENDAN CONNELL** *The Translation of Father Torturo*
**BRENDAN CONNELL** *Unofficial History of Pi Wei*
**BRENDAN CONNELL (editor)**
*The Zinzolin Book of Occult fiction*
**RAFAELA CONTRERAS** *The Turquoise Ring and Other Stories*
**DANIEL CORRICK (editor)**
*Ghosts and Robbers: An Anthology of German Gothic Fiction*
**ADOLFO COUVE** *When I Think of My Missing Head*
**RENÉ CREVEL** *Are You All Crazy?*
**QUENTIN S. CRISP** *Aiaigasa*
**LUCIE DELARUE-MARDRUS** *The Last Siren and Other Stories*
**LADY DILKE** *The Outcast Spirit and Other Stories*
**CATHERINE DOUSTEYSSIER-KHOZE**
*The Beauty of the Death Cap*
**ÉDOUARD DUJARDIN** *Hauntings*
**BERIT ELLINGSEN** *Now We Can See the Moon*
**ERCKMANN-CHATRIAN** *A Malediction*
**ALPHONSE ESQUIROS** *The Enchanted Castle*
**ENRIQUE GÓMEZ CARRILLO** *Sentimental Stories*
**DELPHI FABRICE** *Flowers of Ether*
**DELPHI FABRICE** *The Red Sorcerer*
**DELPHI FABRICE** *The Red Spider*
**BENJAMIN GASTINEAU** *The Reign of Satan*
**EDMOND AND JULES DE GONCOURT** *Manette Salomon*
**REMY DE GOURMONT** *From a Faraway Land*
**REMY DE GOURMONT** *Morose Vignettes*
**GUIDO GOZZANO** *Alcina and Other Stories*
**GUSTAVE GUICHES** *The Modesty of Sodom*
**EDWARD HERON-ALLEN** *The Complete Shorter Fiction*
**EDWARD HERON-ALLEN** *Three Ghost-Written Novels*